SCHOOL FOR
EXTRATERRESTRIAL
GIRLS

PAPERCUTZ

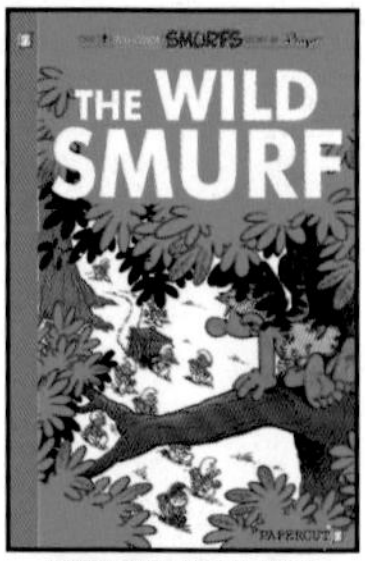
THE WILD SMURF
PAPERCUTZ

THE SMURFS #21

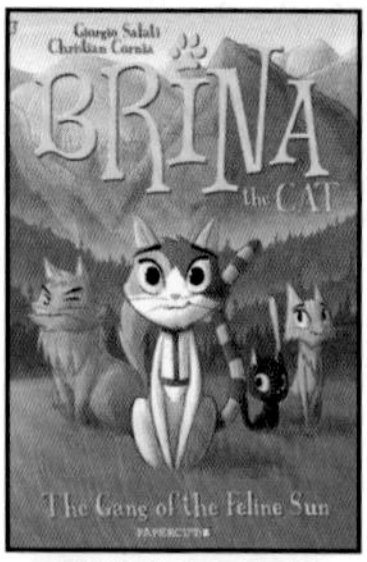
BRINA the CAT
The Gang of the Feline Sun
PAPERCUTZ

BRINA THE CAT #1

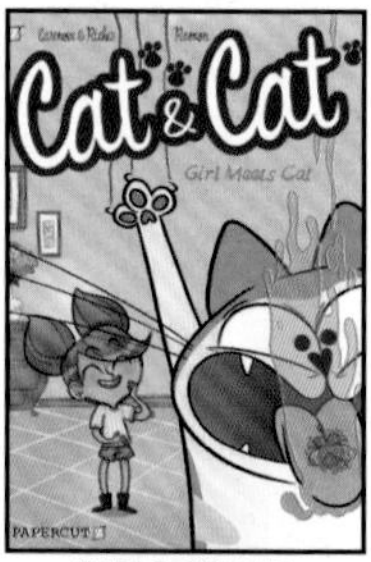
Cat & Cat
Girl Meets Cat
PAPERCUTZ

CAT & CAT #1

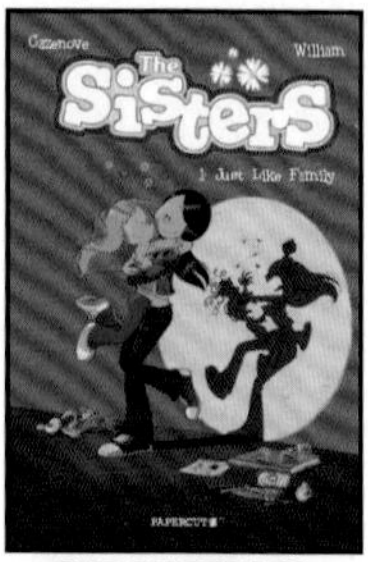
Cazenove
William
The Sisters
PAPERCUTZ

THE SISTERS #1

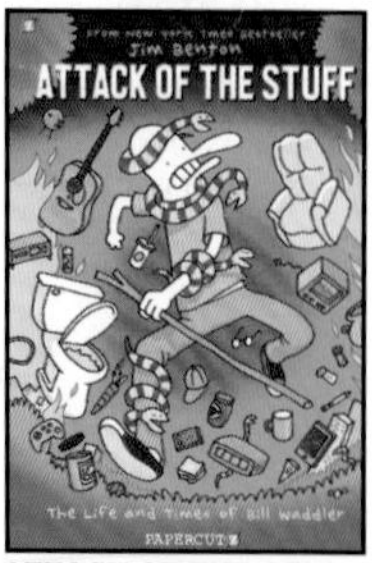
ATTACK OF THE STUFF
PAPERCUTZ

ATTACK OF THE STUFF

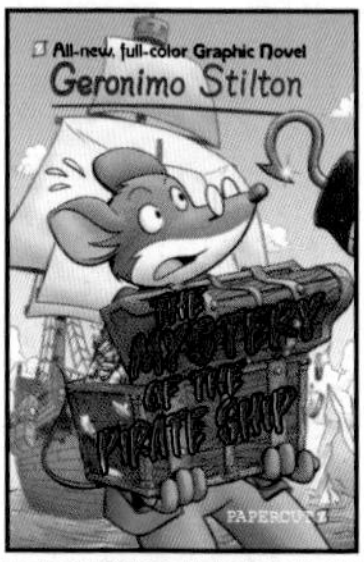
All-new, full-color Graphic Novel
Geronimo Stilton
PAPERCUTZ

GERONIMO STILTON #17

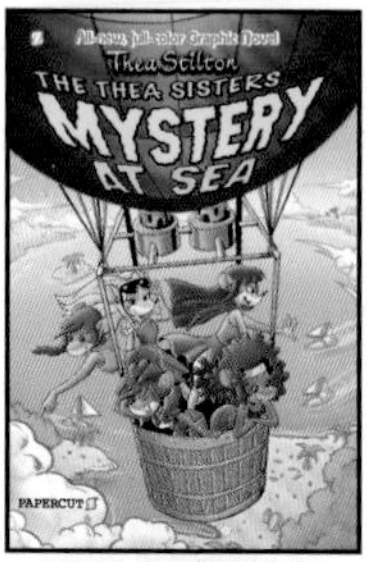
Thea Stilton
THE THEA SISTERS
MYSTERY AT SEA
PAPERCUTZ

THEA STILTON #6

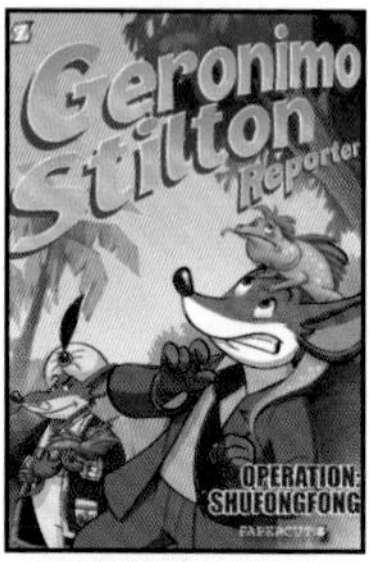
Geronimo Stilton
Reporter
OPERATION: SHUFONGFONG
PAPERCUTZ

GERONIMO STILTON RREPORTER #1

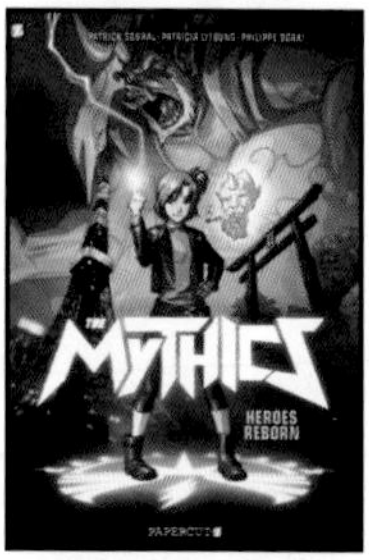
MYTHICS
HEROES REBORN
PAPERCUTZ

THE MYTHICS #1

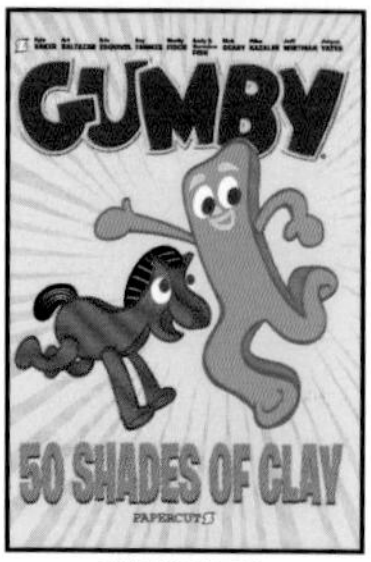
GUMBY
50 SHADES OF CLAY
PAPERCUTZ

GUMBY #1

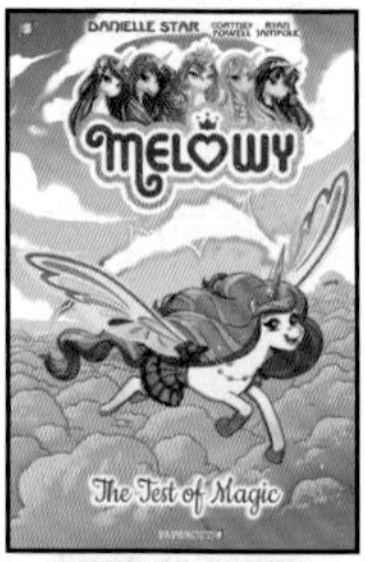
DANIELLE STAR
MELOWY
The Test of Magic
PAPERCUTZ

ANNE OF GREEN BAGELS #1

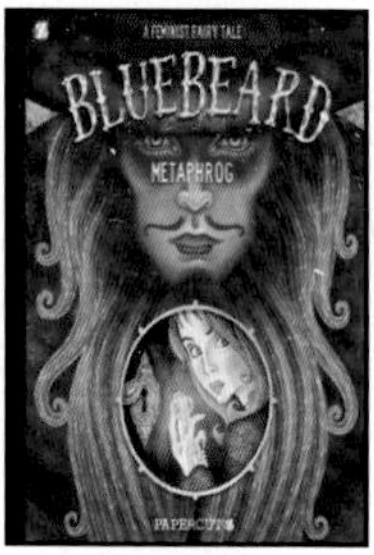
A FEMINIST FAIRY TALE
BLUEBEARD
METAPHROG
PAPERCUTZ

BLUEBEARD

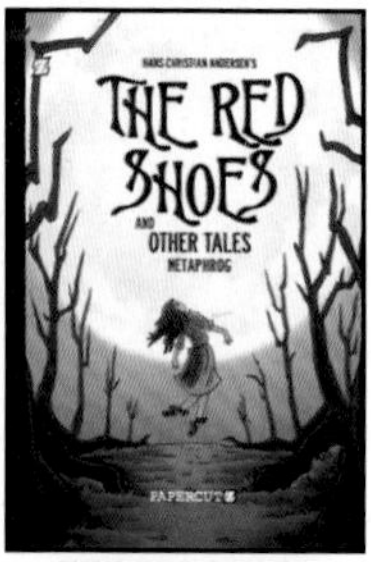
THE RED SHOES
AND OTHER TALES
METAPHROG
PAPERCUTZ

THE RED SHOES

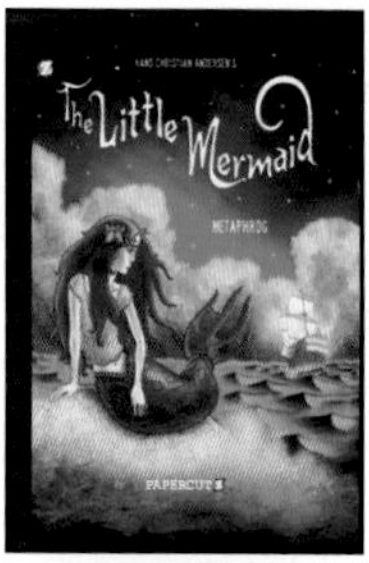
The Little Mermaid
METAPHROG
PAPERCUTZ

THE LITTLE MERMAID

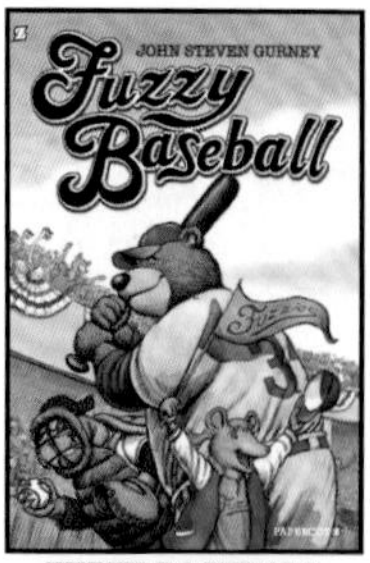
JOHN STEVEN GURNEY
Fuzzy Baseball
PAPERCUTZ

FUZZY BASEBALL

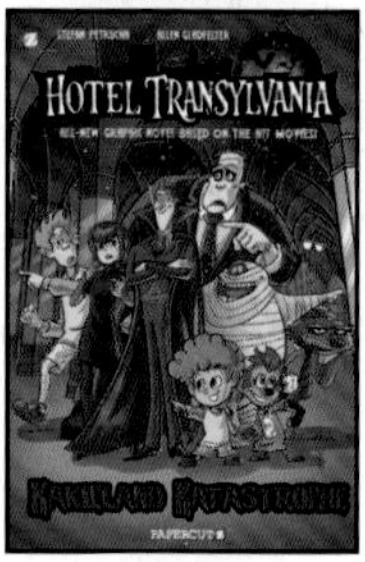
HOTEL TRANSYLVANIA
PAPERCUTZ

HOTEL TRANSYLVANIA #1

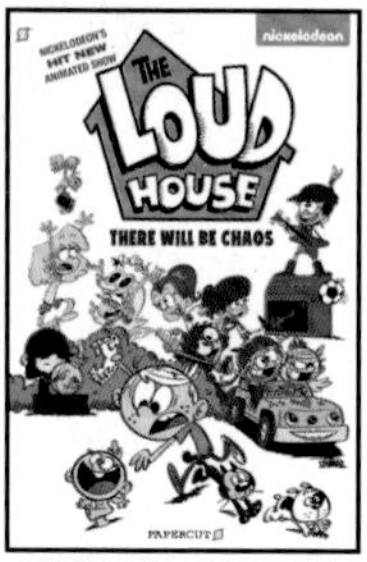
nickelodeon
THE LOUD HOUSE
THERE WILL BE CHAOS
PAPERCUTZ

THE LOUD HOUSE #1

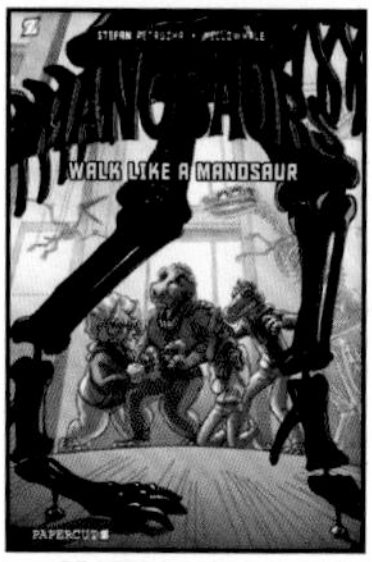
WALK LIKE A MANOSAUR
PAPERCUTZ

MANOSAURS #1

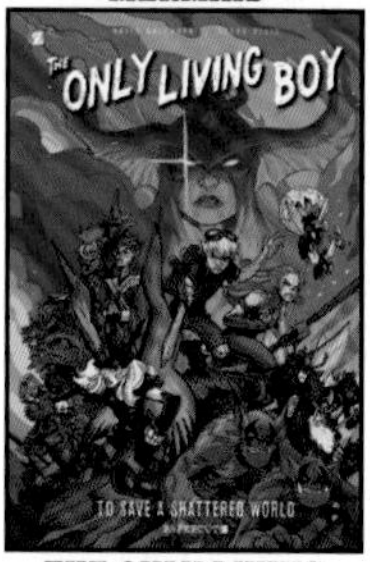
THE ONLY LIVING BOY
TO SAVE A SHATTERED WORLD

THE ONLY LIVING BOY #5

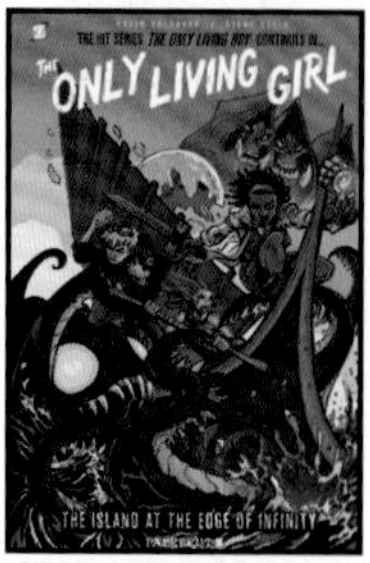
THE ONLY LIVING GIRL
THE ISLAND AT THE EDGE OF INFINITY

ONLY LIVING GIRL #1

SCHOOL FOR EXTRATERRESTRIAL GIRLS

GIRL ON FIRE

JEREMY WHITLEY   JAMIE NOGUCHI

PAPERCUTZ

NEW YORK

School for Extraterrestrial Girls
#1 "Girl on Fire"

By Jeremy Whitley and Jamie Noguchi
©2020 Jeremy Whitley and Jamie Noguchi
All other editorial material © Papercutz.
Written by Jeremy Whitley
Art and color by Jamie Noguchi
Coloring assists by Shannon Lilly
Lettering by Wilson Ramos Jr.

Special thanks to Moe Ferrara

Managing Editor — Jeff Whitman
Editorial Interns — Eric Storms, Izzy Boyce-Blanchard
Jim Salicrup
Editor-in-Chief

Papercutz books may be purchased for business or promotional use. For information on bulk purchases please contact Macmillan Corporate and Premium Sales Department at (800) 221-795 x5442.

Hardcover ISBN: 978-1-5458-0492-6
Paperback ISBN: 978-1-5458-0493-3

Printed in Turkey
August 2020

Distributed by Macmillan
First Printing

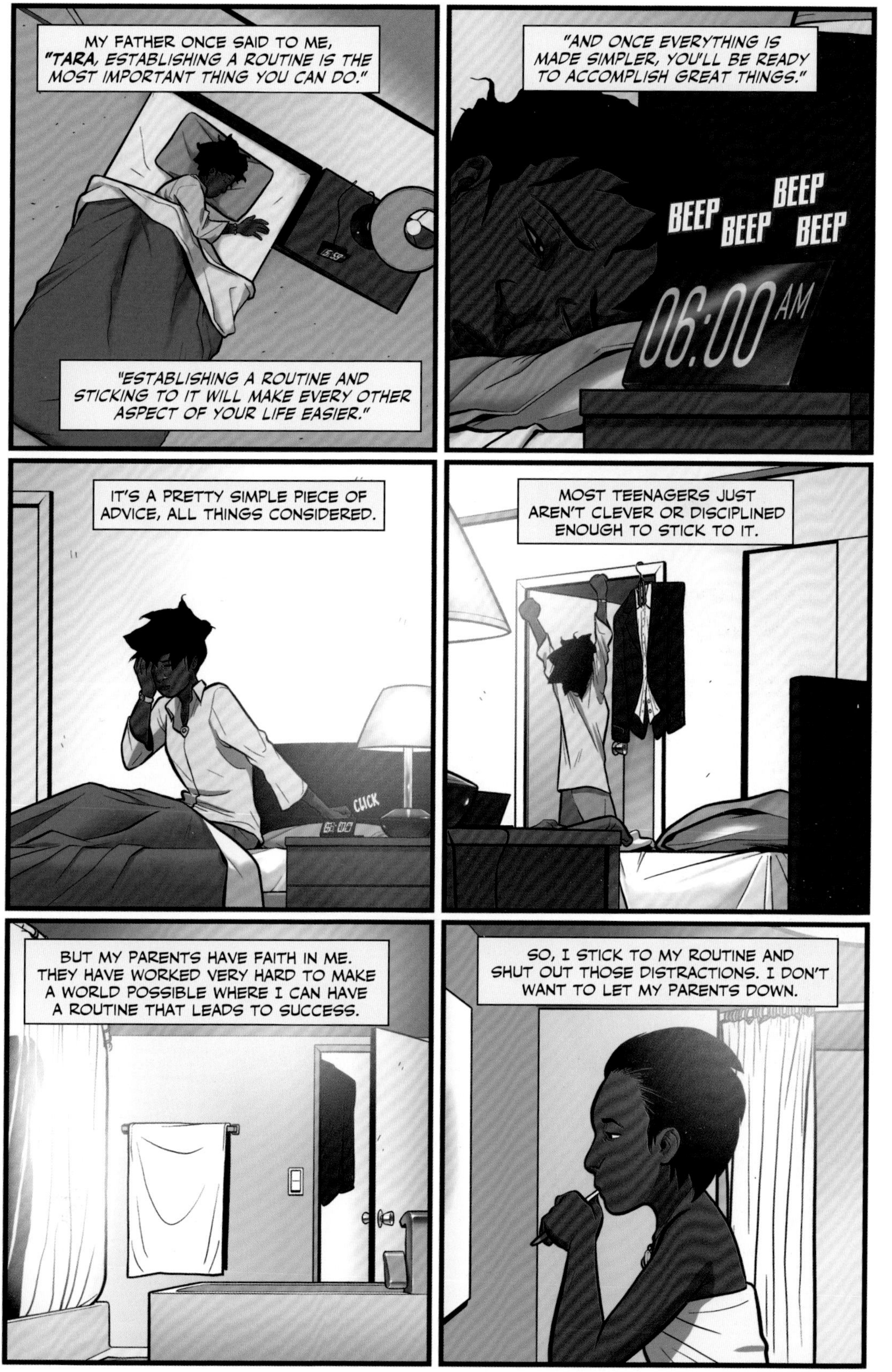

MY FATHER ONCE SAID TO ME, "TARA, ESTABLISHING A ROUTINE IS THE MOST IMPORTANT THING YOU CAN DO."
"ESTABLISHING A ROUTINE AND STICKING TO IT WILL MAKE EVERY OTHER ASPECT OF YOUR LIFE EASIER."
"AND ONCE EVERYTHING IS MADE SIMPLER, YOU'LL BE READY TO ACCOMPLISH GREAT THINGS."
BEEP BEEP BEEP BEEP
06:00 AM
IT'S A PRETTY SIMPLE PIECE OF ADVICE, ALL THINGS CONSIDERED.
CLICK
MOST TEENAGERS JUST AREN'T CLEVER OR DISCIPLINED ENOUGH TO STICK TO IT.
BUT MY PARENTS HAVE FAITH IN ME. THEY HAVE WORKED VERY HARD TO MAKE A WORLD POSSIBLE WHERE I CAN HAVE A ROUTINE THAT LEADS TO SUCCESS.
SO, I STICK TO MY ROUTINE AND SHUT OUT THOSE DISTRACTIONS. I DON'T WANT TO LET MY PARENTS DOWN.

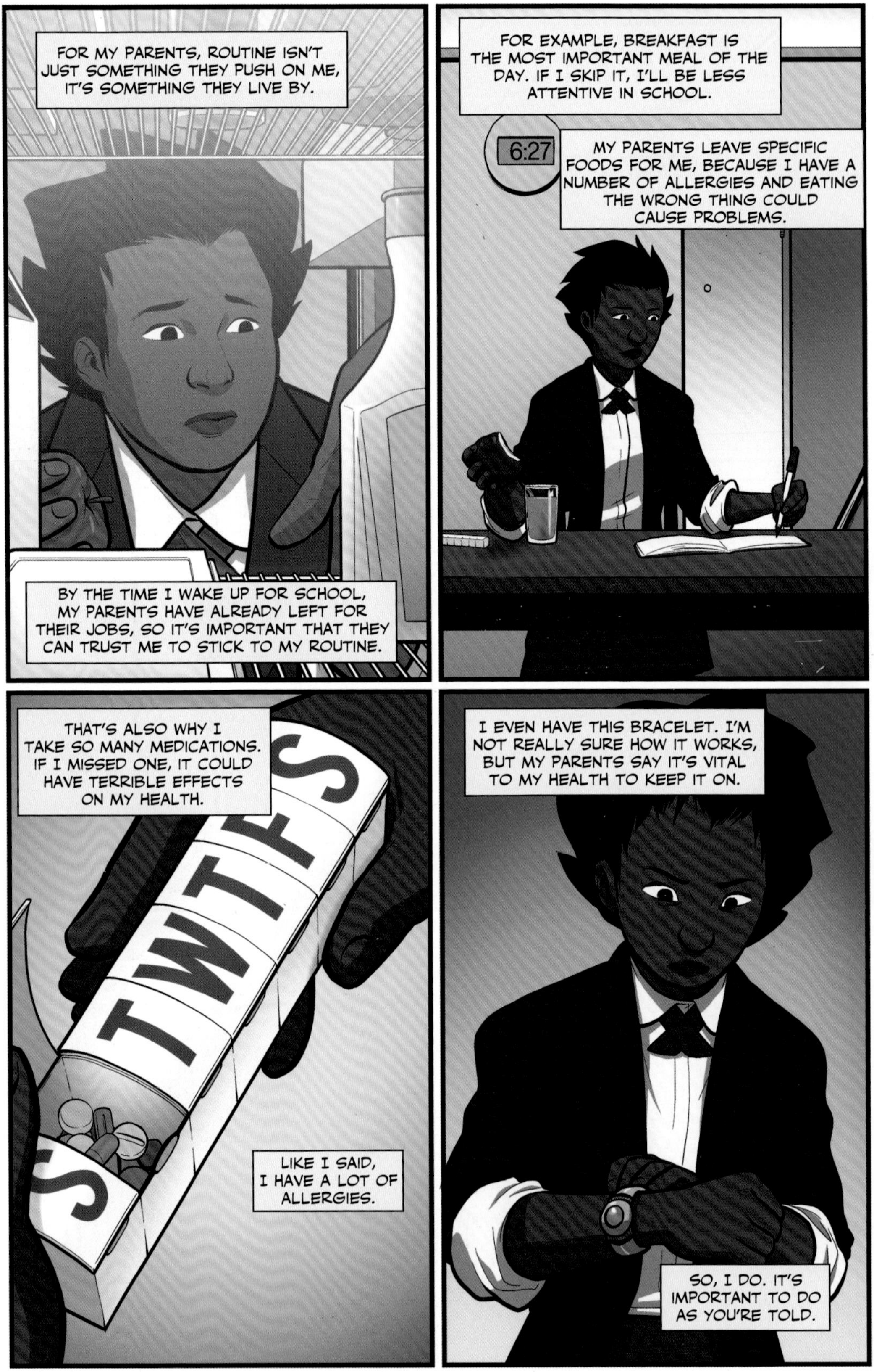
FOR MY PARENTS, ROUTINE ISN'T JUST SOMETHING THEY PUSH ON ME, IT'S SOMETHING THEY LIVE BY.
BY THE TIME I WAKE UP FOR SCHOOL, MY PARENTS HAVE ALREADY LEFT FOR THEIR JOBS, SO IT'S IMPORTANT THAT THEY CAN TRUST ME TO STICK TO MY ROUTINE.
FOR EXAMPLE, BREAKFAST IS THE MOST IMPORTANT MEAL OF THE DAY. IF I SKIP IT, I'LL BE LESS ATTENTIVE IN SCHOOL.
6:27
MY PARENTS LEAVE SPECIFIC FOODS FOR ME, BECAUSE I HAVE A NUMBER OF ALLERGIES AND EATING THE WRONG THING COULD CAUSE PROBLEMS.
THAT'S ALSO WHY I TAKE SO MANY MEDICATIONS. IF I MISSED ONE, IT COULD HAVE TERRIBLE EFFECTS ON MY HEALTH.
S
T W T F S
LIKE I SAID, I HAVE A LOT OF ALLERGIES.
I EVEN HAVE THIS BRACELET. I'M NOT REALLY SURE HOW IT WORKS, BUT MY PARENTS SAY IT'S VITAL TO MY HEALTH TO KEEP IT ON.
SO, I DO. IT'S IMPORTANT TO DO AS YOU'RE TOLD.

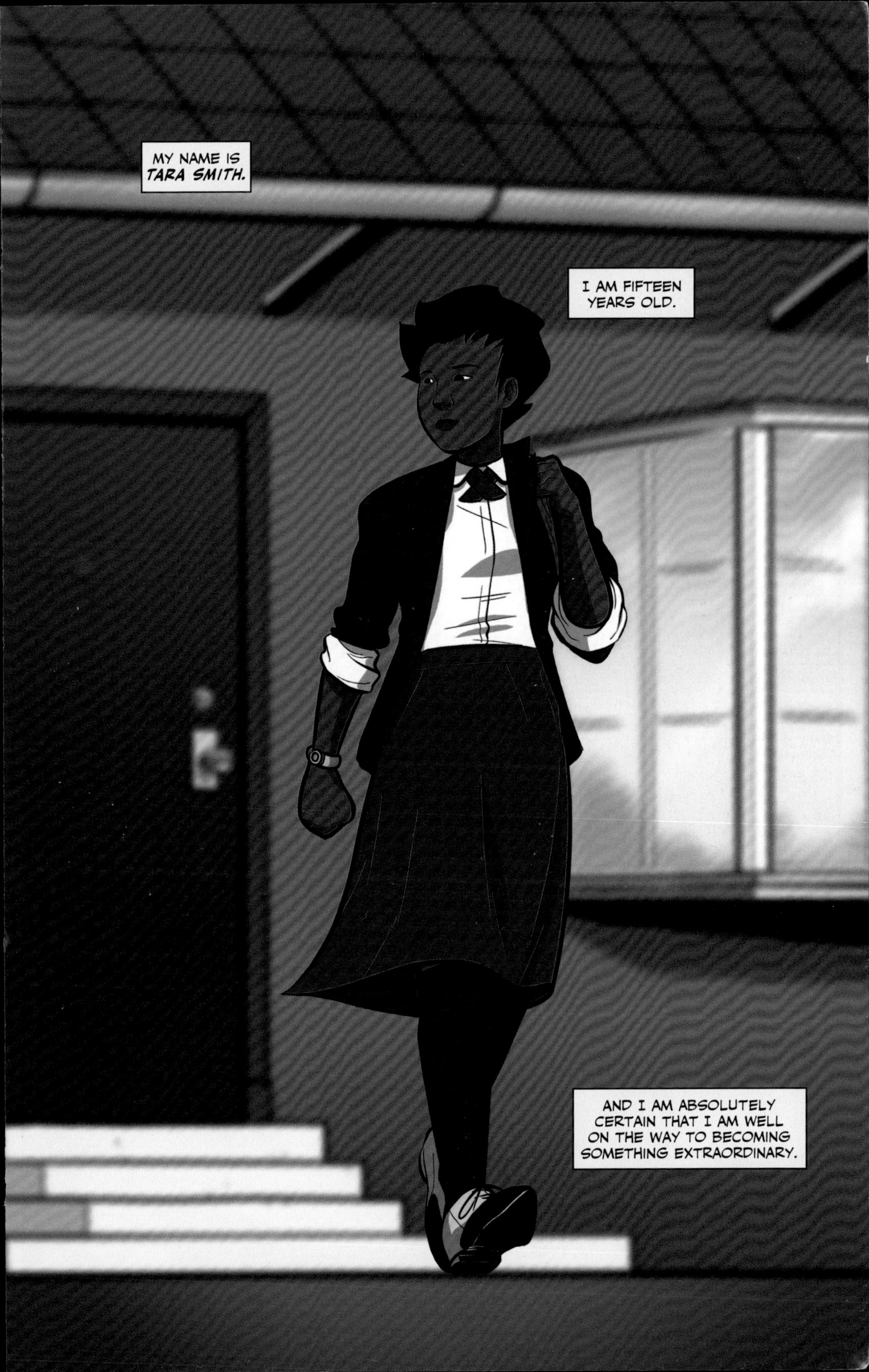
MY NAME IS *TARA SMITH.*
I AM FIFTEEN YEARS OLD.
AND I AM ABSOLUTELY CERTAIN THAT I AM WELL ON THE WAY TO BECOMING SOMETHING EXTRAORDINARY.

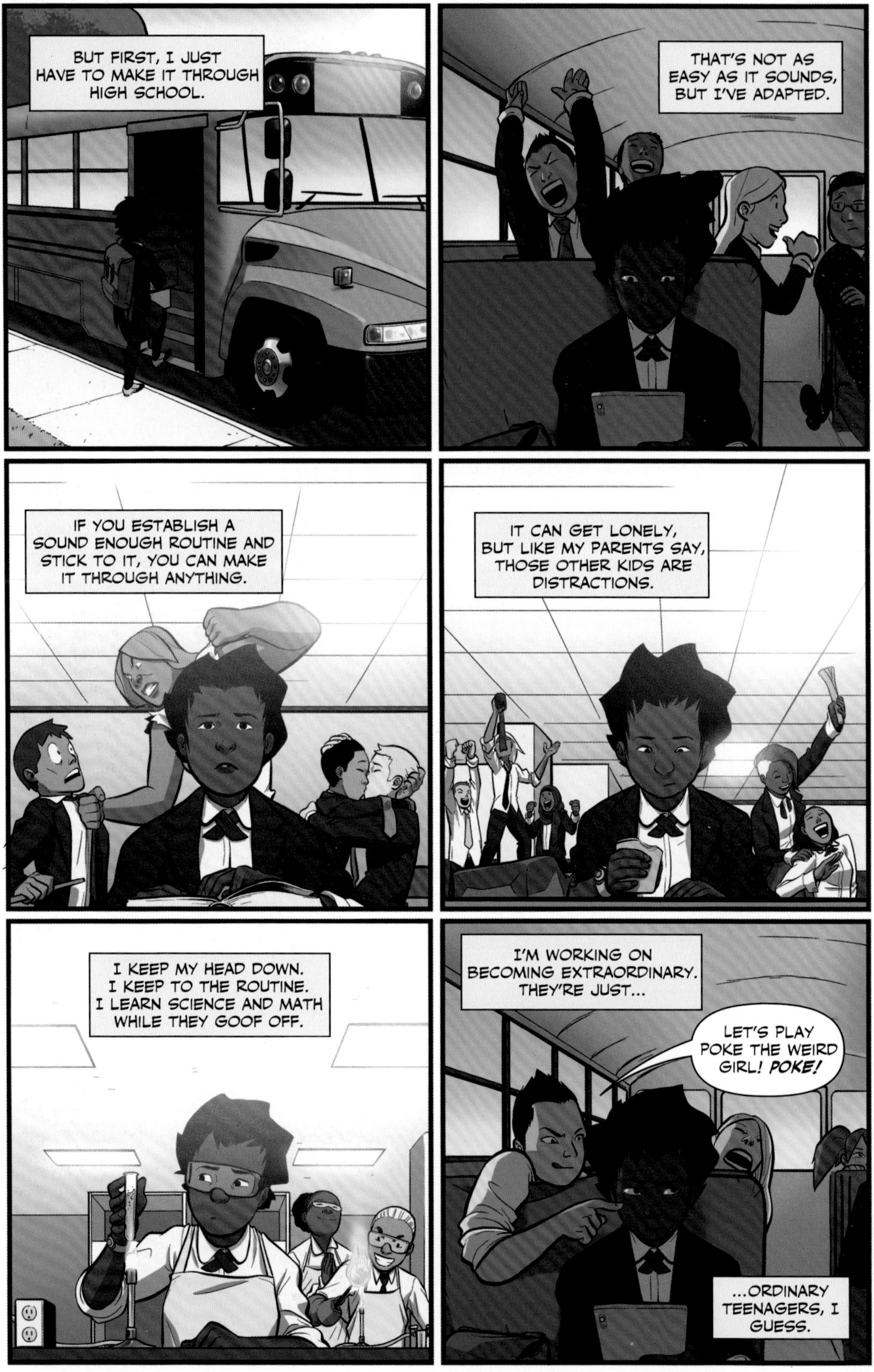
BUT FIRST, I JUST HAVE TO MAKE IT THROUGH HIGH SCHOOL.
THAT'S NOT AS EASY AS IT SOUNDS, BUT I'VE ADAPTED.
IF YOU ESTABLISH A SOUND ENOUGH ROUTINE AND STICK TO IT, YOU CAN MAKE IT THROUGH ANYTHING.
IT CAN GET LONELY, BUT LIKE MY PARENTS SAY, THOSE OTHER KIDS ARE DISTRACTIONS.
I KEEP MY HEAD DOWN. I KEEP TO THE ROUTINE. I LEARN SCIENCE AND MATH WHILE THEY GOOF OFF.
I'M WORKING ON BECOMING EXTRAORDINARY. THEY'RE JUST...
LET'S PLAY POKE THE WEIRD GIRL! *POKE!*
...ORDINARY TEENAGERS, I GUESS.

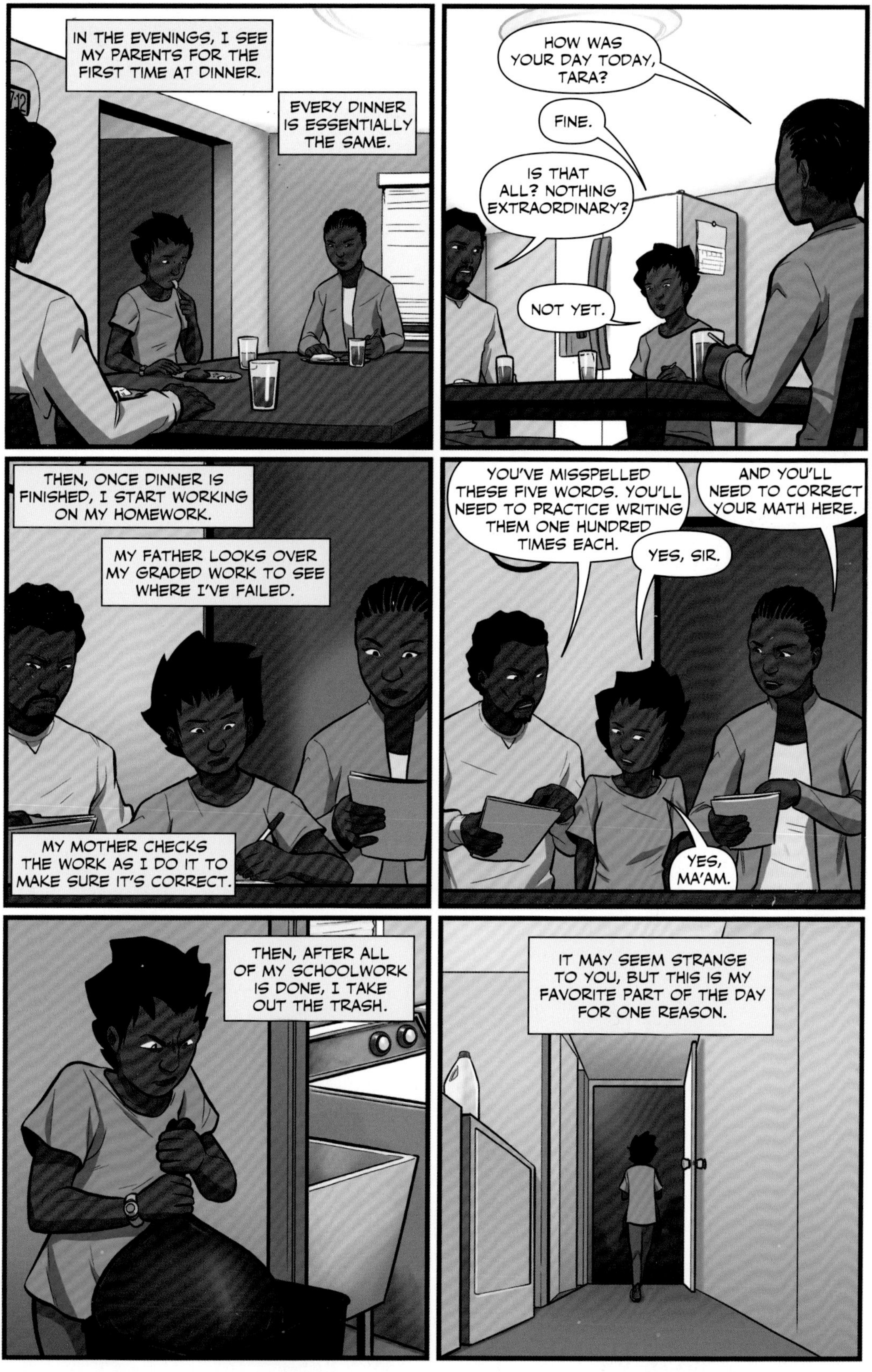
IN THE EVENINGS, I SEE MY PARENTS FOR THE FIRST TIME AT DINNER.
EVERY DINNER IS ESSENTIALLY THE SAME.
HOW WAS YOUR DAY TODAY, TARA?
FINE.
IS THAT ALL? NOTHING EXTRAORDINARY?
NOT YET.
THEN, ONCE DINNER IS FINISHED, I START WORKING ON MY HOMEWORK.
MY FATHER LOOKS OVER MY GRADED WORK TO SEE WHERE I'VE FAILED.
MY MOTHER CHECKS THE WORK AS I DO IT TO MAKE SURE IT'S CORRECT.
YOU'VE MISSPELLED THESE FIVE WORDS. YOU'LL NEED TO PRACTICE WRITING THEM ONE HUNDRED TIMES EACH.
AND YOU'LL NEED TO CORRECT YOUR MATH HERE.
YES, SIR.
YES, MA'AM.
THEN, AFTER ALL OF MY SCHOOLWORK IS DONE, I TAKE OUT THE TRASH.
IT MAY SEEM STRANGE TO YOU, BUT THIS IS MY FAVORITE PART OF THE DAY FOR ONE REASON.

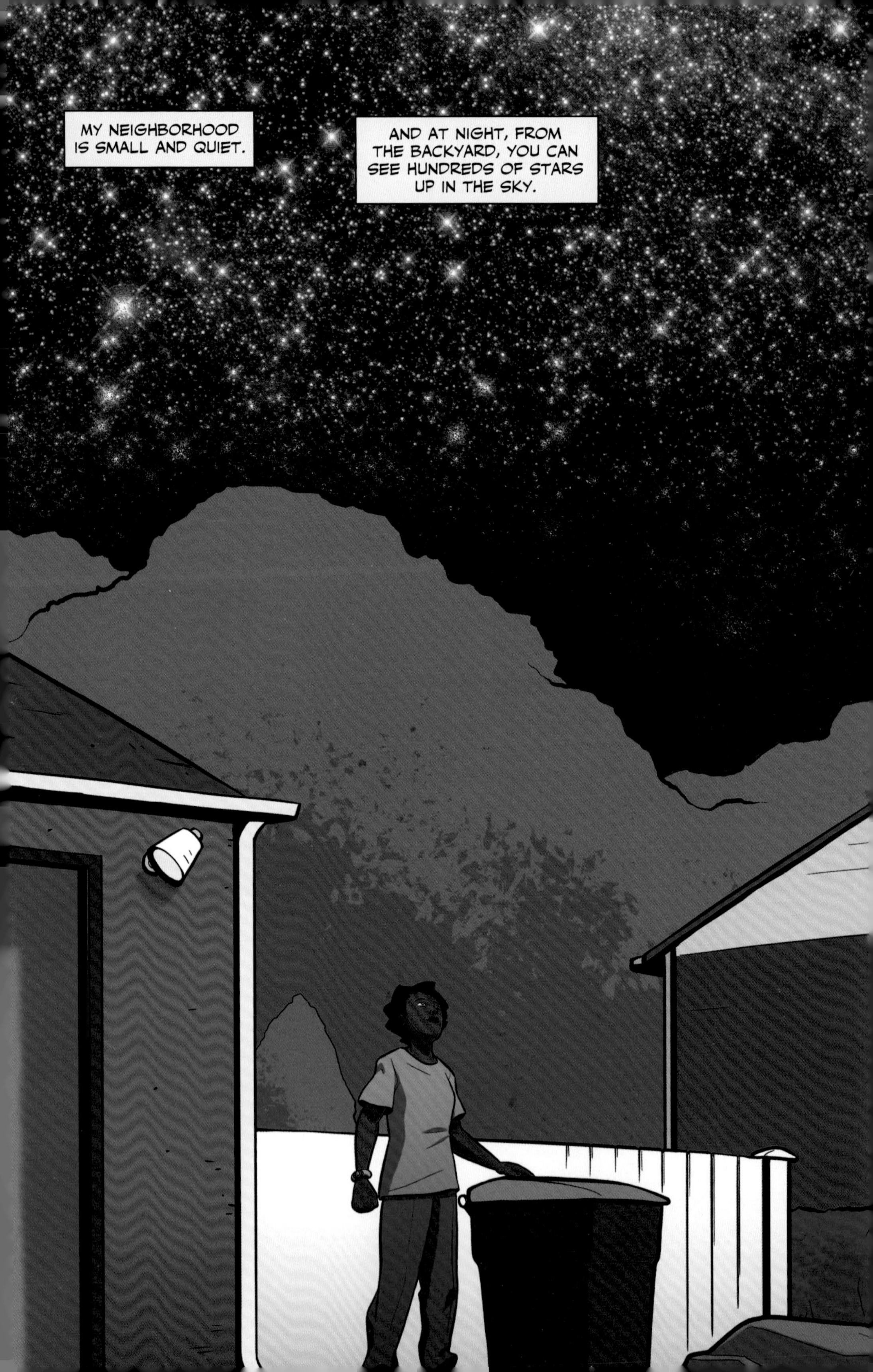
MY NEIGHBORHOOD IS SMALL AND QUIET.
AND AT NIGHT, FROM THE BACKYARD, YOU CAN SEE HUNDREDS OF STARS UP IN THE SKY.

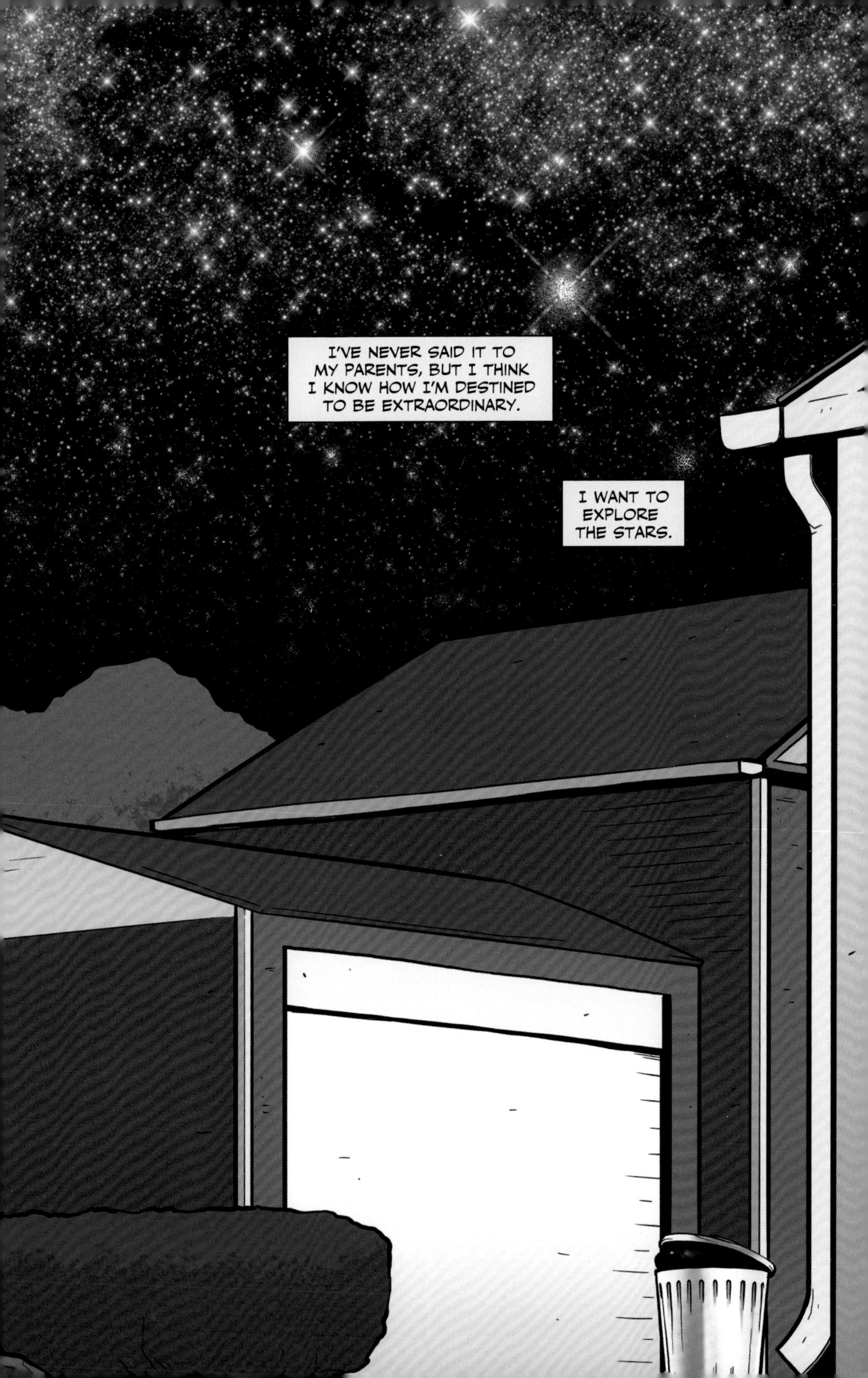
I'VE NEVER SAID IT TO MY PARENTS, BUT I THINK I KNOW HOW I'M DESTINED TO BE EXTRAORDINARY.
I WANT TO EXPLORE THE STARS.

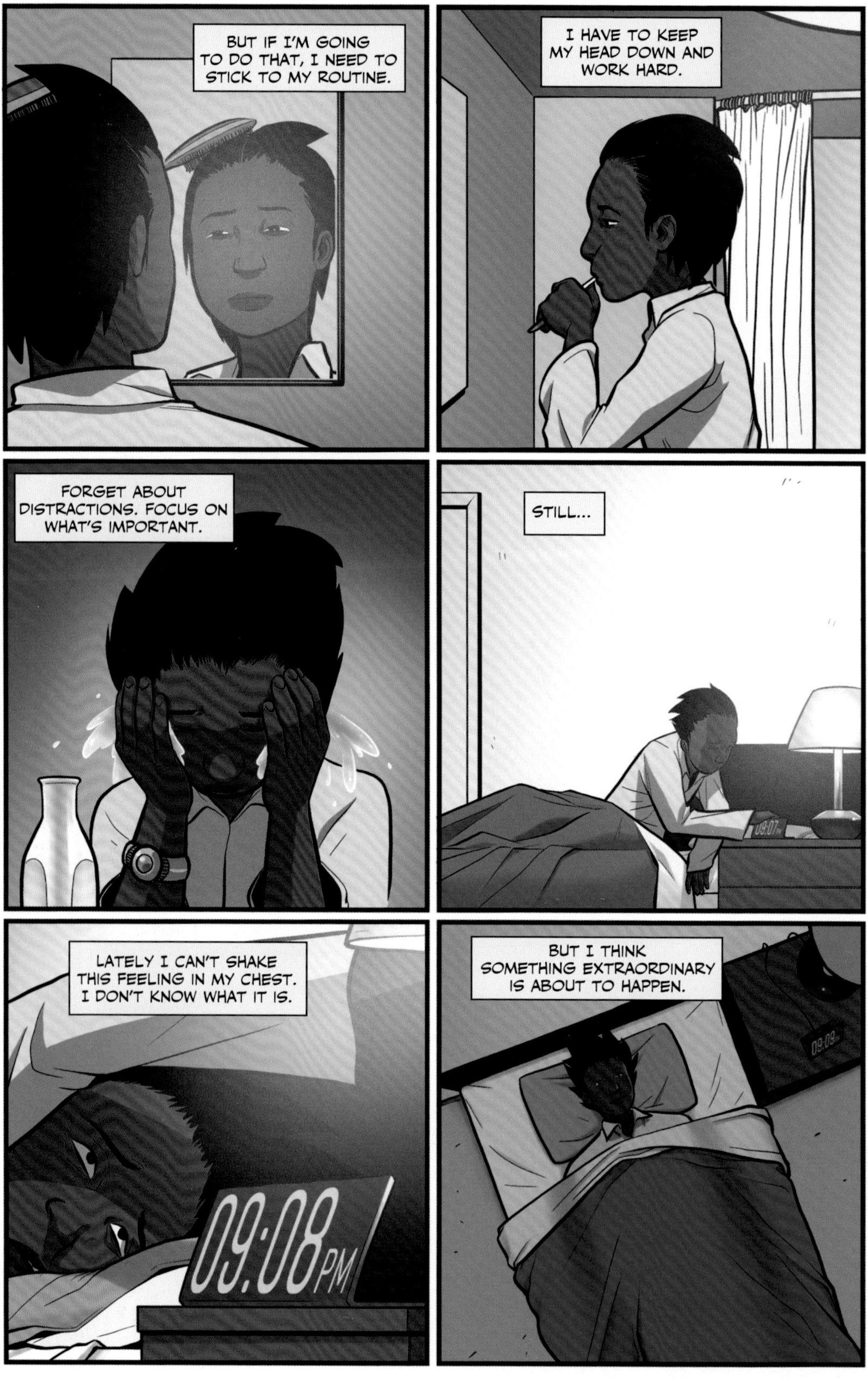
BUT IF I'M GOING TO DO THAT, I NEED TO STICK TO MY ROUTINE.
I HAVE TO KEEP MY HEAD DOWN AND WORK HARD.
FORGET ABOUT DISTRACTIONS. FOCUS ON WHAT'S IMPORTANT.
STILL...
LATELY I CAN'T SHAKE THIS FEELING IN MY CHEST. I DON'T KNOW WHAT IT IS.
09:08PM
BUT I THINK SOMETHING EXTRAORDINARY IS ABOUT TO HAPPEN.

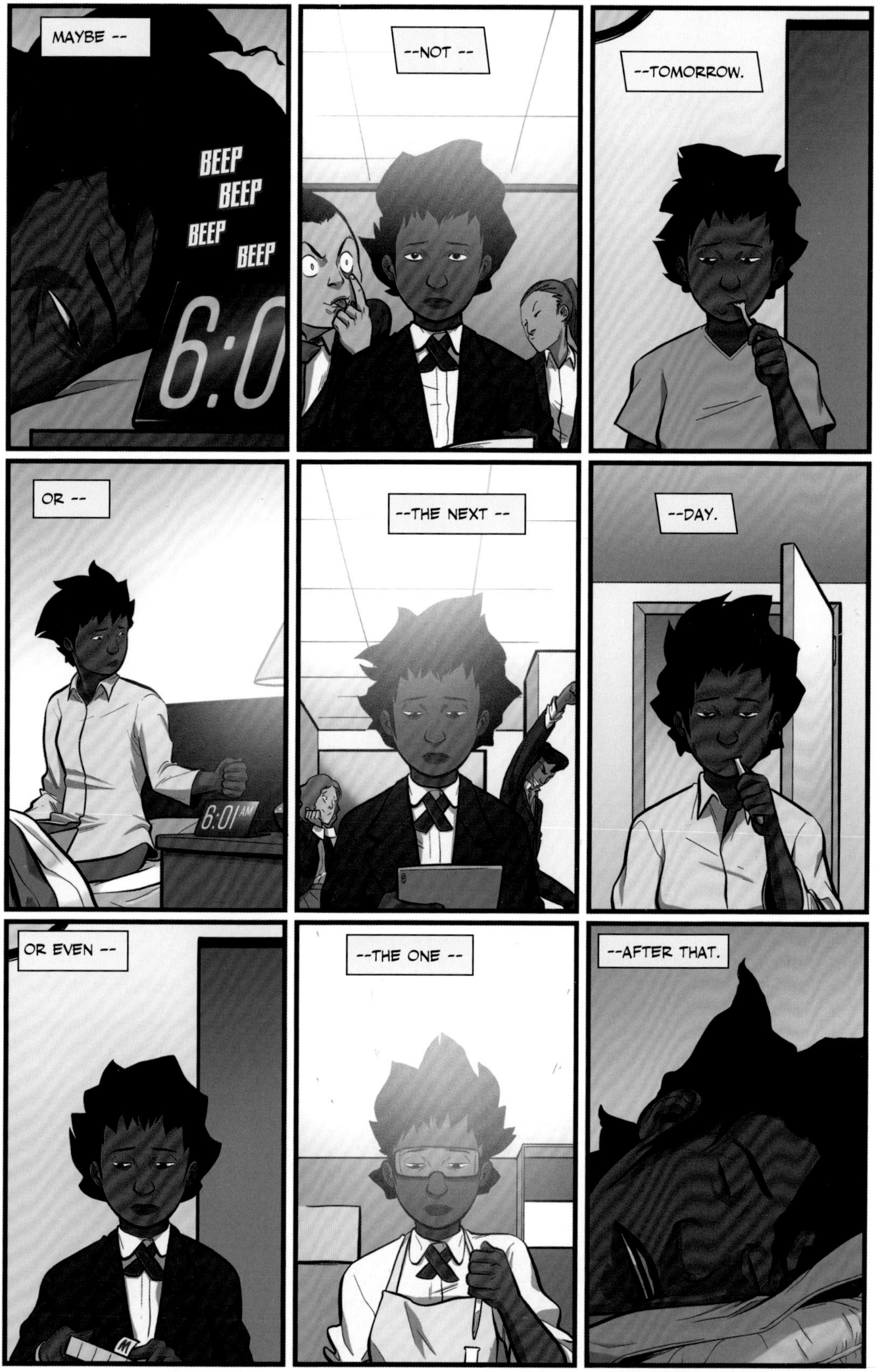
MAYBE --
BEEP
BEEP
BEEP
BEEP
6:0
--NOT --
--TOMORROW.
OR --
6:01 AM
--THE NEXT --
--DAY.
OR EVEN --
--THE ONE --
--AFTER THAT.

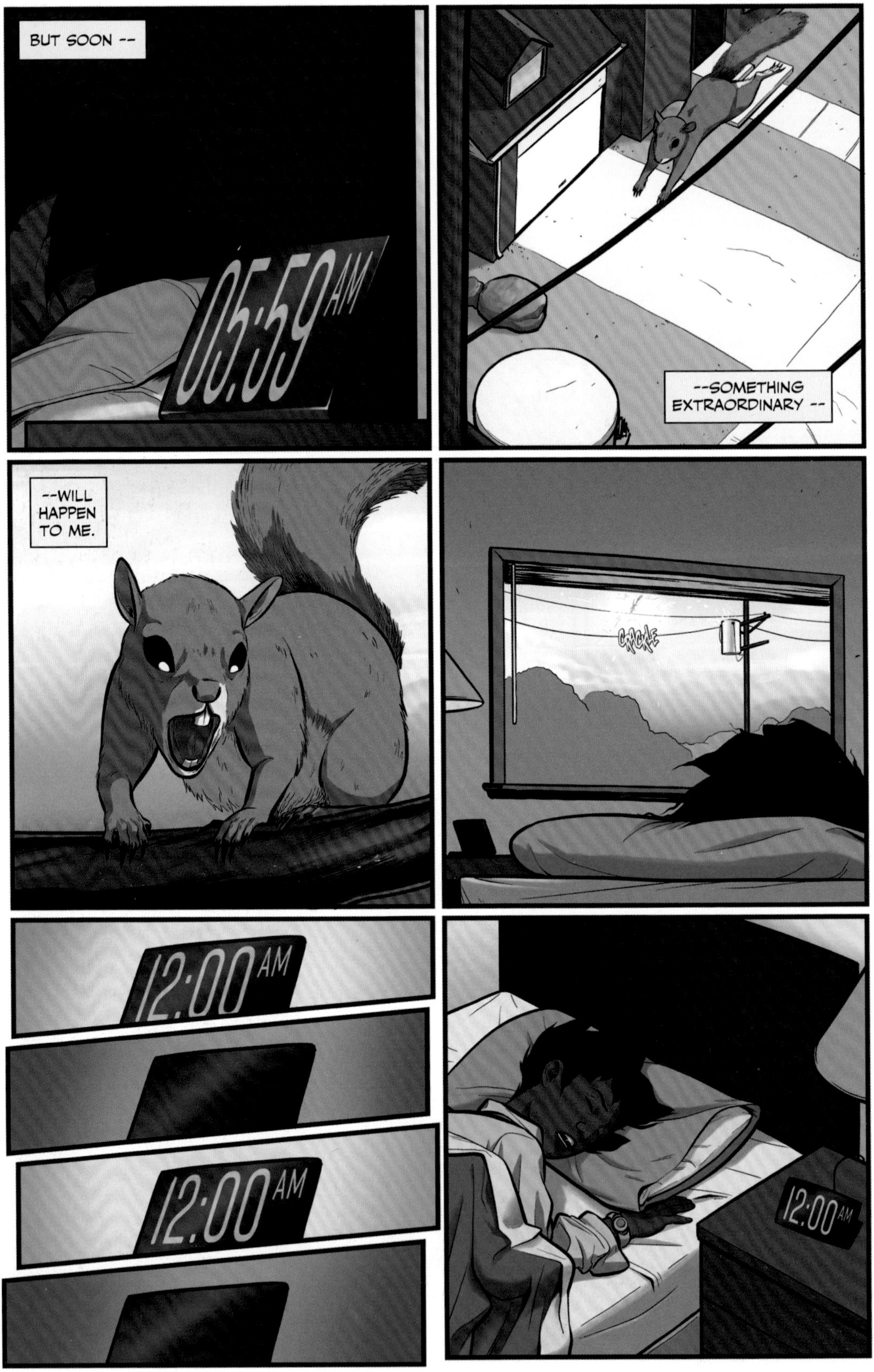
BUT SOON --
05:59 AM
--SOMETHING EXTRAORDINARY --
--WILL HAPPEN TO ME.
CRACKLE
12:00 AM
12:00 AM
12:00 AM

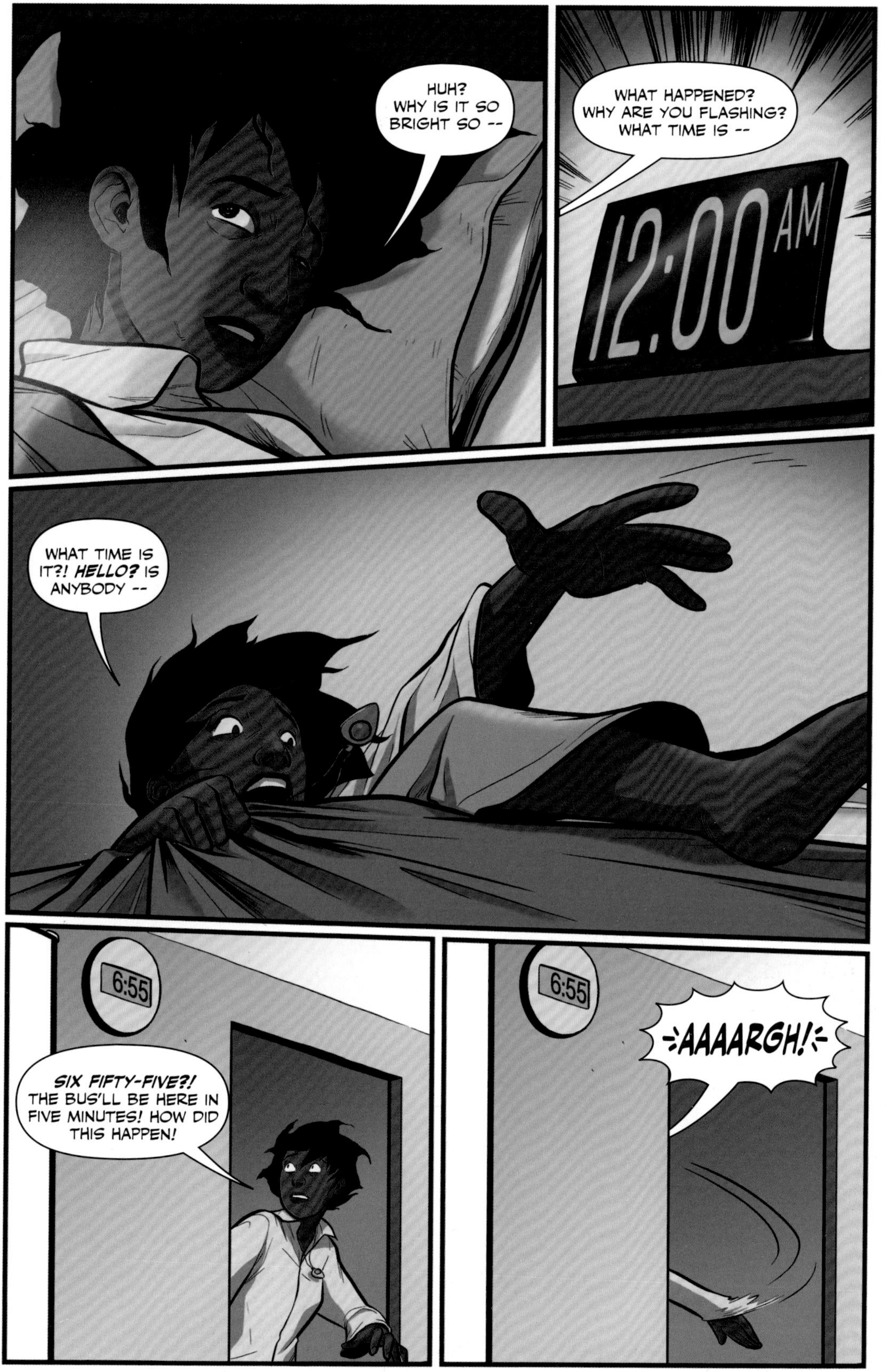
HUH? WHY IS IT SO BRIGHT SO --
WHAT HAPPENED? WHY ARE YOU FLASHING? WHAT TIME IS --
12:00 AM
WHAT TIME IS IT?! *HELLO?* IS ANYBODY --
6:55
SIX FIFTY-FIVE?! THE BUS'LL BE HERE IN FIVE MINUTES! HOW DID THIS HAPPEN!
6:55
AAAARGH!

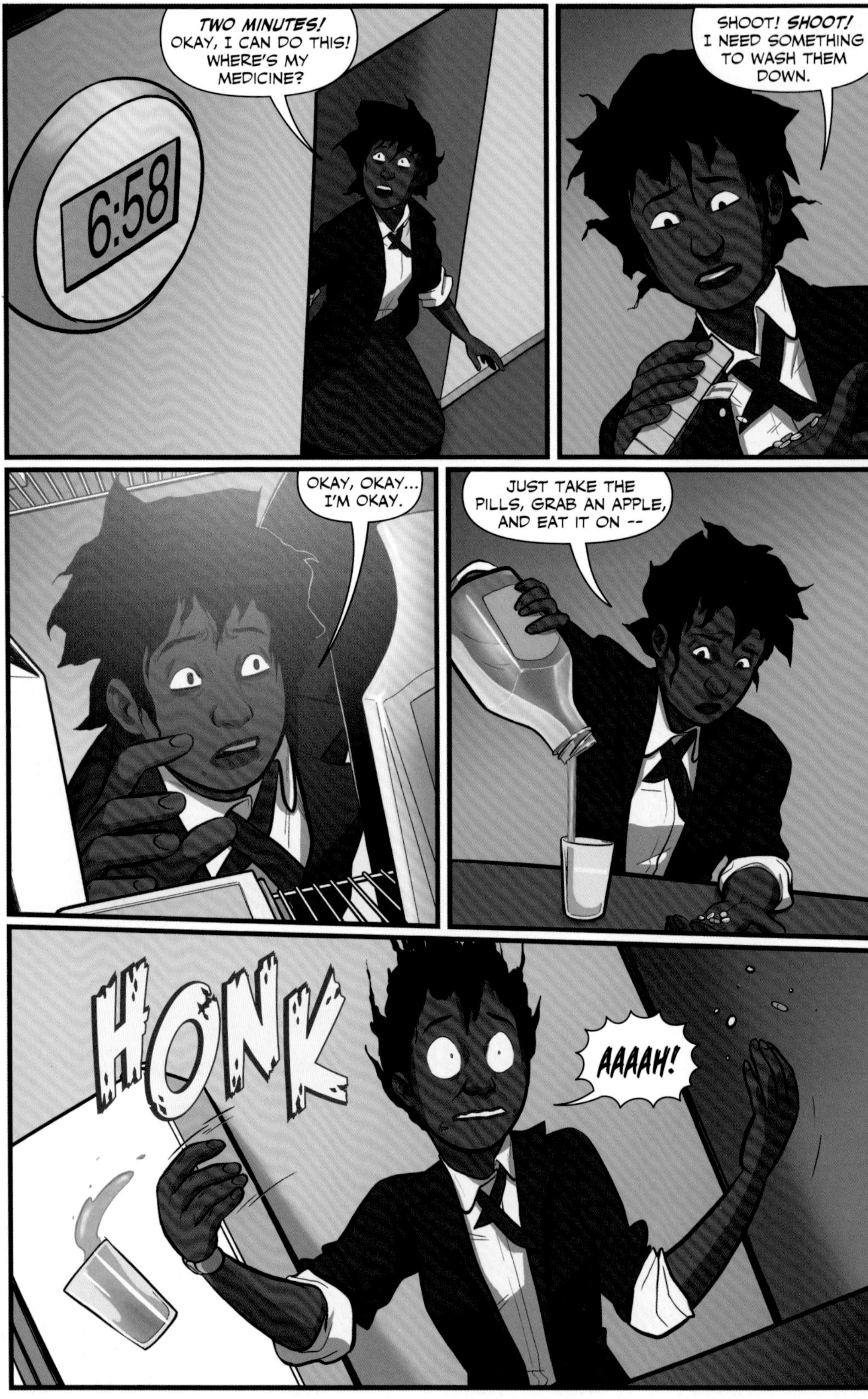
TWO MINUTES! OKAY, I CAN DO THIS! WHERE'S MY MEDICINE?
6:58
SHOOT! SHOOT! I NEED SOMETHING TO WASH THEM DOWN.
OKAY, OKAY... I'M OKAY.
JUST TAKE THE PILLS, GRAB AN APPLE, AND EAT IT ON --
HONK
AAAAH!

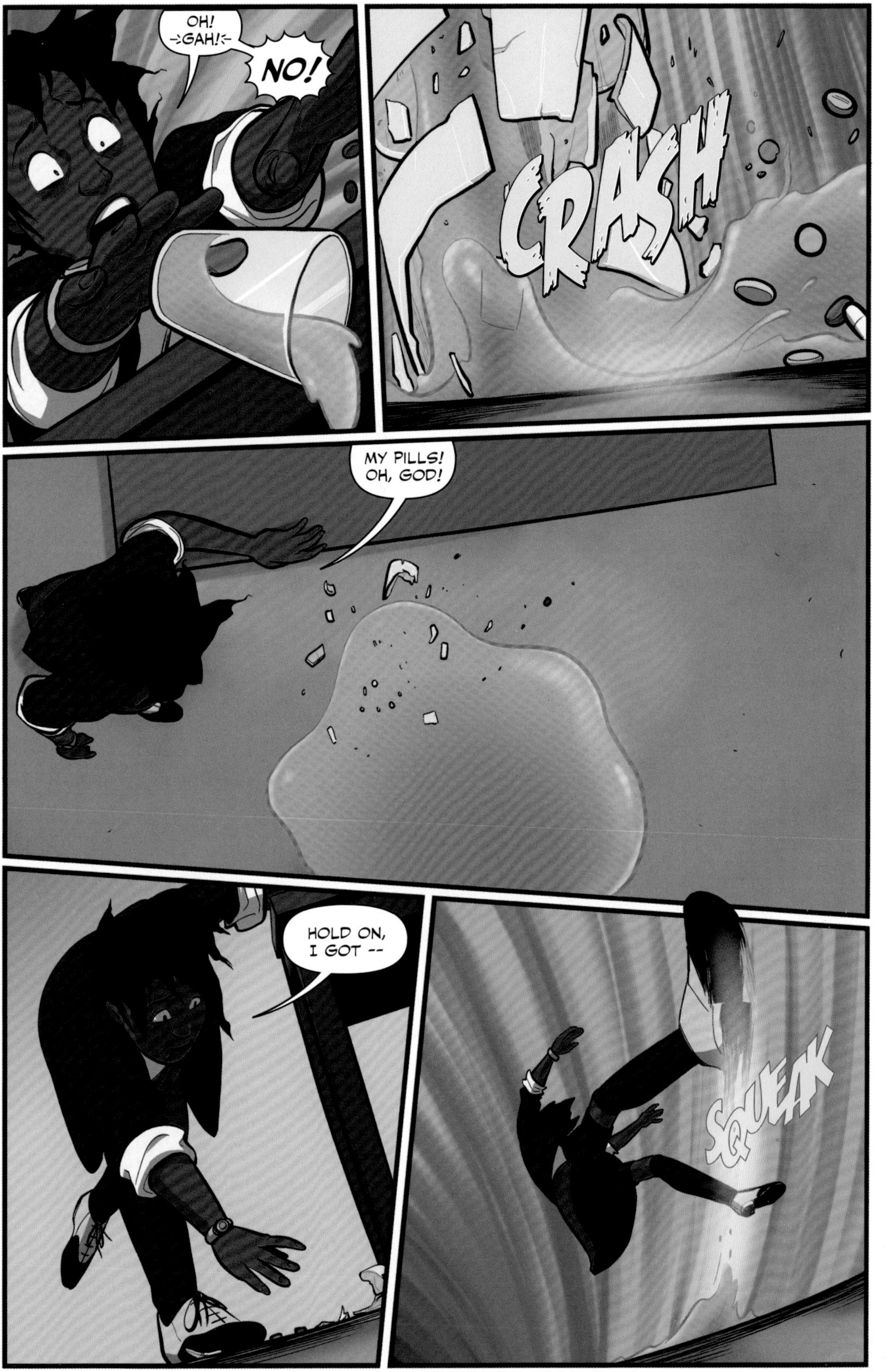
OH!
-GAH!-
NO!
CRASH
MY PILLS! OH, GOD!
HOLD ON, I GOT --
SQUEAK

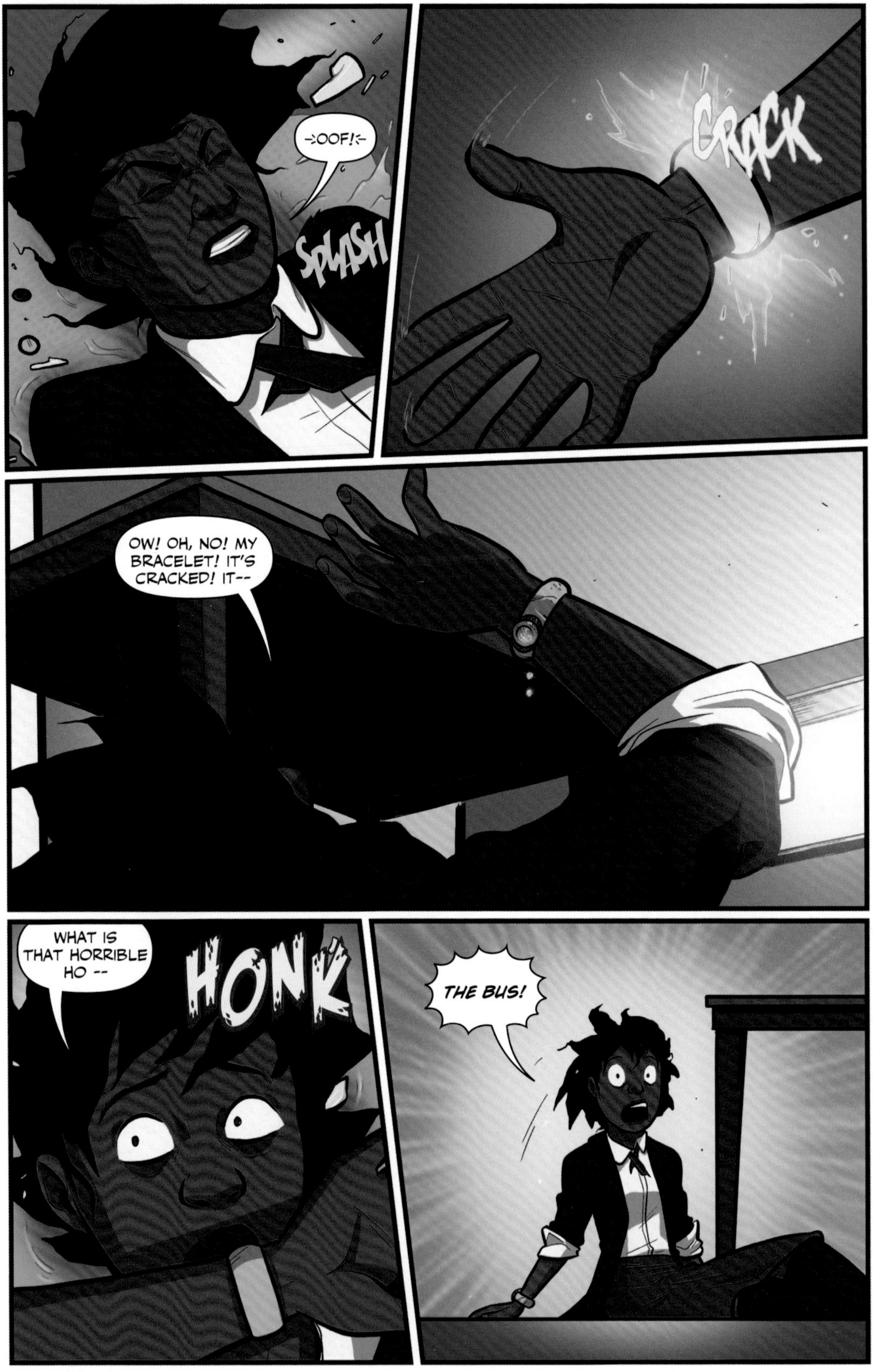

-OOF!-
SPLASH
CRACK
OW! OH, NO! MY BRACELET! IT'S CRACKED! IT--
WHAT IS THAT HORRIBLE HO --
HONK
THE BUS!

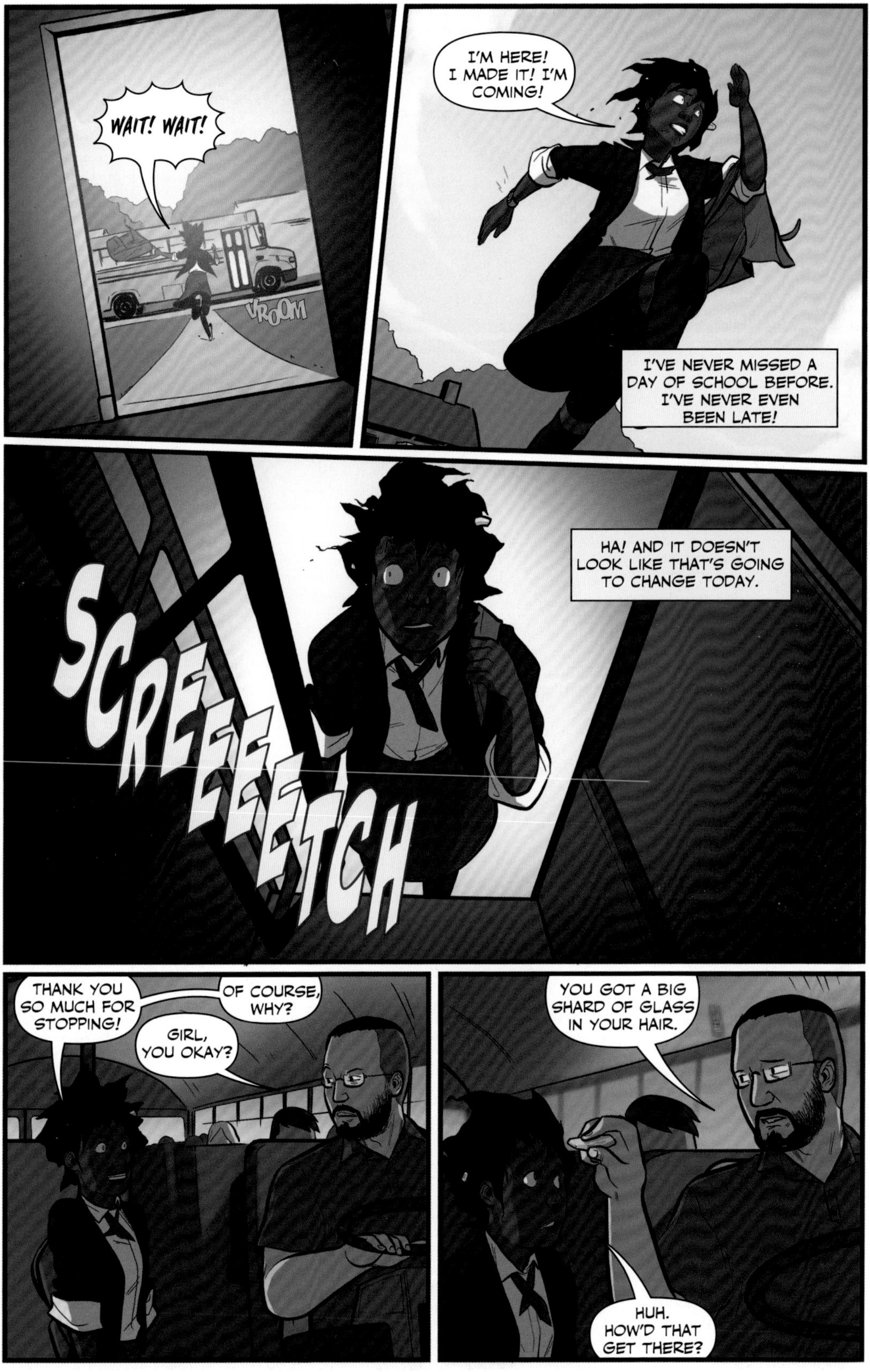
WAIT! WAIT!
VROOM
I'M HERE! I MADE IT! I'M COMING!
I'VE NEVER MISSED A DAY OF SCHOOL BEFORE. I'VE NEVER EVEN BEEN LATE!
HA! AND IT DOESN'T LOOK LIKE THAT'S GOING TO CHANGE TODAY.
SCREEEEETCH
THANK YOU SO MUCH FOR STOPPING!
OF COURSE, WHY?
GIRL, YOU OKAY?
YOU GOT A BIG SHARD OF GLASS IN YOUR HAIR.
HUH. HOW'D THAT GET THERE?

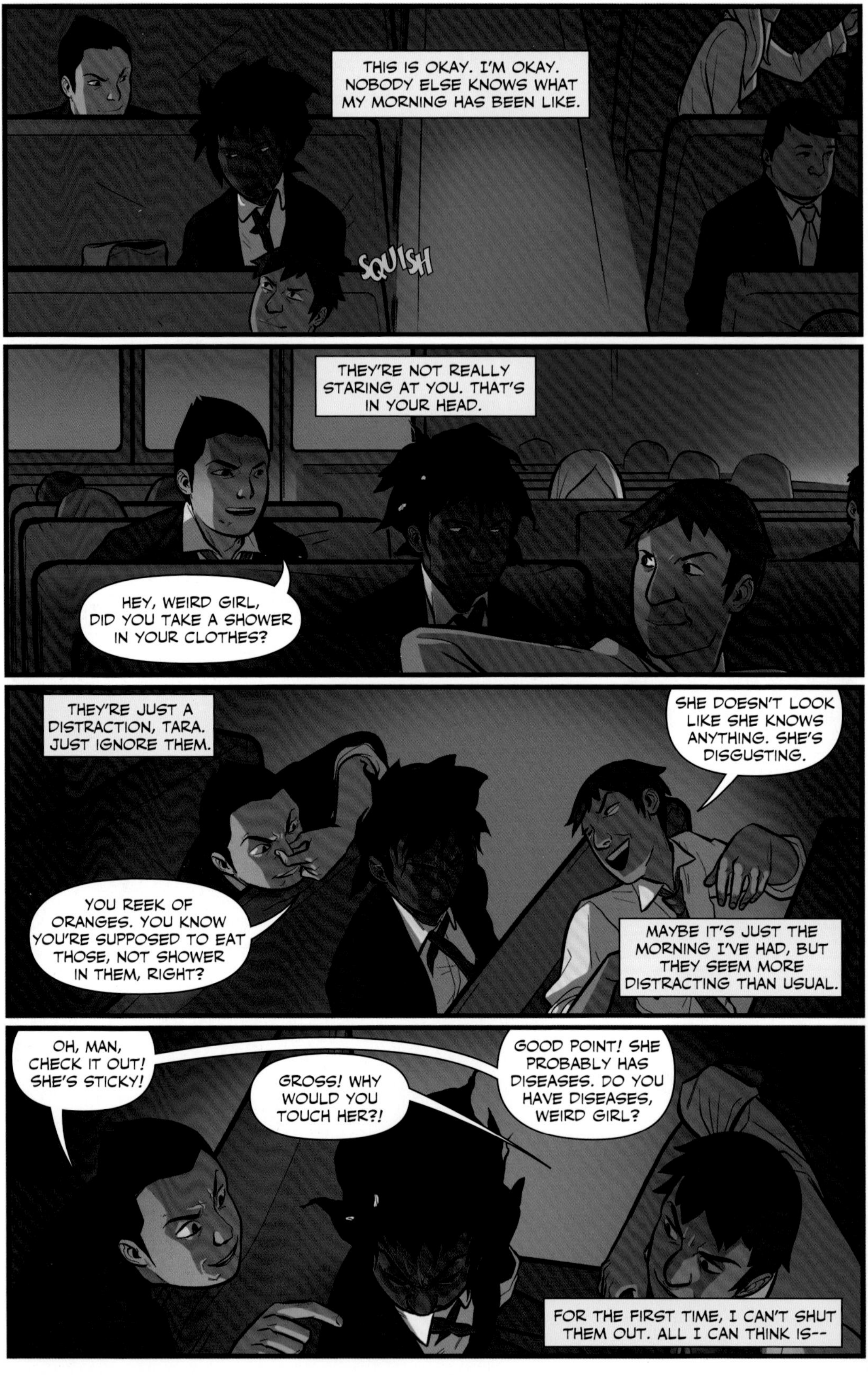
THIS IS OKAY. I'M OKAY. NOBODY ELSE KNOWS WHAT MY MORNING HAS BEEN LIKE.
SQUISH
THEY'RE NOT REALLY STARING AT YOU. THAT'S IN YOUR HEAD.
HEY, WEIRD GIRL, DID YOU TAKE A SHOWER IN YOUR CLOTHES?
THEY'RE JUST A DISTRACTION, TARA. JUST IGNORE THEM.
SHE DOESN'T LOOK LIKE SHE KNOWS ANYTHING. SHE'S DISGUSTING.
YOU REEK OF ORANGES. YOU KNOW YOU'RE SUPPOSED TO EAT THOSE, NOT SHOWER IN THEM, RIGHT?
MAYBE IT'S JUST THE MORNING I'VE HAD, BUT THEY SEEM MORE DISTRACTING THAN USUAL.
OH, MAN, CHECK IT OUT! SHE'S STICKY!
GROSS! WHY WOULD YOU TOUCH HER?!
GOOD POINT! SHE PROBABLY HAS DISEASES. DO YOU HAVE DISEASES, WEIRD GIRL?
FOR THE FIRST TIME, I CAN'T SHUT THEM OUT. ALL I CAN THINK IS--

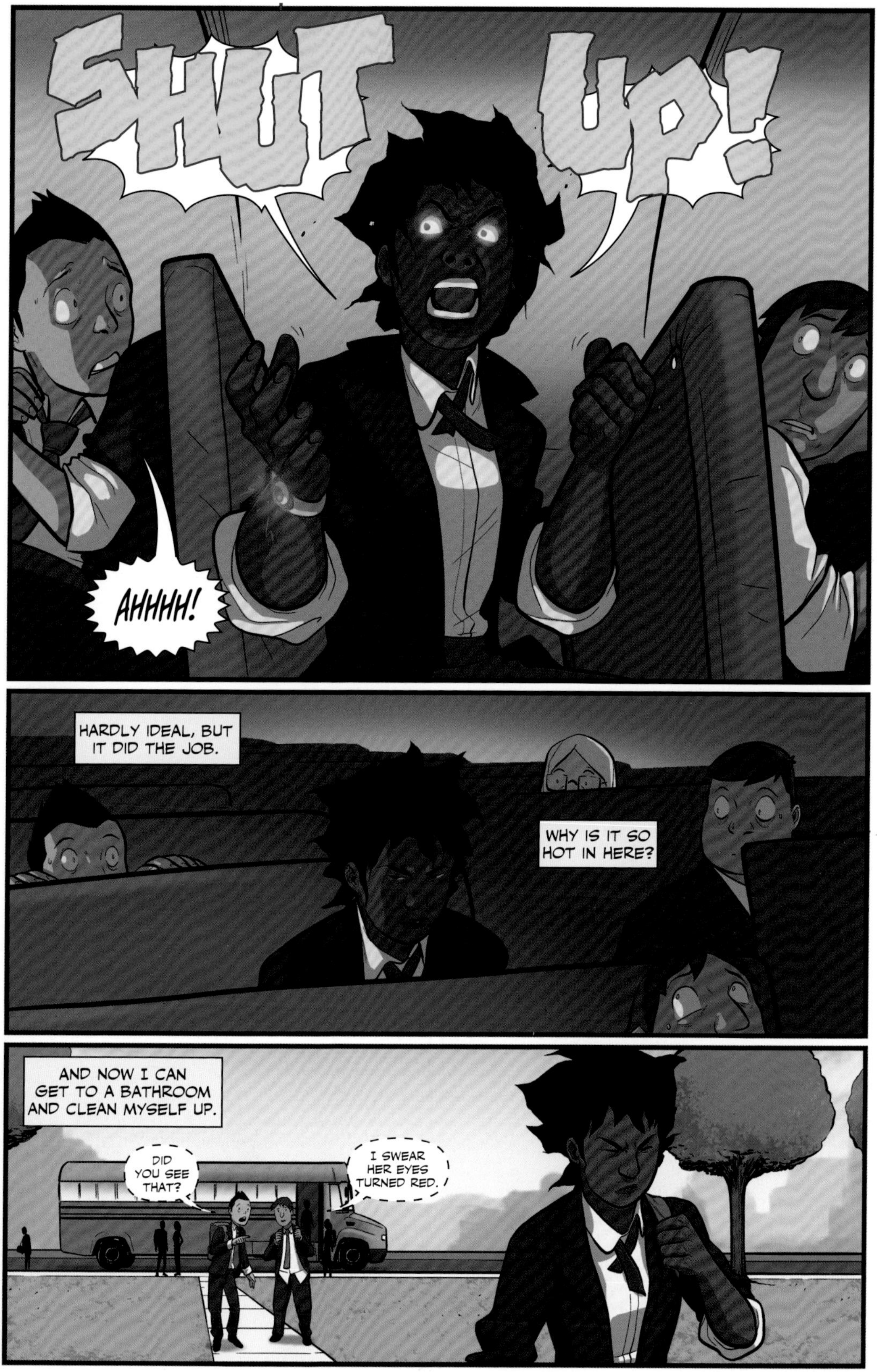
SHUT UP!
AHHHH!
HARDLY IDEAL, BUT IT DID THE JOB.
WHY IS IT SO HOT IN HERE?
AND NOW I CAN GET TO A BATHROOM AND CLEAN MYSELF UP.
DID YOU SEE THAT?
I SWEAR HER EYES TURNED RED.

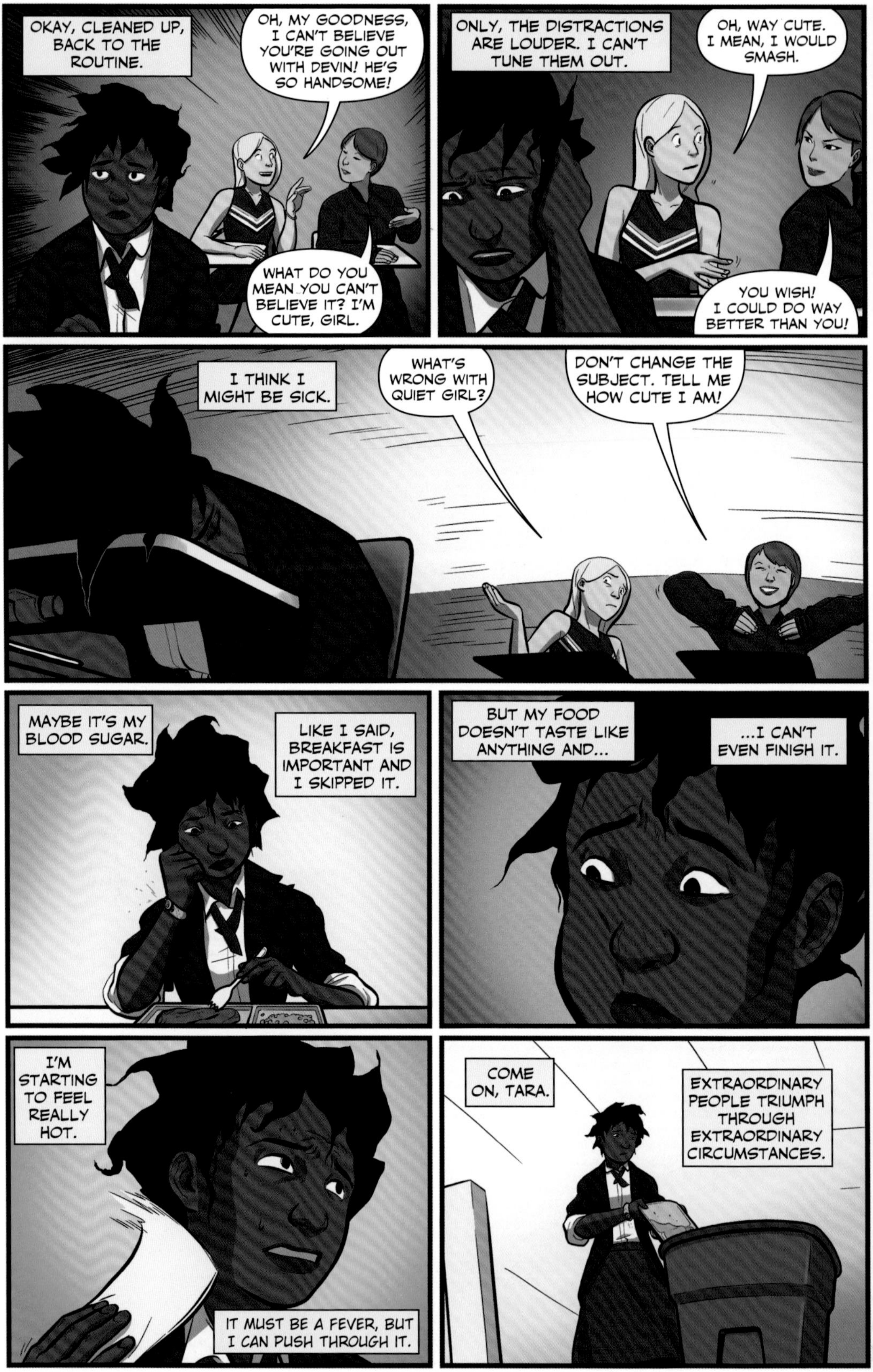
OKAY, CLEANED UP, BACK TO THE ROUTINE.
OH, MY GOODNESS, I CAN'T BELIEVE YOU'RE GOING OUT WITH DEVIN! HE'S SO HANDSOME!
WHAT DO YOU MEAN YOU CAN'T BELIEVE IT? I'M CUTE, GIRL.
ONLY, THE DISTRACTIONS ARE LOUDER. I CAN'T TUNE THEM OUT.
OH, WAY CUTE. I MEAN, I WOULD SMASH.
YOU WISH! I COULD DO WAY BETTER THAN YOU!
I THINK I MIGHT BE SICK.
WHAT'S WRONG WITH QUIET GIRL?
DON'T CHANGE THE SUBJECT. TELL ME HOW CUTE I AM!
MAYBE IT'S MY BLOOD SUGAR.
LIKE I SAID, BREAKFAST IS IMPORTANT AND I SKIPPED IT.
BUT MY FOOD DOESN'T TASTE LIKE ANYTHING AND...
...I CAN'T EVEN FINISH IT.
I'M STARTING TO FEEL REALLY HOT.
IT MUST BE A FEVER, BUT I CAN PUSH THROUGH IT.
COME ON, TARA.
EXTRAORDINARY PEOPLE TRIUMPH THROUGH EXTRAORDINARY CIRCUMSTANCES.

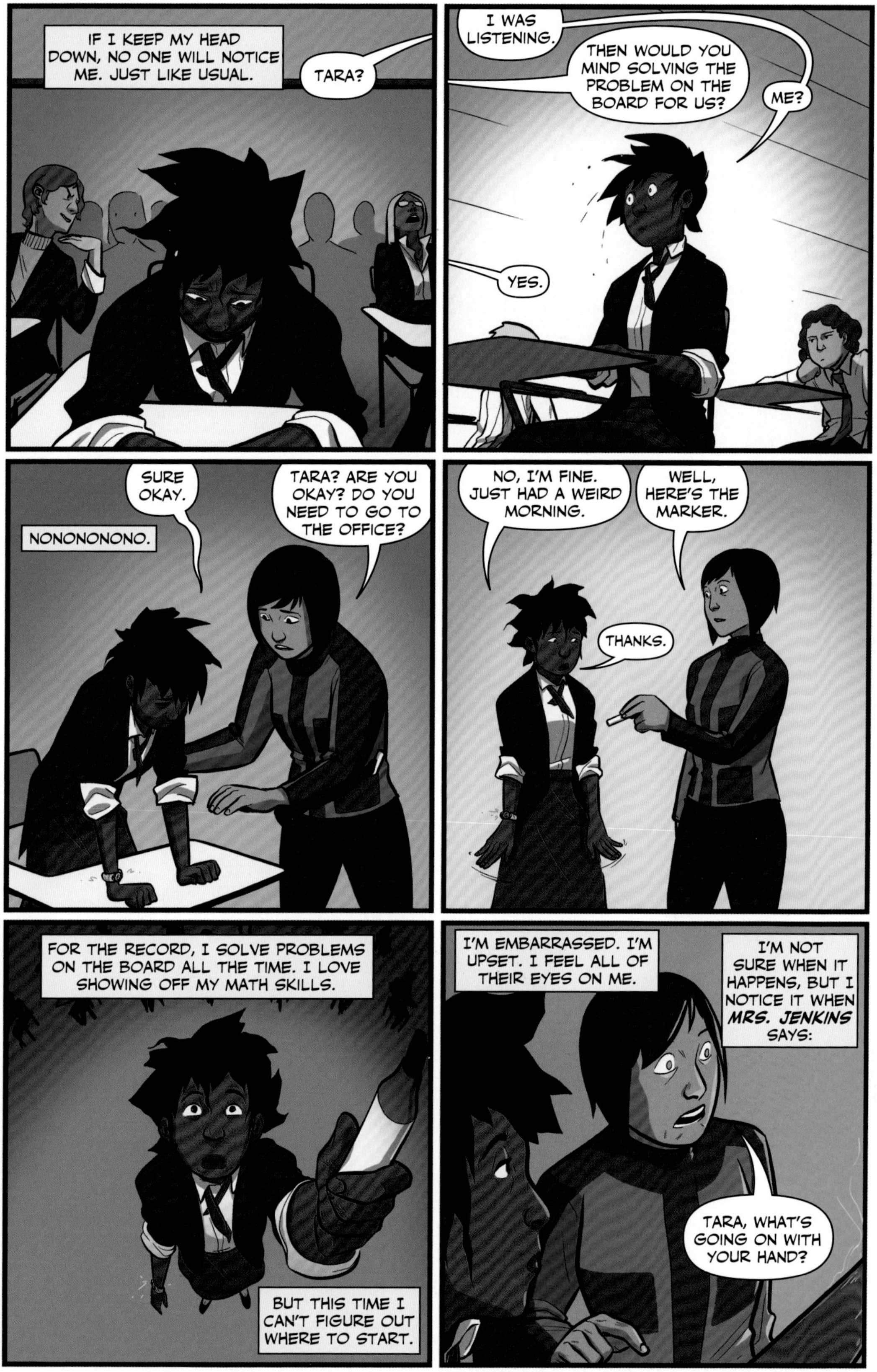
IF I KEEP MY HEAD DOWN, NO ONE WILL NOTICE ME. JUST LIKE USUAL.
TARA?
I WAS LISTENING.
THEN WOULD YOU MIND SOLVING THE PROBLEM ON THE BOARD FOR US?
ME?
YES.
NONONONONO.
SURE OKAY.
TARA? ARE YOU OKAY? DO YOU NEED TO GO TO THE OFFICE?
NO, I'M FINE. JUST HAD A WEIRD MORNING.
WELL, HERE'S THE MARKER.
THANKS.
FOR THE RECORD, I SOLVE PROBLEMS ON THE BOARD ALL THE TIME. I LOVE SHOWING OFF MY MATH SKILLS.
BUT THIS TIME I CAN'T FIGURE OUT WHERE TO START.
I'M EMBARRASSED. I'M UPSET. I FEEL ALL OF THEIR EYES ON ME.
I'M NOT SURE WHEN IT HAPPENS, BUT I NOTICE IT WHEN MRS. JENKINS SAYS:
TARA, WHAT'S GOING ON WITH YOUR HAND?

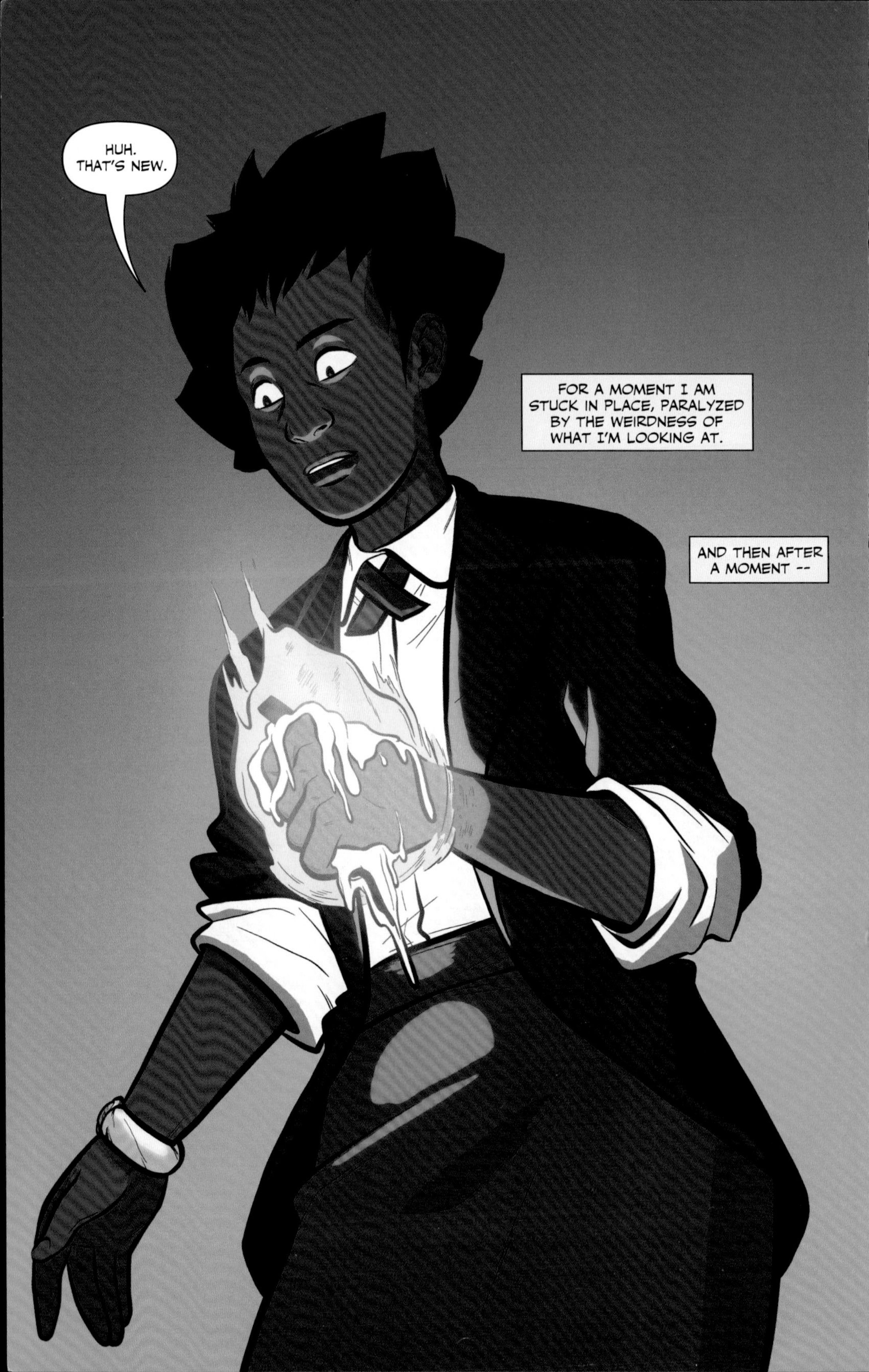
HUH. THAT'S NEW.
FOR A MOMENT I AM STUCK IN PLACE, PARALYZED BY THE WEIRDNESS OF WHAT I'M LOOKING AT.
AND THEN AFTER A MOMENT --

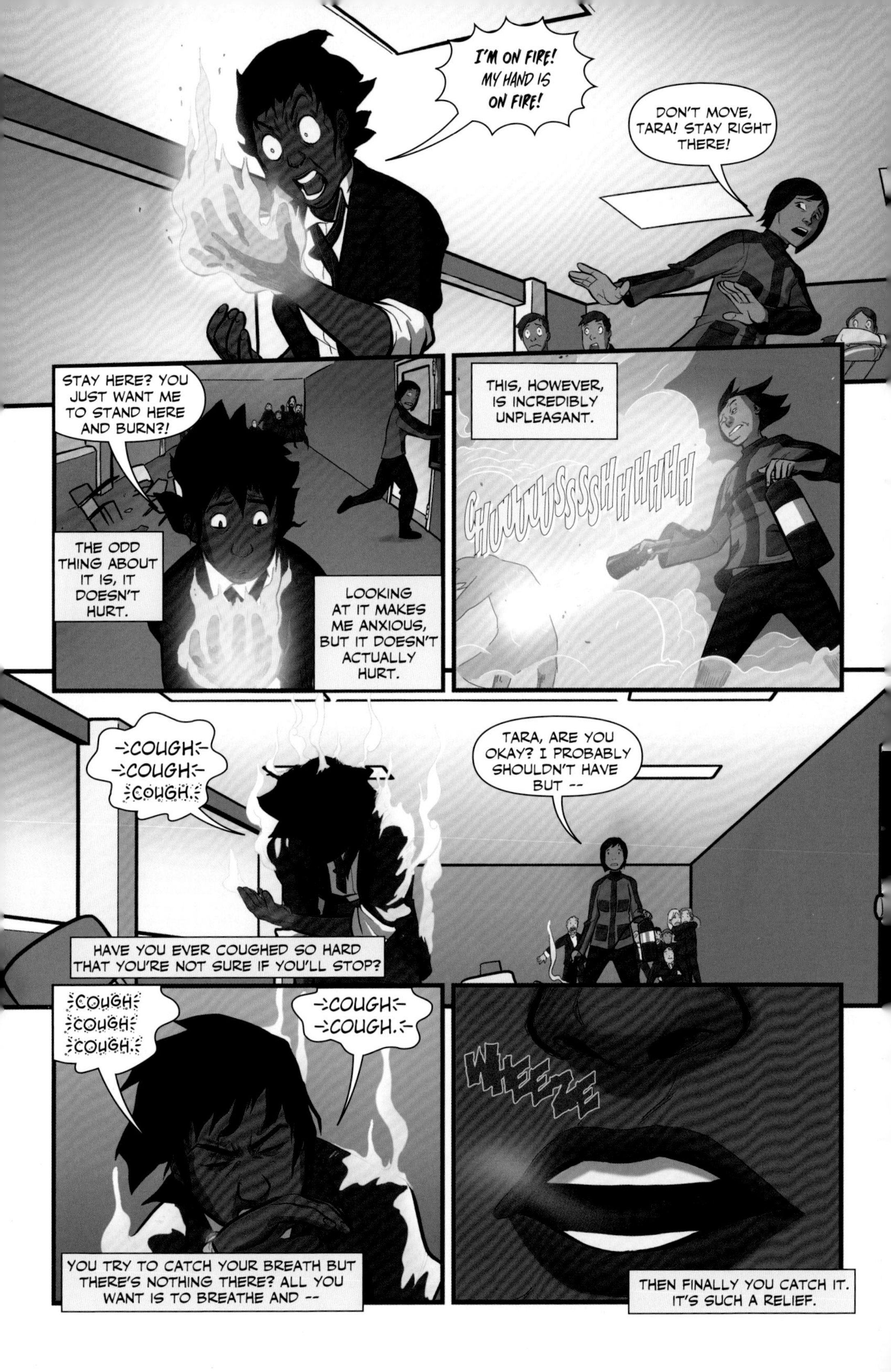

I'M ON FIRE! MY HAND IS ON FIRE!
DON'T MOVE, TARA! STAY RIGHT THERE!
STAY HERE? YOU JUST WANT ME TO STAND HERE AND BURN?!
THE ODD THING ABOUT IT IS, IT DOESN'T HURT.
LOOKING AT IT MAKES ME ANXIOUS, BUT IT DOESN'T ACTUALLY HURT.
THIS, HOWEVER, IS INCREDIBLY UNPLEASANT.
CHUUUUSSSSHHHHHH
COUGH COUGH COUGH.
TARA, ARE YOU OKAY? I PROBABLY SHOULDN'T HAVE BUT --
HAVE YOU EVER COUGHED SO HARD THAT YOU'RE NOT SURE IF YOU'LL STOP?
COUGH COUGH COUGH.
COUGH COUGH.
YOU TRY TO CATCH YOUR BREATH BUT THERE'S NOTHING THERE? ALL YOU WANT IS TO BREATHE AND --
WHEEZE
THEN FINALLY YOU CATCH IT. IT'S SUCH A RELIEF.

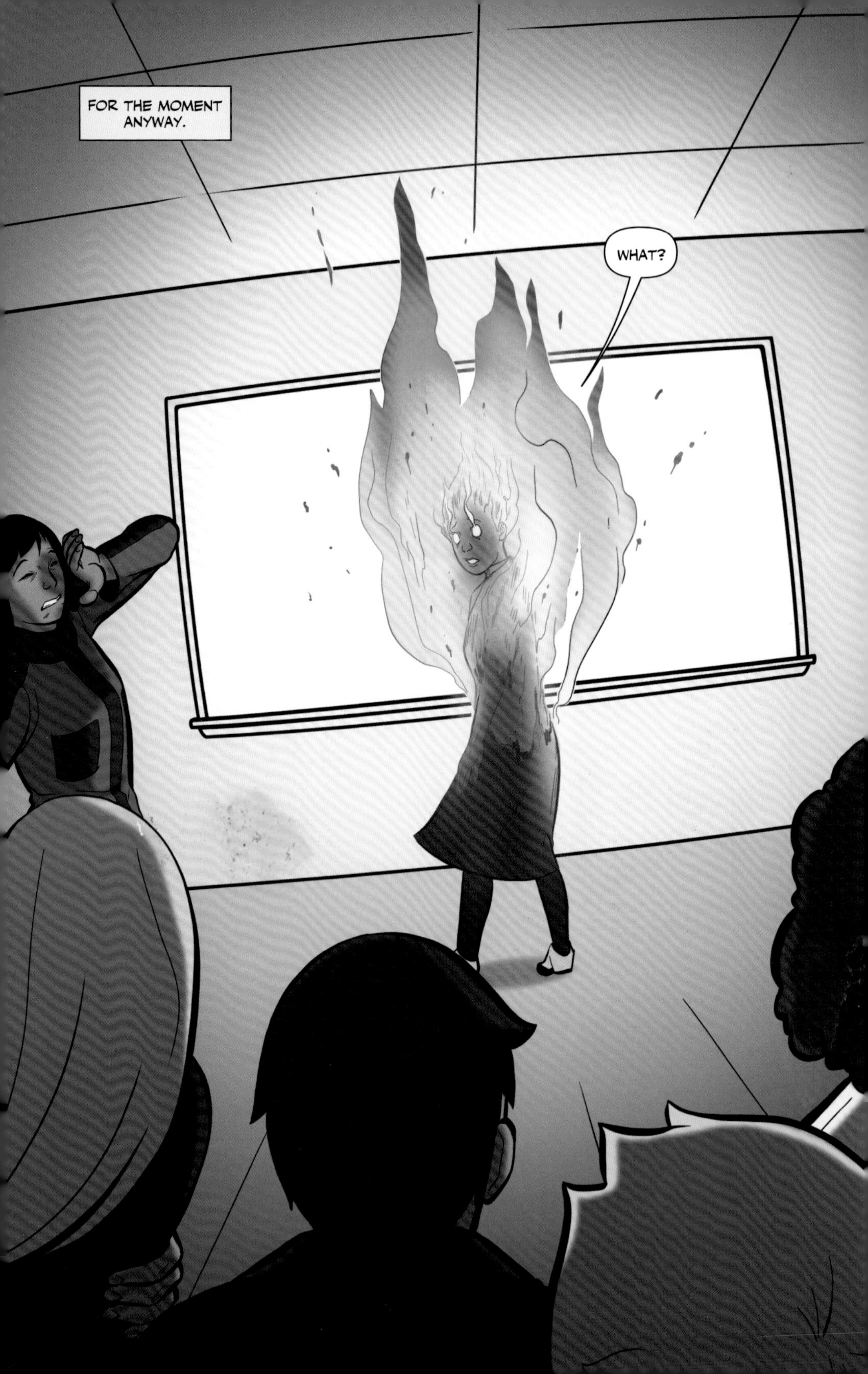
FOR THE MOMENT ANYWAY.
WHAT?

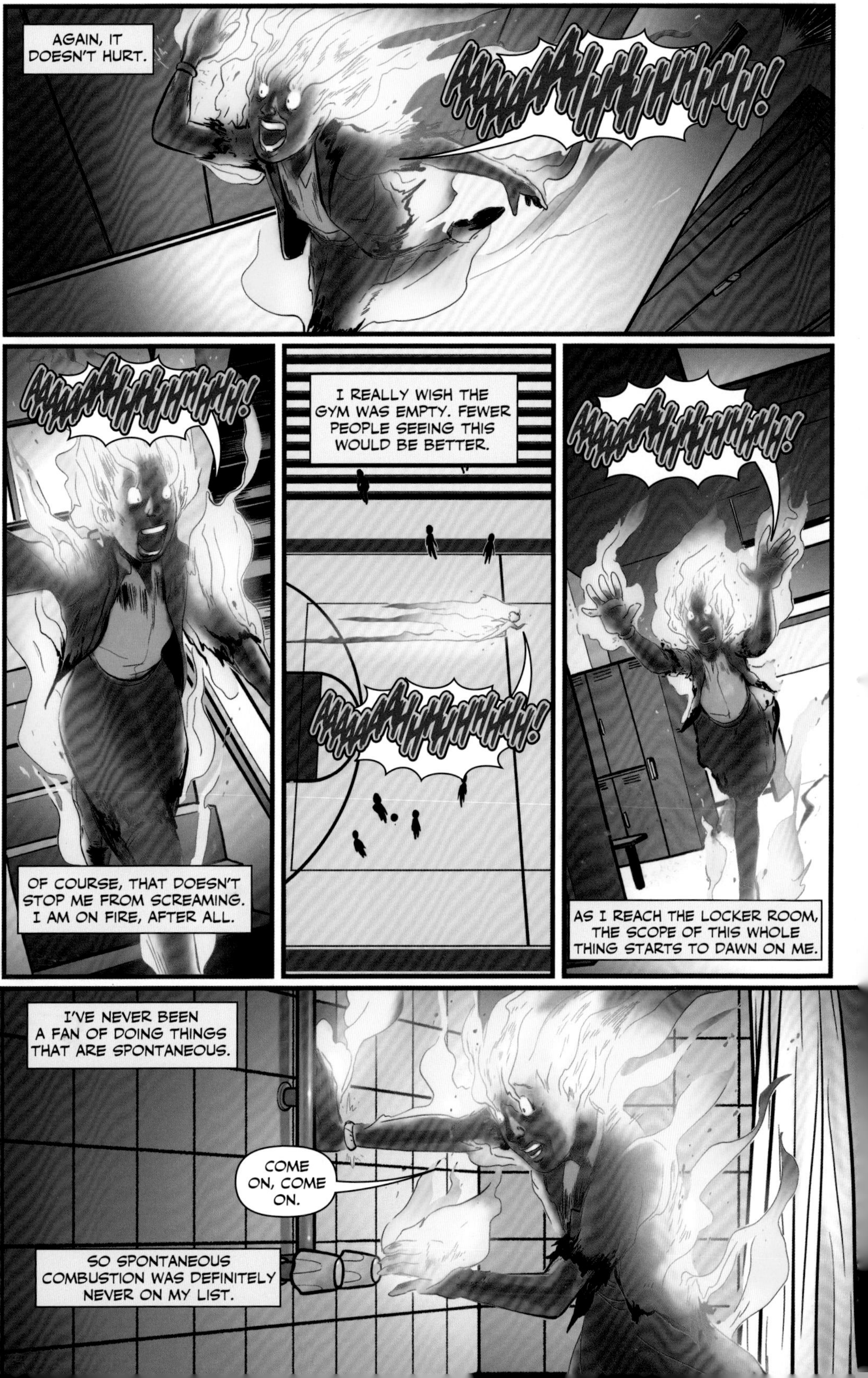
AGAIN, IT DOESN'T HURT.
AAAAAAAAHHHHHHHHH!
AAAAAAAAHHHHHHHHH!
OF COURSE, THAT DOESN'T STOP ME FROM SCREAMING. I AM ON FIRE, AFTER ALL.
I REALLY WISH THE GYM WAS EMPTY. FEWER PEOPLE SEEING THIS WOULD BE BETTER.
AAAAAAAAHHHHHHHHH!
AAAAAAAAHHHHHHHHH!
AS I REACH THE LOCKER ROOM, THE SCOPE OF THIS WHOLE THING STARTS TO DAWN ON ME.
I'VE NEVER BEEN A FAN OF DOING THINGS THAT ARE SPONTANEOUS.
COME ON, COME ON.
SO SPONTANEOUS COMBUSTION WAS DEFINITELY NEVER ON MY LIST.

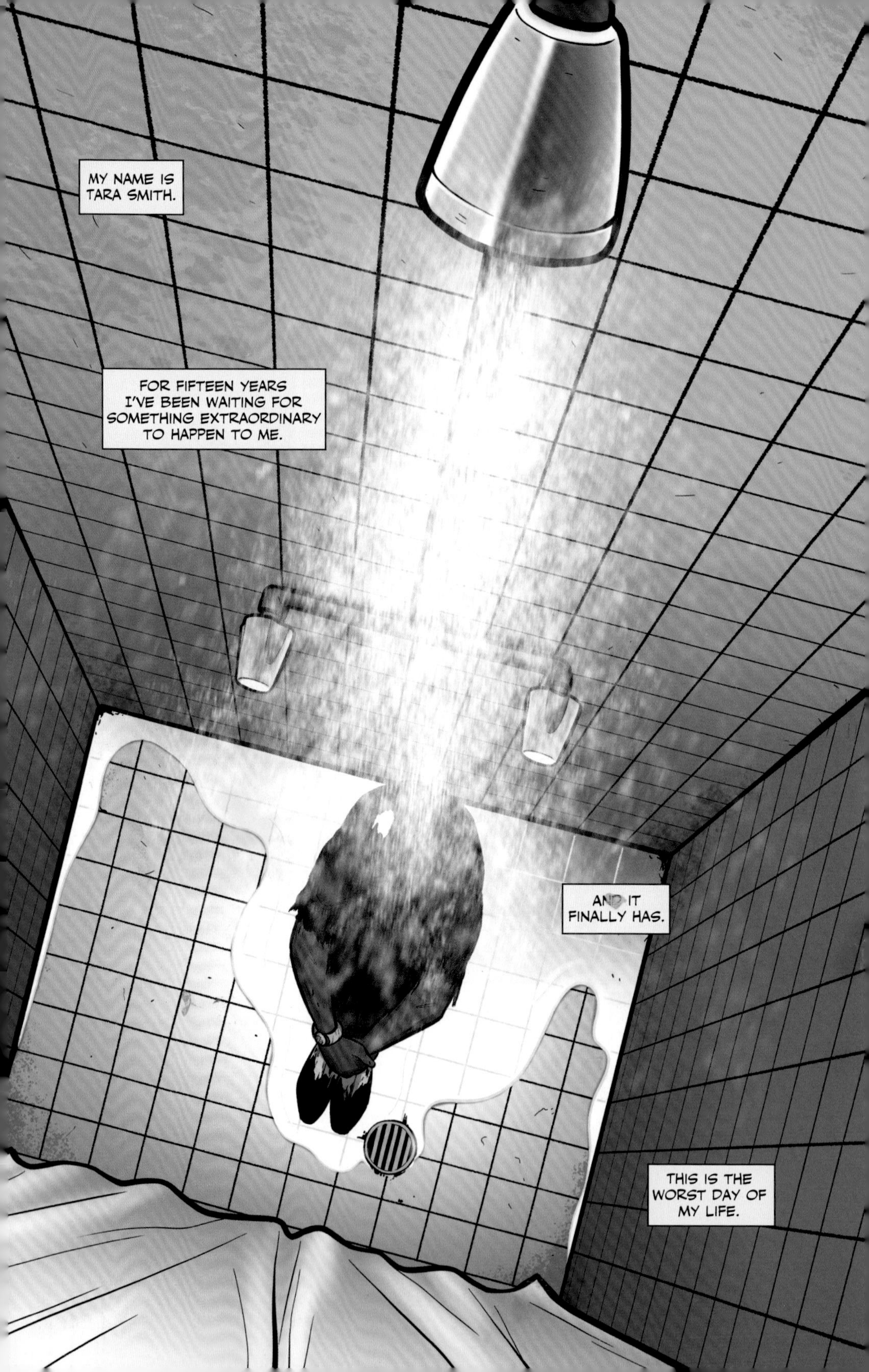
MY NAME IS TARA SMITH.
FOR FIFTEEN YEARS I'VE BEEN WAITING FOR SOMETHING EXTRAORDINARY TO HAPPEN TO ME.
AND IT FINALLY HAS.
THIS IS THE WORST DAY OF MY LIFE.

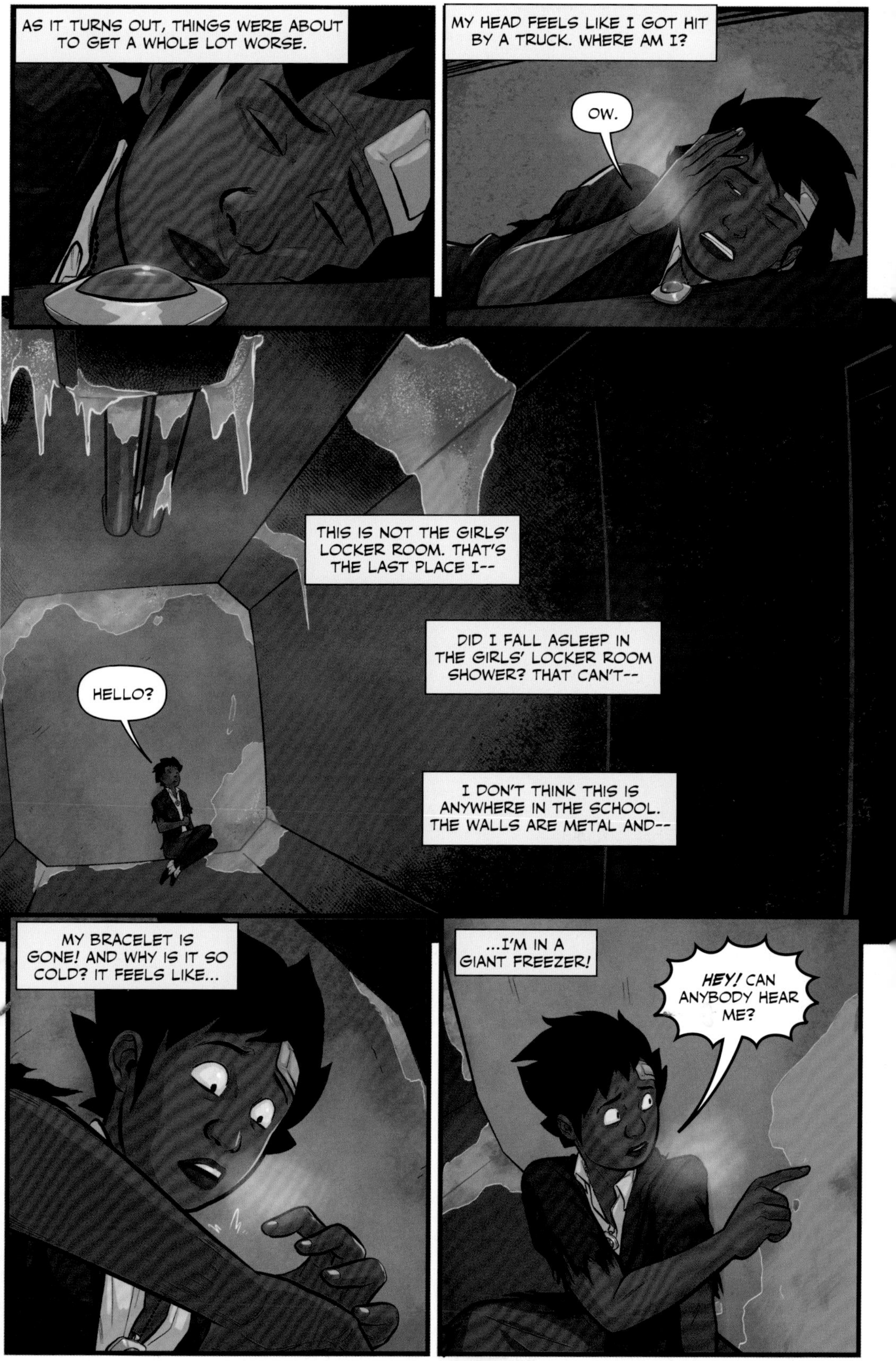
AS IT TURNS OUT, THINGS WERE ABOUT TO GET A WHOLE LOT WORSE.
MY HEAD FEELS LIKE I GOT HIT BY A TRUCK. WHERE AM I?
OW.
THIS IS NOT THE GIRLS' LOCKER ROOM. THAT'S THE LAST PLACE I--
HELLO?
DID I FALL ASLEEP IN THE GIRLS' LOCKER ROOM SHOWER? THAT CAN'T--
I DON'T THINK THIS IS ANYWHERE IN THE SCHOOL. THE WALLS ARE METAL AND--
MY BRACELET IS GONE! AND WHY IS IT SO COLD? IT FEELS LIKE...
...I'M IN A GIANT FREEZER!
HEY! CAN ANYBODY HEAR ME?

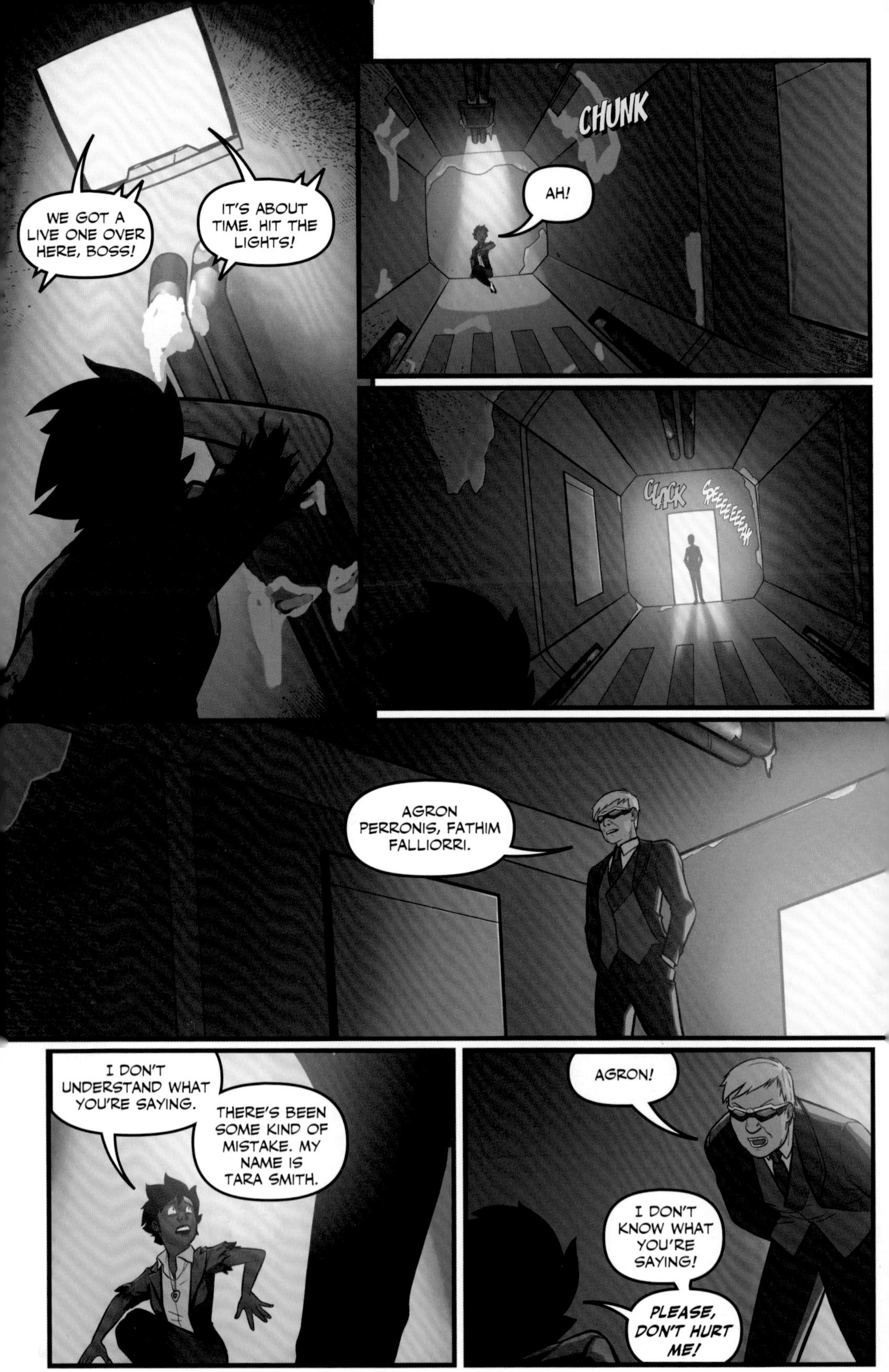
WE GOT A LIVE ONE OVER HERE, BOSS!
IT'S ABOUT TIME. HIT THE LIGHTS!
CHUNK
AH!
CLACK
SPEEEEEEEAK
AGRON PERRONIS, FATHIM FALLIORRI.
I DON'T UNDERSTAND WHAT YOU'RE SAYING.
THERE'S BEEN SOME KIND OF MISTAKE. MY NAME IS TARA SMITH.
AGRON!
I DON'T KNOW WHAT YOU'RE SAYING!
PLEASE, DON'T HURT ME!

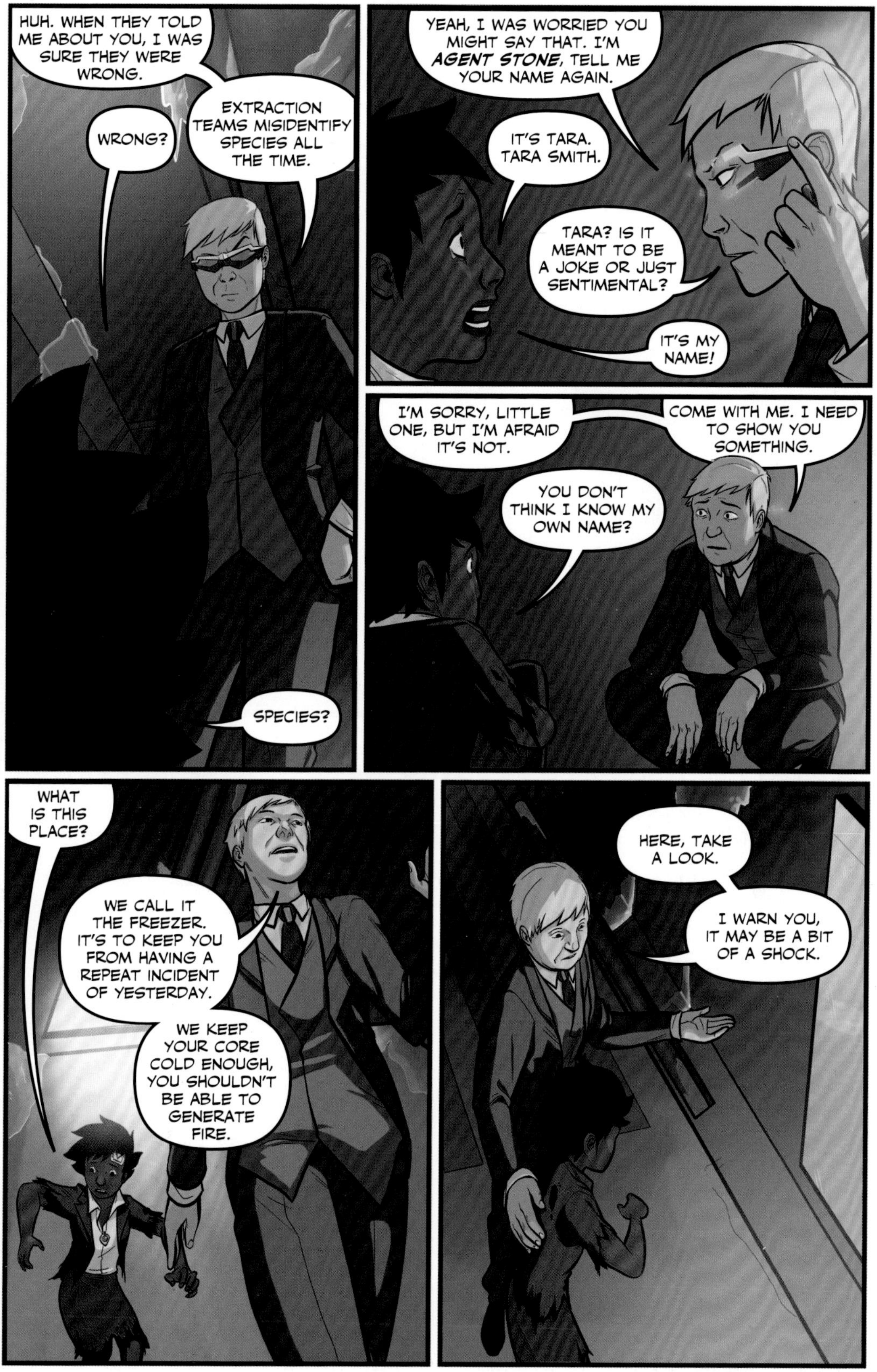
HUH. WHEN THEY TOLD ME ABOUT YOU, I WAS SURE THEY WERE WRONG.
WRONG?
EXTRACTION TEAMS MISIDENTIFY SPECIES ALL THE TIME.
SPECIES?
YEAH, I WAS WORRIED YOU MIGHT SAY THAT. I'M AGENT STONE, TELL ME YOUR NAME AGAIN.
IT'S TARA. TARA SMITH.
TARA? IS IT MEANT TO BE A JOKE OR JUST SENTIMENTAL?
IT'S MY NAME!
I'M SORRY, LITTLE ONE, BUT I'M AFRAID IT'S NOT.
YOU DON'T THINK I KNOW MY OWN NAME?
COME WITH ME. I NEED TO SHOW YOU SOMETHING.
WHAT IS THIS PLACE?
WE CALL IT THE FREEZER. IT'S TO KEEP YOU FROM HAVING A REPEAT INCIDENT OF YESTERDAY.
WE KEEP YOUR CORE COLD ENOUGH, YOU SHOULDN'T BE ABLE TO GENERATE FIRE.
HERE, TAKE A LOOK.
I WARN YOU, IT MAY BE A BIT OF A SHOCK.

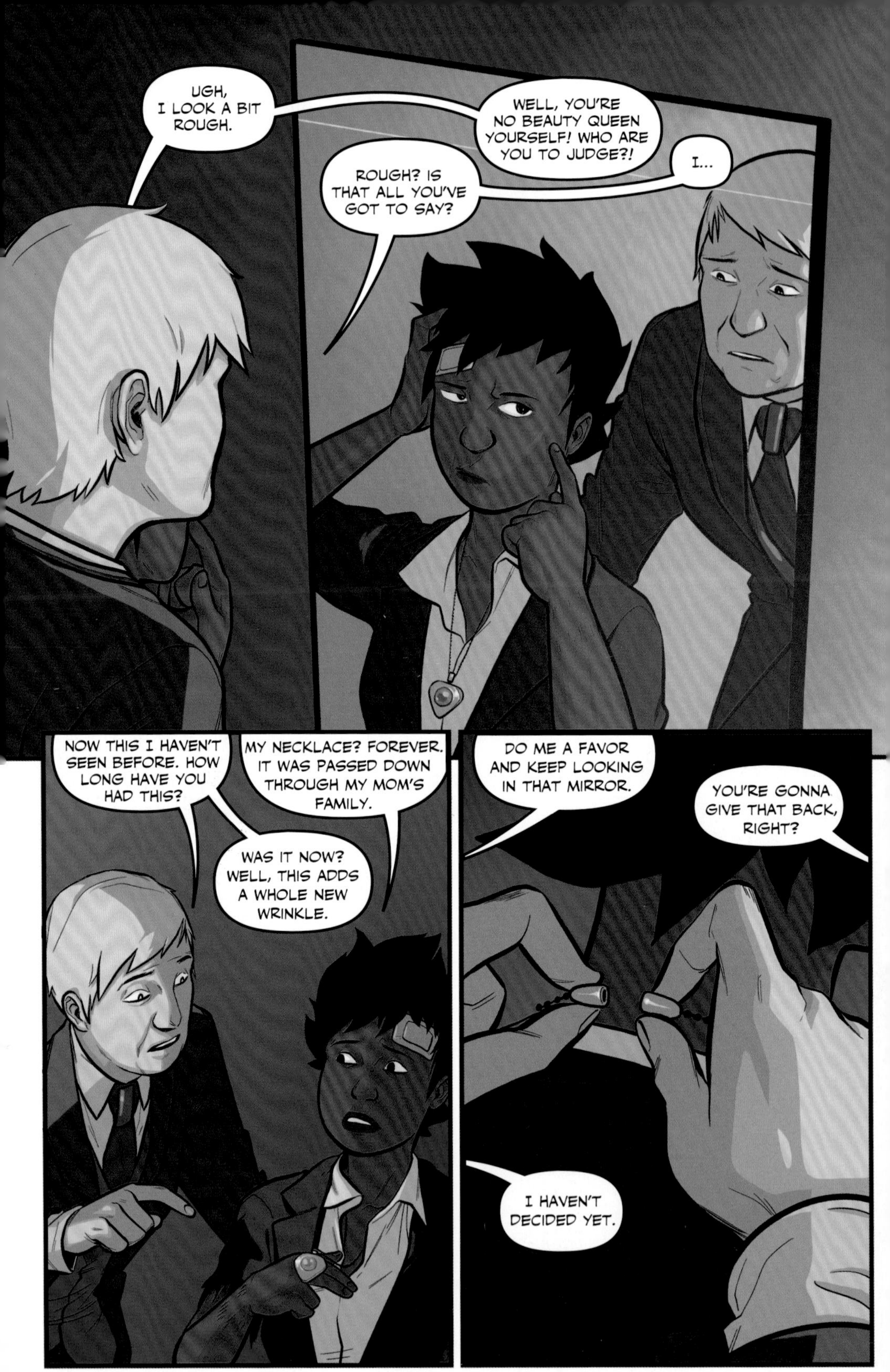
UGH, I LOOK A BIT ROUGH.
WELL, YOU'RE NO BEAUTY QUEEN YOURSELF! WHO ARE YOU TO JUDGE?!
ROUGH? IS THAT ALL YOU'VE GOT TO SAY?
I...
NOW THIS I HAVEN'T SEEN BEFORE. HOW LONG HAVE YOU HAD THIS?
MY NECKLACE? FOREVER. IT WAS PASSED DOWN THROUGH MY MOM'S FAMILY.
WAS IT NOW? WELL, THIS ADDS A WHOLE NEW WRINKLE.
DO ME A FAVOR AND KEEP LOOKING IN THAT MIRROR.
YOU'RE GONNA GIVE THAT BACK, RIGHT?
I HAVEN'T DECIDED YET.

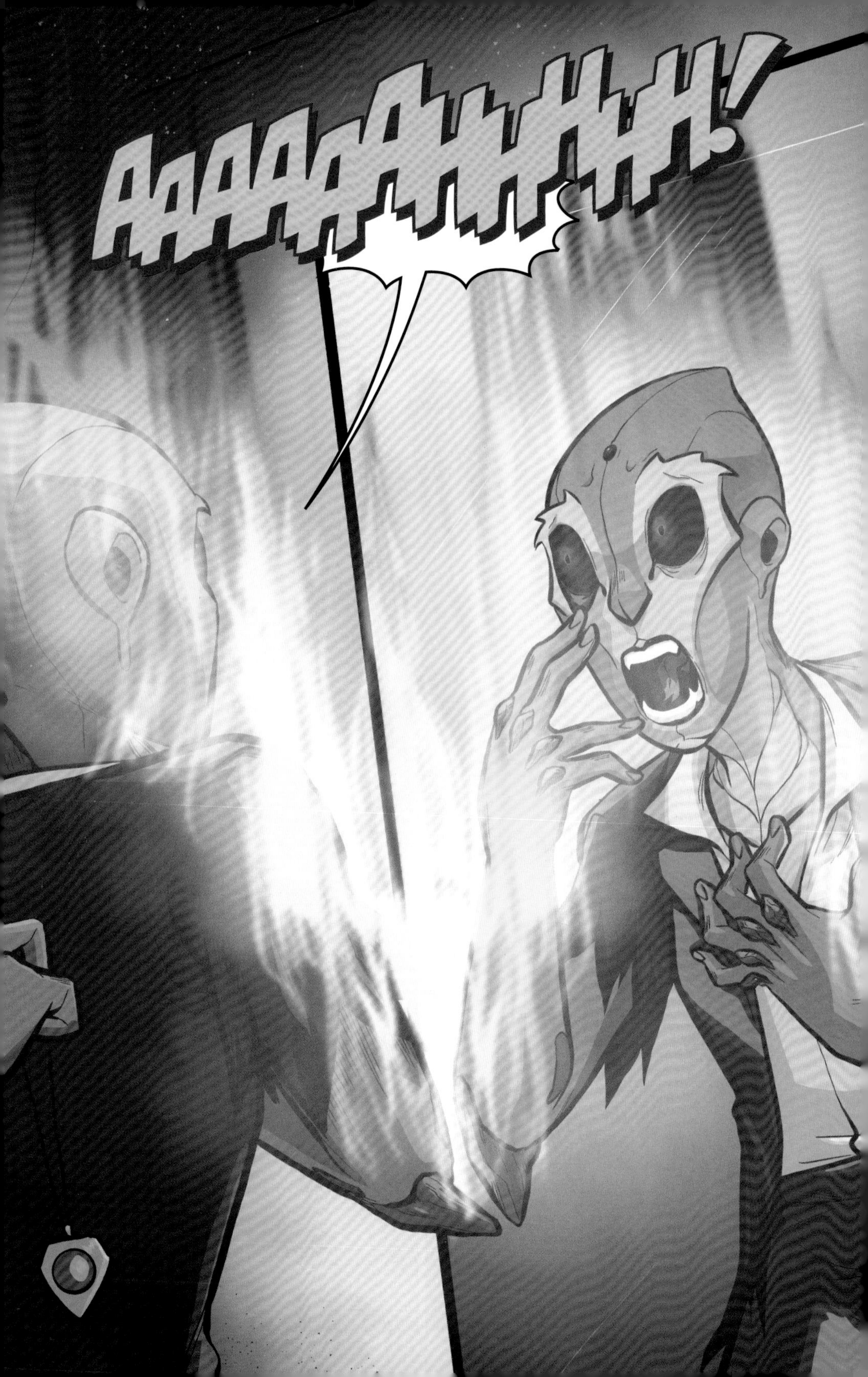
AAAAAHHHH!

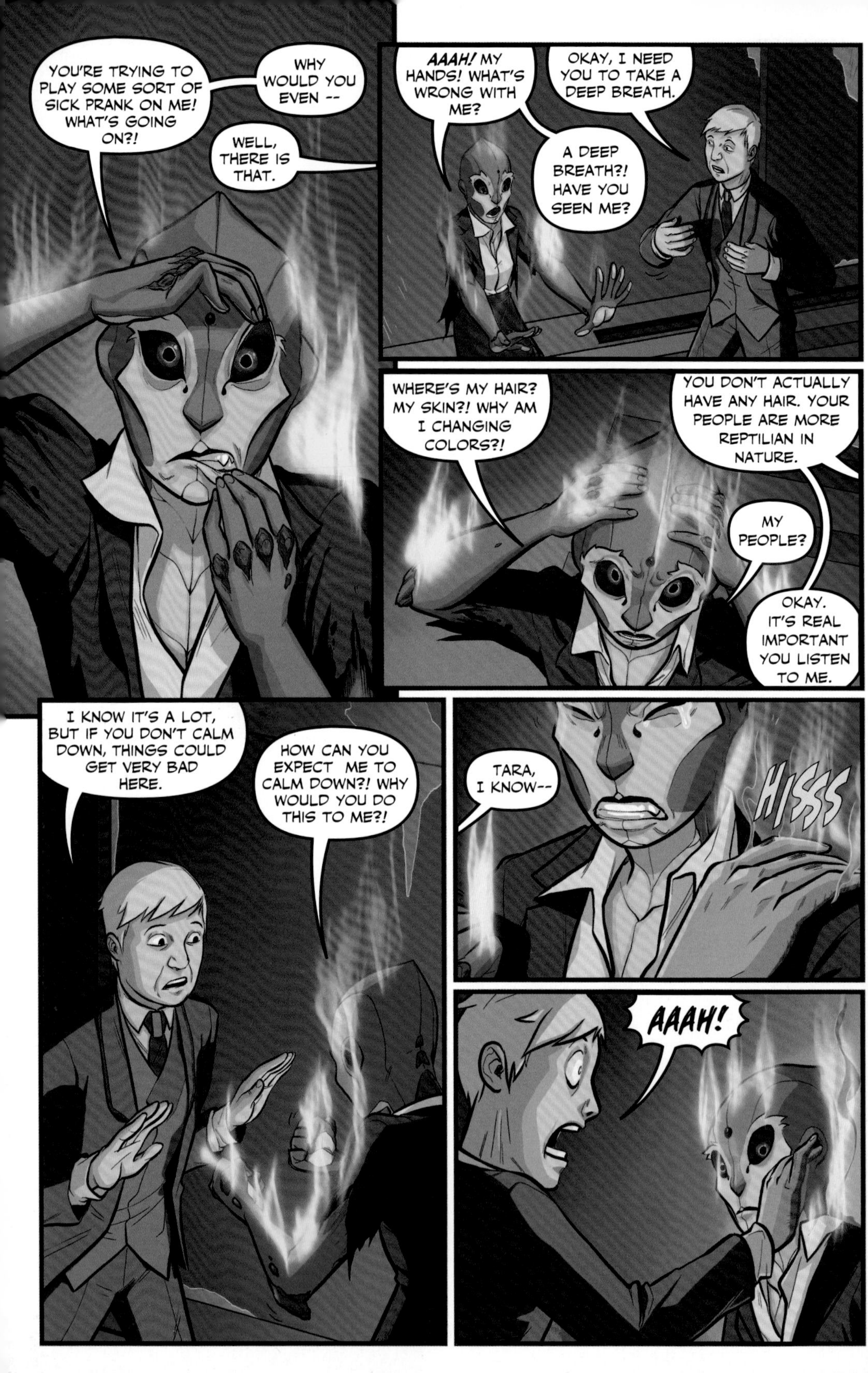
YOU'RE TRYING TO PLAY SOME SORT OF SICK PRANK ON ME! WHAT'S GOING ON?!
WHY WOULD YOU EVEN --
WELL, THERE IS THAT.
AAAH! MY HANDS! WHAT'S WRONG WITH ME?
OKAY, I NEED YOU TO TAKE A DEEP BREATH.
A DEEP BREATH?! HAVE YOU SEEN ME?
WHERE'S MY HAIR? MY SKIN?! WHY AM I CHANGING COLORS?!
YOU DON'T ACTUALLY HAVE ANY HAIR. YOUR PEOPLE ARE MORE REPTILIAN IN NATURE.
MY PEOPLE?
OKAY. IT'S REAL IMPORTANT YOU LISTEN TO ME.
I KNOW IT'S A LOT, BUT IF YOU DON'T CALM DOWN, THINGS COULD GET VERY BAD HERE.
HOW CAN YOU EXPECT ME TO CALM DOWN?! WHY WOULD YOU DO THIS TO ME?!
TARA, I KNOW--
HISSS
AAAH!

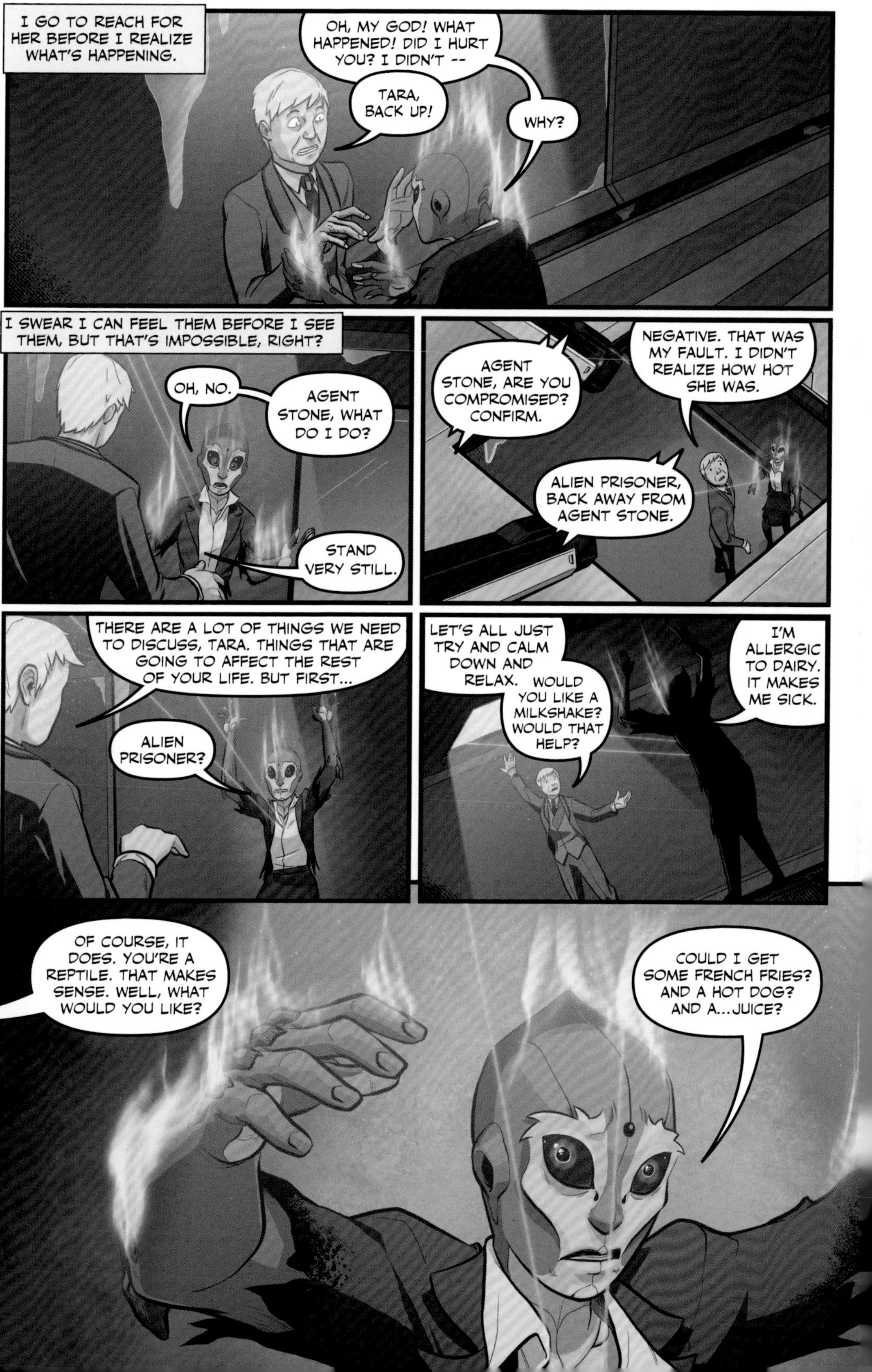
I GO TO REACH FOR HER BEFORE I REALIZE WHAT'S HAPPENING.
OH, MY GOD! WHAT HAPPENED! DID I HURT YOU? I DIDN'T --
TARA, BACK UP!
WHY?
I SWEAR I CAN FEEL THEM BEFORE I SEE THEM, BUT THAT'S IMPOSSIBLE, RIGHT?
OH, NO.
AGENT STONE, WHAT DO I DO?
STAND VERY STILL.
AGENT STONE, ARE YOU COMPROMISED? CONFIRM.
NEGATIVE. THAT WAS MY FAULT. I DIDN'T REALIZE HOW HOT SHE WAS.
ALIEN PRISONER, BACK AWAY FROM AGENT STONE.
THERE ARE A LOT OF THINGS WE NEED TO DISCUSS, TARA. THINGS THAT ARE GOING TO AFFECT THE REST OF YOUR LIFE. BUT FIRST...
ALIEN PRISONER?
LET'S ALL JUST TRY AND CALM DOWN AND RELAX.
WOULD YOU LIKE A MILKSHAKE? WOULD THAT HELP?
I'M ALLERGIC TO DAIRY. IT MAKES ME SICK.
OF COURSE, IT DOES. YOU'RE A REPTILE. THAT MAKES SENSE. WELL, WHAT WOULD YOU LIKE?
COULD I GET SOME FRENCH FRIES? AND A HOT DOG? AND A...JUICE?

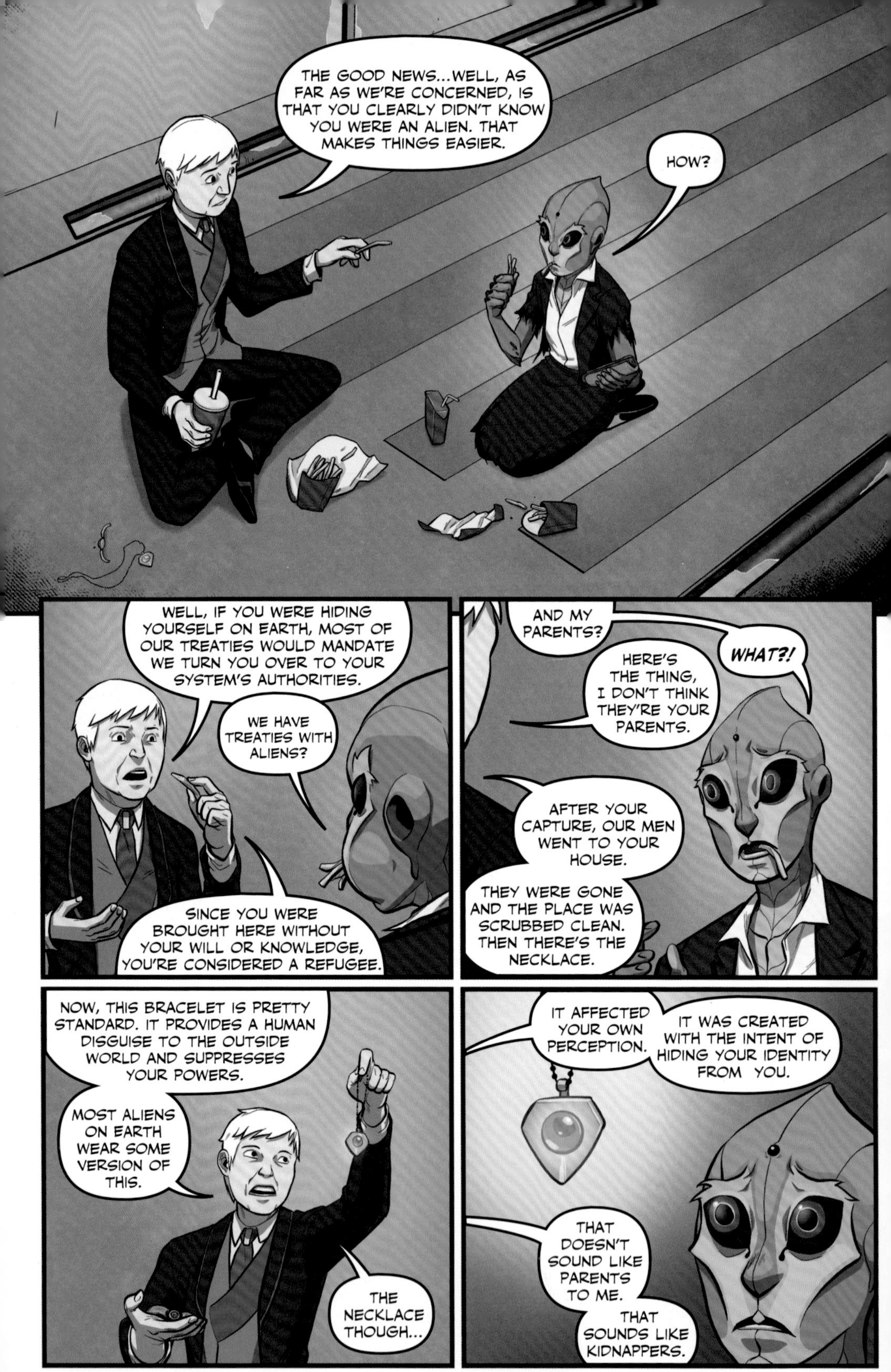
THE GOOD NEWS...WELL, AS FAR AS WE'RE CONCERNED, IS THAT YOU CLEARLY DIDN'T KNOW YOU WERE AN ALIEN. THAT MAKES THINGS EASIER.
HOW?
WELL, IF YOU WERE HIDING YOURSELF ON EARTH, MOST OF OUR TREATIES WOULD MANDATE WE TURN YOU OVER TO YOUR SYSTEM'S AUTHORITIES.
WE HAVE TREATIES WITH ALIENS?
SINCE YOU WERE BROUGHT HERE WITHOUT YOUR WILL OR KNOWLEDGE, YOU'RE CONSIDERED A REFUGEE.
AND MY PARENTS?
HERE'S THE THING, I DON'T THINK THEY'RE YOUR PARENTS.
WHAT?!
AFTER YOUR CAPTURE, OUR MEN WENT TO YOUR HOUSE.
THEY WERE GONE AND THE PLACE WAS SCRUBBED CLEAN. THEN THERE'S THE NECKLACE.
NOW, THIS BRACELET IS PRETTY STANDARD. IT PROVIDES A HUMAN DISGUISE TO THE OUTSIDE WORLD AND SUPPRESSES YOUR POWERS.
MOST ALIENS ON EARTH WEAR SOME VERSION OF THIS.
THE NECKLACE THOUGH...
IT AFFECTED YOUR OWN PERCEPTION.
IT WAS CREATED WITH THE INTENT OF HIDING YOUR IDENTITY FROM YOU.
THAT DOESN'T SOUND LIKE PARENTS TO ME.
THAT SOUNDS LIKE KIDNAPPERS.

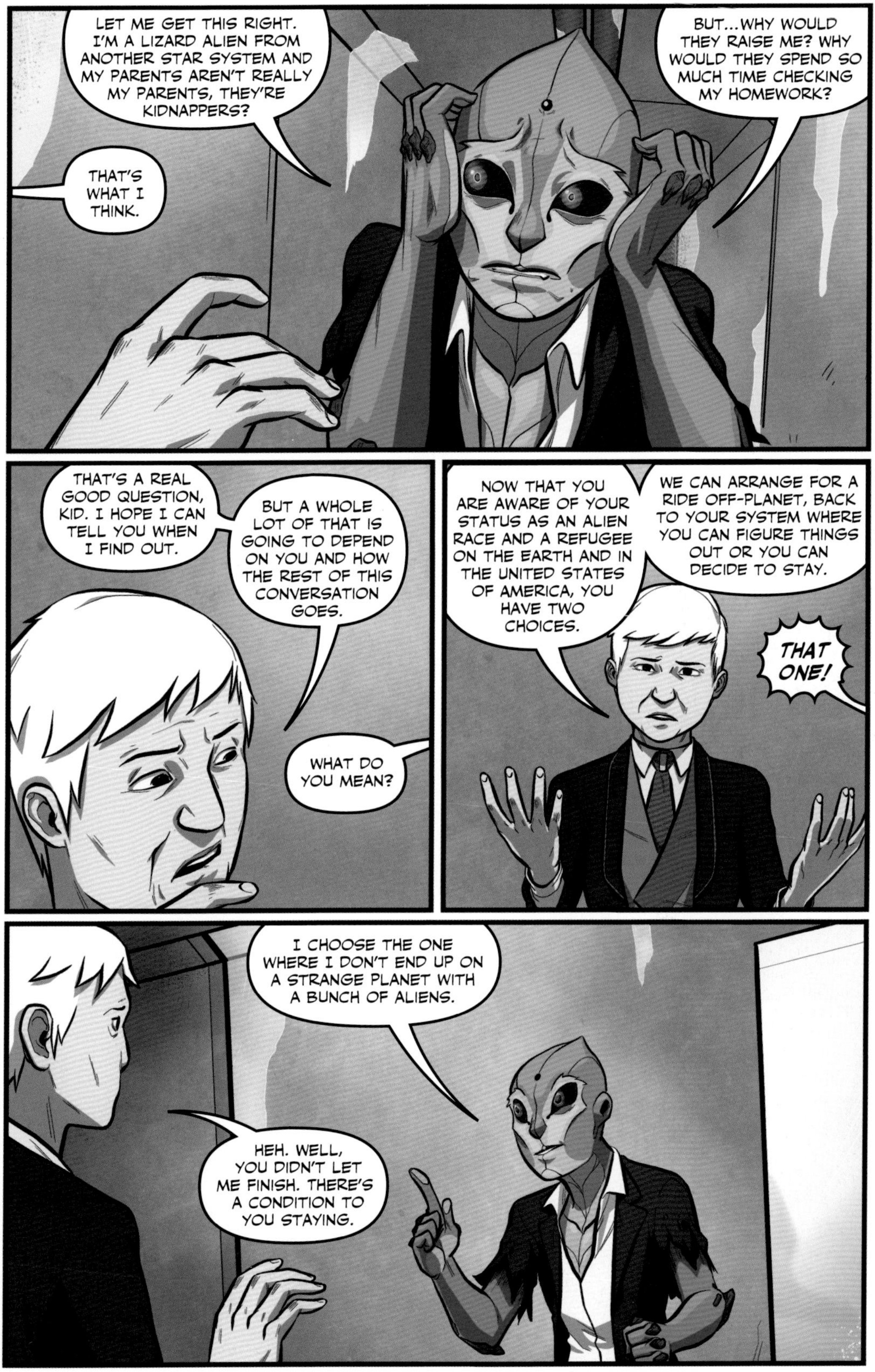

LET ME GET THIS RIGHT. I'M A LIZARD ALIEN FROM ANOTHER STAR SYSTEM AND MY PARENTS AREN'T REALLY MY PARENTS, THEY'RE KIDNAPPERS?
THAT'S WHAT I THINK.
BUT...WHY WOULD THEY RAISE ME? WHY WOULD THEY SPEND SO MUCH TIME CHECKING MY HOMEWORK?
THAT'S A REAL GOOD QUESTION, KID. I HOPE I CAN TELL YOU WHEN I FIND OUT.
BUT A WHOLE LOT OF THAT IS GOING TO DEPEND ON YOU AND HOW THE REST OF THIS CONVERSATION GOES.
WHAT DO YOU MEAN?
NOW THAT YOU ARE AWARE OF YOUR STATUS AS AN ALIEN RACE AND A REFUGEE ON THE EARTH AND IN THE UNITED STATES OF AMERICA, YOU HAVE TWO CHOICES.
WE CAN ARRANGE FOR A RIDE OFF-PLANET, BACK TO YOUR SYSTEM WHERE YOU CAN FIGURE THINGS OUT OR YOU CAN DECIDE TO STAY.
THAT ONE!
I CHOOSE THE ONE WHERE I DON'T END UP ON A STRANGE PLANET WITH A BUNCH OF ALIENS.
HEH. WELL, YOU DIDN'T LET ME FINISH. THERE'S A CONDITION TO YOU STAYING.

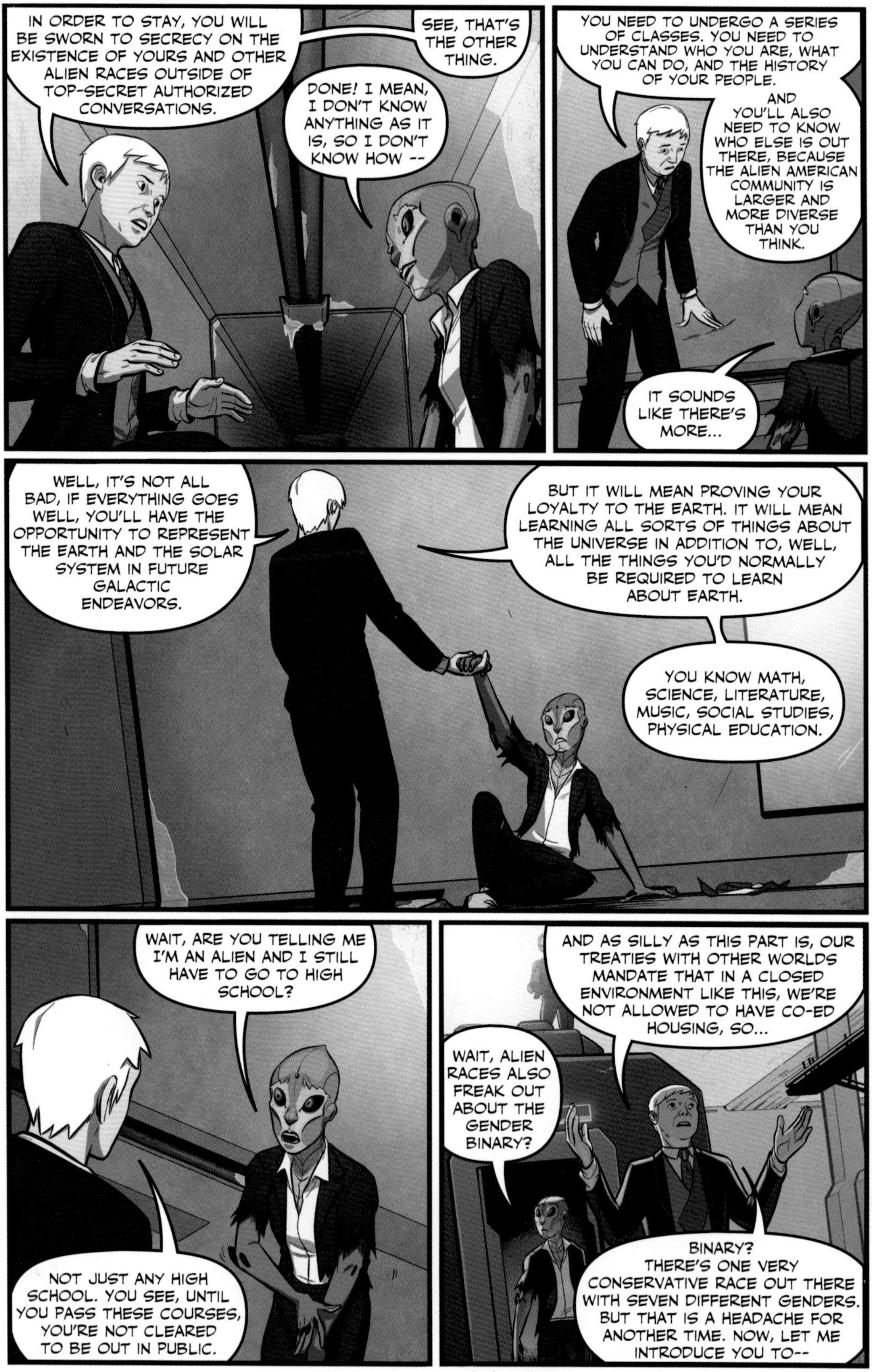
IN ORDER TO STAY, YOU WILL BE SWORN TO SECRECY ON THE EXISTENCE OF YOURS AND OTHER ALIEN RACES OUTSIDE OF TOP-SECRET AUTHORIZED CONVERSATIONS.
SEE, THAT'S THE OTHER THING.
DONE! I MEAN, I DON'T KNOW ANYTHING AS IT IS, SO I DON'T KNOW HOW --
YOU NEED TO UNDERGO A SERIES OF CLASSES. YOU NEED TO UNDERSTAND WHO YOU ARE, WHAT YOU CAN DO, AND THE HISTORY OF YOUR PEOPLE.
AND YOU'LL ALSO NEED TO KNOW WHO ELSE IS OUT THERE, BECAUSE THE ALIEN AMERICAN COMMUNITY IS LARGER AND MORE DIVERSE THAN YOU THINK.
IT SOUNDS LIKE THERE'S MORE...
WELL, IT'S NOT ALL BAD, IF EVERYTHING GOES WELL, YOU'LL HAVE THE OPPORTUNITY TO REPRESENT THE EARTH AND THE SOLAR SYSTEM IN FUTURE GALACTIC ENDEAVORS.
BUT IT WILL MEAN PROVING YOUR LOYALTY TO THE EARTH. IT WILL MEAN LEARNING ALL SORTS OF THINGS ABOUT THE UNIVERSE IN ADDITION TO, WELL, ALL THE THINGS YOU'D NORMALLY BE REQUIRED TO LEARN ABOUT EARTH.
YOU KNOW MATH, SCIENCE, LITERATURE, MUSIC, SOCIAL STUDIES, PHYSICAL EDUCATION.
WAIT, ARE YOU TELLING ME I'M AN ALIEN AND I STILL HAVE TO GO TO HIGH SCHOOL?
NOT JUST ANY HIGH SCHOOL. YOU SEE, UNTIL YOU PASS THESE COURSES, YOU'RE NOT CLEARED TO BE OUT IN PUBLIC.
AND AS SILLY AS THIS PART IS, OUR TREATIES WITH OTHER WORLDS MANDATE THAT IN A CLOSED ENVIRONMENT LIKE THIS, WE'RE NOT ALLOWED TO HAVE CO-ED HOUSING, SO...
WAIT, ALIEN RACES ALSO FREAK OUT ABOUT THE GENDER BINARY?
BINARY? THERE'S ONE VERY CONSERVATIVE RACE OUT THERE WITH SEVEN DIFFERENT GENDERS. BUT THAT IS A HEADACHE FOR ANOTHER TIME. NOW, LET ME INTRODUCE YOU TO--

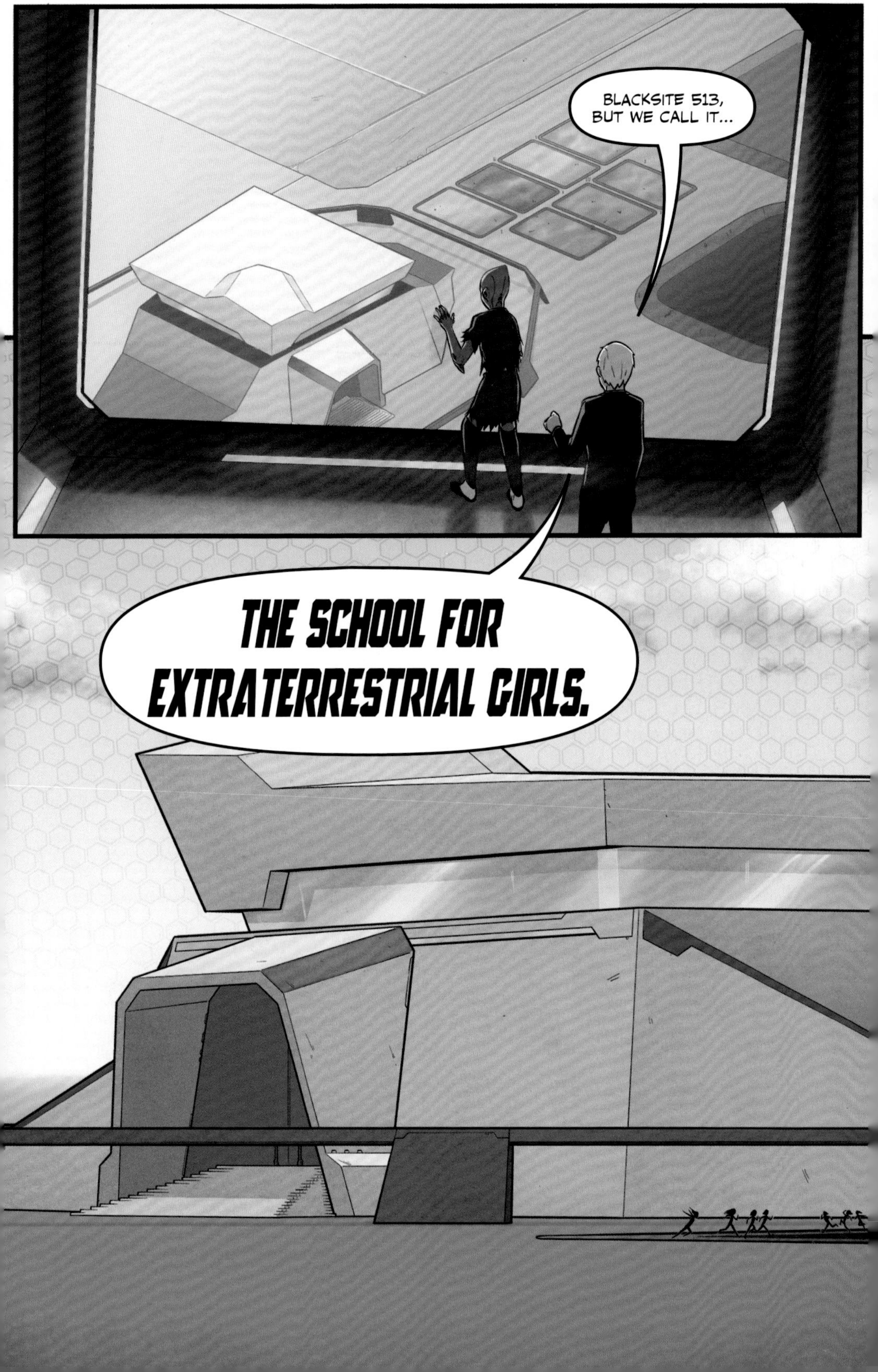
BLACKSITE 513, BUT WE CALL IT...
THE SCHOOL FOR EXTRATERRESTRIAL GIRLS.

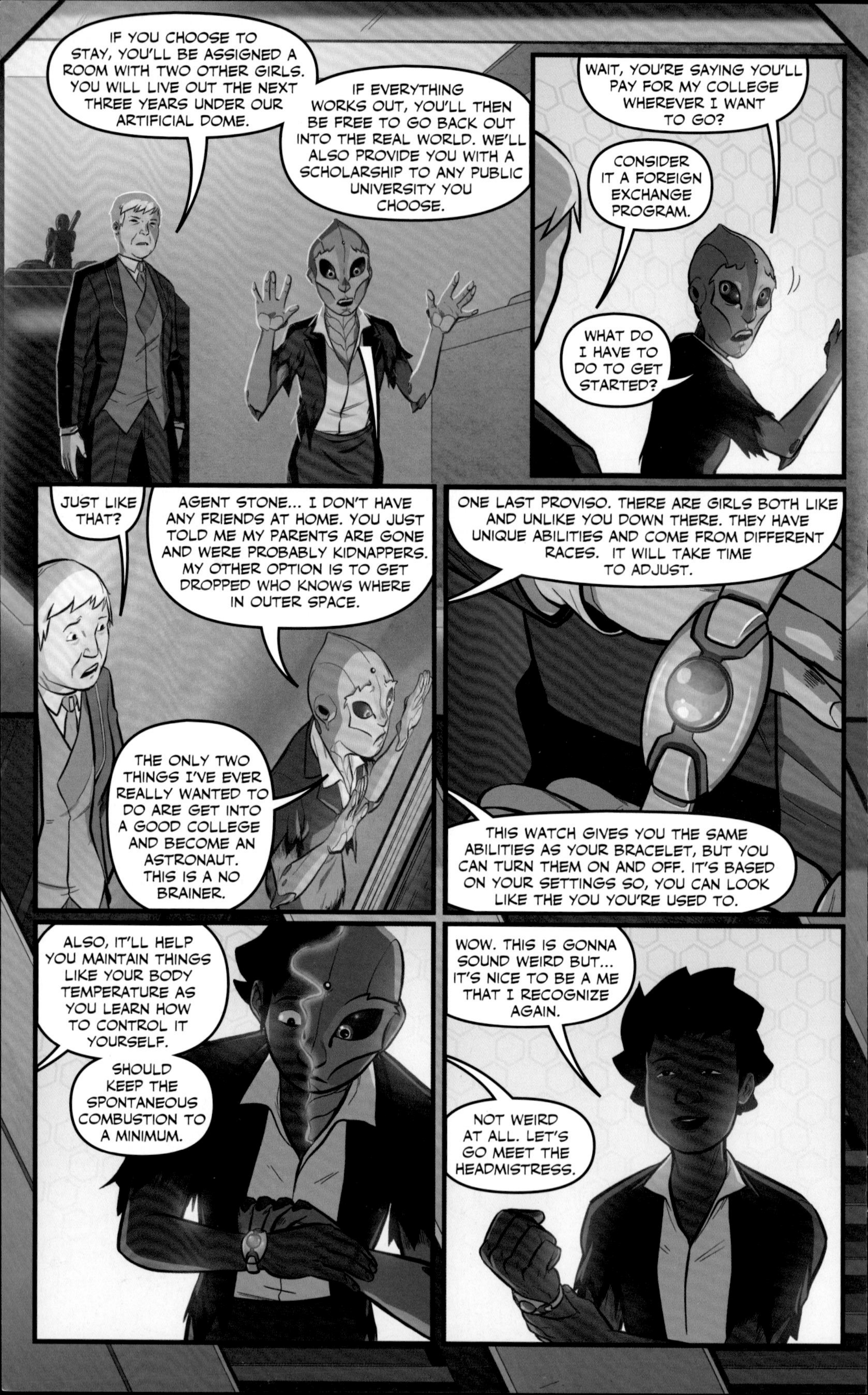
IF YOU CHOOSE TO STAY, YOU'LL BE ASSIGNED A ROOM WITH TWO OTHER GIRLS. YOU WILL LIVE OUT THE NEXT THREE YEARS UNDER OUR ARTIFICIAL DOME.
IF EVERYTHING WORKS OUT, YOU'LL THEN BE FREE TO GO BACK OUT INTO THE REAL WORLD. WE'LL ALSO PROVIDE YOU WITH A SCHOLARSHIP TO ANY PUBLIC UNIVERSITY YOU CHOOSE.
WAIT, YOU'RE SAYING YOU'LL PAY FOR MY COLLEGE WHEREVER I WANT TO GO?
CONSIDER IT A FOREIGN EXCHANGE PROGRAM.
WHAT DO I HAVE TO DO TO GET STARTED?
JUST LIKE THAT?
AGENT STONE... I DON'T HAVE ANY FRIENDS AT HOME. YOU JUST TOLD ME MY PARENTS ARE GONE AND WERE PROBABLY KIDNAPPERS. MY OTHER OPTION IS TO GET DROPPED WHO KNOWS WHERE IN OUTER SPACE.
THE ONLY TWO THINGS I'VE EVER REALLY WANTED TO DO ARE GET INTO A GOOD COLLEGE AND BECOME AN ASTRONAUT. THIS IS A NO BRAINER.
ONE LAST PROVISO. THERE ARE GIRLS BOTH LIKE AND UNLIKE YOU DOWN THERE. THEY HAVE UNIQUE ABILITIES AND COME FROM DIFFERENT RACES. IT WILL TAKE TIME TO ADJUST.
THIS WATCH GIVES YOU THE SAME ABILITIES AS YOUR BRACELET, BUT YOU CAN TURN THEM ON AND OFF. IT'S BASED ON YOUR SETTINGS SO, YOU CAN LOOK LIKE THE YOU YOU'RE USED TO.
ALSO, IT'LL HELP YOU MAINTAIN THINGS LIKE YOUR BODY TEMPERATURE AS YOU LEARN HOW TO CONTROL IT YOURSELF.
SHOULD KEEP THE SPONTANEOUS COMBUSTION TO A MINIMUM.
WOW. THIS IS GONNA SOUND WEIRD BUT... IT'S NICE TO BE A ME THAT I RECOGNIZE AGAIN.
NOT WEIRD AT ALL. LET'S GO MEET THE HEADMISTRESS.

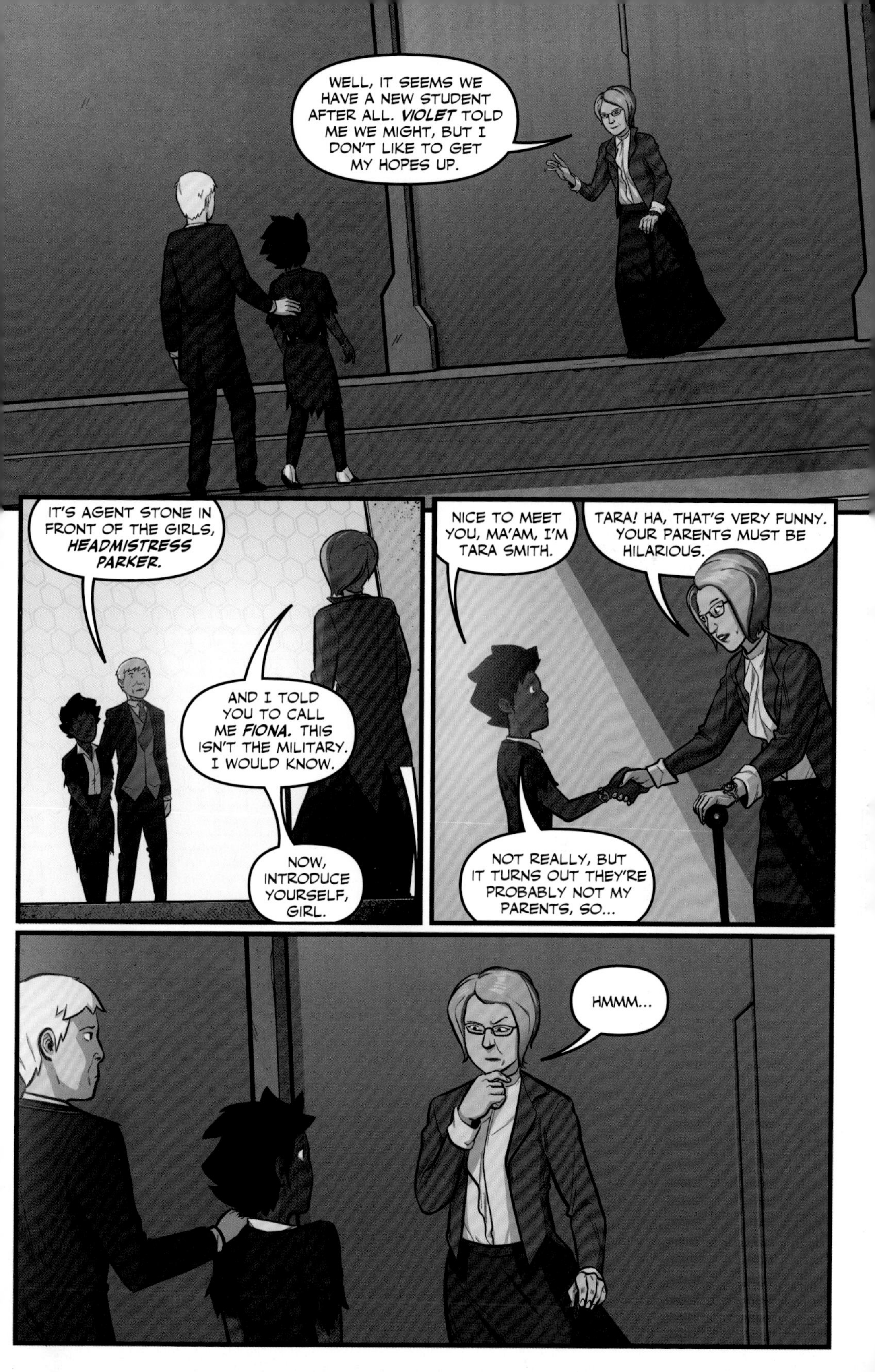
WELL, IT SEEMS WE HAVE A NEW STUDENT AFTER ALL. VIOLET TOLD ME WE MIGHT, BUT I DON'T LIKE TO GET MY HOPES UP.
IT'S AGENT STONE IN FRONT OF THE GIRLS, HEADMISTRESS PARKER.
AND I TOLD YOU TO CALL ME FIONA. THIS ISN'T THE MILITARY. I WOULD KNOW.
NOW, INTRODUCE YOURSELF, GIRL.
NICE TO MEET YOU, MA'AM, I'M TARA SMITH.
TARA! HA, THAT'S VERY FUNNY. YOUR PARENTS MUST BE HILARIOUS.
NOT REALLY, BUT IT TURNS OUT THEY'RE PROBABLY NOT MY PARENTS, SO...
HMMM...

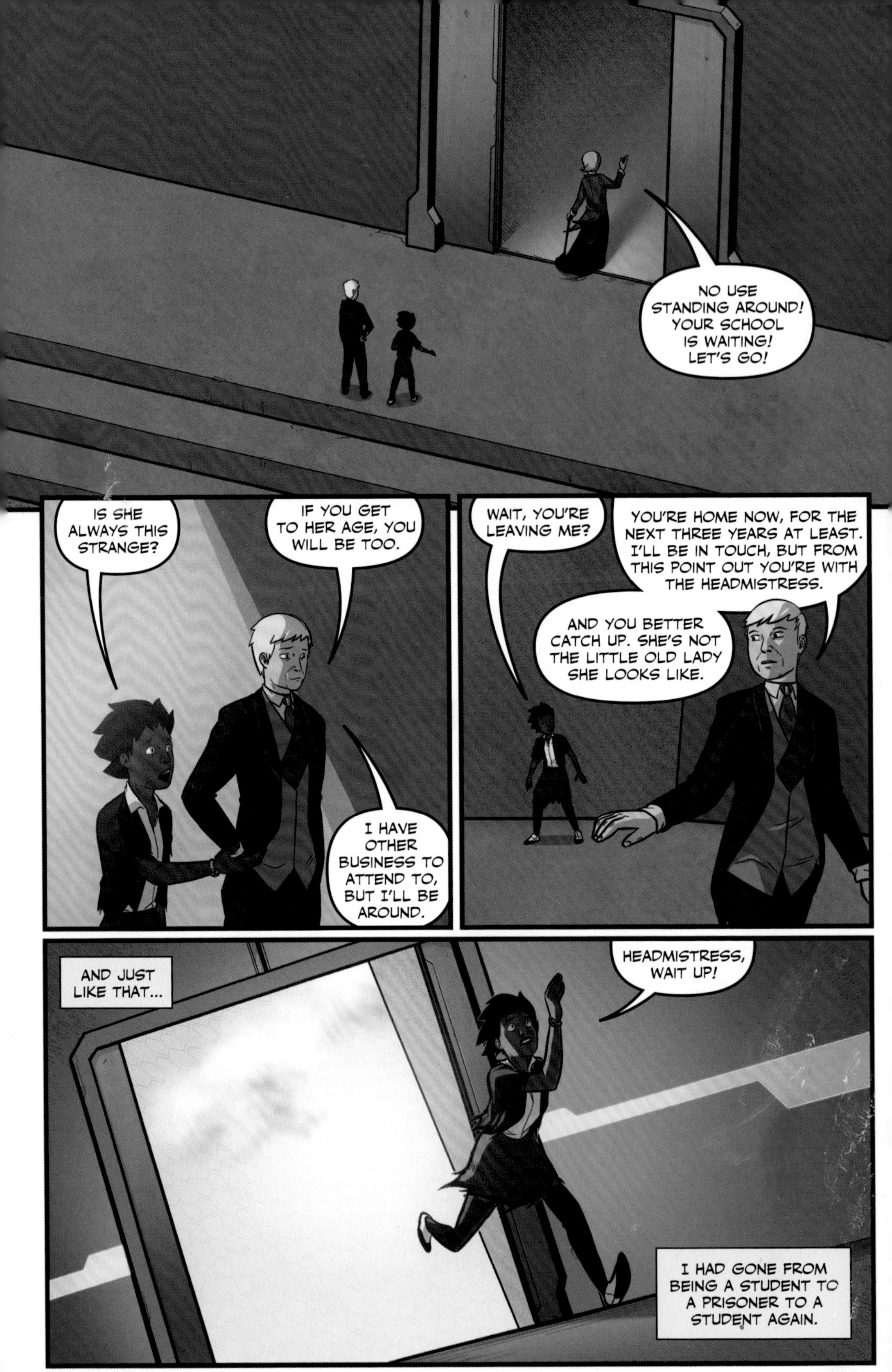
NO USE STANDING AROUND! YOUR SCHOOL IS WAITING! LET'S GO!
IS SHE ALWAYS THIS STRANGE?
IF YOU GET TO HER AGE, YOU WILL BE TOO.
I HAVE OTHER BUSINESS TO ATTEND TO, BUT I'LL BE AROUND.
WAIT, YOU'RE LEAVING ME?
YOU'RE HOME NOW, FOR THE NEXT THREE YEARS AT LEAST. I'LL BE IN TOUCH, BUT FROM THIS POINT OUT YOU'RE WITH THE HEADMISTRESS.
AND YOU BETTER CATCH UP. SHE'S NOT THE LITTLE OLD LADY SHE LOOKS LIKE.
AND JUST LIKE THAT...
HEADMISTRESS, WAIT UP!
I HAD GONE FROM BEING A STUDENT TO A PRISONER TO A STUDENT AGAIN.

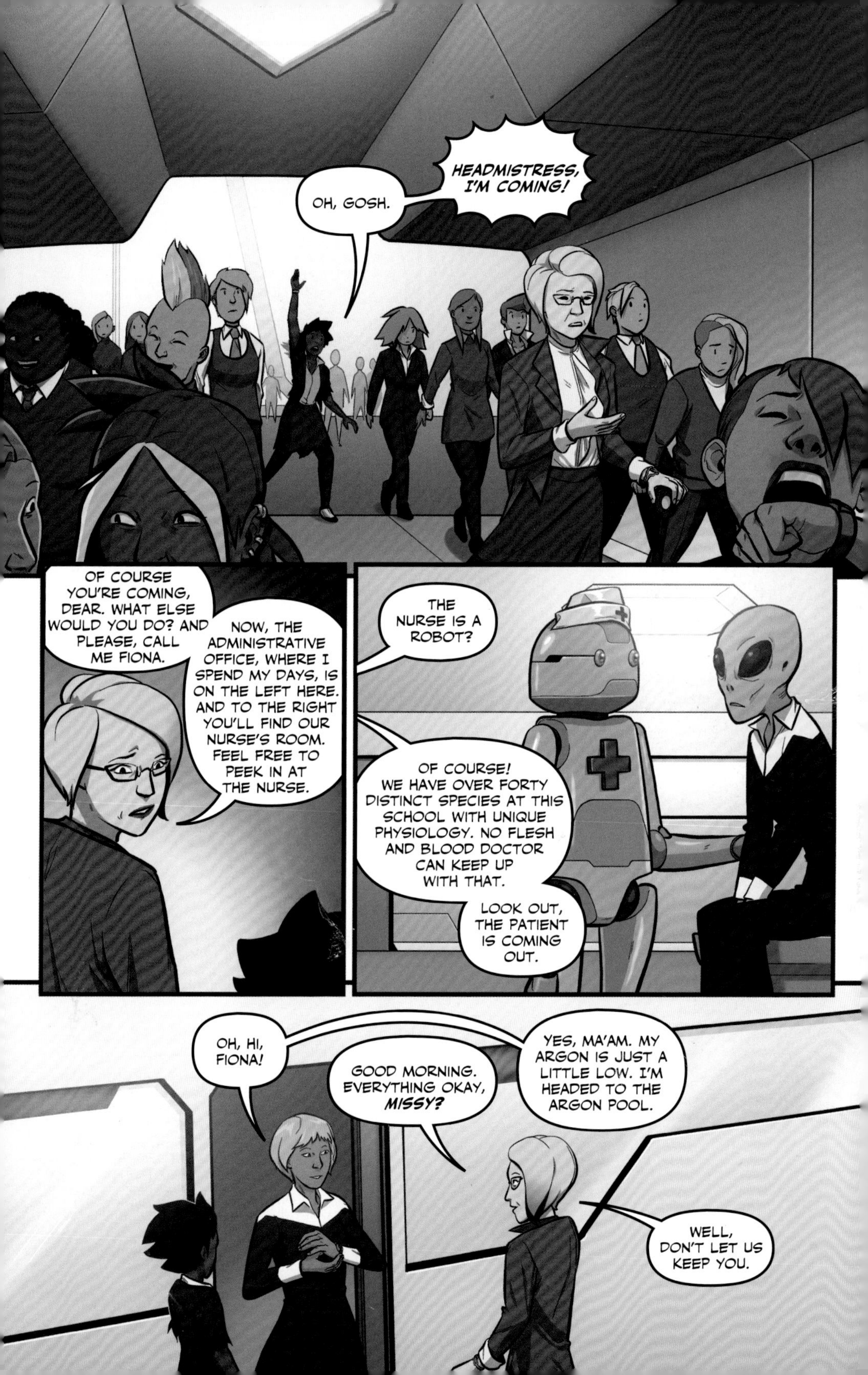
OH, GOSH.
HEADMISTRESS, I'M COMING!
OF COURSE YOU'RE COMING, DEAR. WHAT ELSE WOULD YOU DO? AND PLEASE, CALL ME FIONA.
NOW, THE ADMINISTRATIVE OFFICE, WHERE I SPEND MY DAYS, IS ON THE LEFT HERE. AND TO THE RIGHT YOU'LL FIND OUR NURSE'S ROOM. FEEL FREE TO PEEK IN AT THE NURSE.
THE NURSE IS A ROBOT?
OF COURSE! WE HAVE OVER FORTY DISTINCT SPECIES AT THIS SCHOOL WITH UNIQUE PHYSIOLOGY. NO FLESH AND BLOOD DOCTOR CAN KEEP UP WITH THAT.
LOOK OUT, THE PATIENT IS COMING OUT.
OH, HI, FIONA!
GOOD MORNING. EVERYTHING OKAY, *MISSY?*
YES, MA'AM. MY ARGON IS JUST A LITTLE LOW. I'M HEADED TO THE ARGON POOL.
WELL, DON'T LET US KEEP YOU.

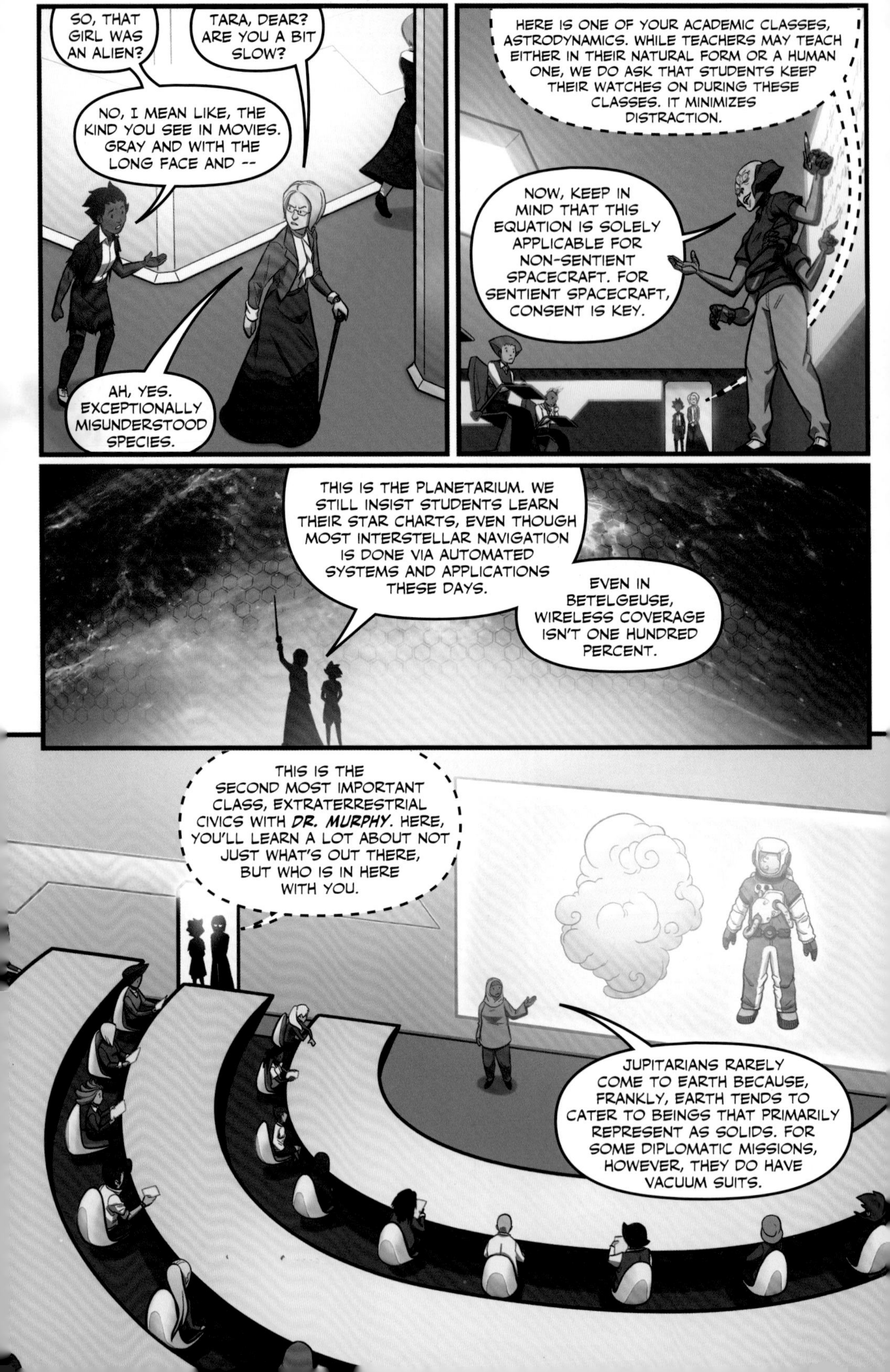
SO, THAT GIRL WAS AN ALIEN?
TARA, DEAR? ARE YOU A BIT SLOW?
NO, I MEAN LIKE, THE KIND YOU SEE IN MOVIES. GRAY AND WITH THE LONG FACE AND --
AH, YES. EXCEPTIONALLY MISUNDERSTOOD SPECIES.
HERE IS ONE OF YOUR ACADEMIC CLASSES, ASTRODYNAMICS. WHILE TEACHERS MAY TEACH EITHER IN THEIR NATURAL FORM OR A HUMAN ONE, WE DO ASK THAT STUDENTS KEEP THEIR WATCHES ON DURING THESE CLASSES. IT MINIMIZES DISTRACTION.
NOW, KEEP IN MIND THAT THIS EQUATION IS SOLELY APPLICABLE FOR NON-SENTIENT SPACECRAFT. FOR SENTIENT SPACECRAFT, CONSENT IS KEY.
THIS IS THE PLANETARIUM. WE STILL INSIST STUDENTS LEARN THEIR STAR CHARTS, EVEN THOUGH MOST INTERSTELLAR NAVIGATION IS DONE VIA AUTOMATED SYSTEMS AND APPLICATIONS THESE DAYS.
EVEN IN BETELGEUSE, WIRELESS COVERAGE ISN'T ONE HUNDRED PERCENT.
THIS IS THE SECOND MOST IMPORTANT CLASS, EXTRATERRESTRIAL CIVICS WITH *DR. MURPHY*. HERE, YOU'LL LEARN A LOT ABOUT NOT JUST WHAT'S OUT THERE, BUT WHO IS IN HERE WITH YOU.
JUPITARIANS RARELY COME TO EARTH BECAUSE, FRANKLY, EARTH TENDS TO CATER TO BEINGS THAT PRIMARILY REPRESENT AS SOLIDS. FOR SOME DIPLOMATIC MISSIONS, HOWEVER, THEY DO HAVE VACUUM SUITS.

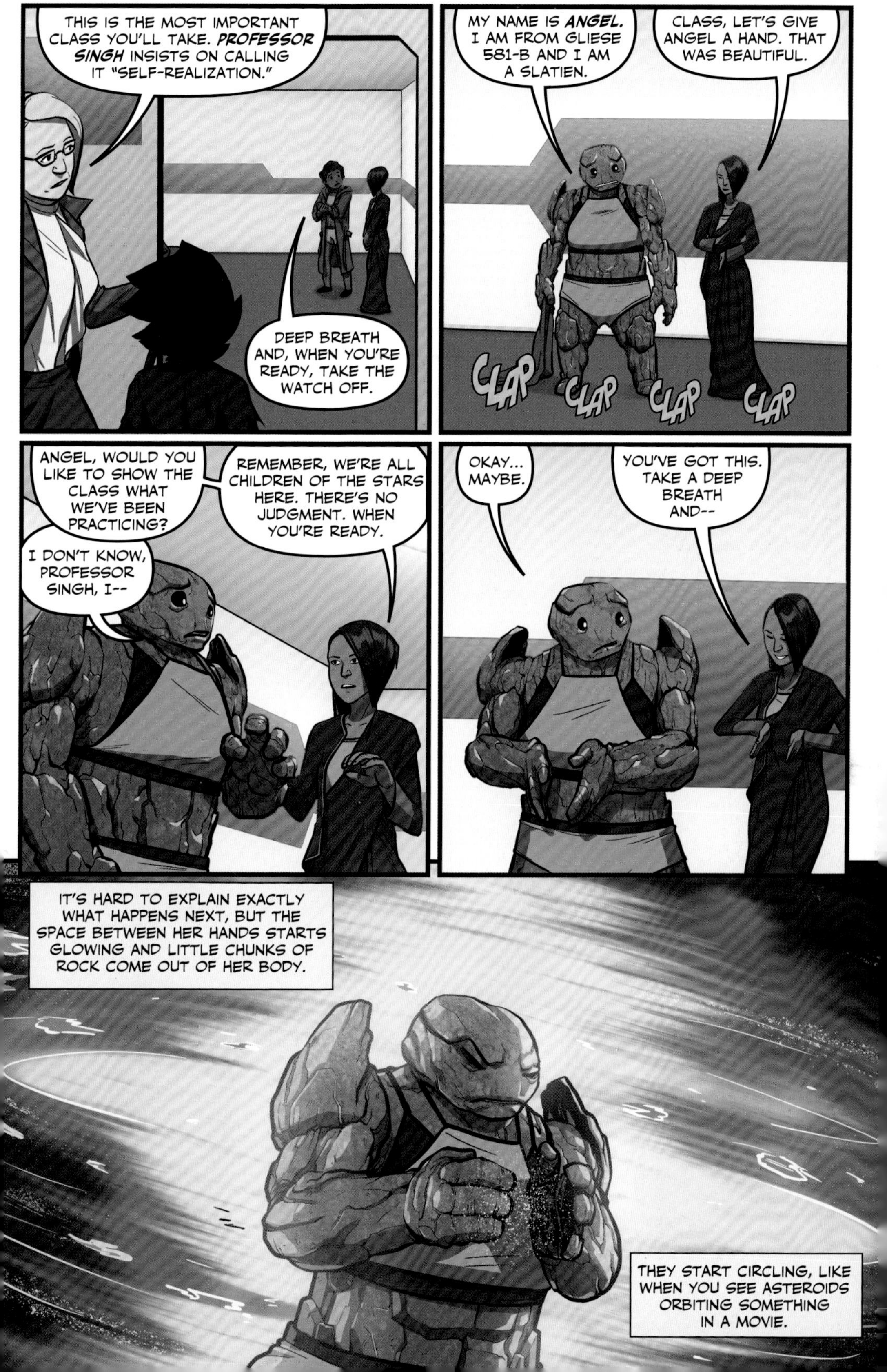
THIS IS THE MOST IMPORTANT CLASS YOU'LL TAKE. ***PROFESSOR SINGH*** INSISTS ON CALLING IT "SELF-REALIZATION."
DEEP BREATH AND, WHEN YOU'RE READY, TAKE THE WATCH OFF.
MY NAME IS ***ANGEL.*** I AM FROM GLIESE 581-B AND I AM A SLATIEN.
CLASS, LET'S GIVE ANGEL A HAND. THAT WAS BEAUTIFUL.
CLAP CLAP CLAP CLAP
ANGEL, WOULD YOU LIKE TO SHOW THE CLASS WHAT WE'VE BEEN PRACTICING?
I DON'T KNOW, PROFESSOR SINGH, I--
REMEMBER, WE'RE ALL CHILDREN OF THE STARS HERE. THERE'S NO JUDGMENT. WHEN YOU'RE READY.
OKAY... MAYBE.
YOU'VE GOT THIS. TAKE A DEEP BREATH AND--
IT'S HARD TO EXPLAIN EXACTLY WHAT HAPPENS NEXT, BUT THE SPACE BETWEEN HER HANDS STARTS GLOWING AND LITTLE CHUNKS OF ROCK COME OUT OF HER BODY.
THEY START CIRCLING, LIKE WHEN YOU SEE ASTEROIDS ORBITING SOMETHING IN A MOVIE.

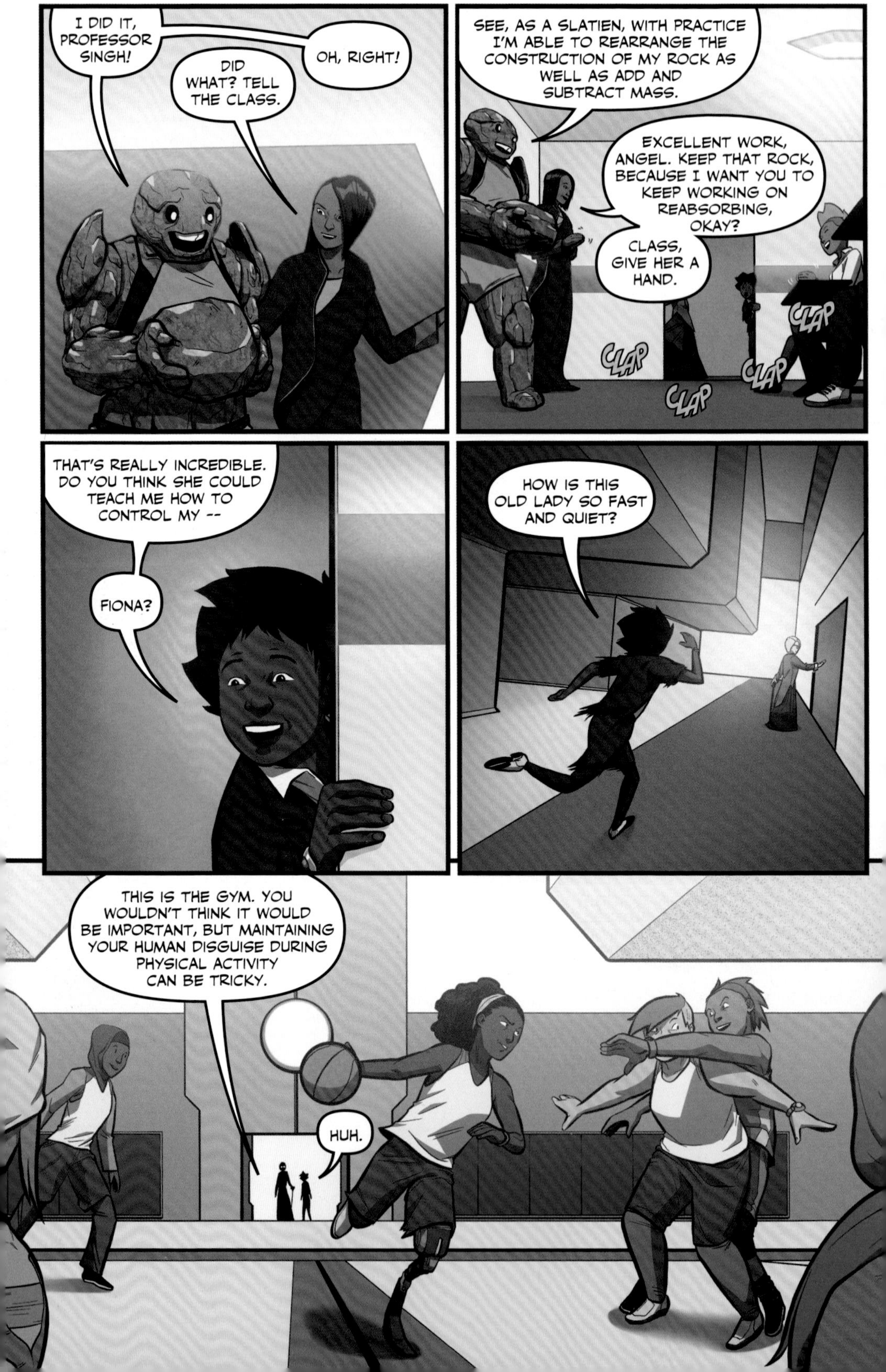
I DID IT, PROFESSOR SINGH!
DID WHAT? TELL THE CLASS.
OH, RIGHT!
SEE, AS A SLATIEN, WITH PRACTICE I'M ABLE TO REARRANGE THE CONSTRUCTION OF MY ROCK AS WELL AS ADD AND SUBTRACT MASS.
EXCELLENT WORK, ANGEL. KEEP THAT ROCK, BECAUSE I WANT YOU TO KEEP WORKING ON REABSORBING, OKAY?
CLASS, GIVE HER A HAND.
CLAP
CLAP
CLAP
CLAP
THAT'S REALLY INCREDIBLE. DO YOU THINK SHE COULD TEACH ME HOW TO CONTROL MY --
FIONA?
HOW IS THIS OLD LADY SO FAST AND QUIET?
THIS IS THE GYM. YOU WOULDN'T THINK IT WOULD BE IMPORTANT, BUT MAINTAINING YOUR HUMAN DISGUISE DURING PHYSICAL ACTIVITY CAN BE TRICKY.
HUH.

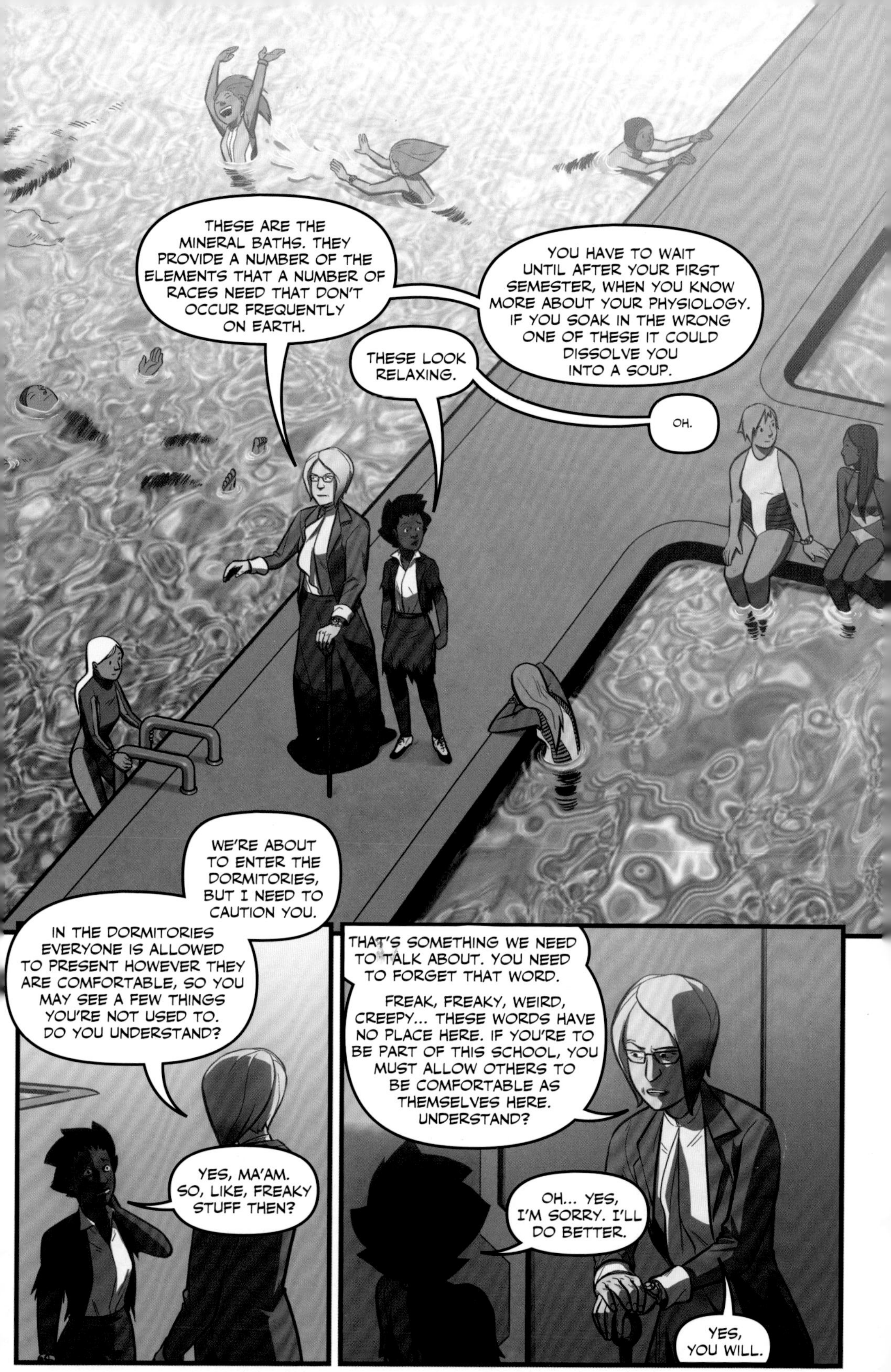
THESE ARE THE MINERAL BATHS. THEY PROVIDE A NUMBER OF THE ELEMENTS THAT A NUMBER OF RACES NEED THAT DON'T OCCUR FREQUENTLY ON EARTH.
YOU HAVE TO WAIT UNTIL AFTER YOUR FIRST SEMESTER, WHEN YOU KNOW MORE ABOUT YOUR PHYSIOLOGY. IF YOU SOAK IN THE WRONG ONE OF THESE IT COULD DISSOLVE YOU INTO A SOUP.
THESE LOOK RELAXING.
OH.
WE'RE ABOUT TO ENTER THE DORMITORIES, BUT I NEED TO CAUTION YOU.
IN THE DORMITORIES EVERYONE IS ALLOWED TO PRESENT HOWEVER THEY ARE COMFORTABLE, SO YOU MAY SEE A FEW THINGS YOU'RE NOT USED TO. DO YOU UNDERSTAND?
YES, MA'AM. SO, LIKE, FREAKY STUFF THEN?
THAT'S SOMETHING WE NEED TO TALK ABOUT. YOU NEED TO FORGET THAT WORD.
FREAK, FREAKY, WEIRD, CREEPY... THESE WORDS HAVE NO PLACE HERE. IF YOU'RE TO BE PART OF THIS SCHOOL, YOU MUST ALLOW OTHERS TO BE COMFORTABLE AS THEMSELVES HERE. UNDERSTAND?
OH... YES, I'M SORRY. I'LL DO BETTER.
YES, YOU WILL.

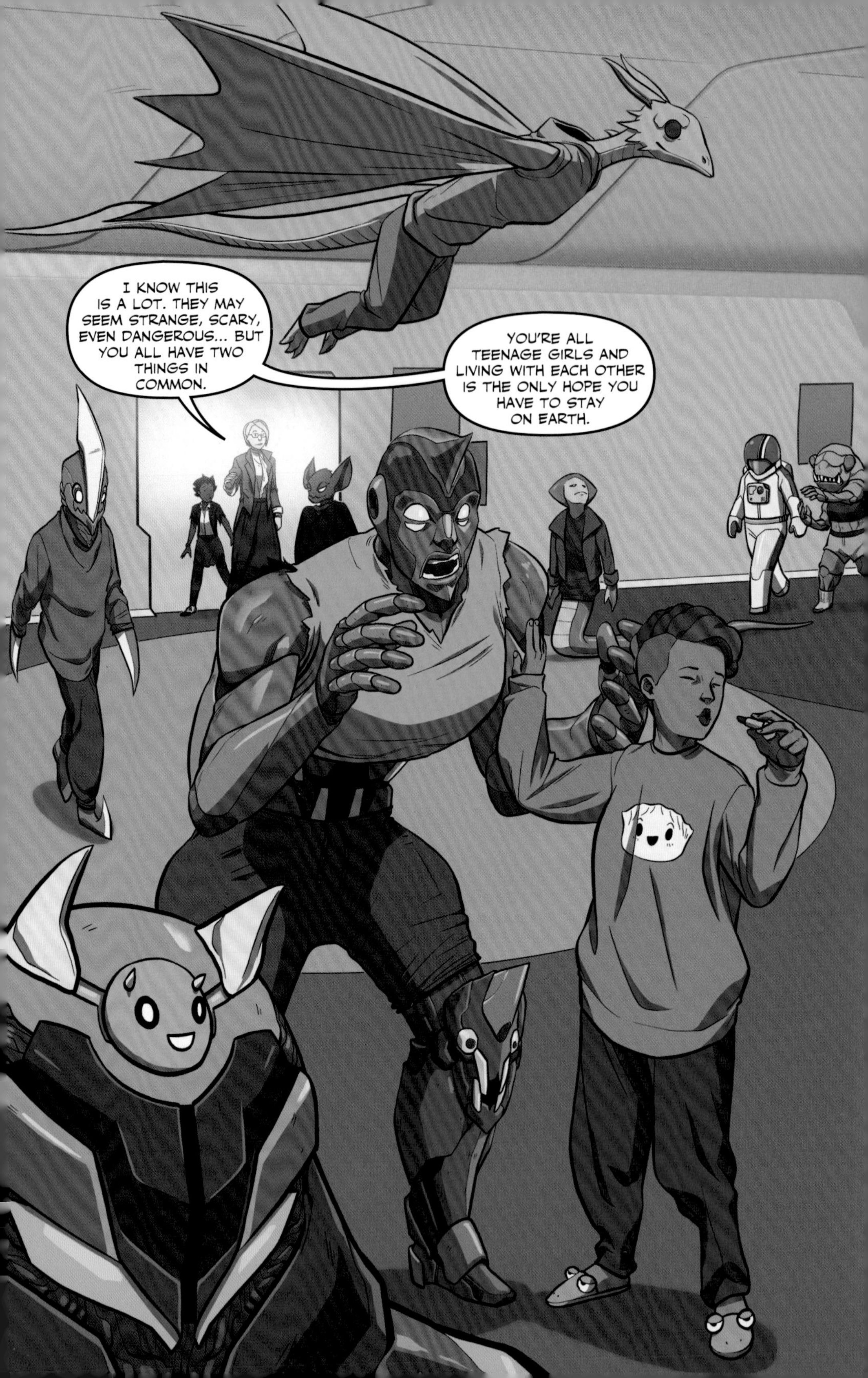
I KNOW THIS IS A LOT. THEY MAY SEEM STRANGE, SCARY, EVEN DANGEROUS... BUT YOU ALL HAVE TWO THINGS IN COMMON.
YOU'RE ALL TEENAGE GIRLS AND LIVING WITH EACH OTHER IS THE ONLY HOPE YOU HAVE TO STAY ON EARTH.

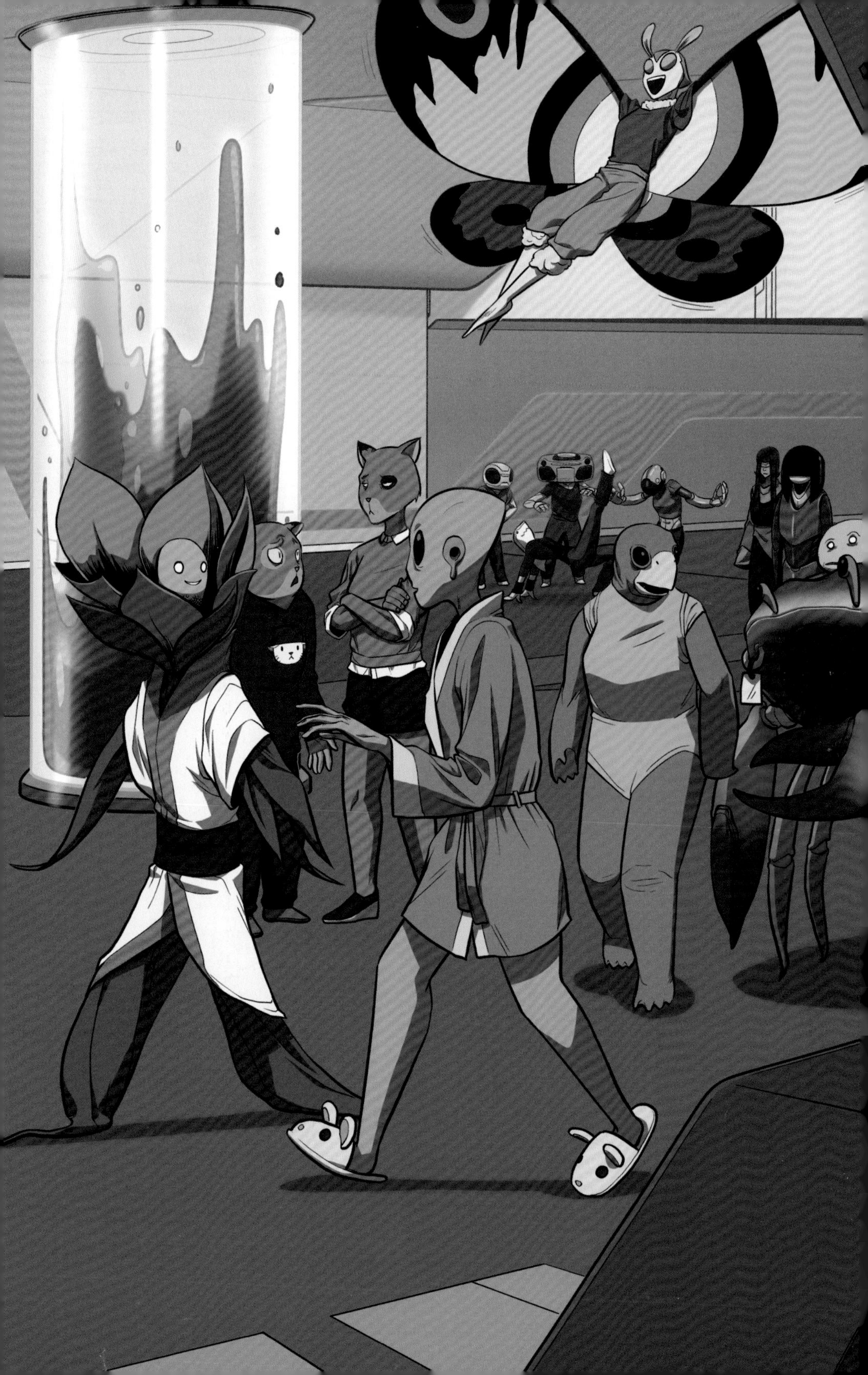

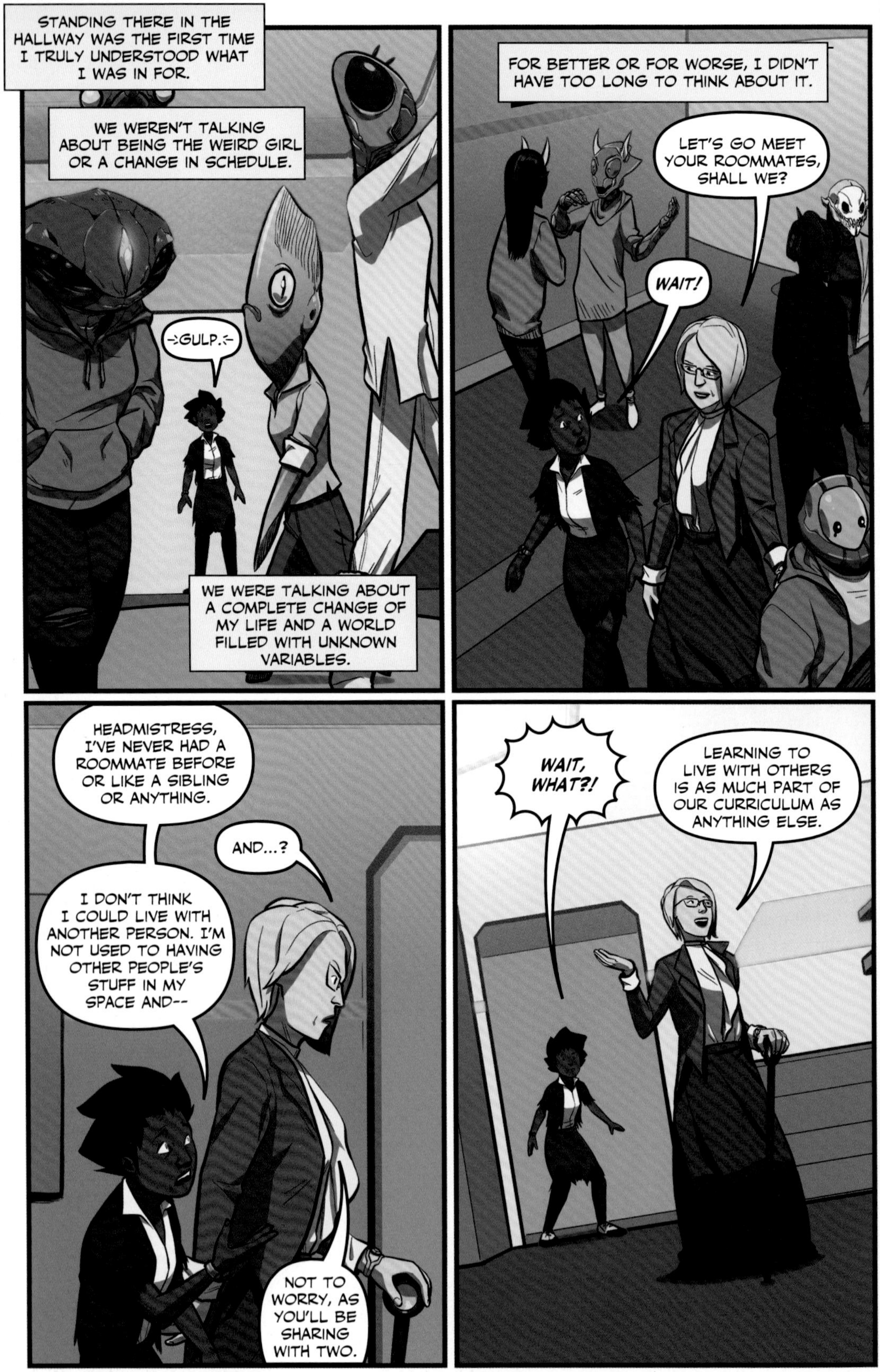
STANDING THERE IN THE HALLWAY WAS THE FIRST TIME I TRULY UNDERSTOOD WHAT I WAS IN FOR.
WE WEREN'T TALKING ABOUT BEING THE WEIRD GIRL OR A CHANGE IN SCHEDULE.
GULP.
WE WERE TALKING ABOUT A COMPLETE CHANGE OF MY LIFE AND A WORLD FILLED WITH UNKNOWN VARIABLES.
FOR BETTER OR FOR WORSE, I DIDN'T HAVE TOO LONG TO THINK ABOUT IT.
LET'S GO MEET YOUR ROOMMATES, SHALL WE?
WAIT!
HEADMISTRESS, I'VE NEVER HAD A ROOMMATE BEFORE OR LIKE A SIBLING OR ANYTHING.
AND...?
I DON'T THINK I COULD LIVE WITH ANOTHER PERSON. I'M NOT USED TO HAVING OTHER PEOPLE'S STUFF IN MY SPACE AND--
NOT TO WORRY, AS YOU'LL BE SHARING WITH TWO.
WAIT, WHAT?!
LEARNING TO LIVE WITH OTHERS IS AS MUCH PART OF OUR CURRICULUM AS ANYTHING ELSE.

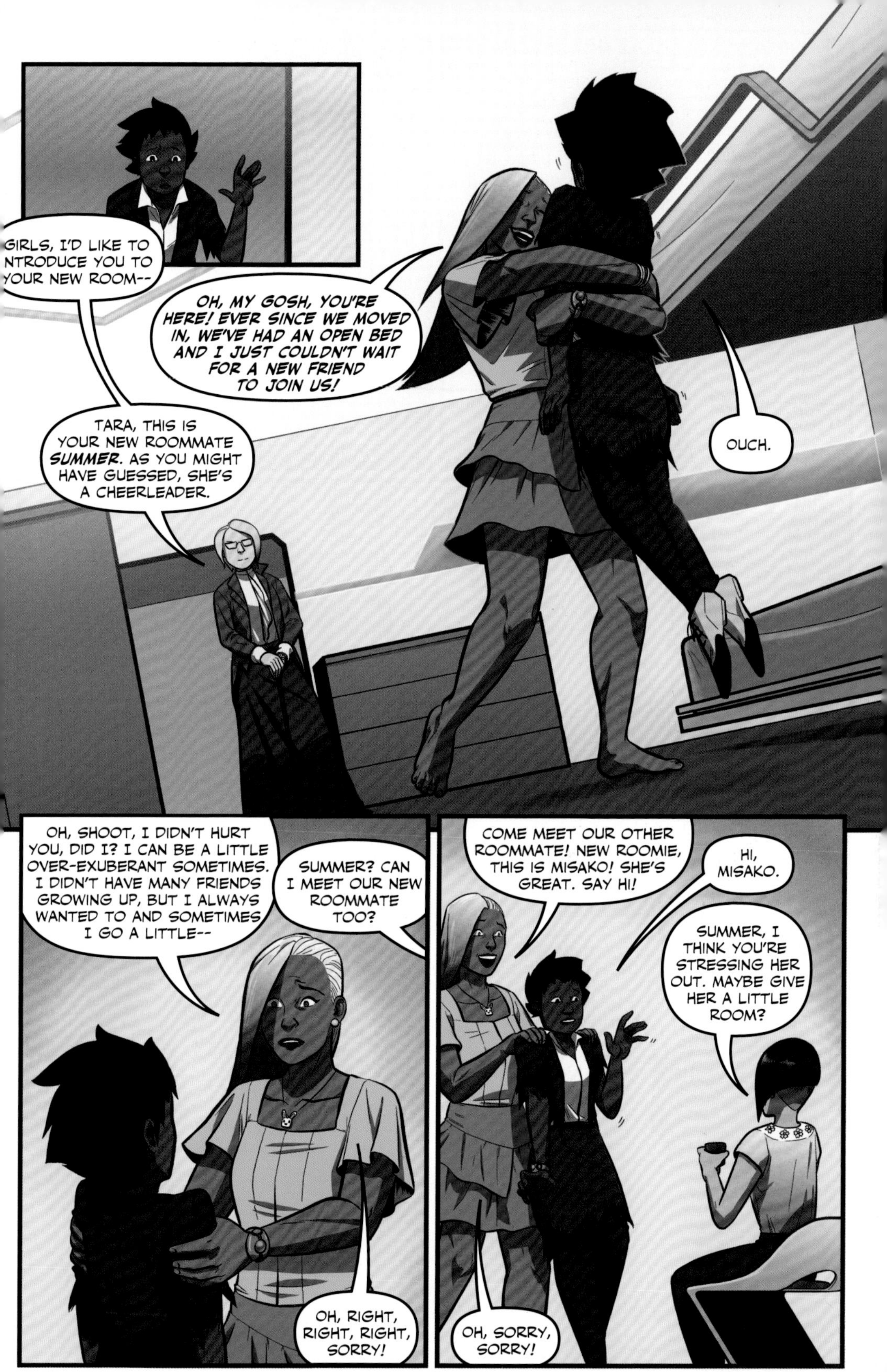
GIRLS, I'D LIKE TO NTRODUCE YOU TO YOUR NEW ROOM--
OH, MY GOSH, YOU'RE HERE! EVER SINCE WE MOVED IN, WE'VE HAD AN OPEN BED AND I JUST COULDN'T WAIT FOR A NEW FRIEND TO JOIN US!
TARA, THIS IS YOUR NEW ROOMMATE SUMMER. AS YOU MIGHT HAVE GUESSED, SHE'S A CHEERLEADER.
OUCH.
OH, SHOOT, I DIDN'T HURT YOU, DID I? I CAN BE A LITTLE OVER-EXUBERANT SOMETIMES. I DIDN'T HAVE MANY FRIENDS GROWING UP, BUT I ALWAYS WANTED TO AND SOMETIMES I GO A LITTLE--
SUMMER? CAN I MEET OUR NEW ROOMMATE TOO?
OH, RIGHT, RIGHT, RIGHT, SORRY!
COME MEET OUR OTHER ROOMMATE! NEW ROOMIE, THIS IS MISAKO! SHE'S GREAT. SAY HI!
HI, MISAKO.
SUMMER, I THINK YOU'RE STRESSING HER OUT. MAYBE GIVE HER A LITTLE ROOM?
OH, SORRY, SORRY!

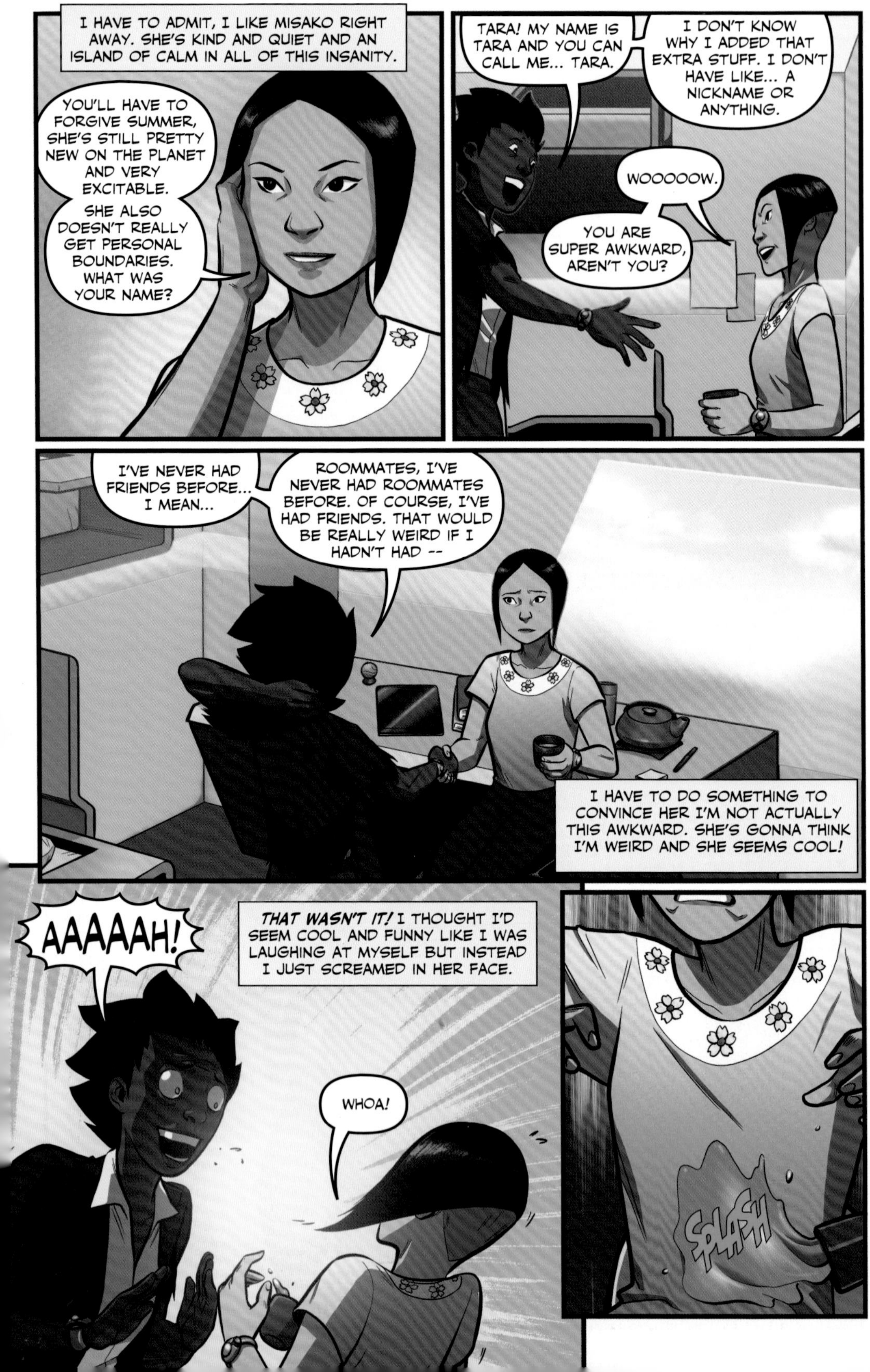
I HAVE TO ADMIT, I LIKE MISAKO RIGHT AWAY. SHE'S KIND AND QUIET AND AN ISLAND OF CALM IN ALL OF THIS INSANITY.
YOU'LL HAVE TO FORGIVE SUMMER, SHE'S STILL PRETTY NEW ON THE PLANET AND VERY EXCITABLE.
SHE ALSO DOESN'T REALLY GET PERSONAL BOUNDARIES. WHAT WAS YOUR NAME?
TARA! MY NAME IS TARA AND YOU CAN CALL ME... TARA.
I DON'T KNOW WHY I ADDED THAT EXTRA STUFF. I DON'T HAVE LIKE... A NICKNAME OR ANYTHING.
WOOOOOW.
YOU ARE SUPER AWKWARD, AREN'T YOU?
I'VE NEVER HAD FRIENDS BEFORE... I MEAN...
ROOMMATES, I'VE NEVER HAD ROOMMATES BEFORE. OF COURSE, I'VE HAD FRIENDS. THAT WOULD BE REALLY WEIRD IF I HADN'T HAD --
I HAVE TO DO SOMETHING TO CONVINCE HER I'M NOT ACTUALLY THIS AWKWARD. SHE'S GONNA THINK I'M WEIRD AND SHE SEEMS COOL!
AAAAAH!
THAT WASN'T IT! I THOUGHT I'D SEEM COOL AND FUNNY LIKE I WAS LAUGHING AT MYSELF BUT INSTEAD I JUST SCREAMED IN HER FACE.
WHOA!
SPLASH

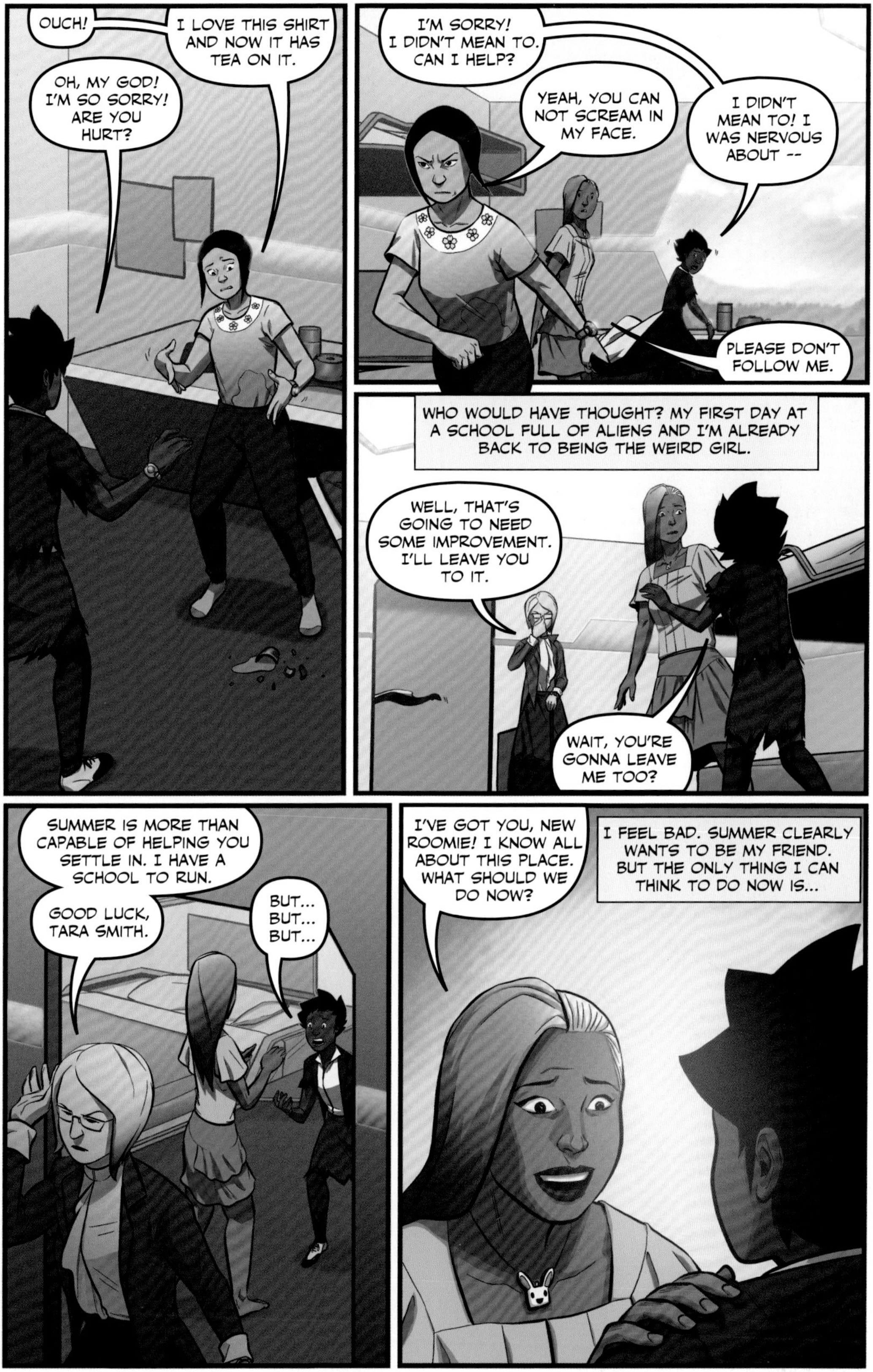
OUCH!
I LOVE THIS SHIRT AND NOW IT HAS TEA ON IT.
OH, MY GOD! I'M SO SORRY! ARE YOU HURT?
I'M SORRY! I DIDN'T MEAN TO. CAN I HELP?
YEAH, YOU CAN NOT SCREAM IN MY FACE.
I DIDN'T MEAN TO! I WAS NERVOUS ABOUT --
PLEASE DON'T FOLLOW ME.
WHO WOULD HAVE THOUGHT? MY FIRST DAY AT A SCHOOL FULL OF ALIENS AND I'M ALREADY BACK TO BEING THE WEIRD GIRL.
WELL, THAT'S GOING TO NEED SOME IMPROVEMENT. I'LL LEAVE YOU TO IT.
WAIT, YOU'RE GONNA LEAVE ME TOO?
SUMMER IS MORE THAN CAPABLE OF HELPING YOU SETTLE IN. I HAVE A SCHOOL TO RUN.
GOOD LUCK, TARA SMITH.
BUT... BUT... BUT...
I'VE GOT YOU, NEW ROOMIE! I KNOW ALL ABOUT THIS PLACE. WHAT SHOULD WE DO NOW?
I FEEL BAD. SUMMER CLEARLY WANTS TO BE MY FRIEND. BUT THE ONLY THING I CAN THINK TO DO NOW IS...

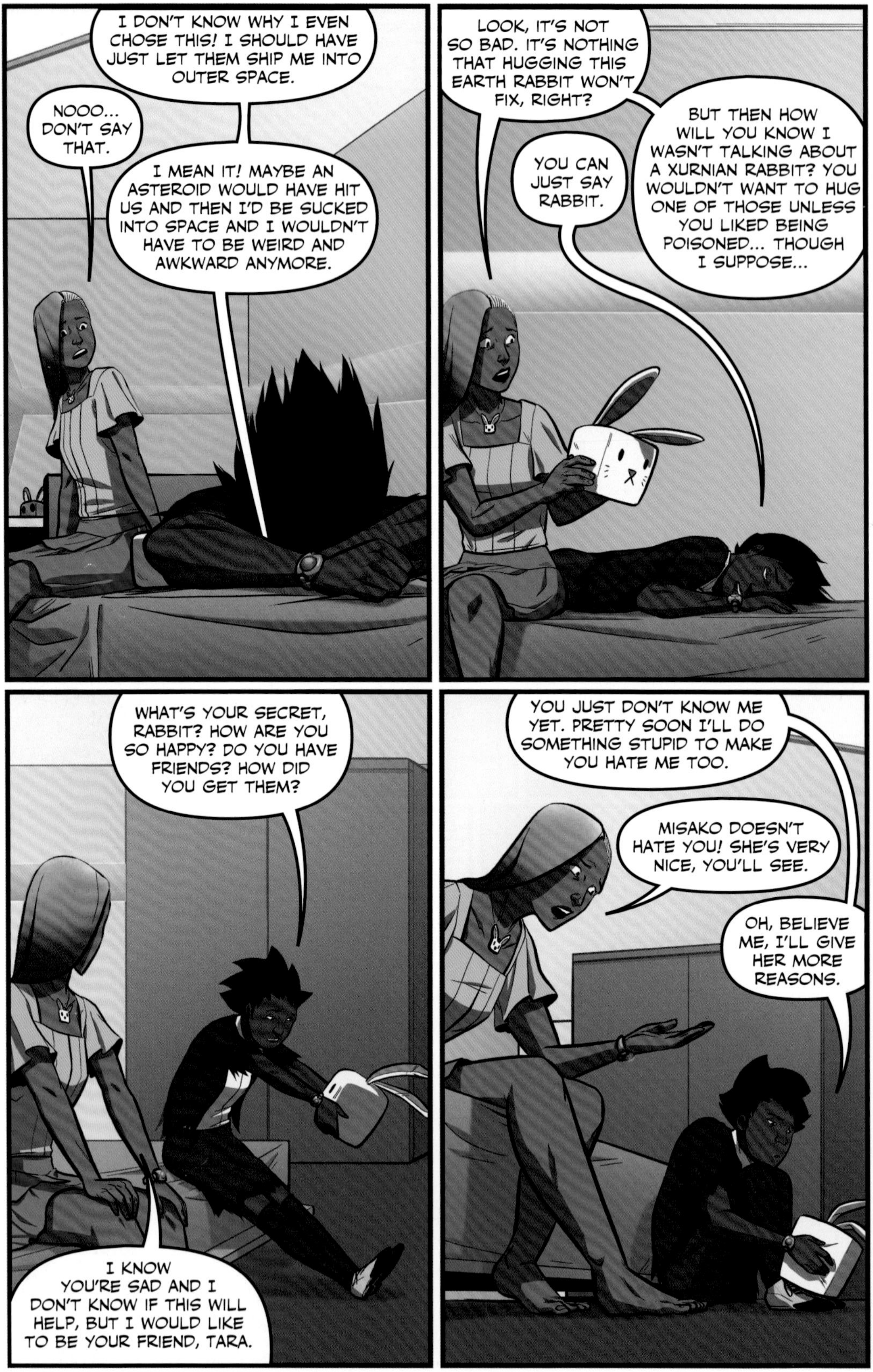
I DON'T KNOW WHY I EVEN CHOSE THIS! I SHOULD HAVE JUST LET THEM SHIP ME INTO OUTER SPACE.
NOOO... DON'T SAY THAT.
I MEAN IT! MAYBE AN ASTEROID WOULD HAVE HIT US AND THEN I'D BE SUCKED INTO SPACE AND I WOULDN'T HAVE TO BE WEIRD AND AWKWARD ANYMORE.
LOOK, IT'S NOT SO BAD. IT'S NOTHING THAT HUGGING THIS EARTH RABBIT WON'T FIX, RIGHT?
YOU CAN JUST SAY RABBIT.
BUT THEN HOW WILL YOU KNOW I WASN'T TALKING ABOUT A XURNIAN RABBIT? YOU WOULDN'T WANT TO HUG ONE OF THOSE UNLESS YOU LIKED BEING POISONED... THOUGH I SUPPOSE...
WHAT'S YOUR SECRET, RABBIT? HOW ARE YOU SO HAPPY? DO YOU HAVE FRIENDS? HOW DID YOU GET THEM?
I KNOW YOU'RE SAD AND I DON'T KNOW IF THIS WILL HELP, BUT I WOULD LIKE TO BE YOUR FRIEND, TARA.
YOU JUST DON'T KNOW ME YET. PRETTY SOON I'LL DO SOMETHING STUPID TO MAKE YOU HATE ME TOO.
MISAKO DOESN'T HATE YOU! SHE'S VERY NICE, YOU'LL SEE.
OH, BELIEVE ME, I'LL GIVE HER MORE REASONS.

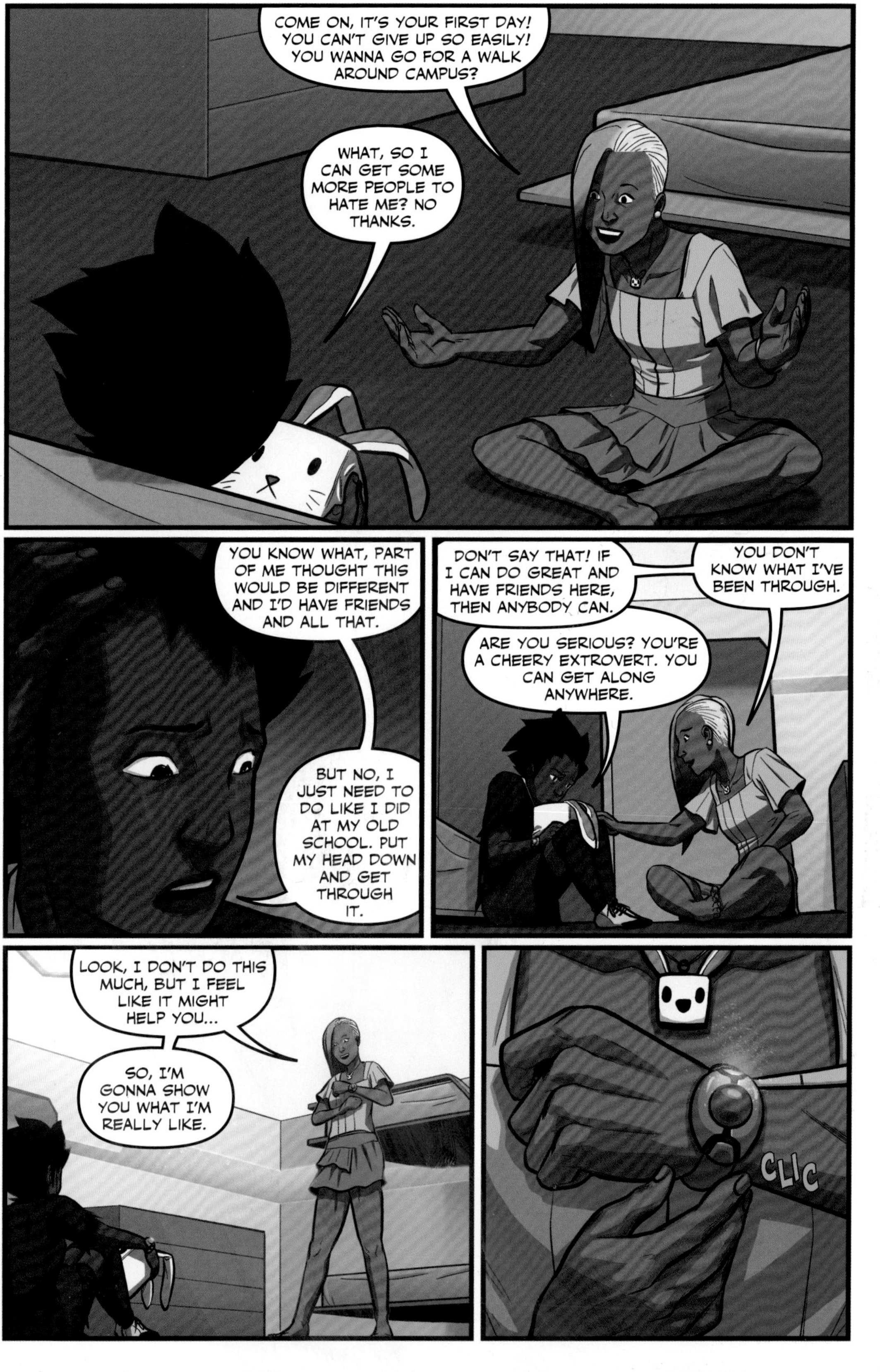
COME ON, IT'S YOUR FIRST DAY! YOU CAN'T GIVE UP SO EASILY! YOU WANNA GO FOR A WALK AROUND CAMPUS?
WHAT, SO I CAN GET SOME MORE PEOPLE TO HATE ME? NO THANKS.
YOU KNOW WHAT, PART OF ME THOUGHT THIS WOULD BE DIFFERENT AND I'D HAVE FRIENDS AND ALL THAT.
BUT NO, I JUST NEED TO DO LIKE I DID AT MY OLD SCHOOL. PUT MY HEAD DOWN AND GET THROUGH IT.
DON'T SAY THAT! IF I CAN DO GREAT AND HAVE FRIENDS HERE, THEN ANYBODY CAN.
ARE YOU SERIOUS? YOU'RE A CHEERY EXTROVERT. YOU CAN GET ALONG ANYWHERE.
YOU DON'T KNOW WHAT I'VE BEEN THROUGH.
LOOK, I DON'T DO THIS MUCH, BUT I FEEL LIKE IT MIGHT HELP YOU...
SO, I'M GONNA SHOW YOU WHAT I'M REALLY LIKE.
CLIC

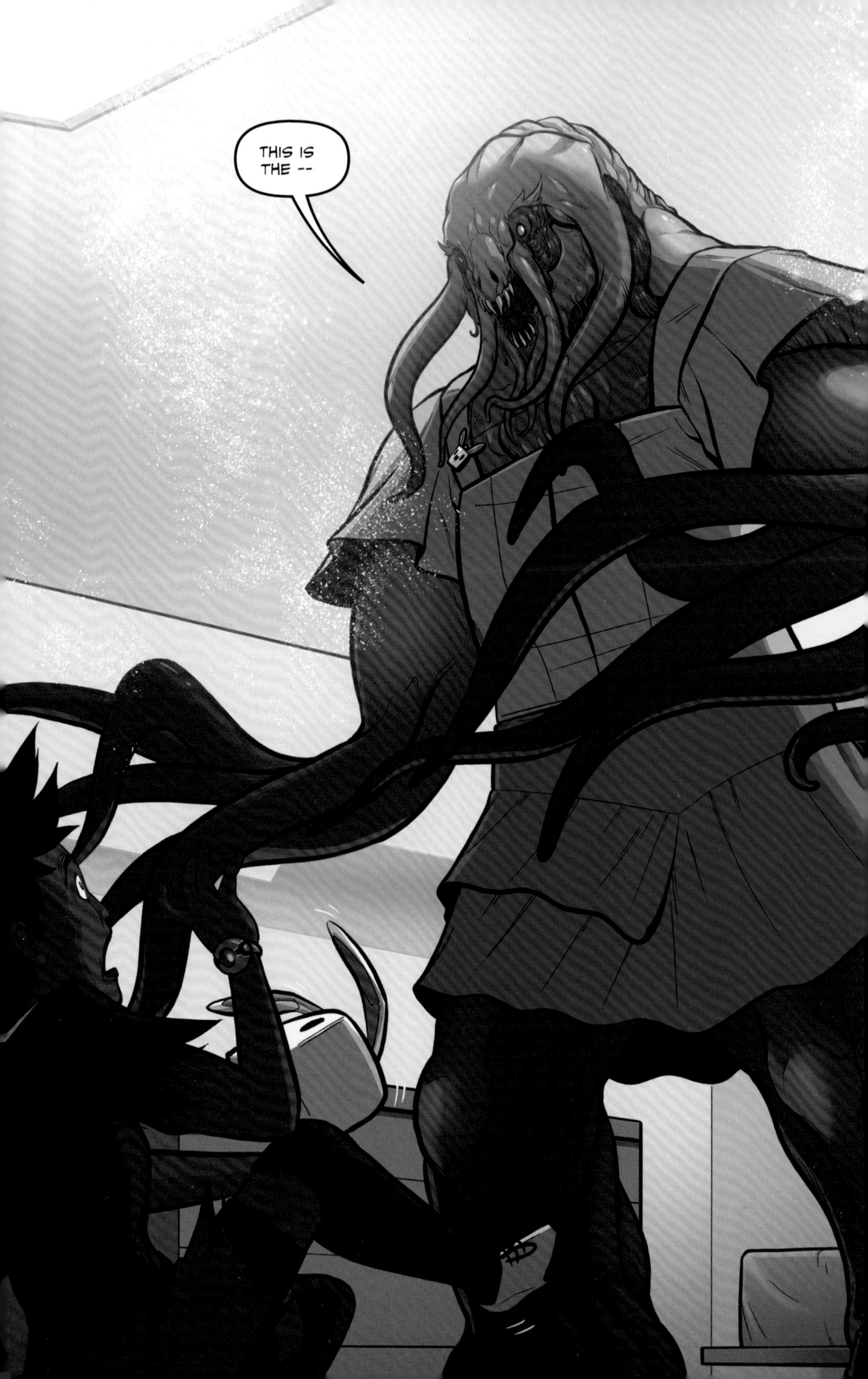
THIS IS THE --

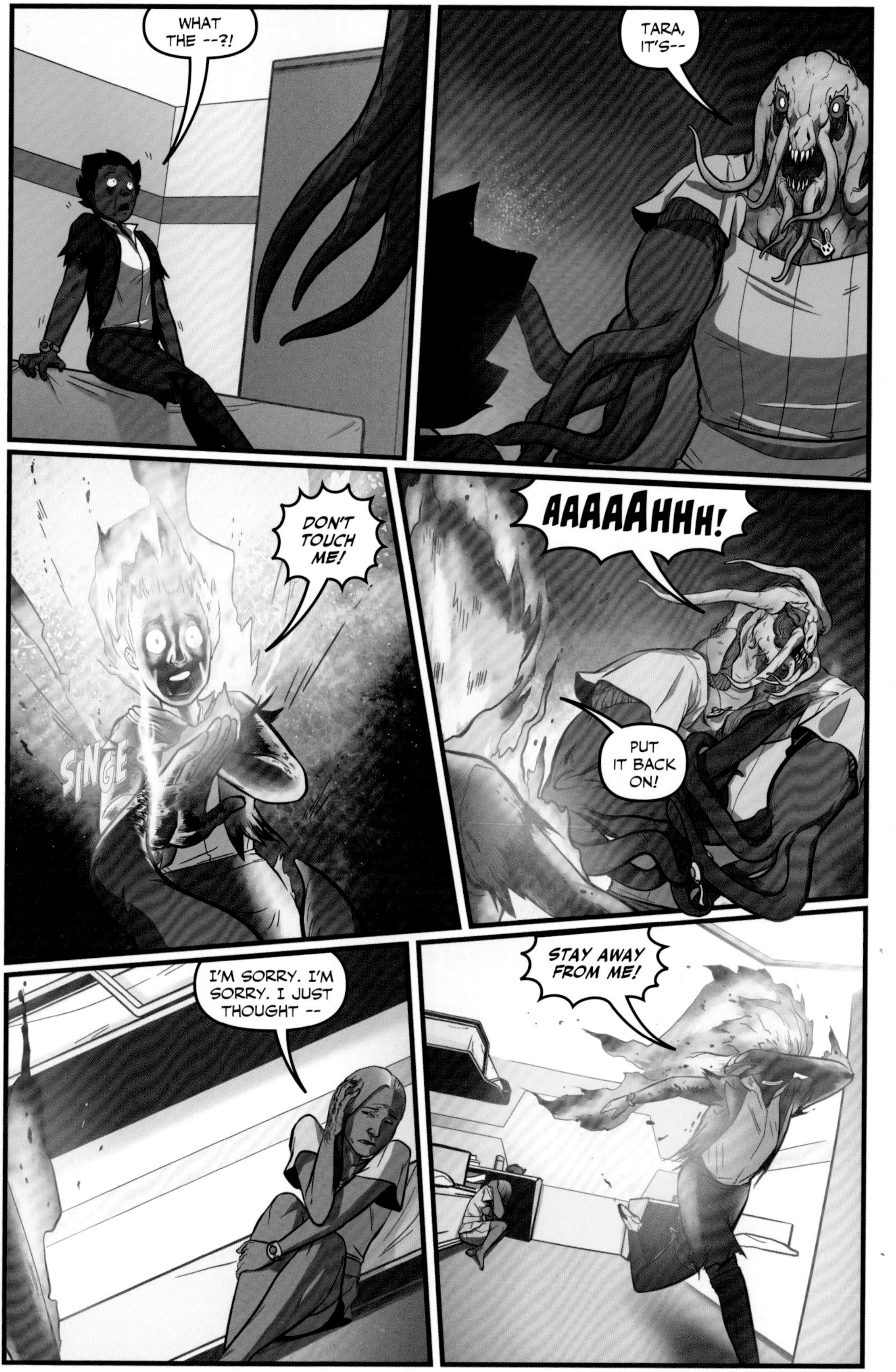
WHAT THE --?!
TARA, IT'S--
DON'T TOUCH ME!
SINGE
AAAAAHHH!
PUT IT BACK ON!
I'M SORRY. I'M SORRY. I JUST THOUGHT --
STAY AWAY FROM ME!

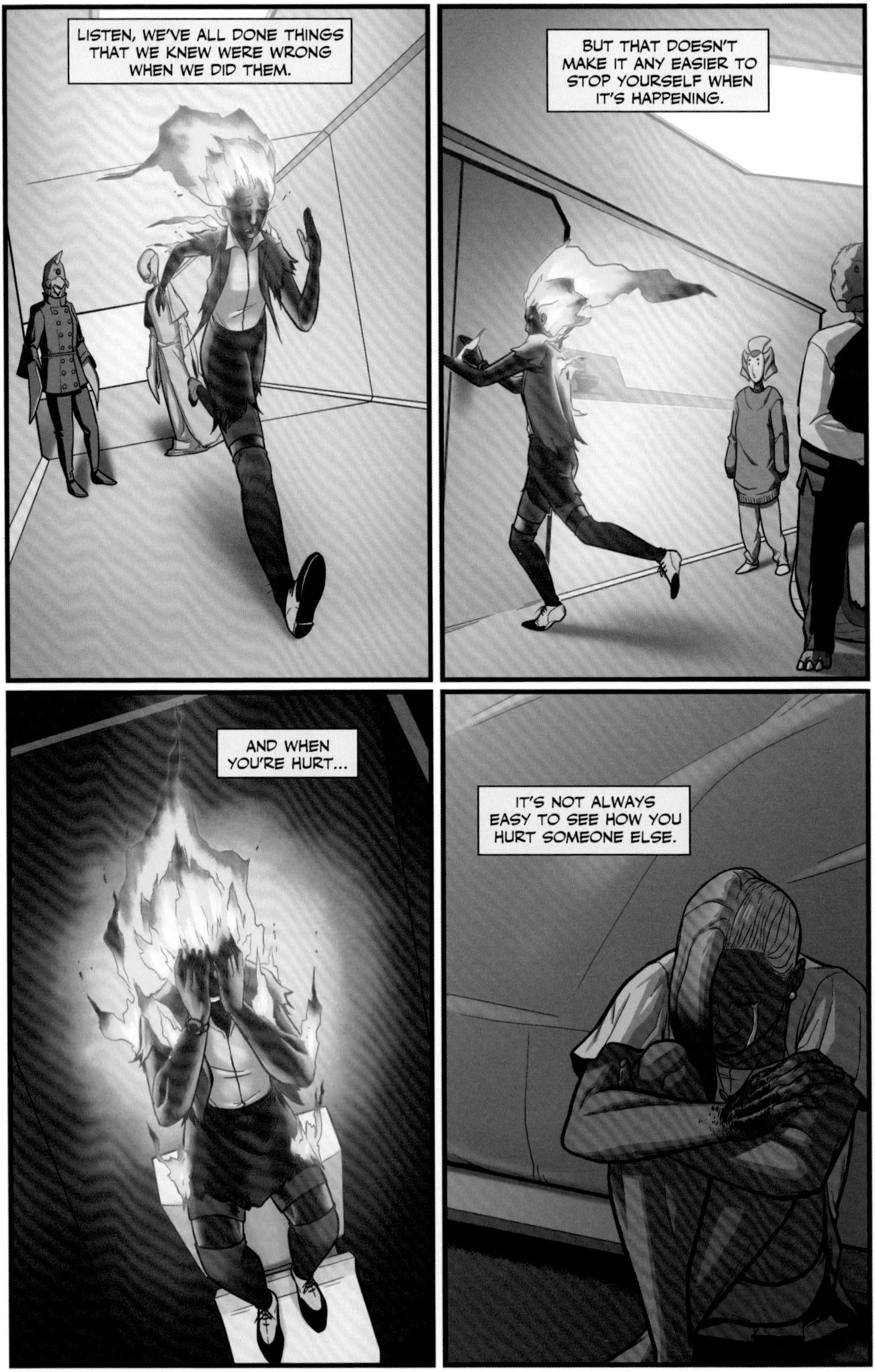
LISTEN, WE'VE ALL DONE THINGS THAT WE KNEW WERE WRONG WHEN WE DID THEM.
BUT THAT DOESN'T MAKE IT ANY EASIER TO STOP YOURSELF WHEN IT'S HAPPENING.
AND WHEN YOU'RE HURT...
IT'S NOT ALWAYS EASY TO SEE HOW YOU HURT SOMEONE ELSE.

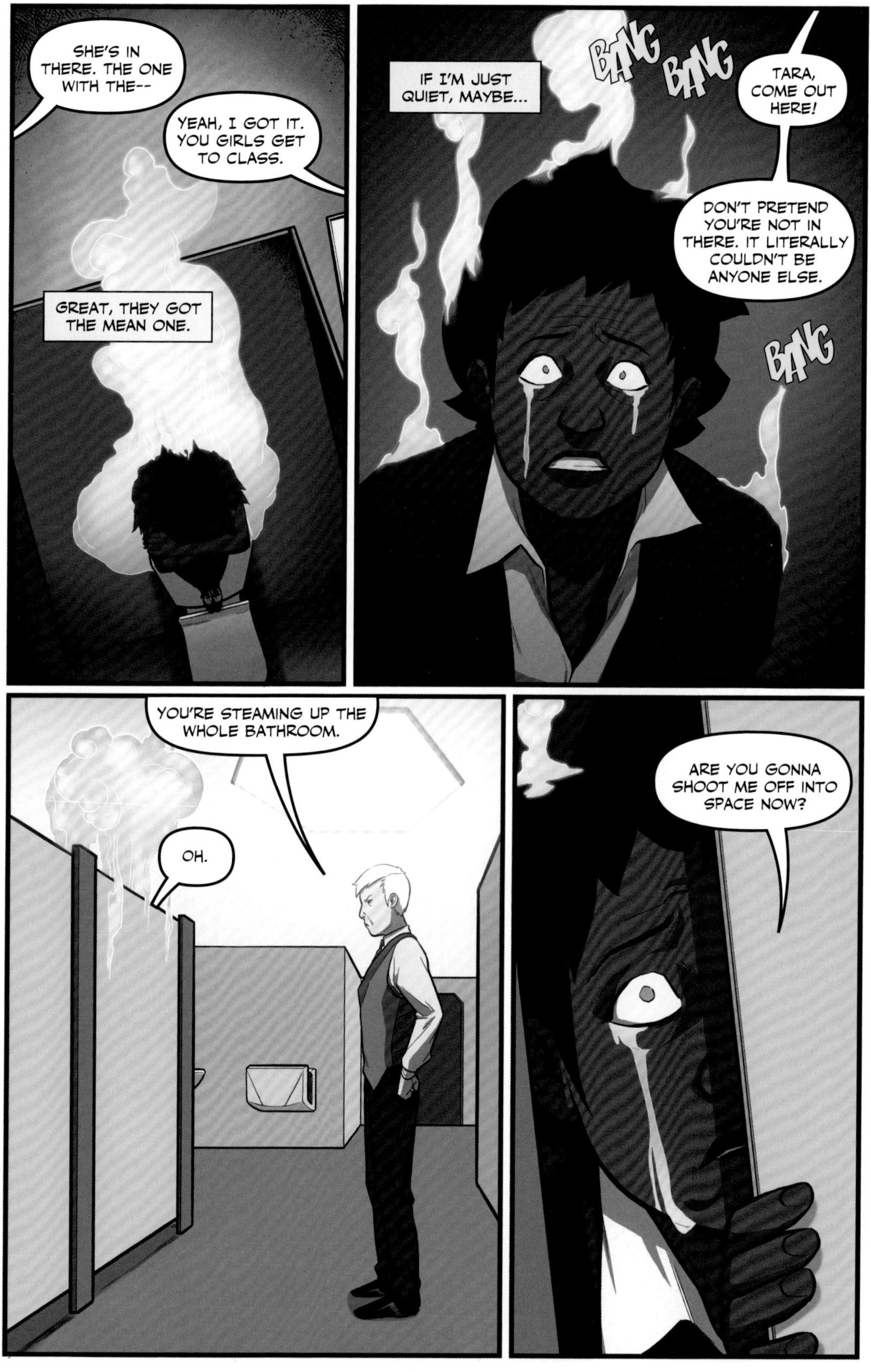
SHE'S IN THERE. THE ONE WITH THE--
YEAH, I GOT IT. YOU GIRLS GET TO CLASS.
GREAT, THEY GOT THE MEAN ONE.
IF I'M JUST QUIET, MAYBE...
BANG
BANG
TARA, COME OUT HERE!
DON'T PRETEND YOU'RE NOT IN THERE. IT LITERALLY COULDN'T BE ANYONE ELSE.
BANG
YOU'RE STEAMING UP THE WHOLE BATHROOM.
OH.
ARE YOU GONNA SHOOT ME OFF INTO SPACE NOW?

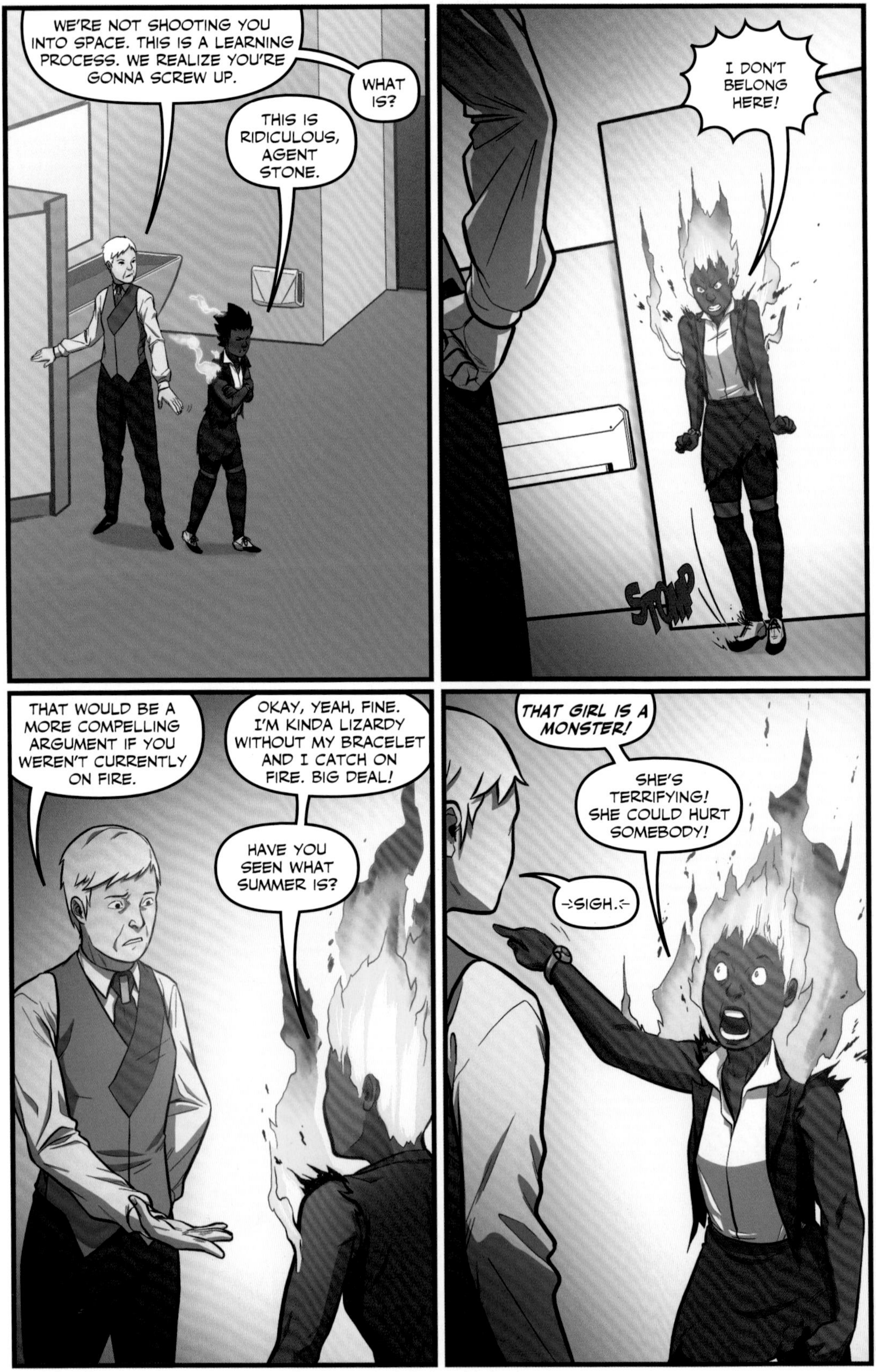
WE'RE NOT SHOOTING YOU INTO SPACE. THIS IS A LEARNING PROCESS. WE REALIZE YOU'RE GONNA SCREW UP.
WHAT IS?
THIS IS RIDICULOUS, AGENT STONE.
I DON'T BELONG HERE!
STOMP
THAT WOULD BE A MORE COMPELLING ARGUMENT IF YOU WEREN'T CURRENTLY ON FIRE.
OKAY, YEAH, FINE. I'M KINDA LIZARDY WITHOUT MY BRACELET AND I CATCH ON FIRE. BIG DEAL!
HAVE YOU SEEN WHAT SUMMER IS?
THAT GIRL IS A MONSTER!
SHE'S TERRIFYING! SHE COULD HURT SOMEBODY!
-SIGH.-

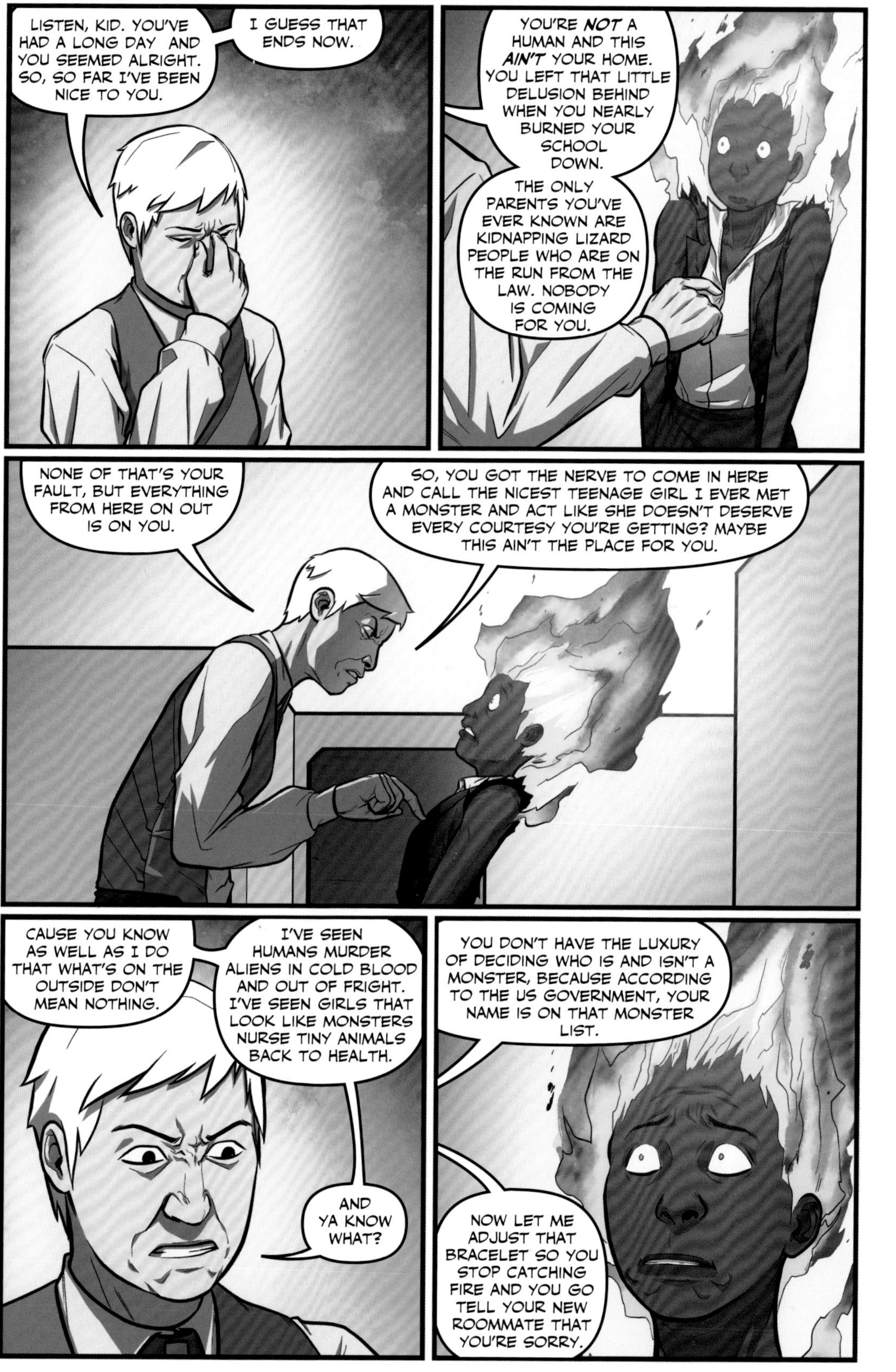
LISTEN, KID. YOU'VE HAD A LONG DAY AND YOU SEEMED ALRIGHT. SO, SO FAR I'VE BEEN NICE TO YOU.
I GUESS THAT ENDS NOW.
YOU'RE NOT A HUMAN AND THIS AIN'T YOUR HOME. YOU LEFT THAT LITTLE DELUSION BEHIND WHEN YOU NEARLY BURNED YOUR SCHOOL DOWN.
THE ONLY PARENTS YOU'VE EVER KNOWN ARE KIDNAPPING LIZARD PEOPLE WHO ARE ON THE RUN FROM THE LAW. NOBODY IS COMING FOR YOU.
NONE OF THAT'S YOUR FAULT, BUT EVERYTHING FROM HERE ON OUT IS ON YOU.
SO, YOU GOT THE NERVE TO COME IN HERE AND CALL THE NICEST TEENAGE GIRL I EVER MET A MONSTER AND ACT LIKE SHE DOESN'T DESERVE EVERY COURTESY YOU'RE GETTING? MAYBE THIS AIN'T THE PLACE FOR YOU.
CAUSE YOU KNOW AS WELL AS I DO THAT WHAT'S ON THE OUTSIDE DON'T MEAN NOTHING.
I'VE SEEN HUMANS MURDER ALIENS IN COLD BLOOD AND OUT OF FRIGHT. I'VE SEEN GIRLS THAT LOOK LIKE MONSTERS NURSE TINY ANIMALS BACK TO HEALTH.
AND YA KNOW WHAT?
YOU DON'T HAVE THE LUXURY OF DECIDING WHO IS AND ISN'T A MONSTER, BECAUSE ACCORDING TO THE US GOVERNMENT, YOUR NAME IS ON THAT MONSTER LIST.
NOW LET ME ADJUST THAT BRACELET SO YOU STOP CATCHING FIRE AND YOU GO TELL YOUR NEW ROOMMATE THAT YOU'RE SORRY.

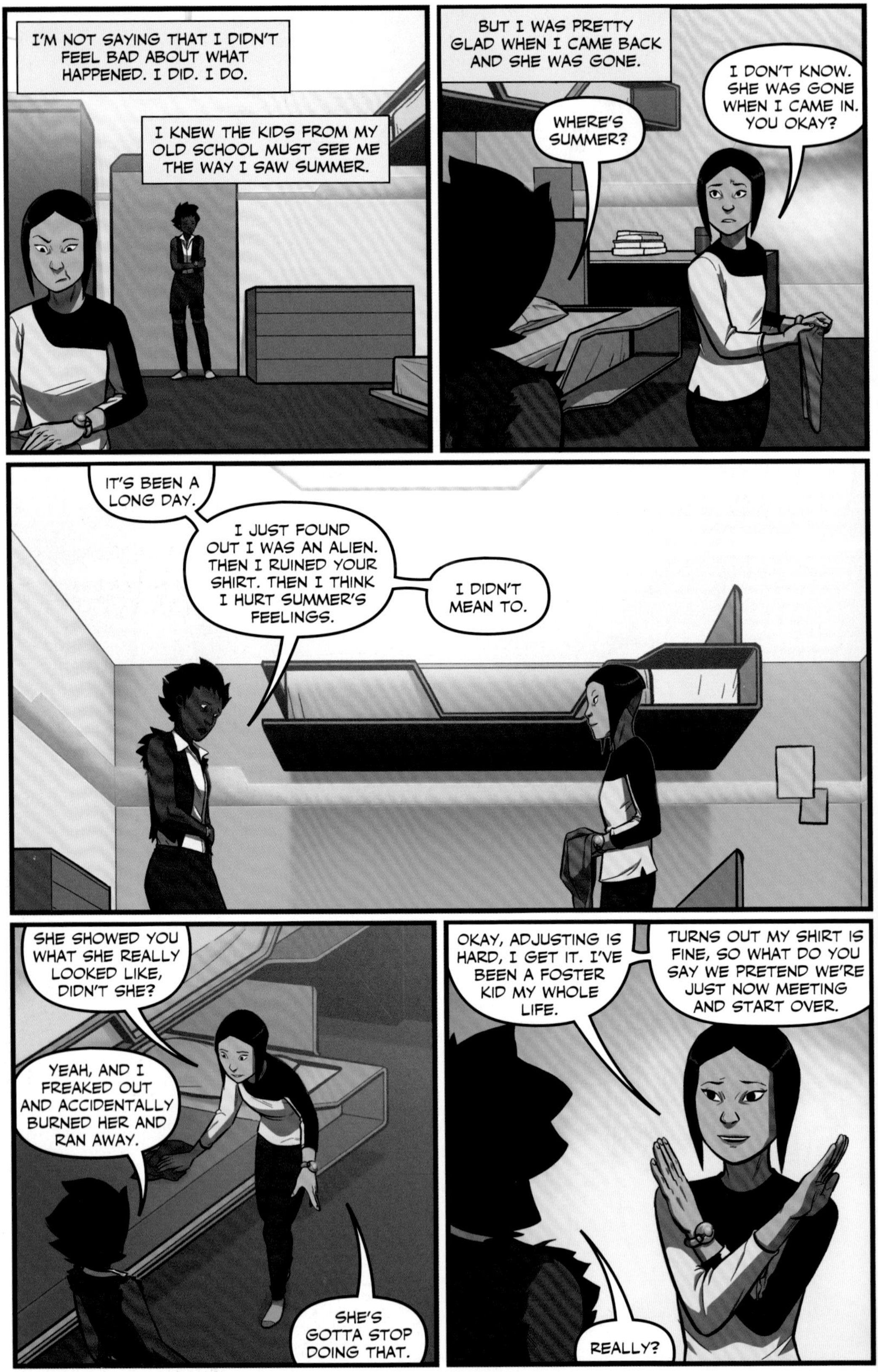
I'M NOT SAYING THAT I DIDN'T FEEL BAD ABOUT WHAT HAPPENED. I DID. I DO.
I KNEW THE KIDS FROM MY OLD SCHOOL MUST SEE ME THE WAY I SAW SUMMER.
BUT I WAS PRETTY GLAD WHEN I CAME BACK AND SHE WAS GONE.
WHERE'S SUMMER?
I DON'T KNOW. SHE WAS GONE WHEN I CAME IN. YOU OKAY?
IT'S BEEN A LONG DAY.
I JUST FOUND OUT I WAS AN ALIEN. THEN I RUINED YOUR SHIRT. THEN I THINK I HURT SUMMER'S FEELINGS.
I DIDN'T MEAN TO.
SHE SHOWED YOU WHAT SHE REALLY LOOKED LIKE, DIDN'T SHE?
YEAH, AND I FREAKED OUT AND ACCIDENTALLY BURNED HER AND RAN AWAY.
SHE'S GOTTA STOP DOING THAT.
OKAY, ADJUSTING IS HARD, I GET IT. I'VE BEEN A FOSTER KID MY WHOLE LIFE.
TURNS OUT MY SHIRT IS FINE, SO WHAT DO YOU SAY WE PRETEND WE'RE JUST NOW MEETING AND START OVER.
REALLY?

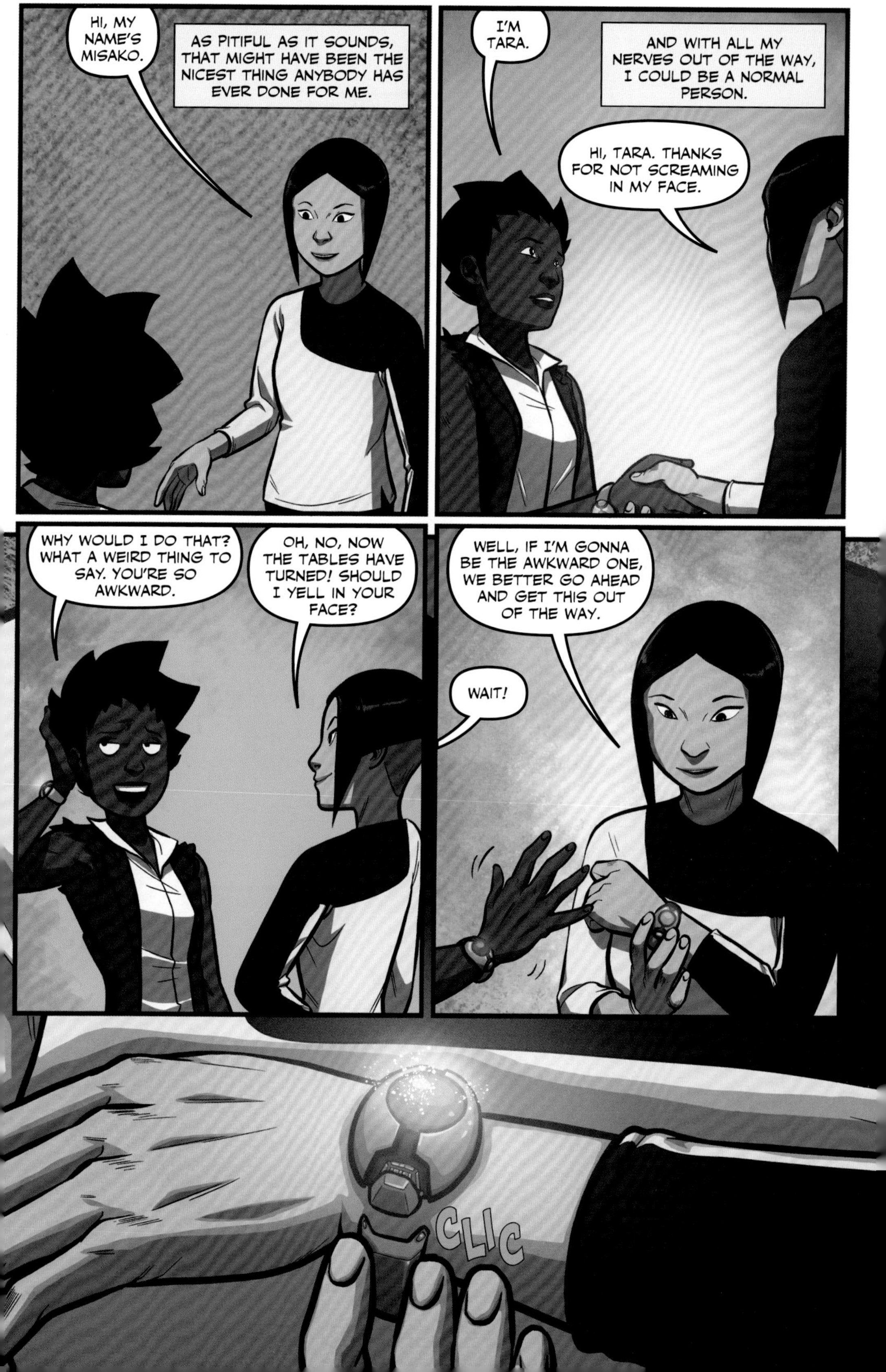
HI, MY NAME'S MISAKO.
AS PITIFUL AS IT SOUNDS, THAT MIGHT HAVE BEEN THE NICEST THING ANYBODY HAS EVER DONE FOR ME.
I'M TARA.
AND WITH ALL MY NERVES OUT OF THE WAY, I COULD BE A NORMAL PERSON.
HI, TARA. THANKS FOR NOT SCREAMING IN MY FACE.
WHY WOULD I DO THAT? WHAT A WEIRD THING TO SAY. YOU'RE SO AWKWARD.
OH, NO, NOW THE TABLES HAVE TURNED! SHOULD I YELL IN YOUR FACE?
WELL, IF I'M GONNA BE THE AWKWARD ONE, WE BETTER GO AHEAD AND GET THIS OUT OF THE WAY.
WAIT!
CLIC

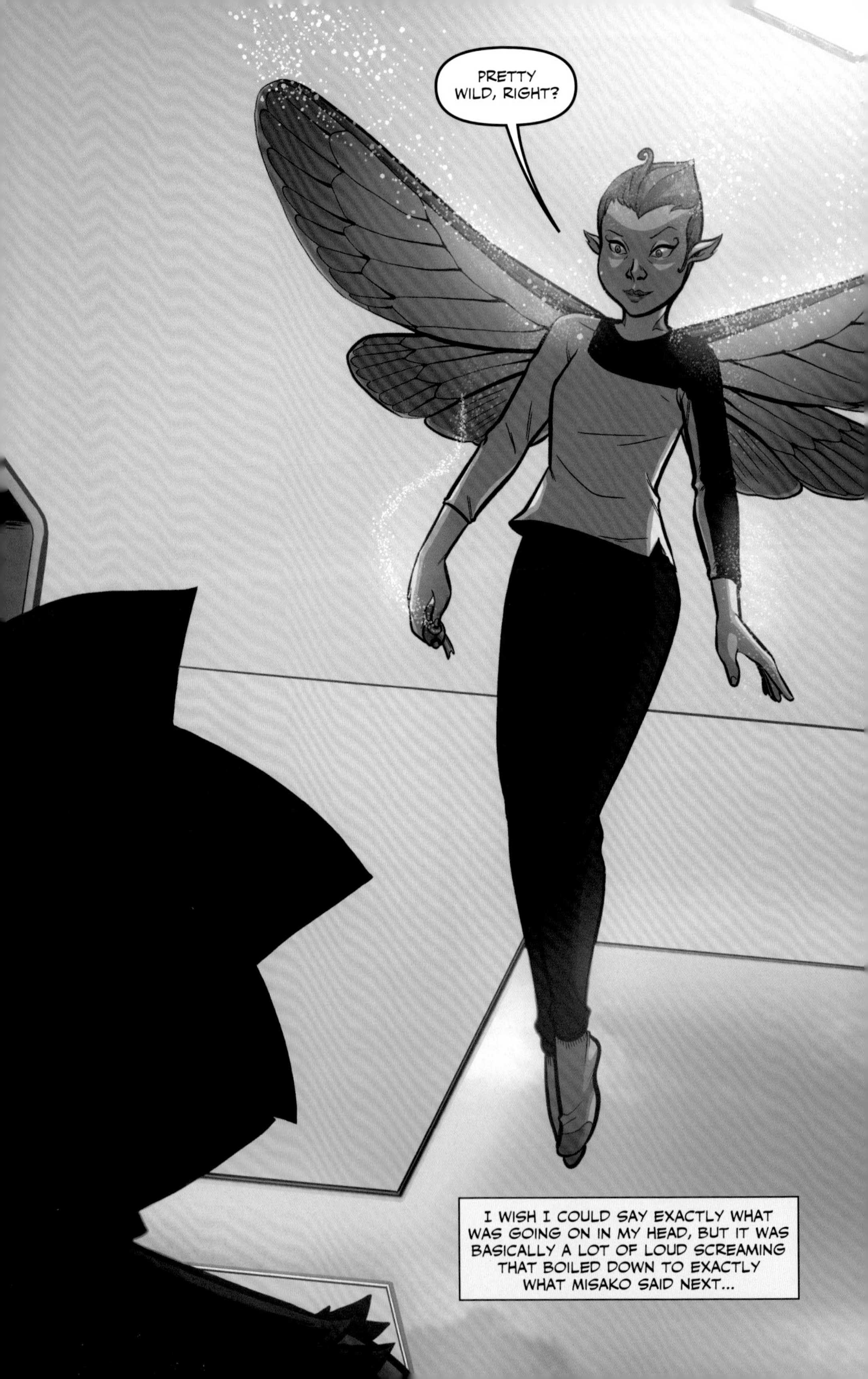
PRETTY WILD, RIGHT?
I WISH I COULD SAY EXACTLY WHAT WAS GOING ON IN MY HEAD, BUT IT WAS BASICALLY A LOT OF LOUD SCREAMING THAT BOILED DOWN TO EXACTLY WHAT MISAKO SAID NEXT...

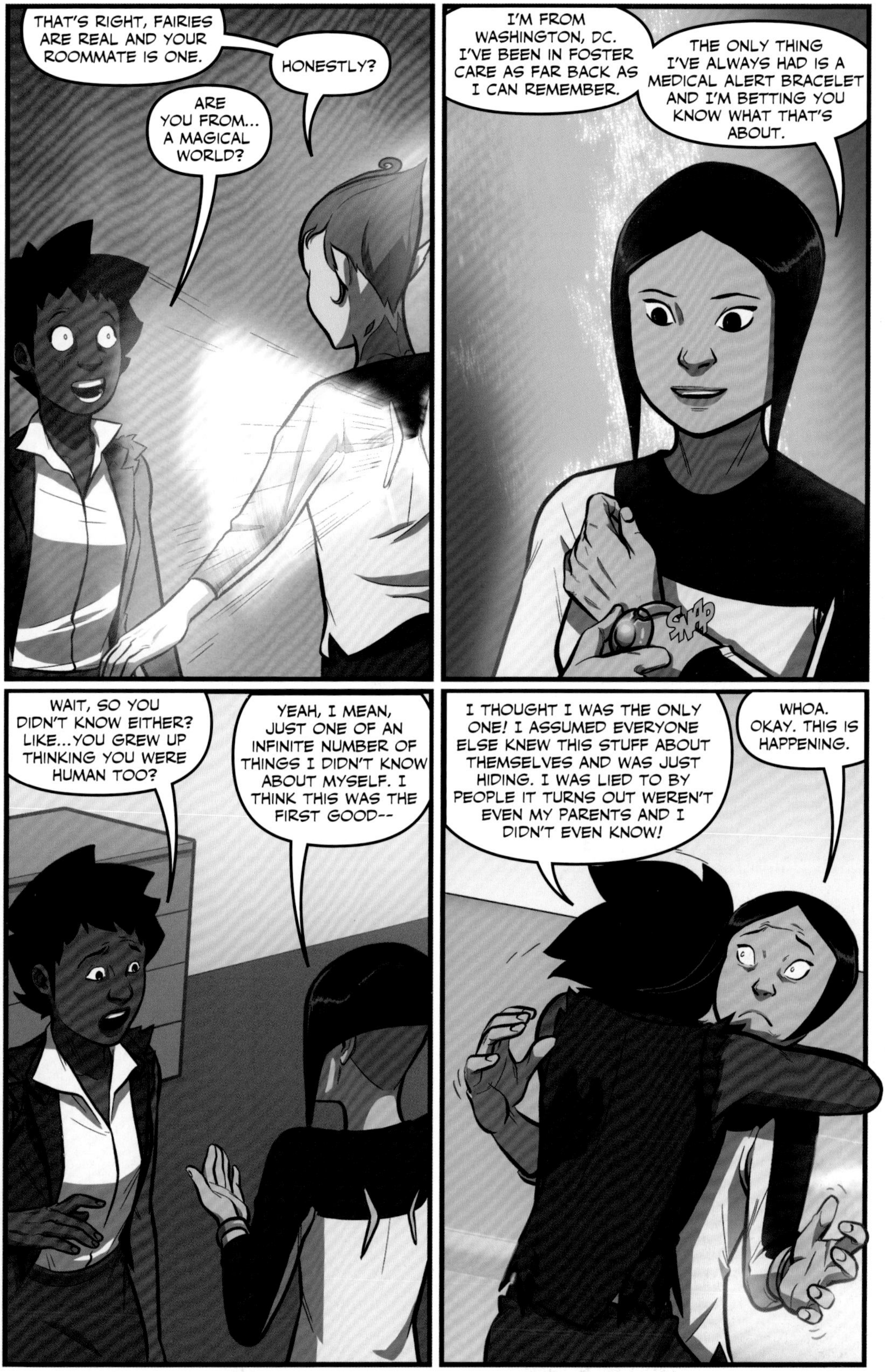
THAT'S RIGHT, FAIRIES ARE REAL AND YOUR ROOMMATE IS ONE.
HONESTLY?
ARE YOU FROM... A MAGICAL WORLD?
I'M FROM WASHINGTON, DC. I'VE BEEN IN FOSTER CARE AS FAR BACK AS I CAN REMEMBER.
THE ONLY THING I'VE ALWAYS HAD IS A MEDICAL ALERT BRACELET AND I'M BETTING YOU KNOW WHAT THAT'S ABOUT.
SNAP
WAIT, SO YOU DIDN'T KNOW EITHER? LIKE...YOU GREW UP THINKING YOU WERE HUMAN TOO?
YEAH, I MEAN, JUST ONE OF AN INFINITE NUMBER OF THINGS I DIDN'T KNOW ABOUT MYSELF. I THINK THIS WAS THE FIRST GOOD--
I THOUGHT I WAS THE ONLY ONE! I ASSUMED EVERYONE ELSE KNEW THIS STUFF ABOUT THEMSELVES AND WAS JUST HIDING. I WAS LIED TO BY PEOPLE IT TURNS OUT WEREN'T EVEN MY PARENTS AND I DIDN'T EVEN KNOW!
WHOA. OKAY. THIS IS HAPPENING.

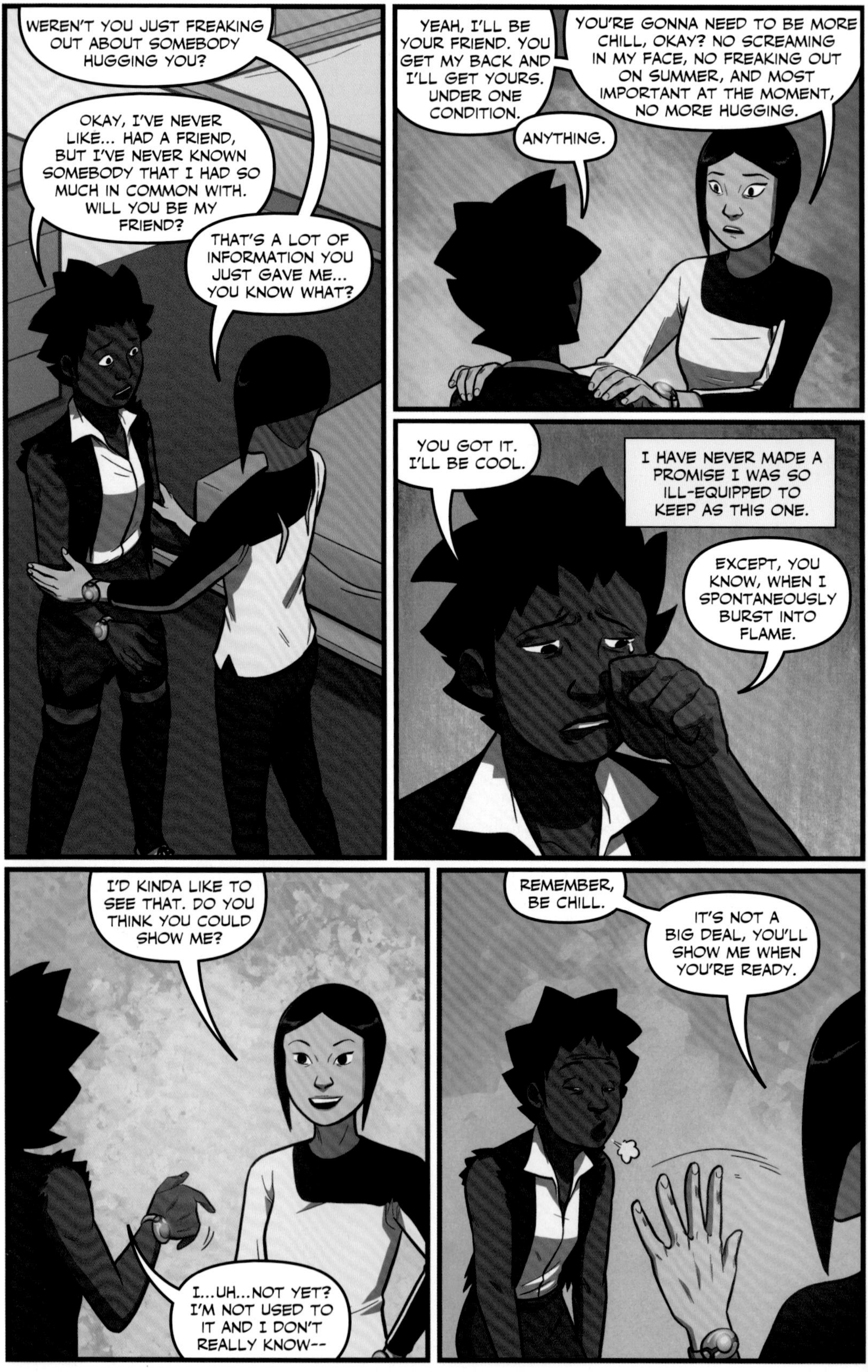
WEREN'T YOU JUST FREAKING OUT ABOUT SOMEBODY HUGGING YOU?
OKAY, I'VE NEVER LIKE... HAD A FRIEND, BUT I'VE NEVER KNOWN SOMEBODY THAT I HAD SO MUCH IN COMMON WITH. WILL YOU BE MY FRIEND?
THAT'S A LOT OF INFORMATION YOU JUST GAVE ME... YOU KNOW WHAT?
YEAH, I'LL BE YOUR FRIEND. YOU GET MY BACK AND I'LL GET YOURS. UNDER ONE CONDITION.
ANYTHING.
YOU'RE GONNA NEED TO BE MORE CHILL, OKAY? NO SCREAMING IN MY FACE, NO FREAKING OUT ON SUMMER, AND MOST IMPORTANT AT THE MOMENT, NO MORE HUGGING.
YOU GOT IT. I'LL BE COOL.
I HAVE NEVER MADE A PROMISE I WAS SO ILL-EQUIPPED TO KEEP AS THIS ONE.
EXCEPT, YOU KNOW, WHEN I SPONTANEOUSLY BURST INTO FLAME.
I'D KINDA LIKE TO SEE THAT. DO YOU THINK YOU COULD SHOW ME?
I...UH...NOT YET? I'M NOT USED TO IT AND I DON'T REALLY KNOW--
REMEMBER, BE CHILL.
IT'S NOT A BIG DEAL, YOU'LL SHOW ME WHEN YOU'RE READY.

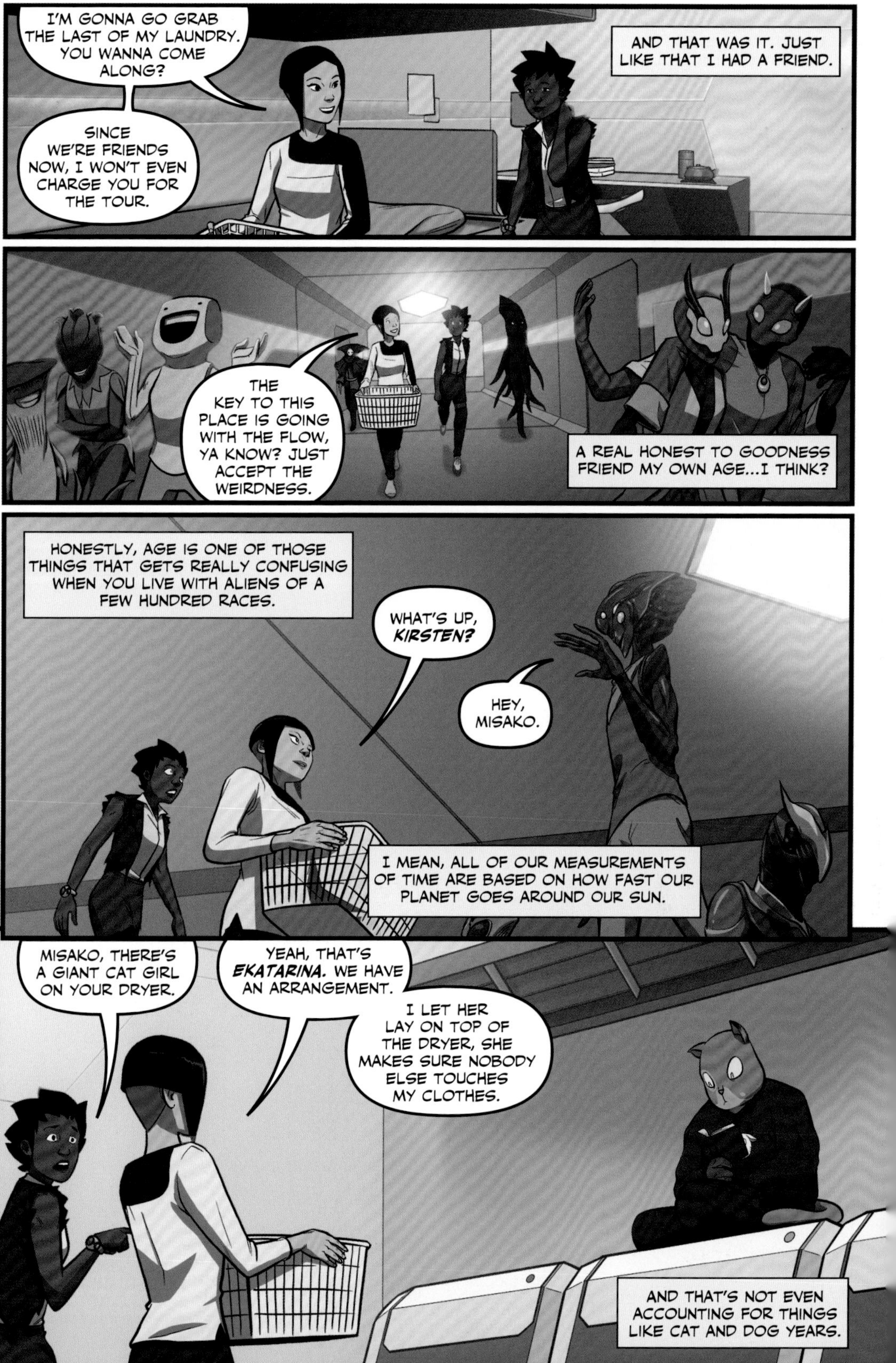
I'M GONNA GO GRAB THE LAST OF MY LAUNDRY. YOU WANNA COME ALONG?
SINCE WE'RE FRIENDS NOW, I WON'T EVEN CHARGE YOU FOR THE TOUR.
AND THAT WAS IT. JUST LIKE THAT I HAD A FRIEND.
THE KEY TO THIS PLACE IS GOING WITH THE FLOW, YA KNOW? JUST ACCEPT THE WEIRDNESS.
A REAL HONEST TO GOODNESS FRIEND MY OWN AGE...I THINK?
HONESTLY, AGE IS ONE OF THOSE THINGS THAT GETS REALLY CONFUSING WHEN YOU LIVE WITH ALIENS OF A FEW HUNDRED RACES.
WHAT'S UP, KIRSTEN?
HEY, MISAKO.
I MEAN, ALL OF OUR MEASUREMENTS OF TIME ARE BASED ON HOW FAST OUR PLANET GOES AROUND OUR SUN.
MISAKO, THERE'S A GIANT CAT GIRL ON YOUR DRYER.
YEAH, THAT'S EKATARINA. WE HAVE AN ARRANGEMENT.
I LET HER LAY ON TOP OF THE DRYER, SHE MAKES SURE NOBODY ELSE TOUCHES MY CLOTHES.
AND THAT'S NOT EVEN ACCOUNTING FOR THINGS LIKE CAT AND DOG YEARS.

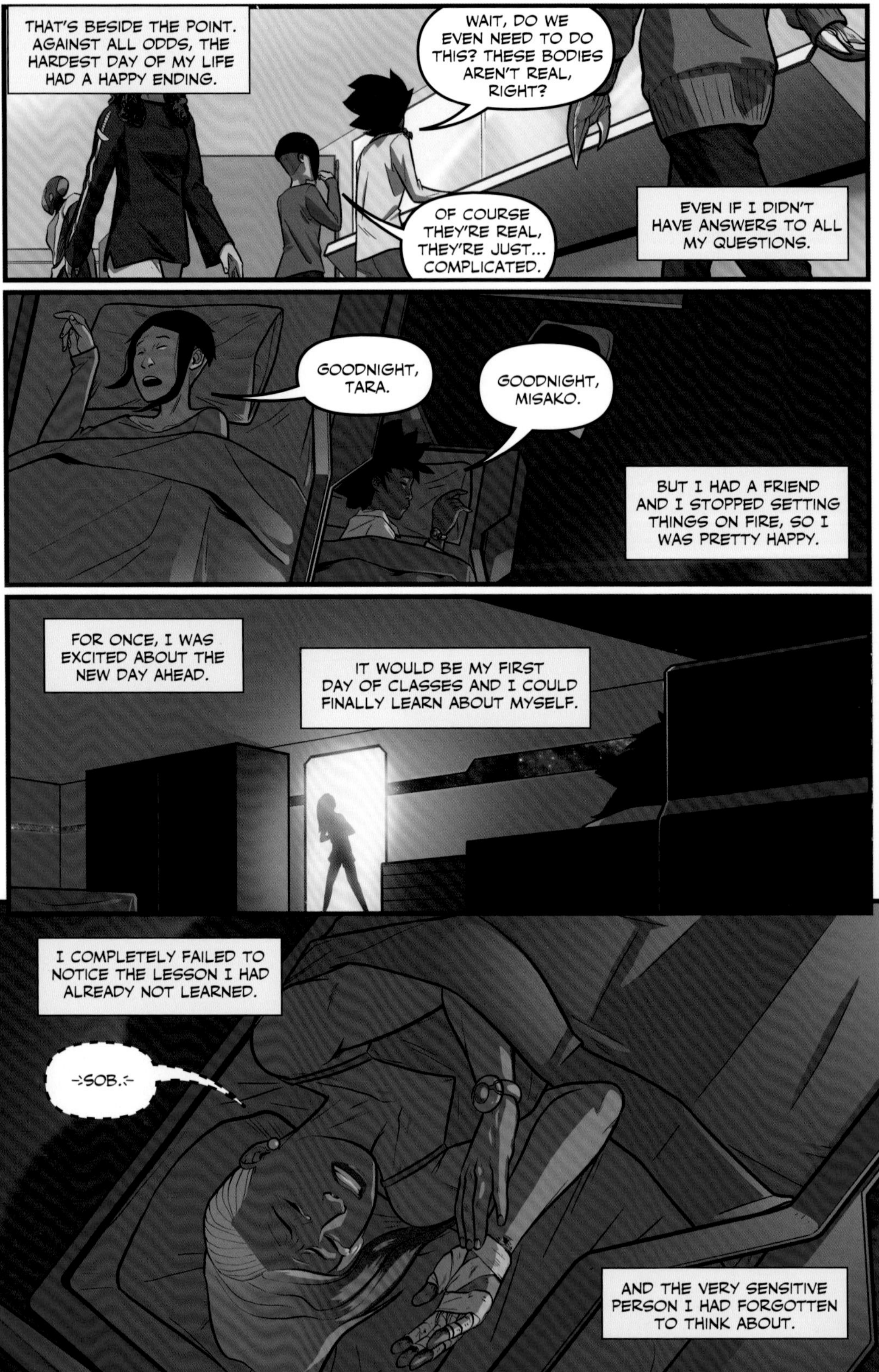
THAT'S BESIDE THE POINT. AGAINST ALL ODDS, THE HARDEST DAY OF MY LIFE HAD A HAPPY ENDING.
WAIT, DO WE EVEN NEED TO DO THIS? THESE BODIES AREN'T REAL, RIGHT?
OF COURSE THEY'RE REAL, THEY'RE JUST... COMPLICATED.
EVEN IF I DIDN'T HAVE ANSWERS TO ALL MY QUESTIONS.
GOODNIGHT, TARA.
GOODNIGHT, MISAKO.
BUT I HAD A FRIEND AND I STOPPED SETTING THINGS ON FIRE, SO I WAS PRETTY HAPPY.
FOR ONCE, I WAS EXCITED ABOUT THE NEW DAY AHEAD.
IT WOULD BE MY FIRST DAY OF CLASSES AND I COULD FINALLY LEARN ABOUT MYSELF.
I COMPLETELY FAILED TO NOTICE THE LESSON I HAD ALREADY NOT LEARNED.
SOB.
AND THE VERY SENSITIVE PERSON I HAD FORGOTTEN TO THINK ABOUT.

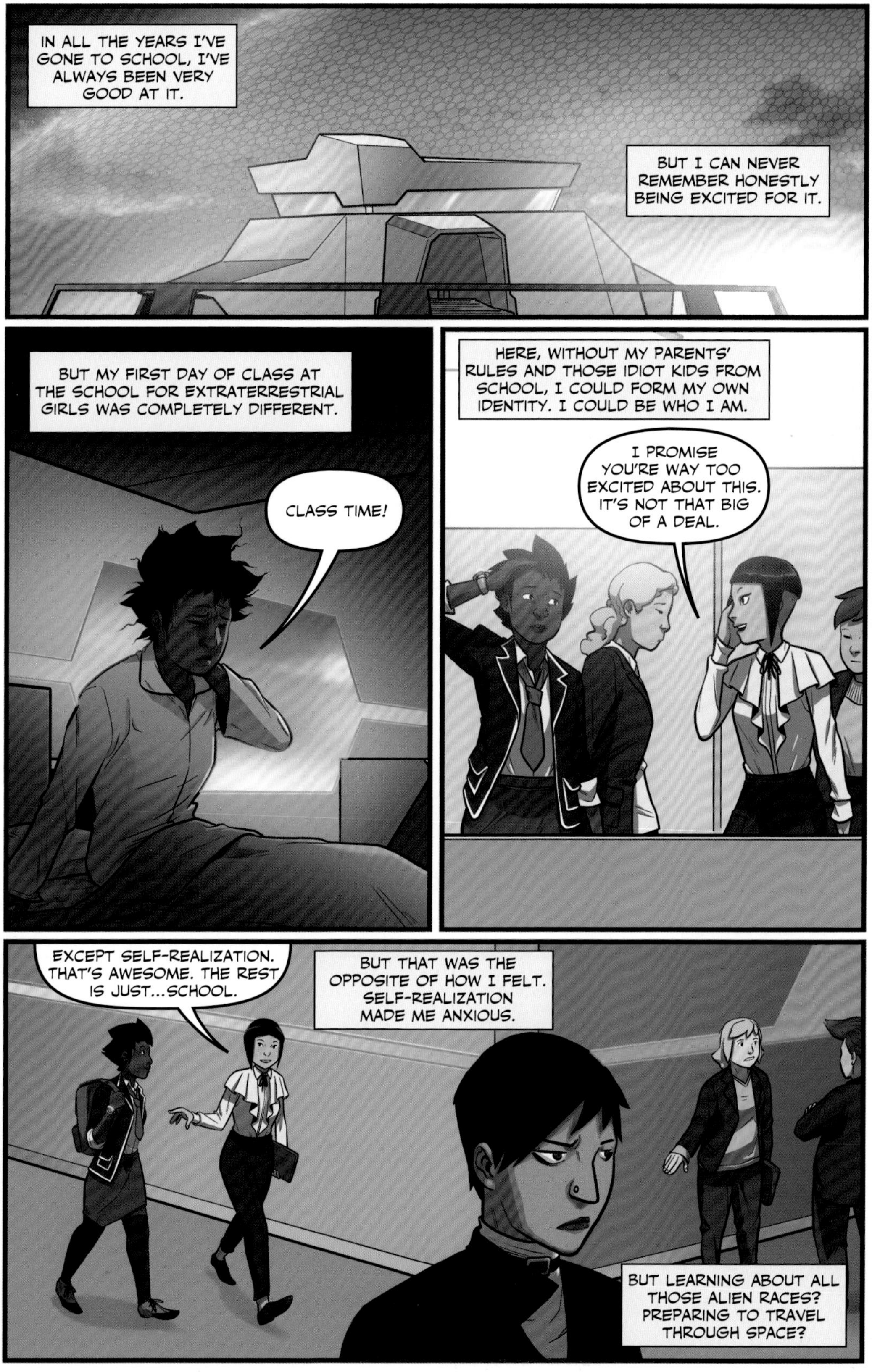
IN ALL THE YEARS I'VE GONE TO SCHOOL, I'VE ALWAYS BEEN VERY GOOD AT IT.
BUT I CAN NEVER REMEMBER HONESTLY BEING EXCITED FOR IT.
BUT MY FIRST DAY OF CLASS AT THE SCHOOL FOR EXTRATERRESTRIAL GIRLS WAS COMPLETELY DIFFERENT.
CLASS TIME!
HERE, WITHOUT MY PARENTS' RULES AND THOSE IDIOT KIDS FROM SCHOOL, I COULD FORM MY OWN IDENTITY. I COULD BE WHO I AM.
I PROMISE YOU'RE WAY TOO EXCITED ABOUT THIS. IT'S NOT THAT BIG OF A DEAL.
EXCEPT SELF-REALIZATION. THAT'S AWESOME. THE REST IS JUST...SCHOOL.
BUT THAT WAS THE OPPOSITE OF HOW I FELT. SELF-REALIZATION MADE ME ANXIOUS.
BUT LEARNING ABOUT ALL THOSE ALIEN RACES? PREPARING TO TRAVEL THROUGH SPACE?

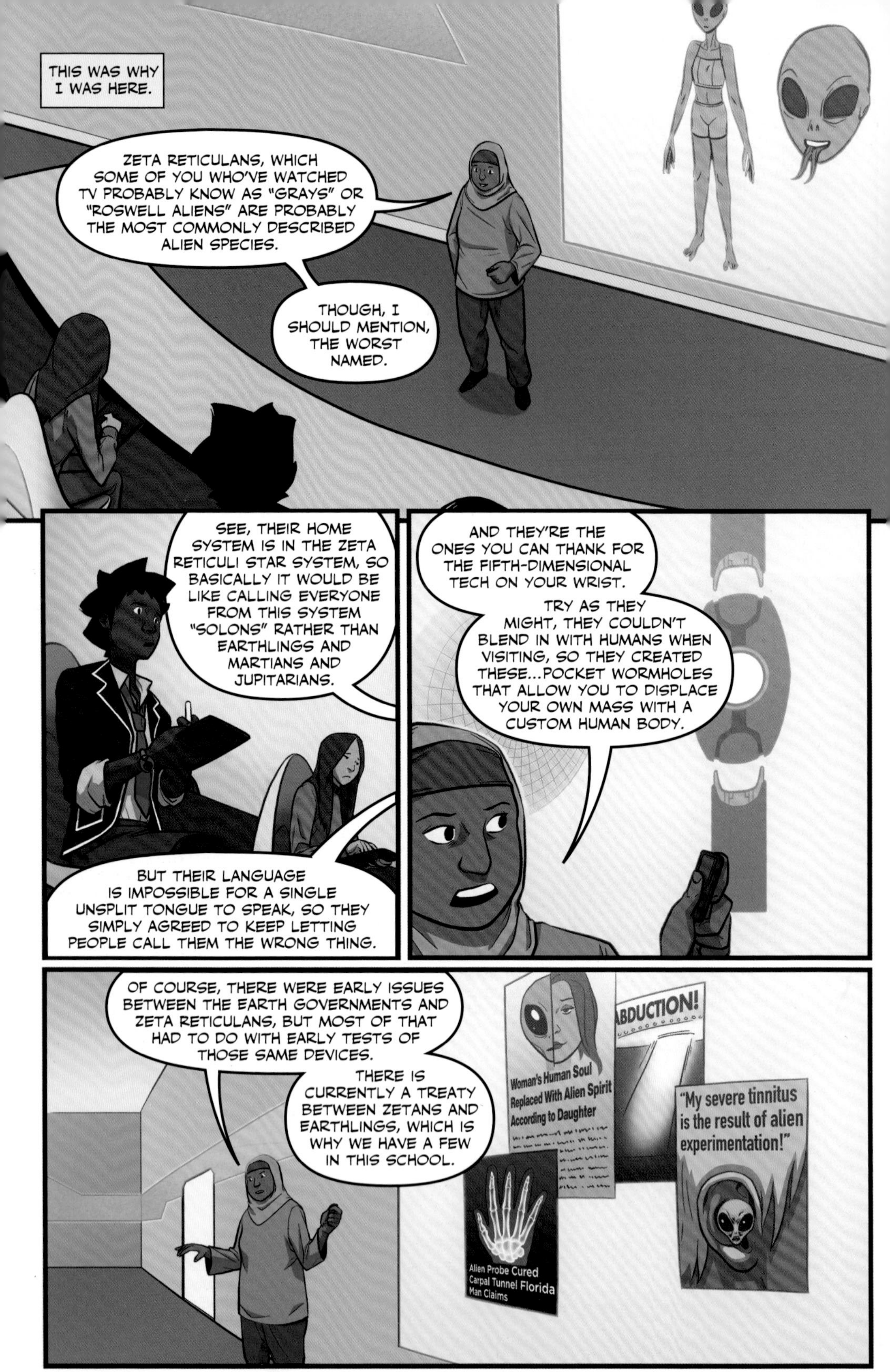
THIS WAS WHY I WAS HERE.
ZETA RETICULANS, WHICH SOME OF YOU WHO'VE WATCHED TV PROBABLY KNOW AS "GRAYS" OR "ROSWELL ALIENS" ARE PROBABLY THE MOST COMMONLY DESCRIBED ALIEN SPECIES.
THOUGH, I SHOULD MENTION, THE WORST NAMED.
SEE, THEIR HOME SYSTEM IS IN THE ZETA RETICULI STAR SYSTEM, SO BASICALLY IT WOULD BE LIKE CALLING EVERYONE FROM THIS SYSTEM "SOLONS" RATHER THAN EARTHLINGS AND MARTIANS AND JUPITARIANS.
BUT THEIR LANGUAGE IS IMPOSSIBLE FOR A SINGLE UNSPLIT TONGUE TO SPEAK, SO THEY SIMPLY AGREED TO KEEP LETTING PEOPLE CALL THEM THE WRONG THING.
AND THEY'RE THE ONES YOU CAN THANK FOR THE FIFTH-DIMENSIONAL TECH ON YOUR WRIST.
TRY AS THEY MIGHT, THEY COULDN'T BLEND IN WITH HUMANS WHEN VISITING, SO THEY CREATED THESE...POCKET WORMHOLES THAT ALLOW YOU TO DISPLACE YOUR OWN MASS WITH A CUSTOM HUMAN BODY.
OF COURSE, THERE WERE EARLY ISSUES BETWEEN THE EARTH GOVERNMENTS AND ZETA RETICULANS, BUT MOST OF THAT HAD TO DO WITH EARLY TESTS OF THOSE SAME DEVICES.
THERE IS CURRENTLY A TREATY BETWEEN ZETANS AND EARTHLINGS, WHICH IS WHY WE HAVE A FEW IN THIS SCHOOL.
Woman's Human Soul Replaced With Alien Spirit According to Daughter
ABDUCTION!
"My severe tinnitus is the result of alien experimentation!"
Alien Probe Cured Carpal Tunnel Florida Man Claims

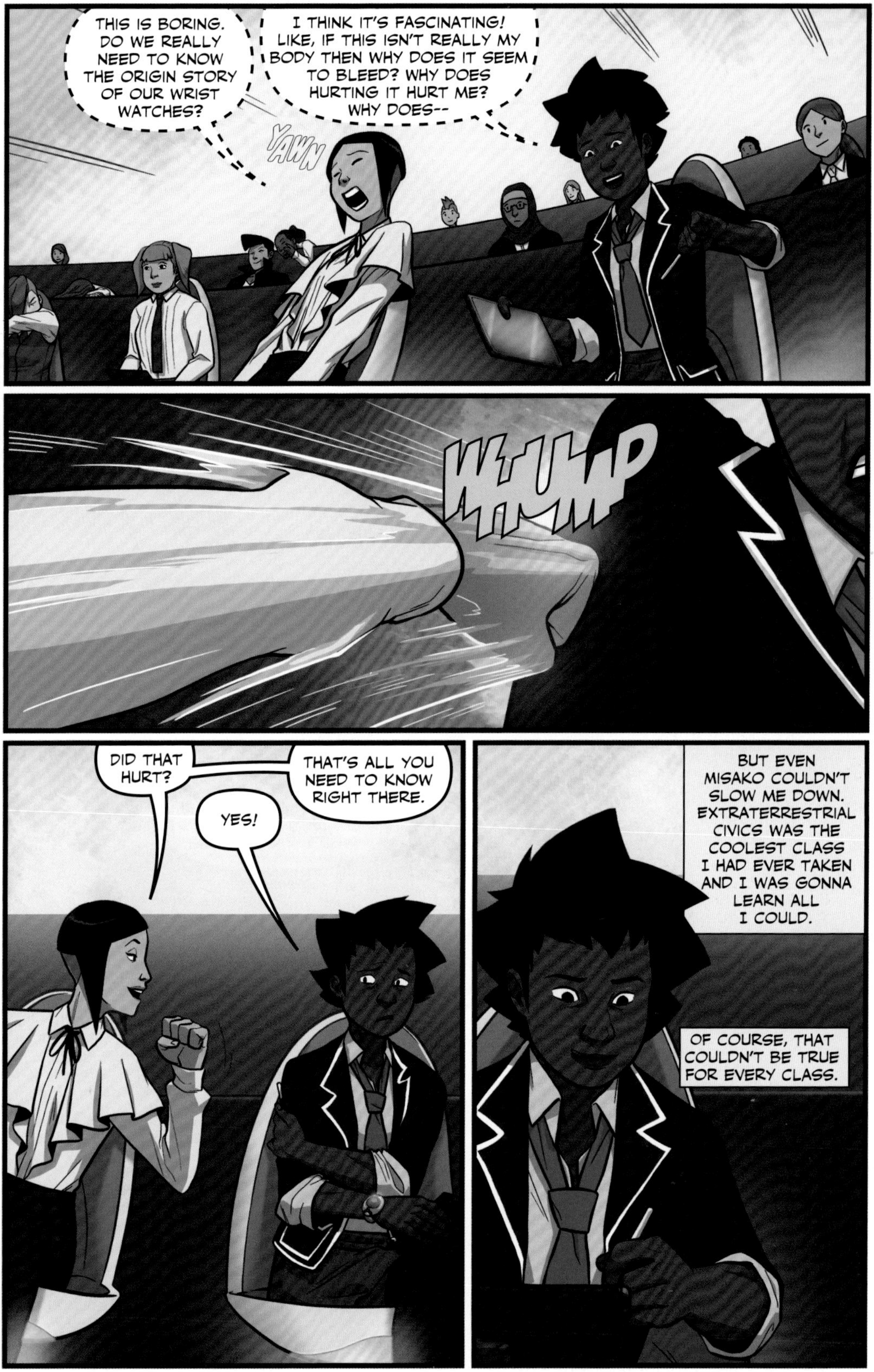
THIS IS BORING. DO WE REALLY NEED TO KNOW THE ORIGIN STORY OF OUR WRIST WATCHES?
I THINK IT'S FASCINATING! LIKE, IF THIS ISN'T REALLY MY BODY THEN WHY DOES IT SEEM TO BLEED? WHY DOES HURTING IT HURT ME? WHY DOES--
YAWN
WHUMP
DID THAT HURT?
YES!
THAT'S ALL YOU NEED TO KNOW RIGHT THERE.
BUT EVEN MISAKO COULDN'T SLOW ME DOWN. EXTRATERRESTRIAL CIVICS WAS THE COOLEST CLASS I HAD EVER TAKEN AND I WAS GONNA LEARN ALL I COULD.
OF COURSE, THAT COULDN'T BE TRUE FOR EVERY CLASS.

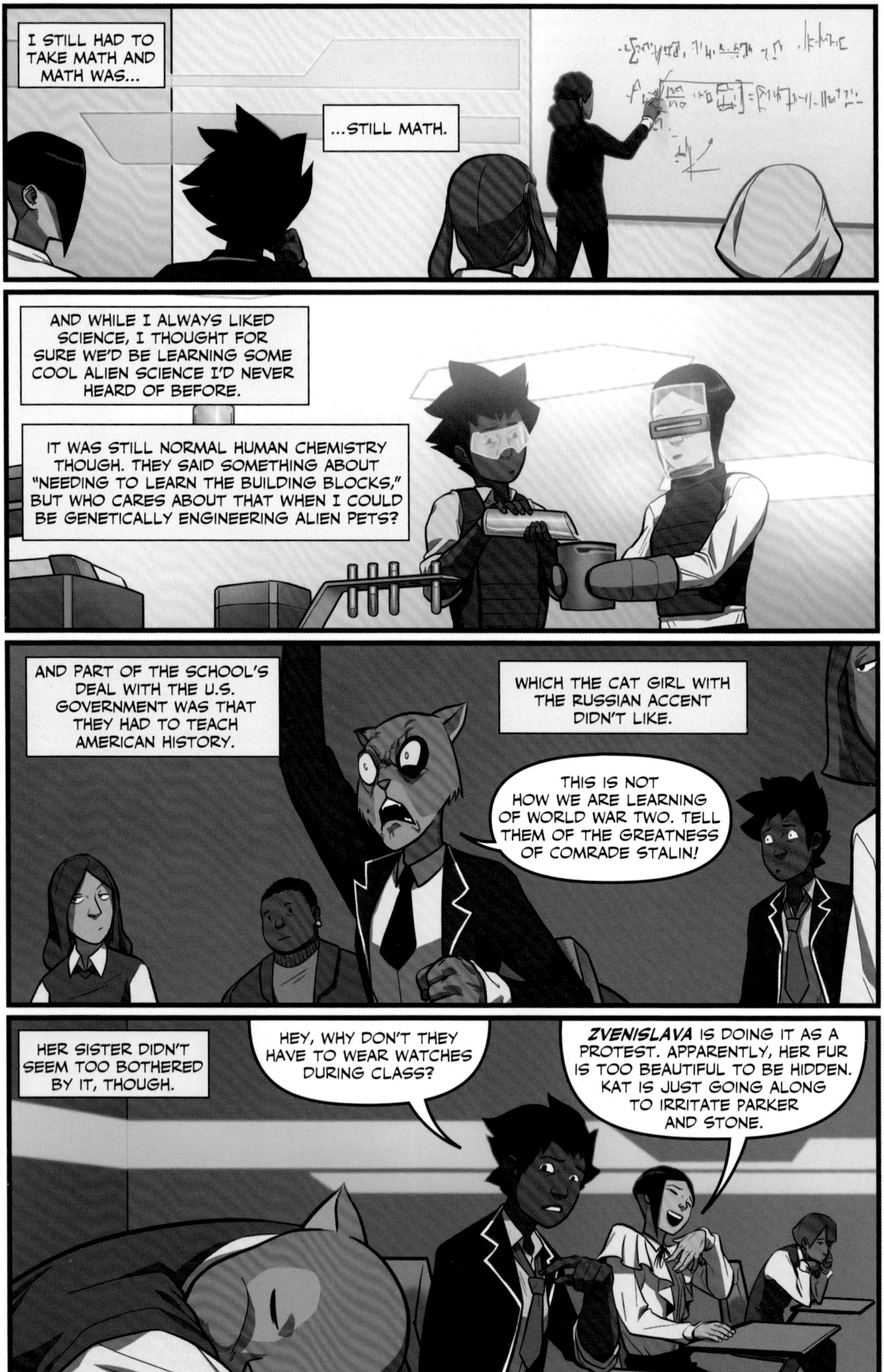
I STILL HAD TO TAKE MATH AND MATH WAS...
...STILL MATH.
AND WHILE I ALWAYS LIKED SCIENCE, I THOUGHT FOR SURE WE'D BE LEARNING SOME COOL ALIEN SCIENCE I'D NEVER HEARD OF BEFORE.
IT WAS STILL NORMAL HUMAN CHEMISTRY THOUGH. THEY SAID SOMETHING ABOUT "NEEDING TO LEARN THE BUILDING BLOCKS," BUT WHO CARES ABOUT THAT WHEN I COULD BE GENETICALLY ENGINEERING ALIEN PETS?
AND PART OF THE SCHOOL'S DEAL WITH THE U.S. GOVERNMENT WAS THAT THEY HAD TO TEACH AMERICAN HISTORY.
WHICH THE CAT GIRL WITH THE RUSSIAN ACCENT DIDN'T LIKE.
THIS IS NOT HOW WE ARE LEARNING OF WORLD WAR TWO. TELL THEM OF THE GREATNESS OF COMRADE STALIN!
HER SISTER DIDN'T SEEM TOO BOTHERED BY IT, THOUGH.
HEY, WHY DON'T THEY HAVE TO WEAR WATCHES DURING CLASS?
ZVENISLAVA IS DOING IT AS A PROTEST. APPARENTLY, HER FUR IS TOO BEAUTIFUL TO BE HIDDEN. KAT IS JUST GOING ALONG TO IRRITATE PARKER AND STONE.

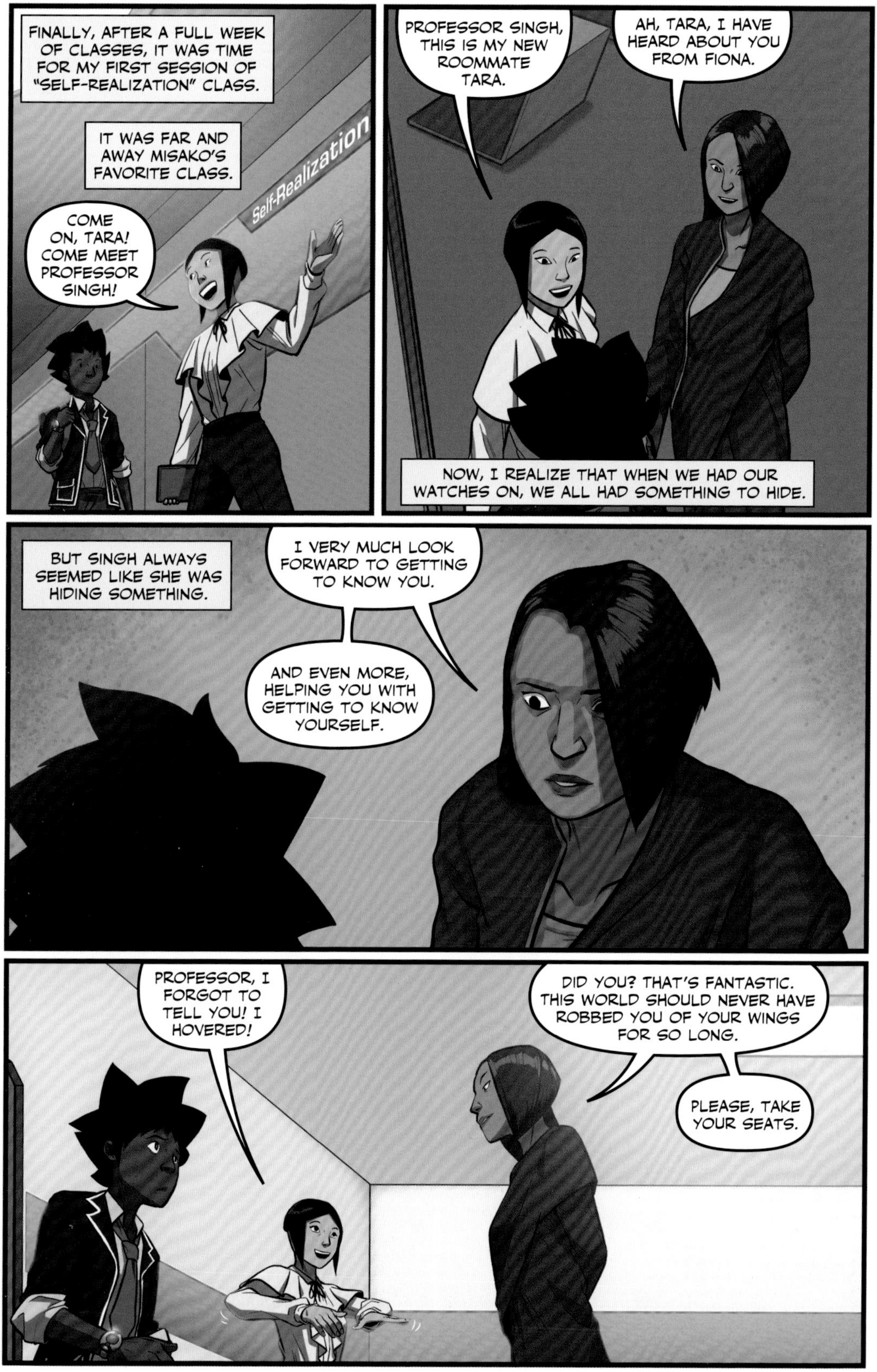
FINALLY, AFTER A FULL WEEK OF CLASSES, IT WAS TIME FOR MY FIRST SESSION OF "SELF-REALIZATION" CLASS.
IT WAS FAR AND AWAY MISAKO'S FAVORITE CLASS.
Self-Realization
COME ON, TARA! COME MEET PROFESSOR SINGH!
PROFESSOR SINGH, THIS IS MY NEW ROOMMATE TARA.
AH, TARA, I HAVE HEARD ABOUT YOU FROM FIONA.
NOW, I REALIZE THAT WHEN WE HAD OUR WATCHES ON, WE ALL HAD SOMETHING TO HIDE.
BUT SINGH ALWAYS SEEMED LIKE SHE WAS HIDING SOMETHING.
I VERY MUCH LOOK FORWARD TO GETTING TO KNOW YOU.
AND EVEN MORE, HELPING YOU WITH GETTING TO KNOW YOURSELF.
PROFESSOR, I FORGOT TO TELL YOU! I HOVERED!
DID YOU? THAT'S FANTASTIC. THIS WORLD SHOULD NEVER HAVE ROBBED YOU OF YOUR WINGS FOR SO LONG.
PLEASE, TAKE YOUR SEATS.

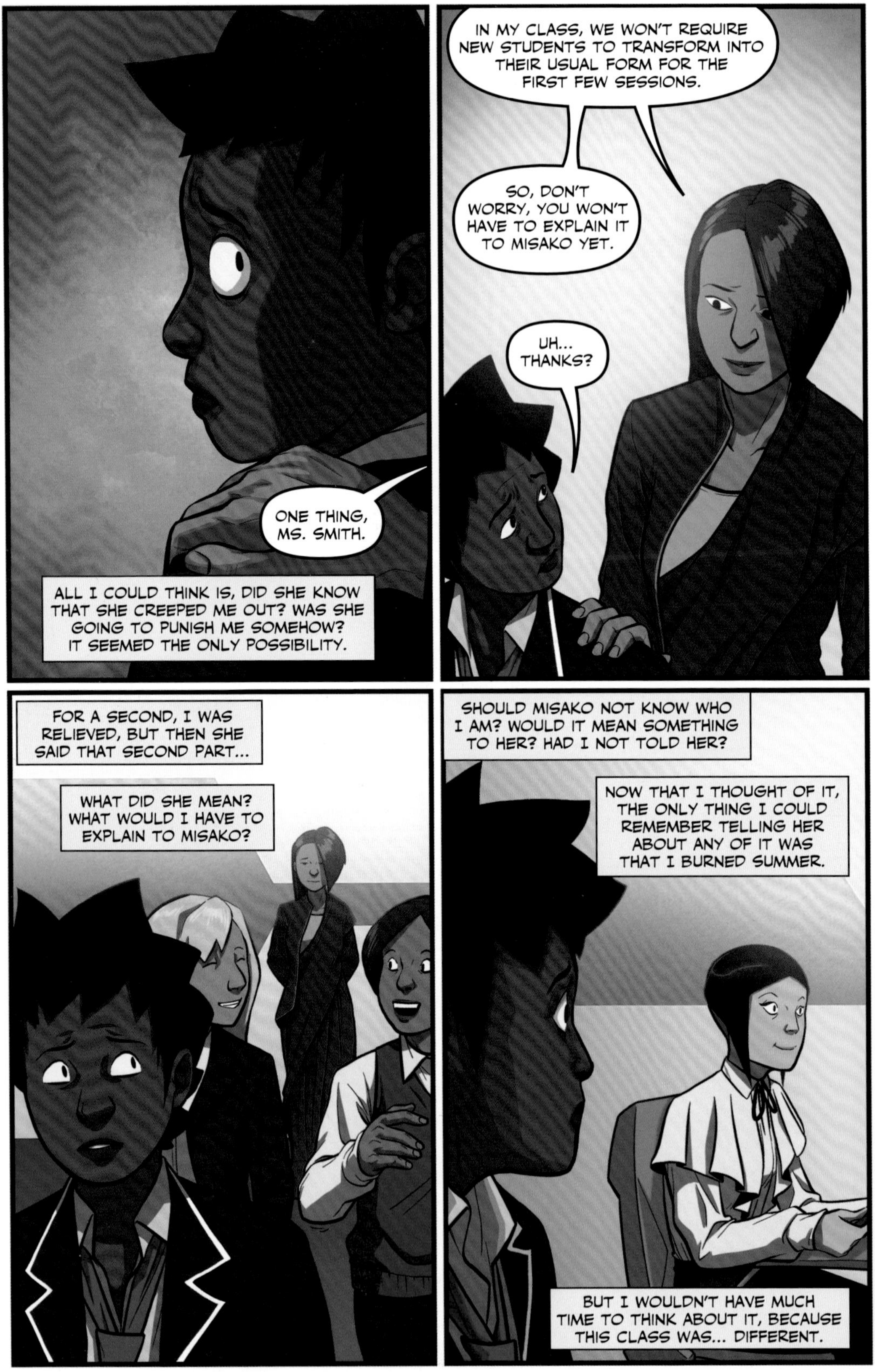
ONE THING, MS. SMITH.
ALL I COULD THINK IS, DID SHE KNOW THAT SHE CREEPED ME OUT? WAS SHE GOING TO PUNISH ME SOMEHOW? IT SEEMED THE ONLY POSSIBILITY.
IN MY CLASS, WE WON'T REQUIRE NEW STUDENTS TO TRANSFORM INTO THEIR USUAL FORM FOR THE FIRST FEW SESSIONS.
SO, DON'T WORRY, YOU WON'T HAVE TO EXPLAIN IT TO MISAKO YET.
UH... THANKS?
FOR A SECOND, I WAS RELIEVED, BUT THEN SHE SAID THAT SECOND PART...
WHAT DID SHE MEAN? WHAT WOULD I HAVE TO EXPLAIN TO MISAKO?
SHOULD MISAKO NOT KNOW WHO I AM? WOULD IT MEAN SOMETHING TO HER? HAD I NOT TOLD HER?
NOW THAT I THOUGHT OF IT, THE ONLY THING I COULD REMEMBER TELLING HER ABOUT ANY OF IT WAS THAT I BURNED SUMMER.
BUT I WOULDN'T HAVE MUCH TIME TO THINK ABOUT IT, BECAUSE THIS CLASS WAS... DIFFERENT.

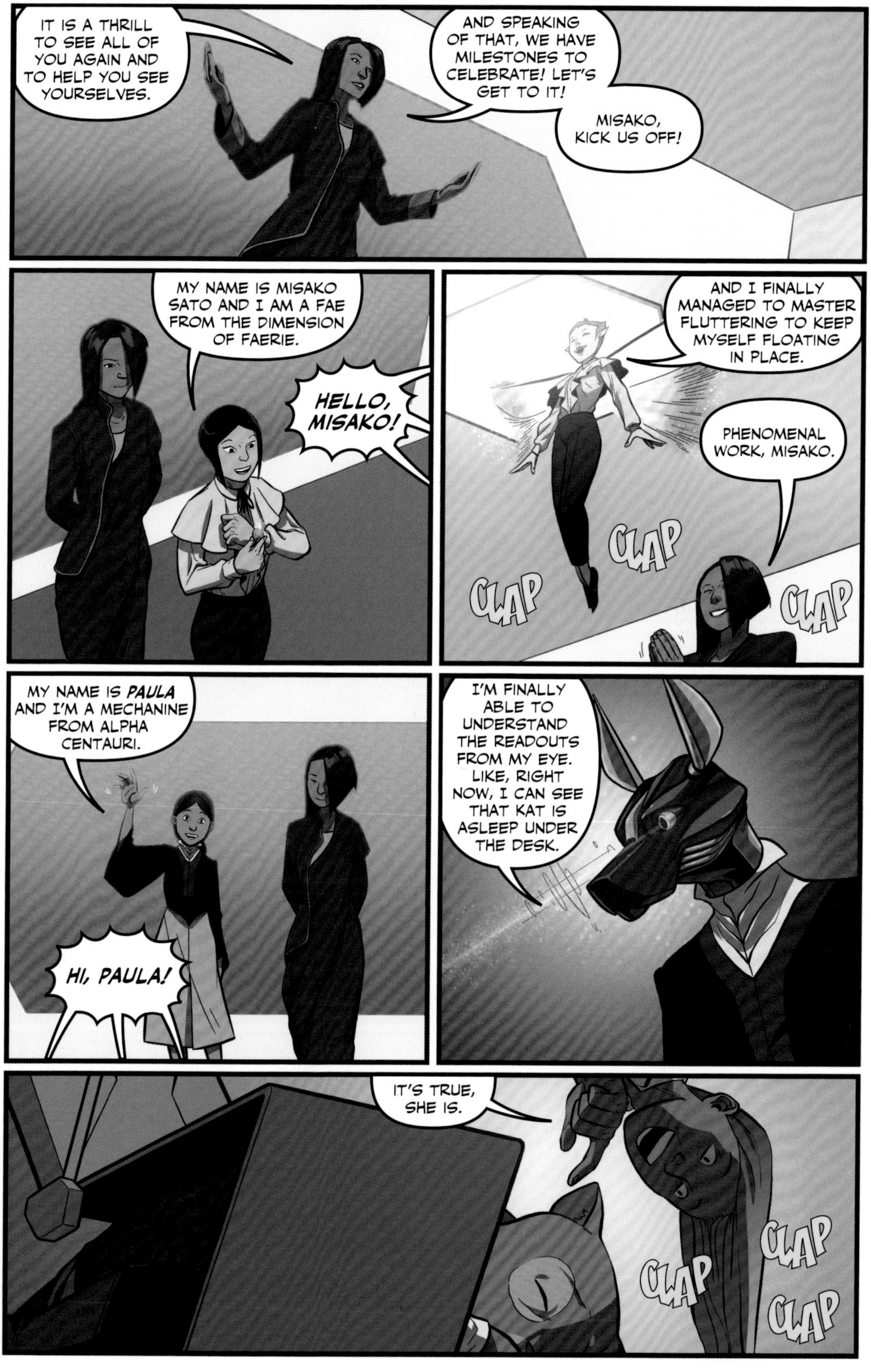
IT IS A THRILL TO SEE ALL OF YOU AGAIN AND TO HELP YOU SEE YOURSELVES.
AND SPEAKING OF THAT, WE HAVE MILESTONES TO CELEBRATE! LET'S GET TO IT!
MISAKO, KICK US OFF!
MY NAME IS MISAKO SATO AND I AM A FAE FROM THE DIMENSION OF FAERIE.
HELLO, MISAKO!
AND I FINALLY MANAGED TO MASTER FLUTTERING TO KEEP MYSELF FLOATING IN PLACE.
PHENOMENAL WORK, MISAKO.
CLAP
CLAP
CLAP
MY NAME IS PAULA AND I'M A MECHANINE FROM ALPHA CENTAURI.
HI, PAULA!
I'M FINALLY ABLE TO UNDERSTAND THE READOUTS FROM MY EYE. LIKE, RIGHT NOW, I CAN SEE THAT KAT IS ASLEEP UNDER THE DESK.
IT'S TRUE, SHE IS.
CLAP
CLAP
CLAP

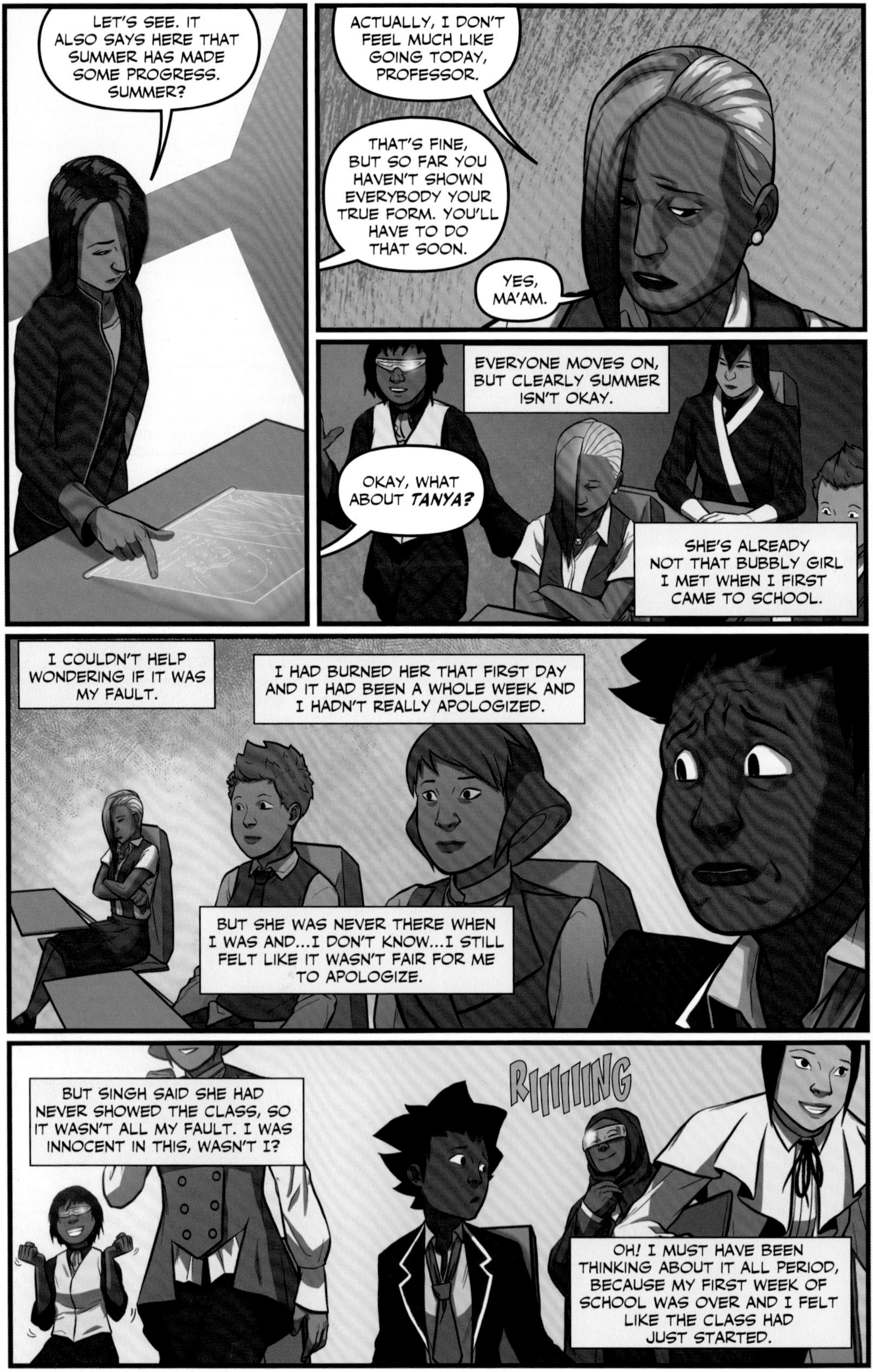
LET'S SEE. IT ALSO SAYS HERE THAT SUMMER HAS MADE SOME PROGRESS. SUMMER?
ACTUALLY, I DON'T FEEL MUCH LIKE GOING TODAY, PROFESSOR.
THAT'S FINE, BUT SO FAR YOU HAVEN'T SHOWN EVERYBODY YOUR TRUE FORM. YOU'LL HAVE TO DO THAT SOON.
YES, MA'AM.
EVERYONE MOVES ON, BUT CLEARLY SUMMER ISN'T OKAY.
OKAY, WHAT ABOUT *TANYA?*
SHE'S ALREADY NOT THAT BUBBLY GIRL I MET WHEN I FIRST CAME TO SCHOOL.
I COULDN'T HELP WONDERING IF IT WAS MY FAULT.
I HAD BURNED HER THAT FIRST DAY AND IT HAD BEEN A WHOLE WEEK AND I HADN'T REALLY APOLOGIZED.
BUT SHE WAS NEVER THERE WHEN I WAS AND...I DON'T KNOW...I STILL FELT LIKE IT WASN'T FAIR FOR ME TO APOLOGIZE.
BUT SINGH SAID SHE HAD NEVER SHOWED THE CLASS, SO IT WASN'T ALL MY FAULT. I WAS INNOCENT IN THIS, WASN'T I?
RIIIIIING
OH! I MUST HAVE BEEN THINKING ABOUT IT ALL PERIOD, BECAUSE MY FIRST WEEK OF SCHOOL WAS OVER AND I FELT LIKE THE CLASS HAD JUST STARTED.

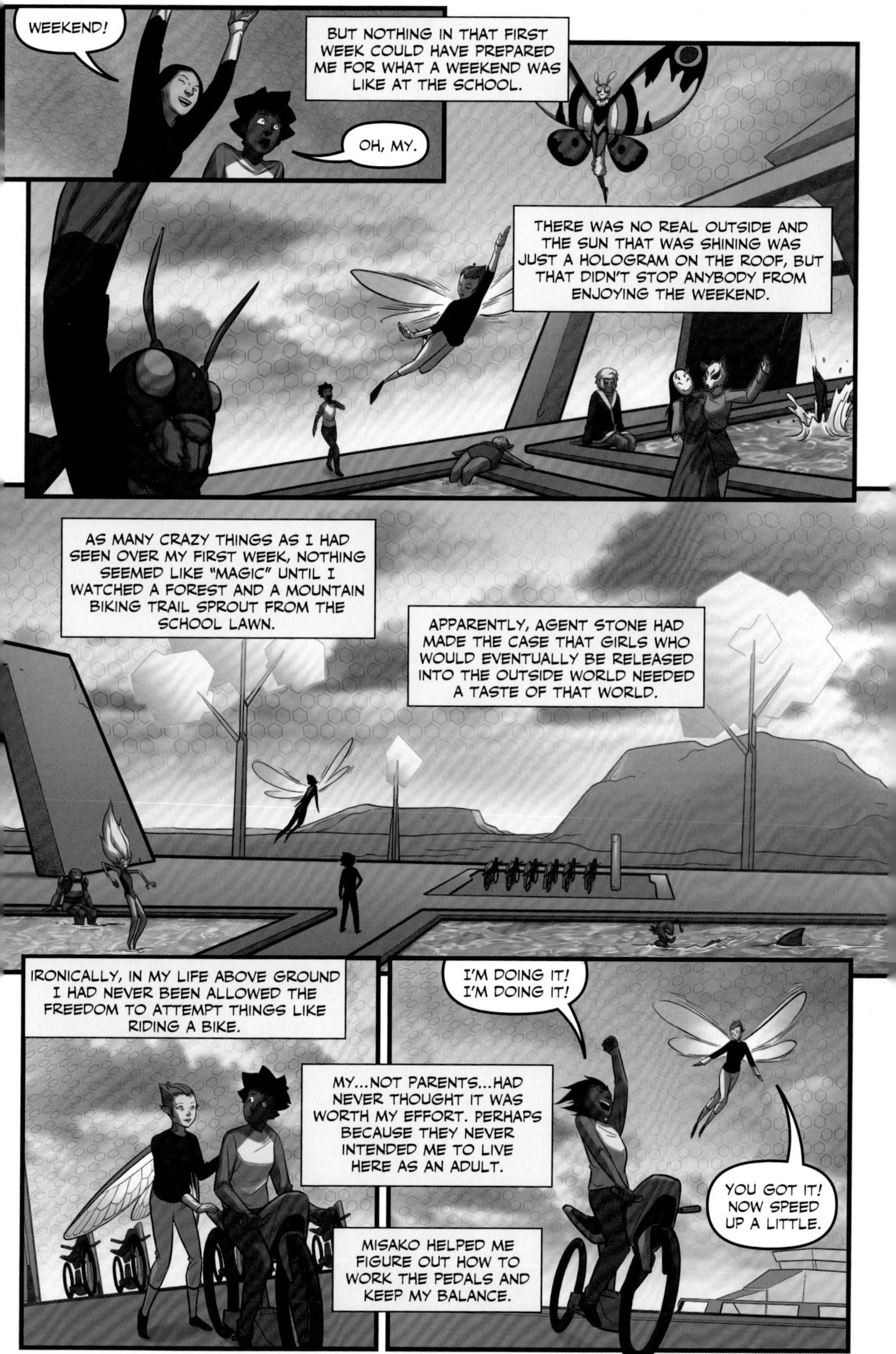
WEEKEND!
BUT NOTHING IN THAT FIRST WEEK COULD HAVE PREPARED ME FOR WHAT A WEEKEND WAS LIKE AT THE SCHOOL.
OH, MY.
THERE WAS NO REAL OUTSIDE AND THE SUN THAT WAS SHINING WAS JUST A HOLOGRAM ON THE ROOF, BUT THAT DIDN'T STOP ANYBODY FROM ENJOYING THE WEEKEND.
AS MANY CRAZY THINGS AS I HAD SEEN OVER MY FIRST WEEK, NOTHING SEEMED LIKE "MAGIC" UNTIL I WATCHED A FOREST AND A MOUNTAIN BIKING TRAIL SPROUT FROM THE SCHOOL LAWN.
APPARENTLY, AGENT STONE HAD MADE THE CASE THAT GIRLS WHO WOULD EVENTUALLY BE RELEASED INTO THE OUTSIDE WORLD NEEDED A TASTE OF THAT WORLD.
IRONICALLY, IN MY LIFE ABOVE GROUND I HAD NEVER BEEN ALLOWED THE FREEDOM TO ATTEMPT THINGS LIKE RIDING A BIKE.
MY...NOT PARENTS...HAD NEVER THOUGHT IT WAS WORTH MY EFFORT. PERHAPS BECAUSE THEY NEVER INTENDED ME TO LIVE HERE AS AN ADULT.
MISAKO HELPED ME FIGURE OUT HOW TO WORK THE PEDALS AND KEEP MY BALANCE.
I'M DOING IT! I'M DOING IT!
YOU GOT IT! NOW SPEED UP A LITTLE.

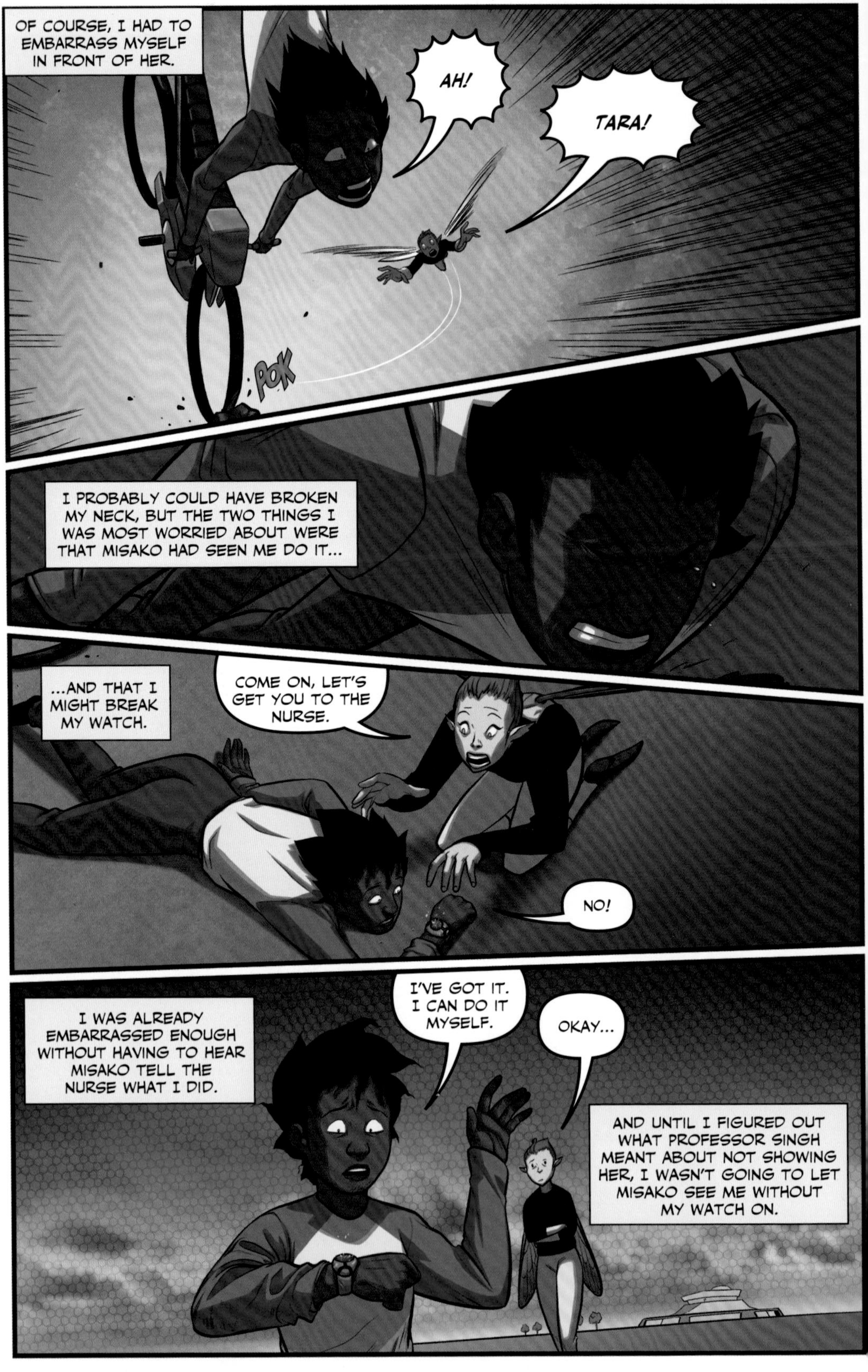
OF COURSE, I HAD TO EMBARRASS MYSELF IN FRONT OF HER.
AH!
TARA!
POK
I PROBABLY COULD HAVE BROKEN MY NECK, BUT THE TWO THINGS I WAS MOST WORRIED ABOUT WERE THAT MISAKO HAD SEEN ME DO IT...
...AND THAT I MIGHT BREAK MY WATCH.
COME ON, LET'S GET YOU TO THE NURSE.
NO!
I WAS ALREADY EMBARRASSED ENOUGH WITHOUT HAVING TO HEAR MISAKO TELL THE NURSE WHAT I DID.
I'VE GOT IT. I CAN DO IT MYSELF.
OKAY...
AND UNTIL I FIGURED OUT WHAT PROFESSOR SINGH MEANT ABOUT NOT SHOWING HER, I WASN'T GOING TO LET MISAKO SEE ME WITHOUT MY WATCH ON.

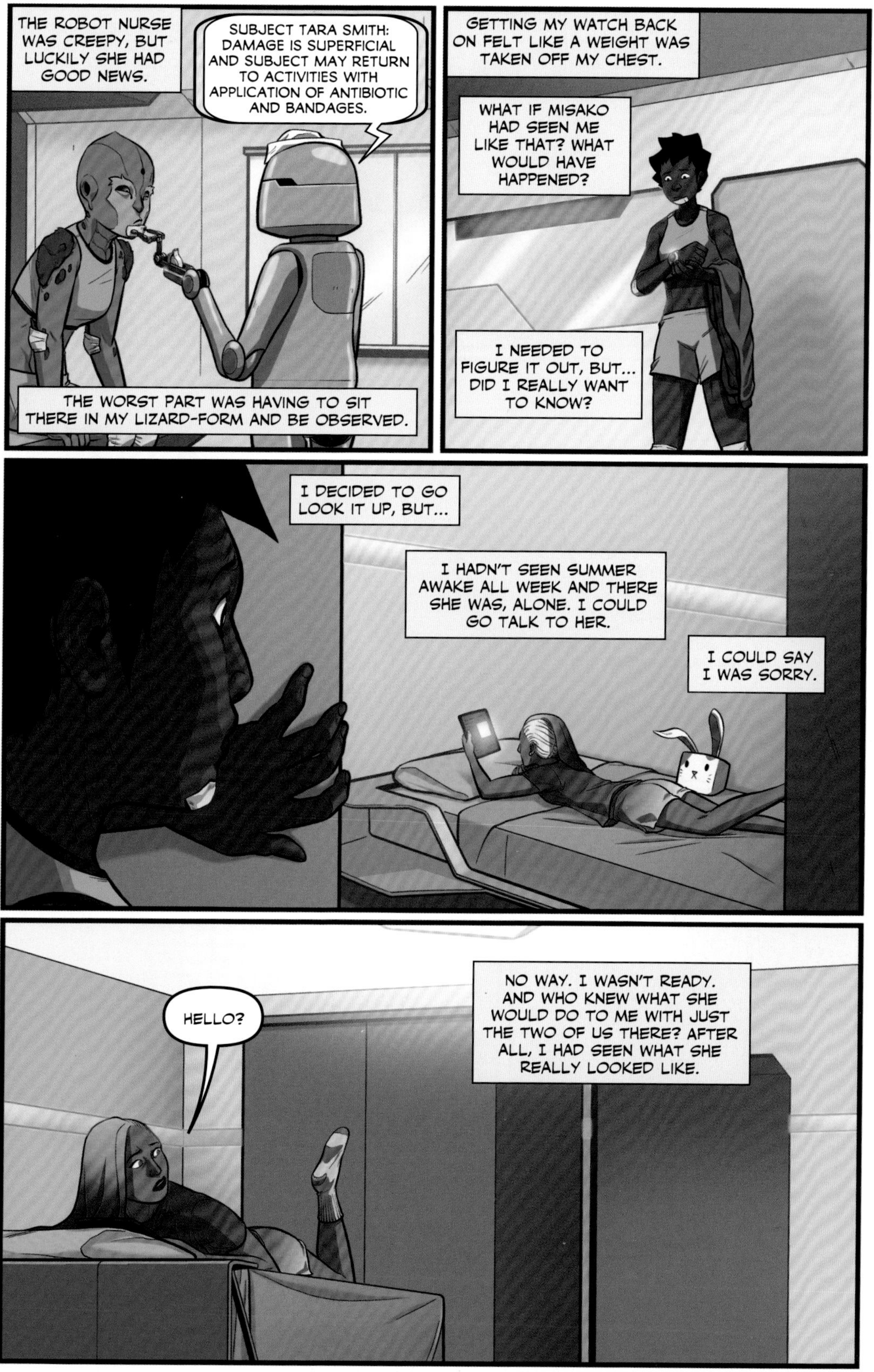
THE ROBOT NURSE WAS CREEPY, BUT LUCKILY SHE HAD GOOD NEWS.
SUBJECT TARA SMITH: DAMAGE IS SUPERFICIAL AND SUBJECT MAY RETURN TO ACTIVITIES WITH APPLICATION OF ANTIBIOTIC AND BANDAGES.
THE WORST PART WAS HAVING TO SIT THERE IN MY LIZARD-FORM AND BE OBSERVED.
GETTING MY WATCH BACK ON FELT LIKE A WEIGHT WAS TAKEN OFF MY CHEST.
WHAT IF MISAKO HAD SEEN ME LIKE THAT? WHAT WOULD HAVE HAPPENED?
I NEEDED TO FIGURE IT OUT, BUT... DID I REALLY WANT TO KNOW?
I DECIDED TO GO LOOK IT UP, BUT...
I HADN'T SEEN SUMMER AWAKE ALL WEEK AND THERE SHE WAS, ALONE. I COULD GO TALK TO HER.
I COULD SAY I WAS SORRY.
HELLO?
NO WAY. I WASN'T READY. AND WHO KNEW WHAT SHE WOULD DO TO ME WITH JUST THE TWO OF US THERE? AFTER ALL, I HAD SEEN WHAT SHE REALLY LOOKED LIKE.

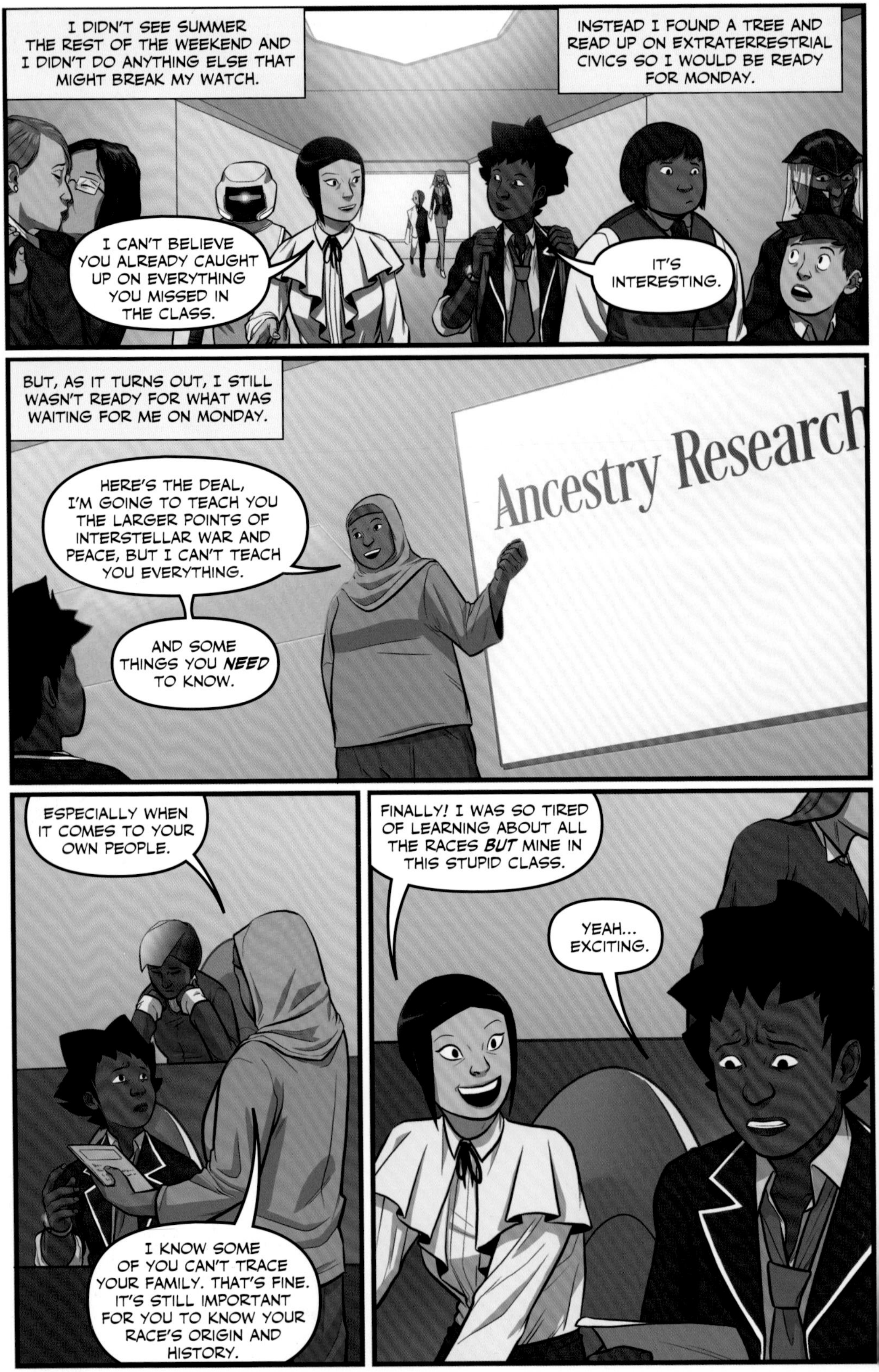
I DIDN'T SEE SUMMER THE REST OF THE WEEKEND AND I DIDN'T DO ANYTHING ELSE THAT MIGHT BREAK MY WATCH.
INSTEAD I FOUND A TREE AND READ UP ON EXTRATERRESTRIAL CIVICS SO I WOULD BE READY FOR MONDAY.
I CAN'T BELIEVE YOU ALREADY CAUGHT UP ON EVERYTHING YOU MISSED IN THE CLASS.
IT'S INTERESTING.
BUT, AS IT TURNS OUT, I STILL WASN'T READY FOR WHAT WAS WAITING FOR ME ON MONDAY.
Ancestry Research
HERE'S THE DEAL, I'M GOING TO TEACH YOU THE LARGER POINTS OF INTERSTELLAR WAR AND PEACE, BUT I CAN'T TEACH YOU EVERYTHING.
AND SOME THINGS YOU *NEED* TO KNOW.
ESPECIALLY WHEN IT COMES TO YOUR OWN PEOPLE.
I KNOW SOME OF YOU CAN'T TRACE YOUR FAMILY. THAT'S FINE. IT'S STILL IMPORTANT FOR YOU TO KNOW YOUR RACE'S ORIGIN AND HISTORY.
FINALLY! I WAS SO TIRED OF LEARNING ABOUT ALL THE RACES *BUT* MINE IN THIS STUPID CLASS.
YEAH... EXCITING.

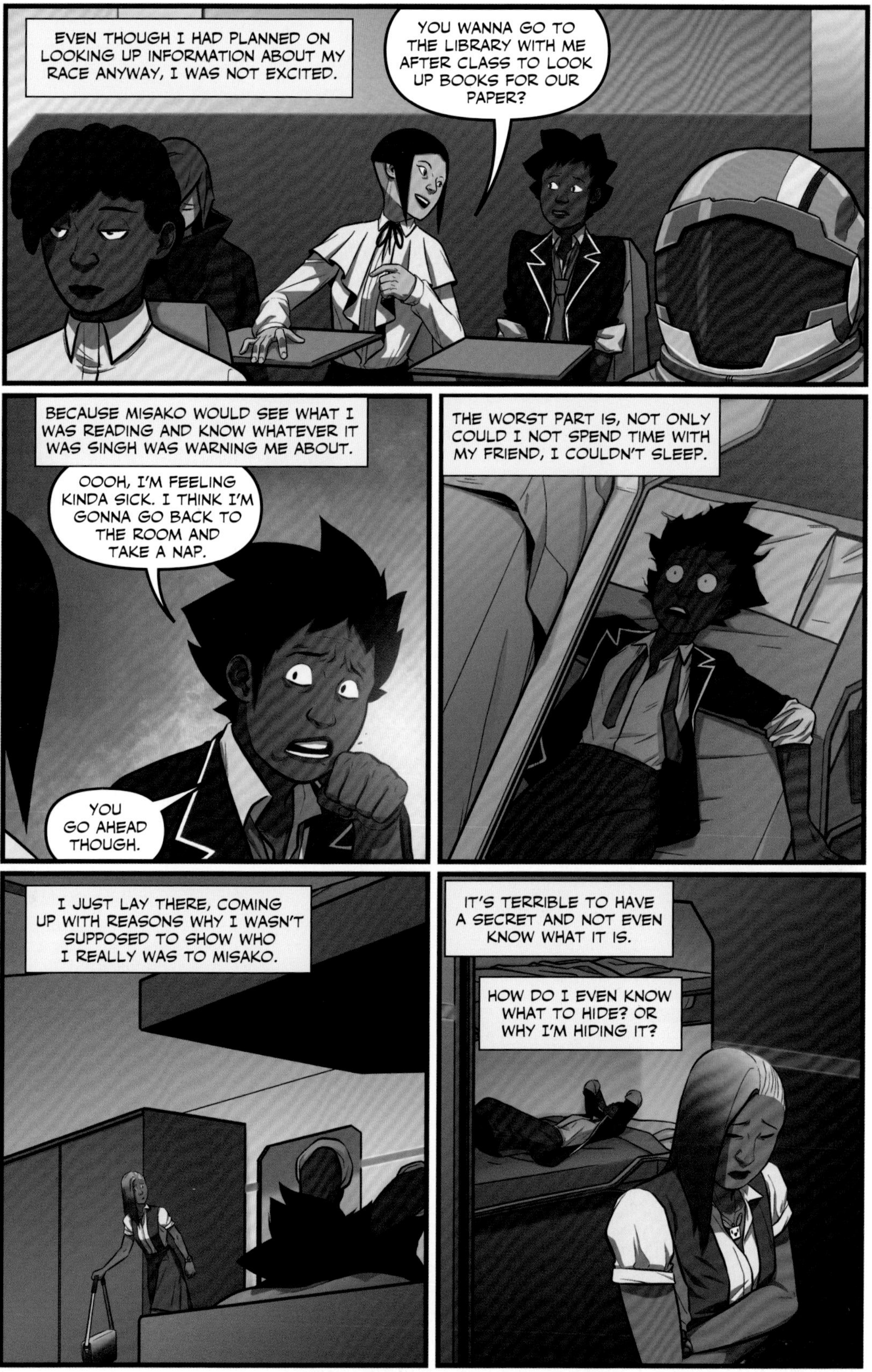

EVEN THOUGH I HAD PLANNED ON LOOKING UP INFORMATION ABOUT MY RACE ANYWAY, I WAS NOT EXCITED.
YOU WANNA GO TO THE LIBRARY WITH ME AFTER CLASS TO LOOK UP BOOKS FOR OUR PAPER?
BECAUSE MISAKO WOULD SEE WHAT I WAS READING AND KNOW WHATEVER IT WAS SINGH WAS WARNING ME ABOUT.
OOOH, I'M FEELING KINDA SICK. I THINK I'M GONNA GO BACK TO THE ROOM AND TAKE A NAP.
YOU GO AHEAD THOUGH.
THE WORST PART IS, NOT ONLY COULD I NOT SPEND TIME WITH MY FRIEND, I COULDN'T SLEEP.
I JUST LAY THERE, COMING UP WITH REASONS WHY I WASN'T SUPPOSED TO SHOW WHO I REALLY WAS TO MISAKO.
IT'S TERRIBLE TO HAVE A SECRET AND NOT EVEN KNOW WHAT IT IS.
HOW DO I EVEN KNOW WHAT TO HIDE? OR WHY I'M HIDING IT?

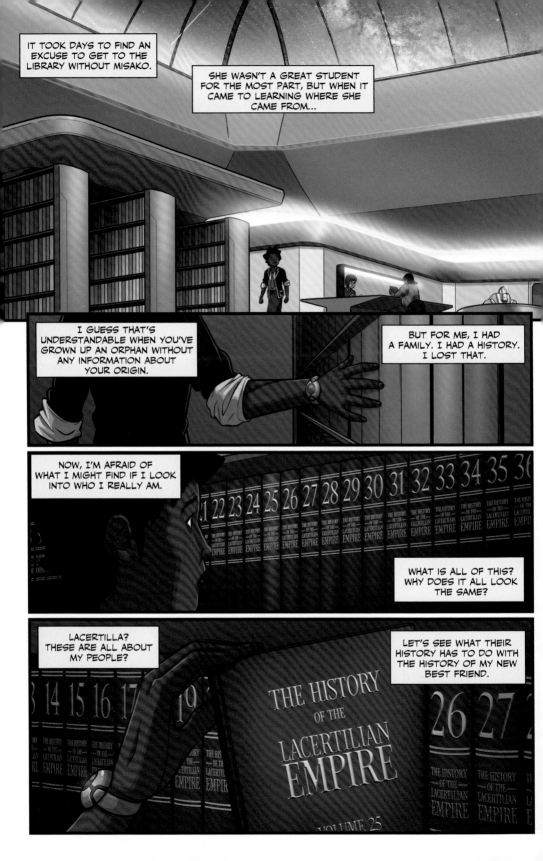

IT TOOK DAYS TO FIND AN EXCUSE TO GET TO THE LIBRARY WITHOUT MISAKO.

SHE WASN'T A GREAT STUDENT FOR THE MOST PART, BUT WHEN IT CAME TO LEARNING WHERE SHE CAME FROM...

I GUESS THAT'S UNDERSTANDABLE WHEN YOU'VE GROWN UP AN ORPHAN WITHOUT ANY INFORMATION ABOUT YOUR ORIGIN.

BUT FOR ME, I HAD A FAMILY. I HAD A HISTORY. I LOST THAT.

NOW, I'M AFRAID OF WHAT I MIGHT FIND IF I LOOK INTO WHO I REALLY AM.

WHAT IS ALL OF THIS? WHY DOES IT ALL LOOK THE SAME?

LACERTILLA? THESE ARE ALL ABOUT MY PEOPLE?

LET'S SEE WHAT THEIR HISTORY HAS TO DO WITH THE HISTORY OF MY NEW BEST FRIEND.

THE HISTORY OF THE LACERTILIAN EMPIRE

VOLUME 25

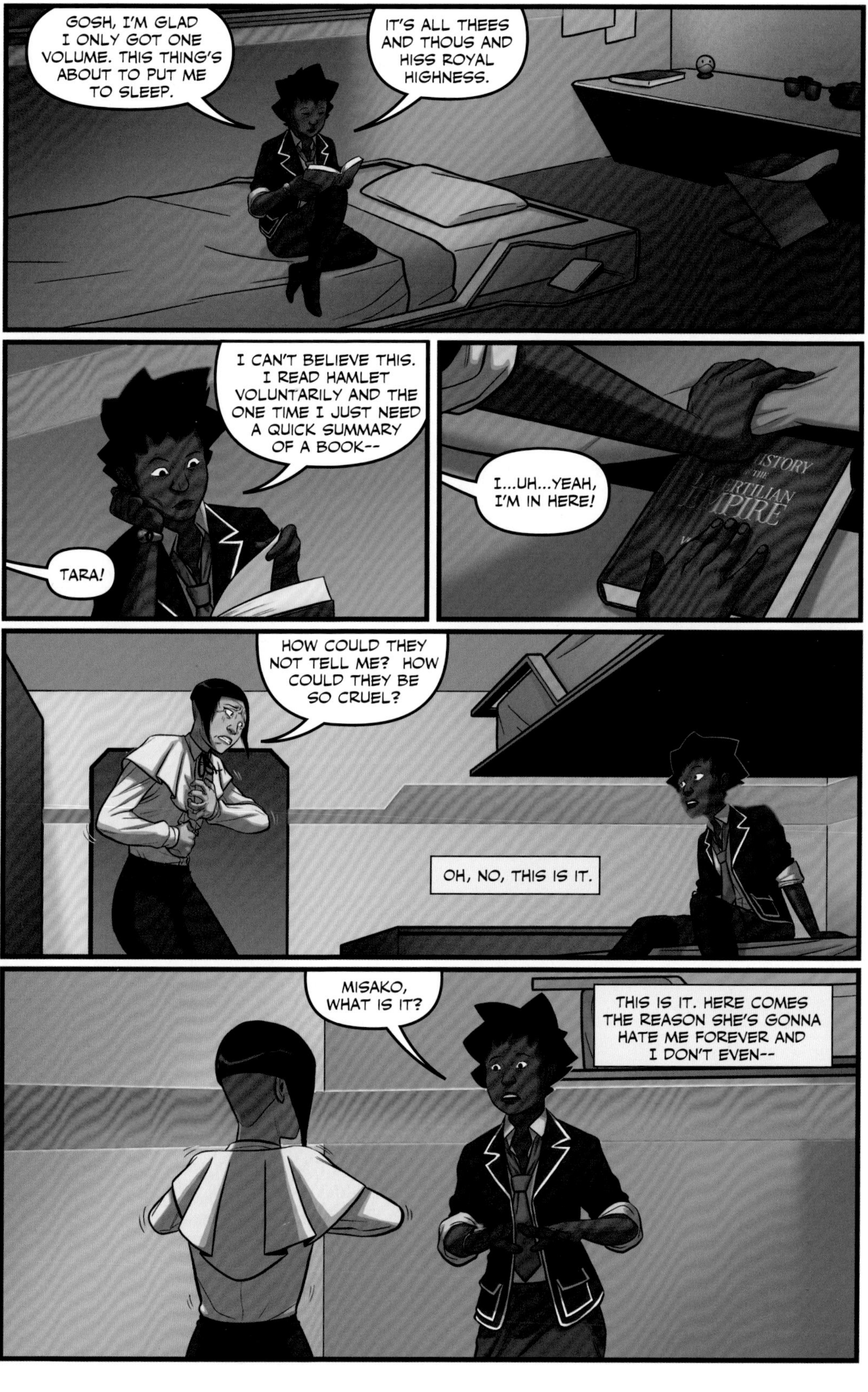
GOSH, I'M GLAD I ONLY GOT ONE VOLUME. THIS THING'S ABOUT TO PUT ME TO SLEEP.
IT'S ALL THEES AND THOUS AND HISS ROYAL HIGHNESS.
I CAN'T BELIEVE THIS. I READ HAMLET VOLUNTARILY AND THE ONE TIME I JUST NEED A QUICK SUMMARY OF A BOOK--
TARA!
I...UH...YEAH, I'M IN HERE!
HOW COULD THEY NOT TELL ME? HOW COULD THEY BE SO CRUEL?
OH, NO, THIS IS IT.
MISAKO, WHAT IS IT?
THIS IS IT. HERE COMES THE REASON SHE'S GONNA HATE ME FOREVER AND I DON'T EVEN--

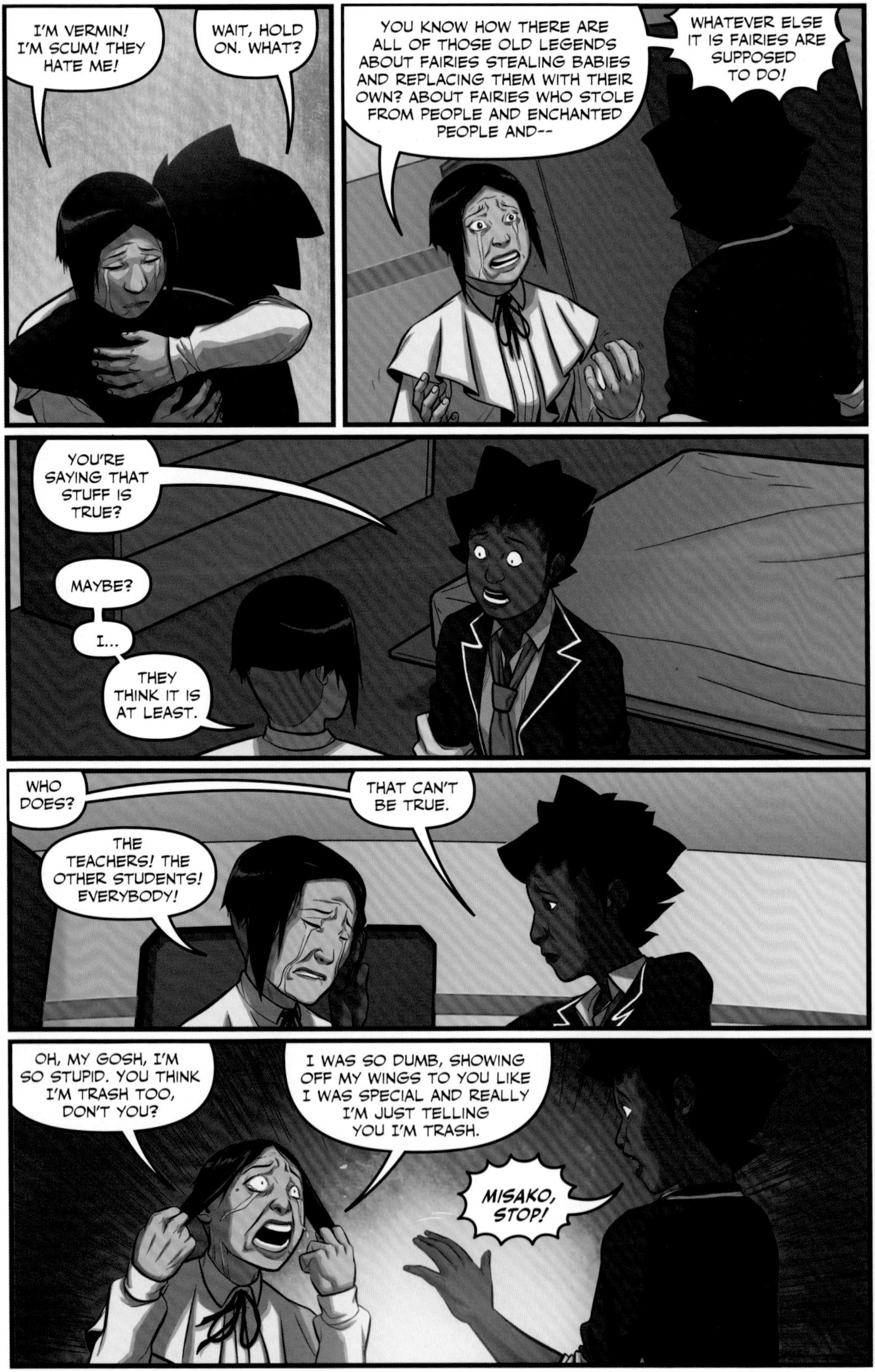
I'M VERMIN! I'M SCUM! THEY HATE ME!
WAIT, HOLD ON. WHAT?
YOU KNOW HOW THERE ARE ALL OF THOSE OLD LEGENDS ABOUT FAIRIES STEALING BABIES AND REPLACING THEM WITH THEIR OWN? ABOUT FAIRIES WHO STOLE FROM PEOPLE AND ENCHANTED PEOPLE AND--
WHATEVER ELSE IT IS FAIRIES ARE SUPPOSED TO DO!
YOU'RE SAYING THAT STUFF IS TRUE?
MAYBE?
I...
THEY THINK IT IS AT LEAST.
WHO DOES?
THAT CAN'T BE TRUE.
THE TEACHERS! THE OTHER STUDENTS! EVERYBODY!
OH, MY GOSH, I'M SO STUPID. YOU THINK I'M TRASH TOO, DON'T YOU?
I WAS SO DUMB, SHOWING OFF MY WINGS TO YOU LIKE I WAS SPECIAL AND REALLY I'M JUST TELLING YOU I'M TRASH.
MISAKO, STOP!

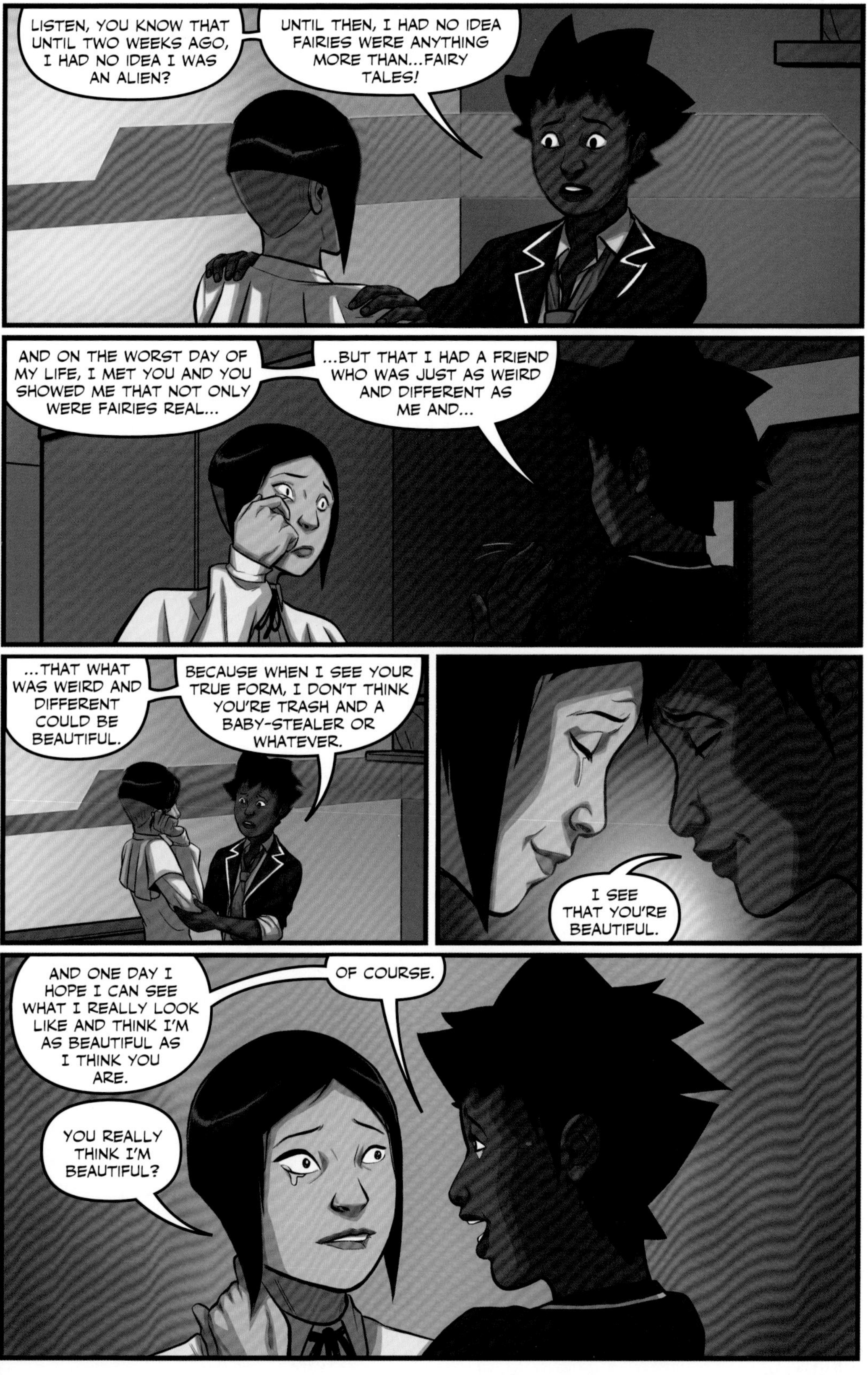
LISTEN, YOU KNOW THAT UNTIL TWO WEEKS AGO, I HAD NO IDEA I WAS AN ALIEN?
UNTIL THEN, I HAD NO IDEA FAIRIES WERE ANYTHING MORE THAN...FAIRY TALES!
AND ON THE WORST DAY OF MY LIFE, I MET YOU AND YOU SHOWED ME THAT NOT ONLY WERE FAIRIES REAL...
...BUT THAT I HAD A FRIEND WHO WAS JUST AS WEIRD AND DIFFERENT AS ME AND...
...THAT WHAT WAS WEIRD AND DIFFERENT COULD BE BEAUTIFUL.
BECAUSE WHEN I SEE YOUR TRUE FORM, I DON'T THINK YOU'RE TRASH AND A BABY-STEALER OR WHATEVER.
I SEE THAT YOU'RE BEAUTIFUL.
YOU REALLY THINK I'M BEAUTIFUL?
OF COURSE.
AND ONE DAY I HOPE I CAN SEE WHAT I REALLY LOOK LIKE AND THINK I'M AS BEAUTIFUL AS I THINK YOU ARE.

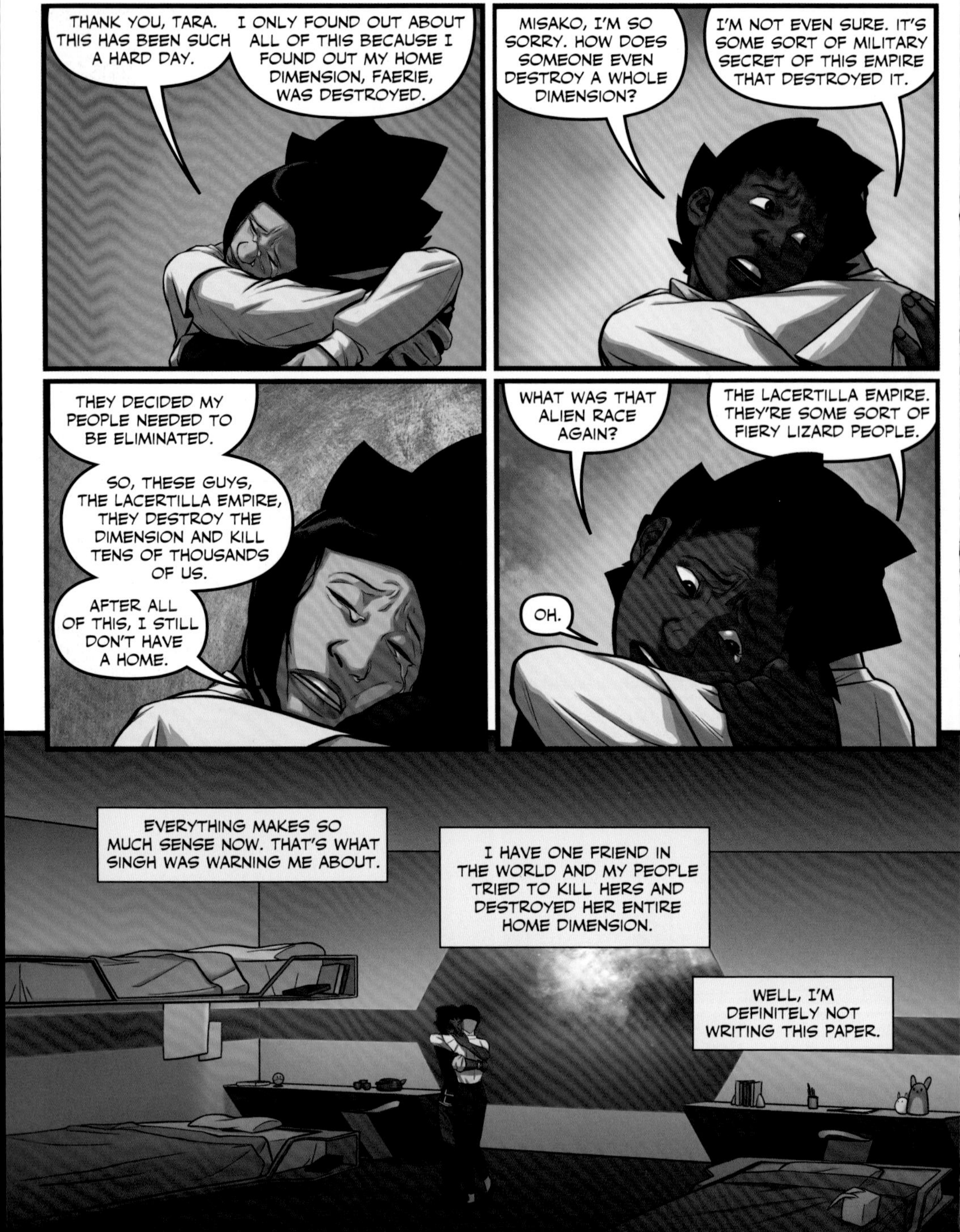

THANK YOU, TARA. THIS HAS BEEN SUCH A HARD DAY.
I ONLY FOUND OUT ABOUT ALL OF THIS BECAUSE I FOUND OUT MY HOME DIMENSION, FAERIE, WAS DESTROYED.
MISAKO, I'M SO SORRY. HOW DOES SOMEONE EVEN DESTROY A WHOLE DIMENSION?
I'M NOT EVEN SURE. IT'S SOME SORT OF MILITARY SECRET OF THIS EMPIRE THAT DESTROYED IT.
THEY DECIDED MY PEOPLE NEEDED TO BE ELIMINATED.
SO, THESE GUYS, THE LACERTILLA EMPIRE, THEY DESTROY THE DIMENSION AND KILL TENS OF THOUSANDS OF US.
AFTER ALL OF THIS, I STILL DON'T HAVE A HOME.
WHAT WAS THAT ALIEN RACE AGAIN?
THE LACERTILLA EMPIRE. THEY'RE SOME SORT OF FIERY LIZARD PEOPLE.
OH.
EVERYTHING MAKES SO MUCH SENSE NOW. THAT'S WHAT SINGH WAS WARNING ME ABOUT.
I HAVE ONE FRIEND IN THE WORLD AND MY PEOPLE TRIED TO KILL HERS AND DESTROYED HER ENTIRE HOME DIMENSION.
WELL, I'M DEFINITELY NOT WRITING THIS PAPER.

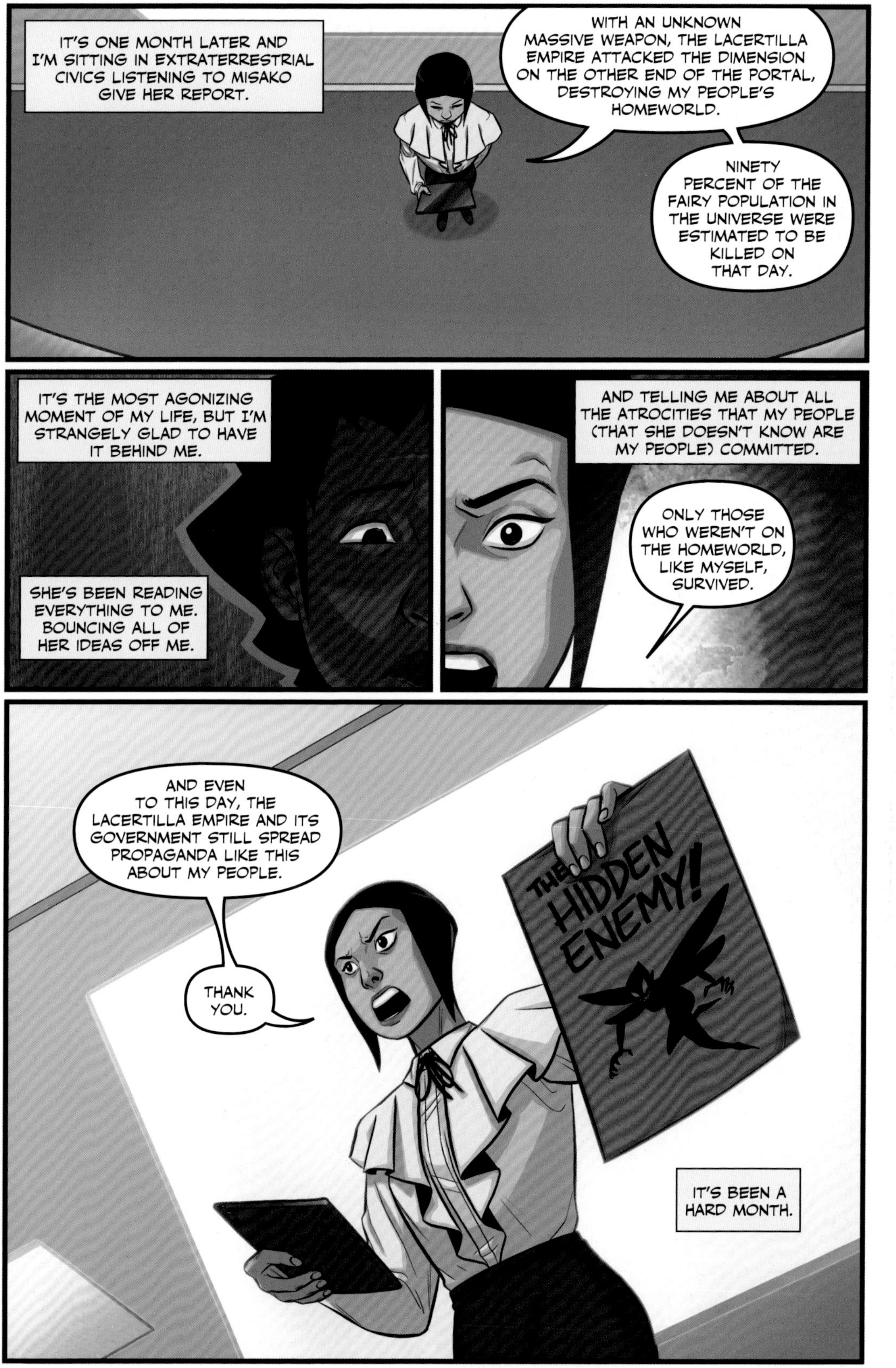
IT'S ONE MONTH LATER AND I'M SITTING IN EXTRATERRESTRIAL CIVICS LISTENING TO MISAKO GIVE HER REPORT.
WITH AN UNKNOWN MASSIVE WEAPON, THE LACERTILLA EMPIRE ATTACKED THE DIMENSION ON THE OTHER END OF THE PORTAL, DESTROYING MY PEOPLE'S HOMEWORLD.
NINETY PERCENT OF THE FAIRY POPULATION IN THE UNIVERSE WERE ESTIMATED TO BE KILLED ON THAT DAY.
IT'S THE MOST AGONIZING MOMENT OF MY LIFE, BUT I'M STRANGELY GLAD TO HAVE IT BEHIND ME.
SHE'S BEEN READING EVERYTHING TO ME. BOUNCING ALL OF HER IDEAS OFF ME.
AND TELLING ME ABOUT ALL THE ATROCITIES THAT MY PEOPLE (THAT SHE DOESN'T KNOW ARE MY PEOPLE) COMMITTED.
ONLY THOSE WHO WEREN'T ON THE HOMEWORLD, LIKE MYSELF, SURVIVED.
AND EVEN TO THIS DAY, THE LACERTILLA EMPIRE AND ITS GOVERNMENT STILL SPREAD PROPAGANDA LIKE THIS ABOUT MY PEOPLE.
THE HIDDEN ENEMY!
THANK YOU.
IT'S BEEN A HARD MONTH.

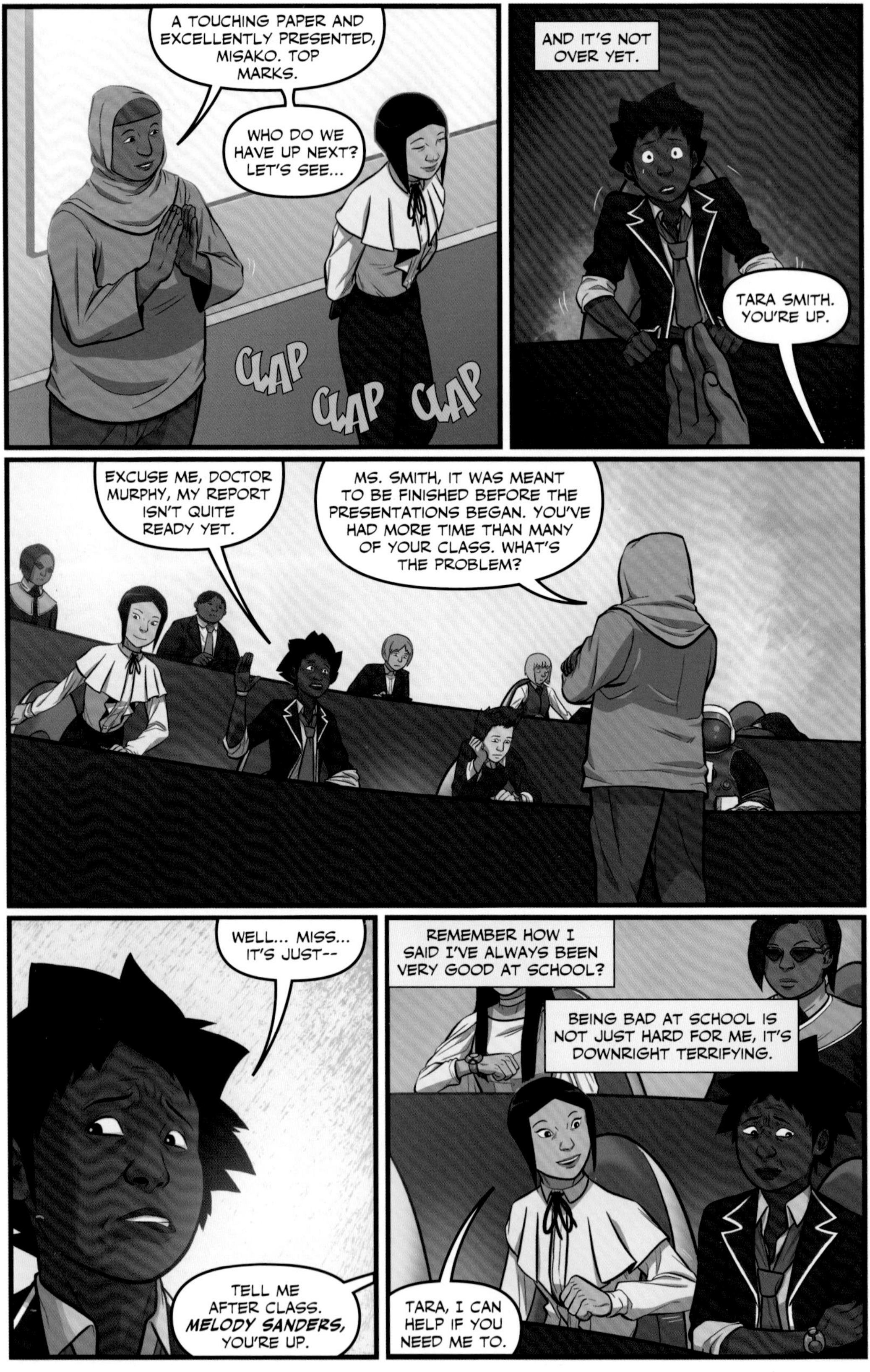

A TOUCHING PAPER AND EXCELLENTLY PRESENTED, MISAKO. TOP MARKS.
WHO DO WE HAVE UP NEXT? LET'S SEE...
CLAP
CLAP
CLAP
AND IT'S NOT OVER YET.
TARA SMITH. YOU'RE UP.
EXCUSE ME, DOCTOR MURPHY, MY REPORT ISN'T QUITE READY YET.
MS. SMITH, IT WAS MEANT TO BE FINISHED BEFORE THE PRESENTATIONS BEGAN. YOU'VE HAD MORE TIME THAN MANY OF YOUR CLASS. WHAT'S THE PROBLEM?
WELL... MISS... IT'S JUST--
TELL ME AFTER CLASS. *MELODY SANDERS,* YOU'RE UP.
REMEMBER HOW I SAID I'VE ALWAYS BEEN VERY GOOD AT SCHOOL?
BEING BAD AT SCHOOL IS NOT JUST HARD FOR ME, IT'S DOWNRIGHT TERRIFYING.
TARA, I CAN HELP IF YOU NEED ME TO.

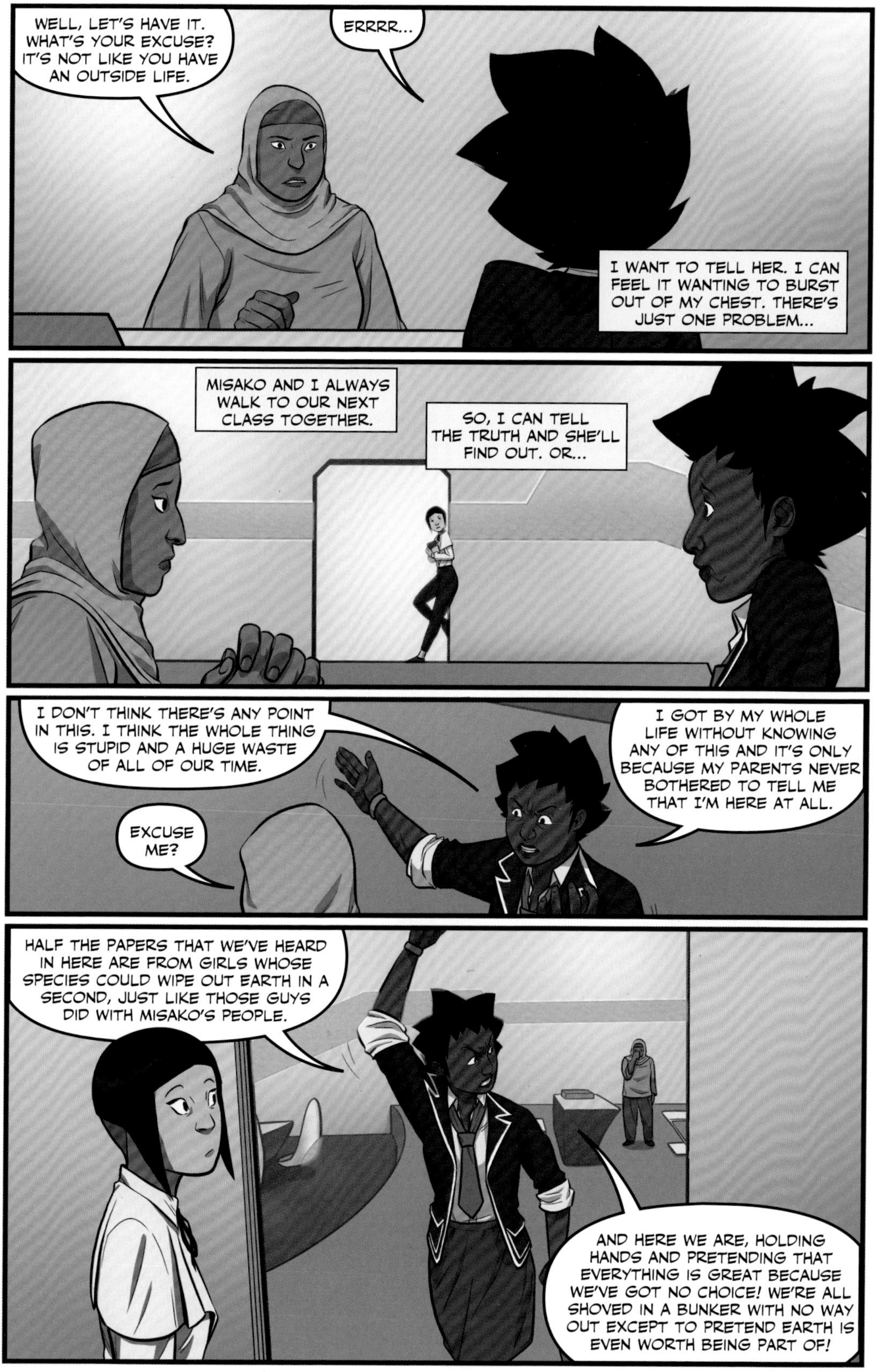
WELL, LET'S HAVE IT. WHAT'S YOUR EXCUSE? IT'S NOT LIKE YOU HAVE AN OUTSIDE LIFE.
ERRRR...
I WANT TO TELL HER. I CAN FEEL IT WANTING TO BURST OUT OF MY CHEST. THERE'S JUST ONE PROBLEM...
MISAKO AND I ALWAYS WALK TO OUR NEXT CLASS TOGETHER.
SO, I CAN TELL THE TRUTH AND SHE'LL FIND OUT. OR...
I DON'T THINK THERE'S ANY POINT IN THIS. I THINK THE WHOLE THING IS STUPID AND A HUGE WASTE OF ALL OF OUR TIME.
EXCUSE ME?
I GOT BY MY WHOLE LIFE WITHOUT KNOWING ANY OF THIS AND IT'S ONLY BECAUSE MY PARENTS NEVER BOTHERED TO TELL ME THAT I'M HERE AT ALL.
HALF THE PAPERS THAT WE'VE HEARD IN HERE ARE FROM GIRLS WHOSE SPECIES COULD WIPE OUT EARTH IN A SECOND, JUST LIKE THOSE GUYS DID WITH MISAKO'S PEOPLE.
AND HERE WE ARE, HOLDING HANDS AND PRETENDING THAT EVERYTHING IS GREAT BECAUSE WE'VE GOT NO CHOICE! WE'RE ALL SHOVED IN A BUNKER WITH NO WAY OUT EXCEPT TO PRETEND EARTH IS EVEN WORTH BEING PART OF!

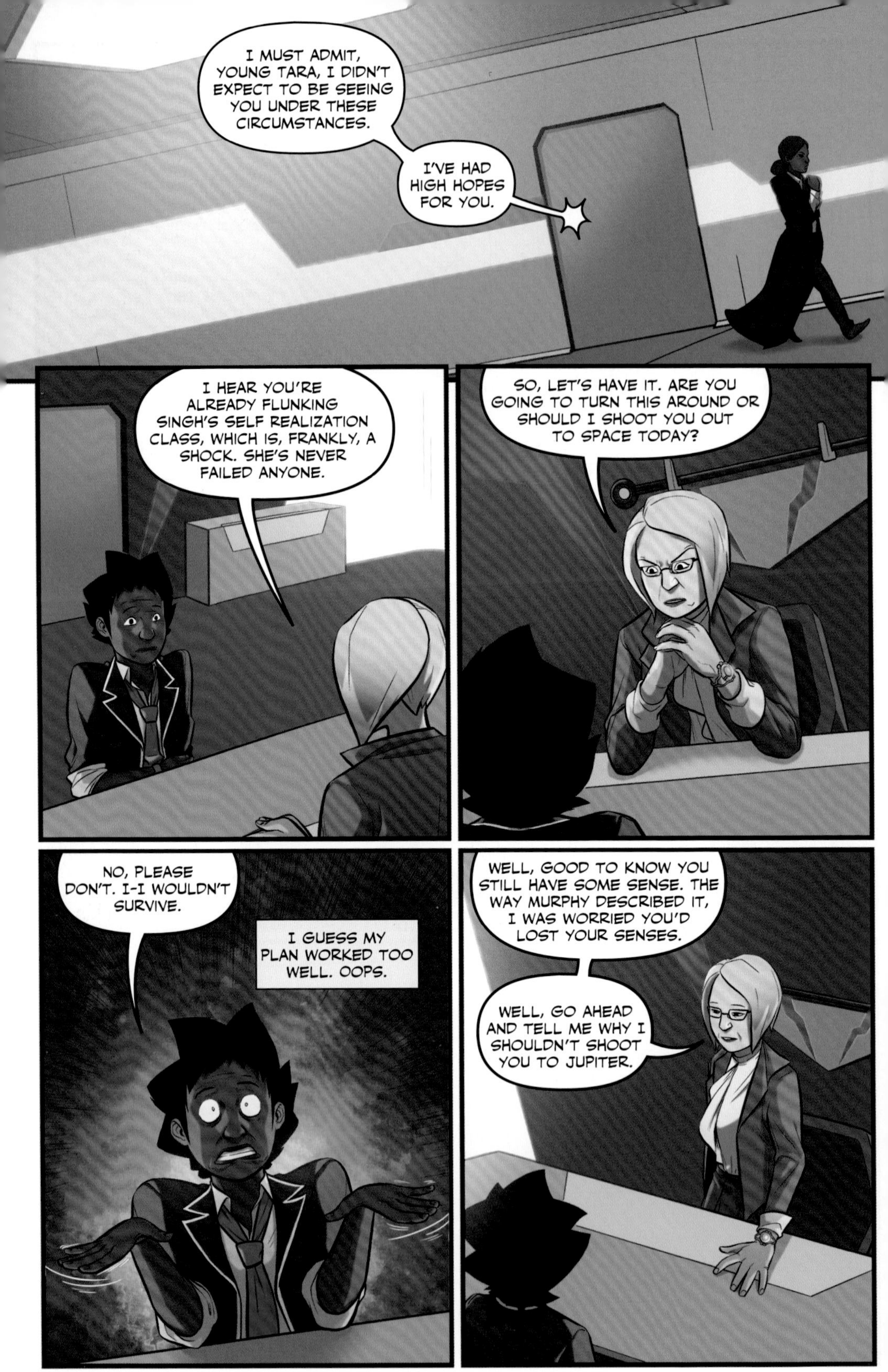
I MUST ADMIT, YOUNG TARA, I DIDN'T EXPECT TO BE SEEING YOU UNDER THESE CIRCUMSTANCES.
I'VE HAD HIGH HOPES FOR YOU.
I HEAR YOU'RE ALREADY FLUNKING SINGH'S SELF REALIZATION CLASS, WHICH IS, FRANKLY, A SHOCK. SHE'S NEVER FAILED ANYONE.
SO, LET'S HAVE IT. ARE YOU GOING TO TURN THIS AROUND OR SHOULD I SHOOT YOU OUT TO SPACE TODAY?
NO, PLEASE DON'T. I-I WOULDN'T SURVIVE.
I GUESS MY PLAN WORKED TOO WELL. OOPS.
WELL, GOOD TO KNOW YOU STILL HAVE SOME SENSE. THE WAY MURPHY DESCRIBED IT, I WAS WORRIED YOU'D LOST YOUR SENSES.
WELL, GO AHEAD AND TELL ME WHY I SHOULDN'T SHOOT YOU TO JUPITER.

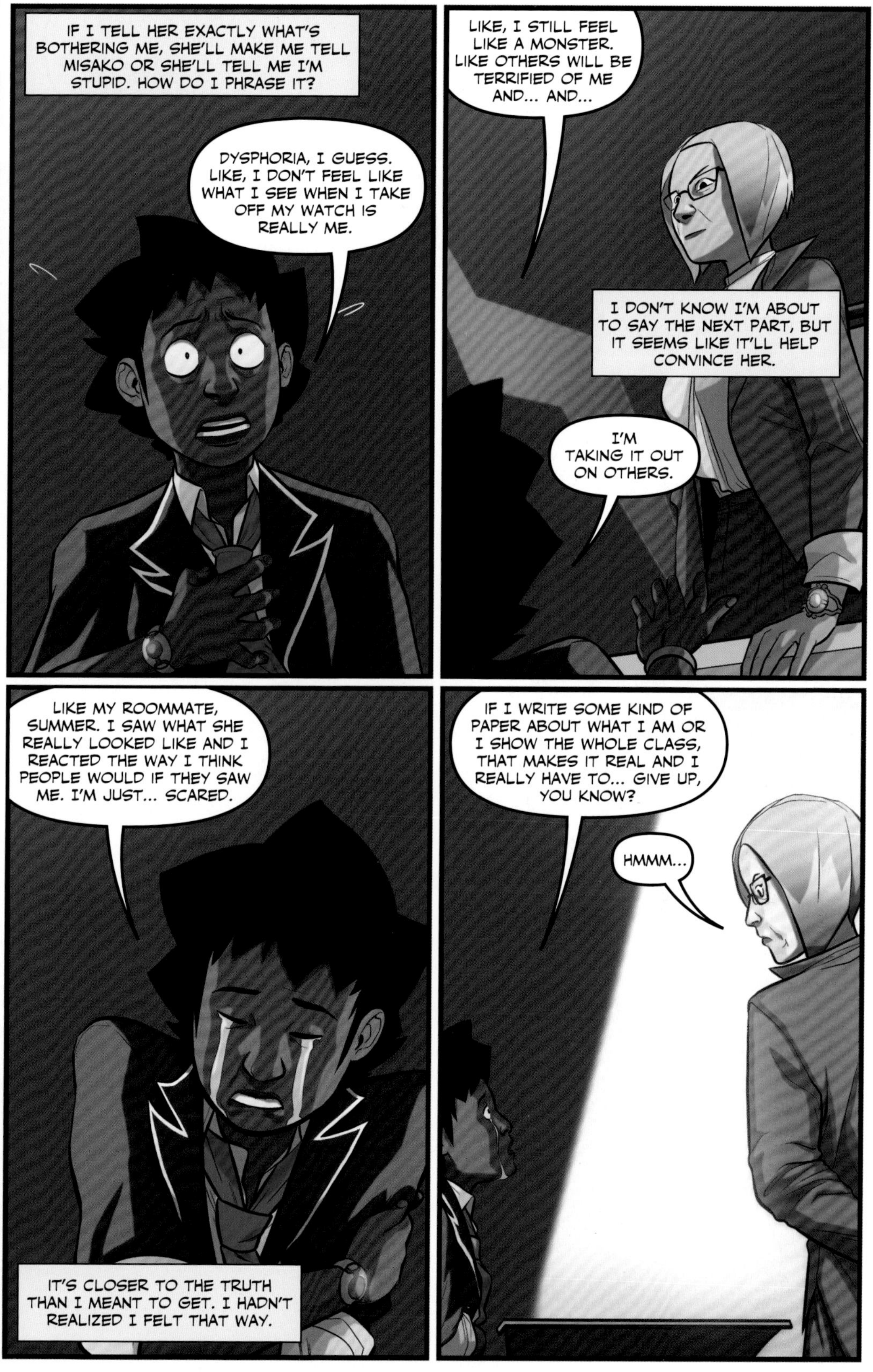
IF I TELL HER EXACTLY WHAT'S BOTHERING ME, SHE'LL MAKE ME TELL MISAKO OR SHE'LL TELL ME I'M STUPID. HOW DO I PHRASE IT?
DYSPHORIA, I GUESS. LIKE, I DON'T FEEL LIKE WHAT I SEE WHEN I TAKE OFF MY WATCH IS REALLY ME.
LIKE, I STILL FEEL LIKE A MONSTER. LIKE OTHERS WILL BE TERRIFIED OF ME AND... AND...
I DON'T KNOW I'M ABOUT TO SAY THE NEXT PART, BUT IT SEEMS LIKE IT'LL HELP CONVINCE HER.
I'M TAKING IT OUT ON OTHERS.
LIKE MY ROOMMATE, SUMMER. I SAW WHAT SHE REALLY LOOKED LIKE AND I REACTED THE WAY I THINK PEOPLE WOULD IF THEY SAW ME. I'M JUST... SCARED.
IT'S CLOSER TO THE TRUTH THAN I MEANT TO GET. I HADN'T REALIZED I FELT THAT WAY.
IF I WRITE SOME KIND OF PAPER ABOUT WHAT I AM OR I SHOW THE WHOLE CLASS, THAT MAKES IT REAL AND I REALLY HAVE TO... GIVE UP, YOU KNOW?
HMMM...

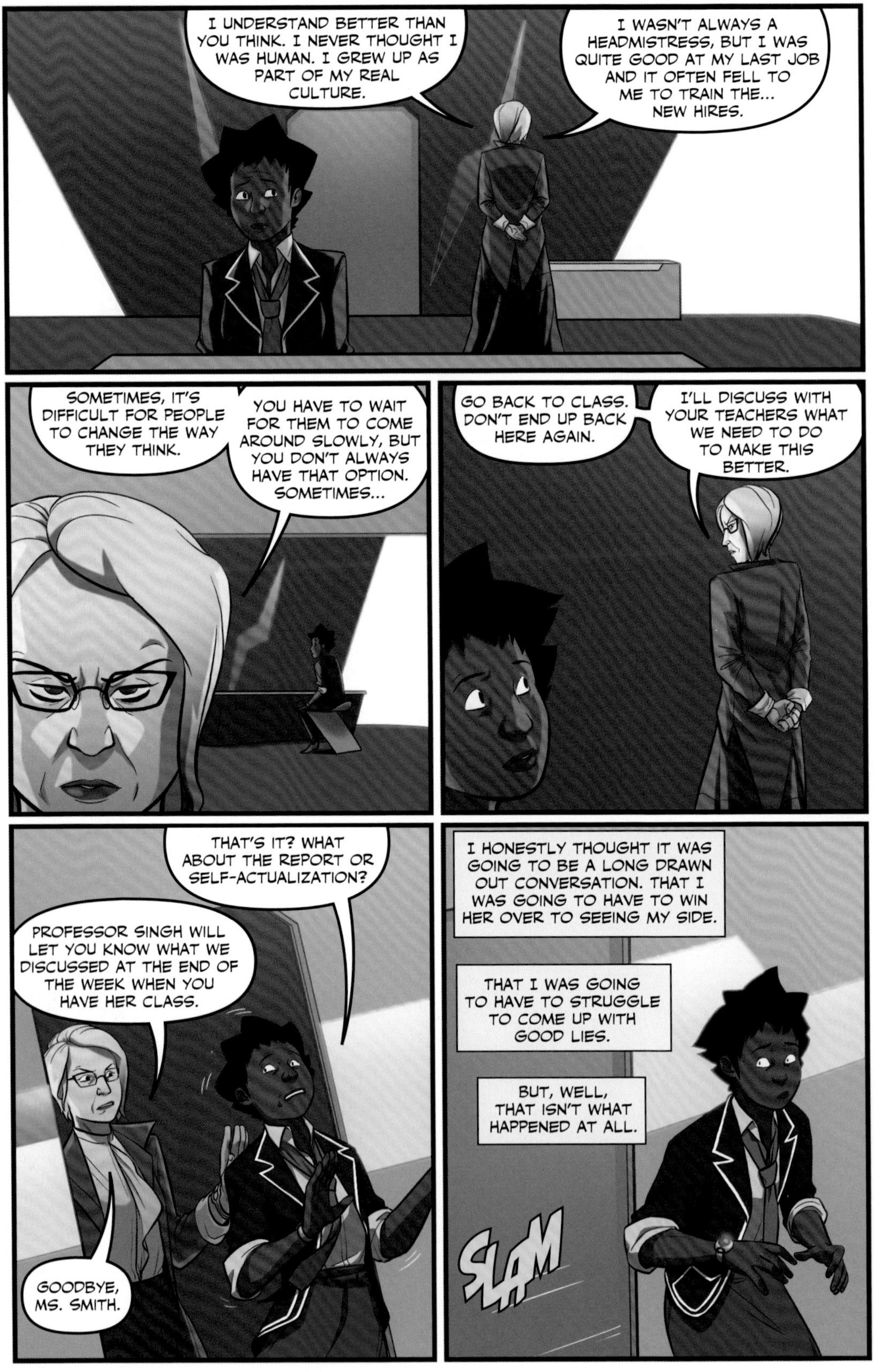
I UNDERSTAND BETTER THAN YOU THINK. I NEVER THOUGHT I WAS HUMAN. I GREW UP AS PART OF MY REAL CULTURE.
I WASN'T ALWAYS A HEADMISTRESS, BUT I WAS QUITE GOOD AT MY LAST JOB AND IT OFTEN FELL TO ME TO TRAIN THE... NEW HIRES.
SOMETIMES, IT'S DIFFICULT FOR PEOPLE TO CHANGE THE WAY THEY THINK.
YOU HAVE TO WAIT FOR THEM TO COME AROUND SLOWLY, BUT YOU DON'T ALWAYS HAVE THAT OPTION. SOMETIMES...
GO BACK TO CLASS. DON'T END UP BACK HERE AGAIN.
I'LL DISCUSS WITH YOUR TEACHERS WHAT WE NEED TO DO TO MAKE THIS BETTER.
THAT'S IT? WHAT ABOUT THE REPORT OR SELF-ACTUALIZATION?
PROFESSOR SINGH WILL LET YOU KNOW WHAT WE DISCUSSED AT THE END OF THE WEEK WHEN YOU HAVE HER CLASS.
GOODBYE, MS. SMITH.
I HONESTLY THOUGHT IT WAS GOING TO BE A LONG DRAWN OUT CONVERSATION. THAT I WAS GOING TO HAVE TO WIN HER OVER TO SEEING MY SIDE.
THAT I WAS GOING TO HAVE TO STRUGGLE TO COME UP WITH GOOD LIES.
BUT, WELL, THAT ISN'T WHAT HAPPENED AT ALL.
SLAM

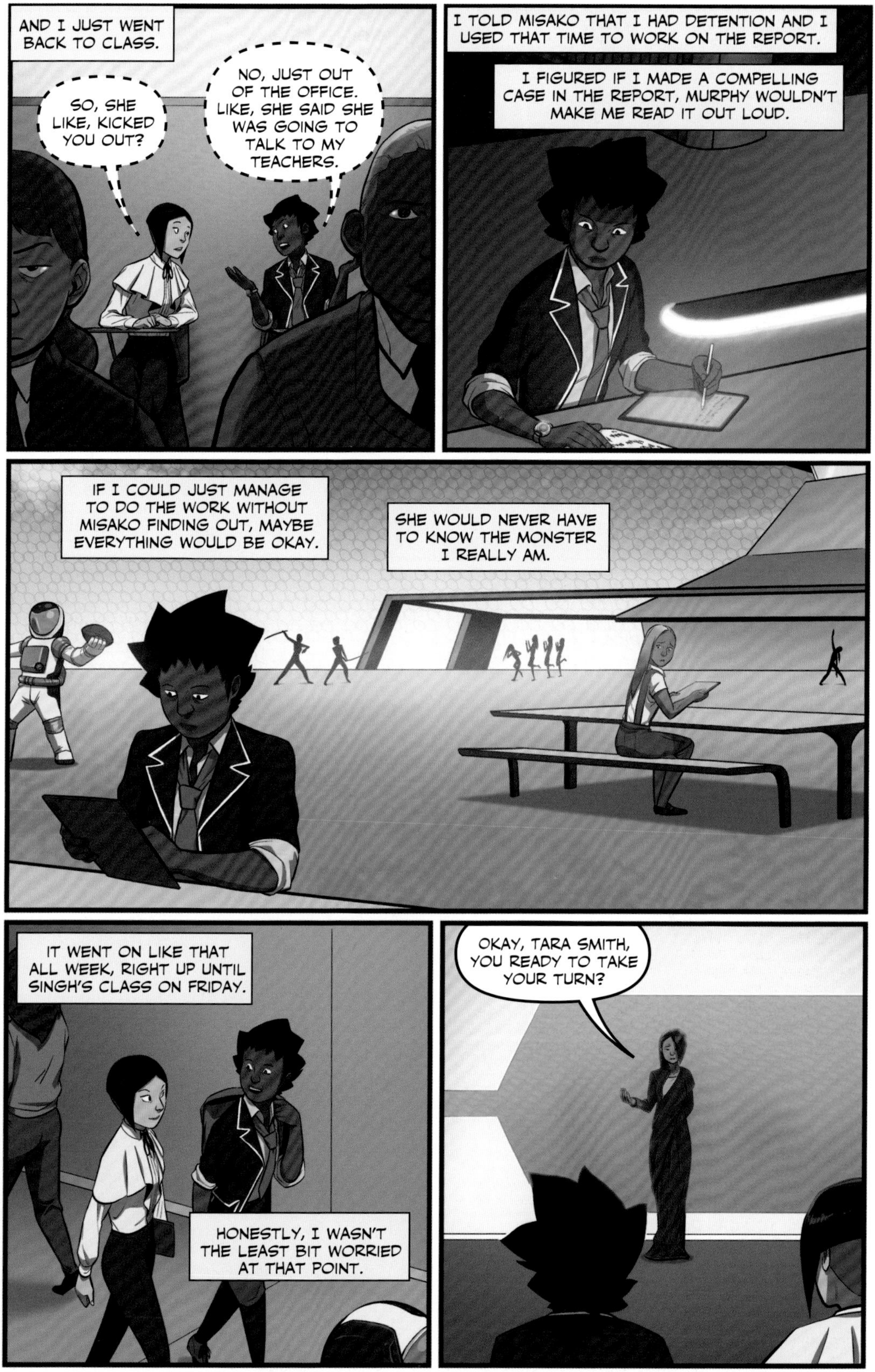
AND I JUST WENT BACK TO CLASS.
SO, SHE LIKE, KICKED YOU OUT?
NO, JUST OUT OF THE OFFICE. LIKE, SHE SAID SHE WAS GOING TO TALK TO MY TEACHERS.
I TOLD MISAKO THAT I HAD DETENTION AND I USED THAT TIME TO WORK ON THE REPORT.
I FIGURED IF I MADE A COMPELLING CASE IN THE REPORT, MURPHY WOULDN'T MAKE ME READ IT OUT LOUD.
IF I COULD JUST MANAGE TO DO THE WORK WITHOUT MISAKO FINDING OUT, MAYBE EVERYTHING WOULD BE OKAY.
SHE WOULD NEVER HAVE TO KNOW THE MONSTER I REALLY AM.
IT WENT ON LIKE THAT ALL WEEK, RIGHT UP UNTIL SINGH'S CLASS ON FRIDAY.
HONESTLY, I WASN'T THE LEAST BIT WORRIED AT THAT POINT.
OKAY, TARA SMITH, YOU READY TO TAKE YOUR TURN?

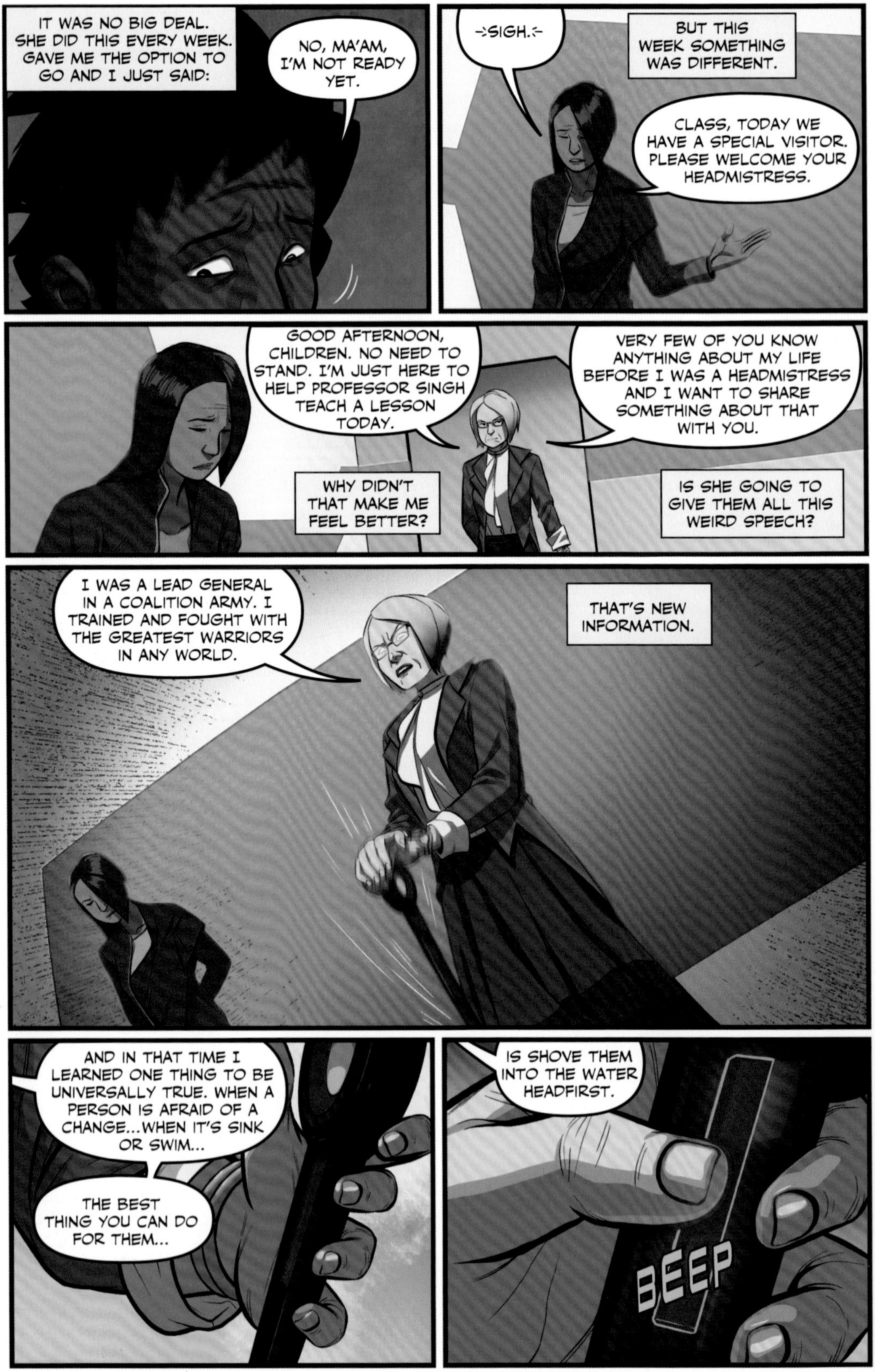

IT WAS NO BIG DEAL. SHE DID THIS EVERY WEEK. GAVE ME THE OPTION TO GO AND I JUST SAID:
NO, MA'AM, I'M NOT READY YET.
-SIGH.-
BUT THIS WEEK SOMETHING WAS DIFFERENT.
CLASS, TODAY WE HAVE A SPECIAL VISITOR. PLEASE WELCOME YOUR HEADMISTRESS.
GOOD AFTERNOON, CHILDREN. NO NEED TO STAND. I'M JUST HERE TO HELP PROFESSOR SINGH TEACH A LESSON TODAY.
WHY DIDN'T THAT MAKE ME FEEL BETTER?
VERY FEW OF YOU KNOW ANYTHING ABOUT MY LIFE BEFORE I WAS A HEADMISTRESS AND I WANT TO SHARE SOMETHING ABOUT THAT WITH YOU.
IS SHE GOING TO GIVE THEM ALL THIS WEIRD SPEECH?
I WAS A LEAD GENERAL IN A COALITION ARMY. I TRAINED AND FOUGHT WITH THE GREATEST WARRIORS IN ANY WORLD.
THAT'S NEW INFORMATION.
AND IN THAT TIME I LEARNED ONE THING TO BE UNIVERSALLY TRUE. WHEN A PERSON IS AFRAID OF A CHANGE...WHEN IT'S SINK OR SWIM...
THE BEST THING YOU CAN DO FOR THEM...
IS SHOVE THEM INTO THE WATER HEADFIRST.
BEEP

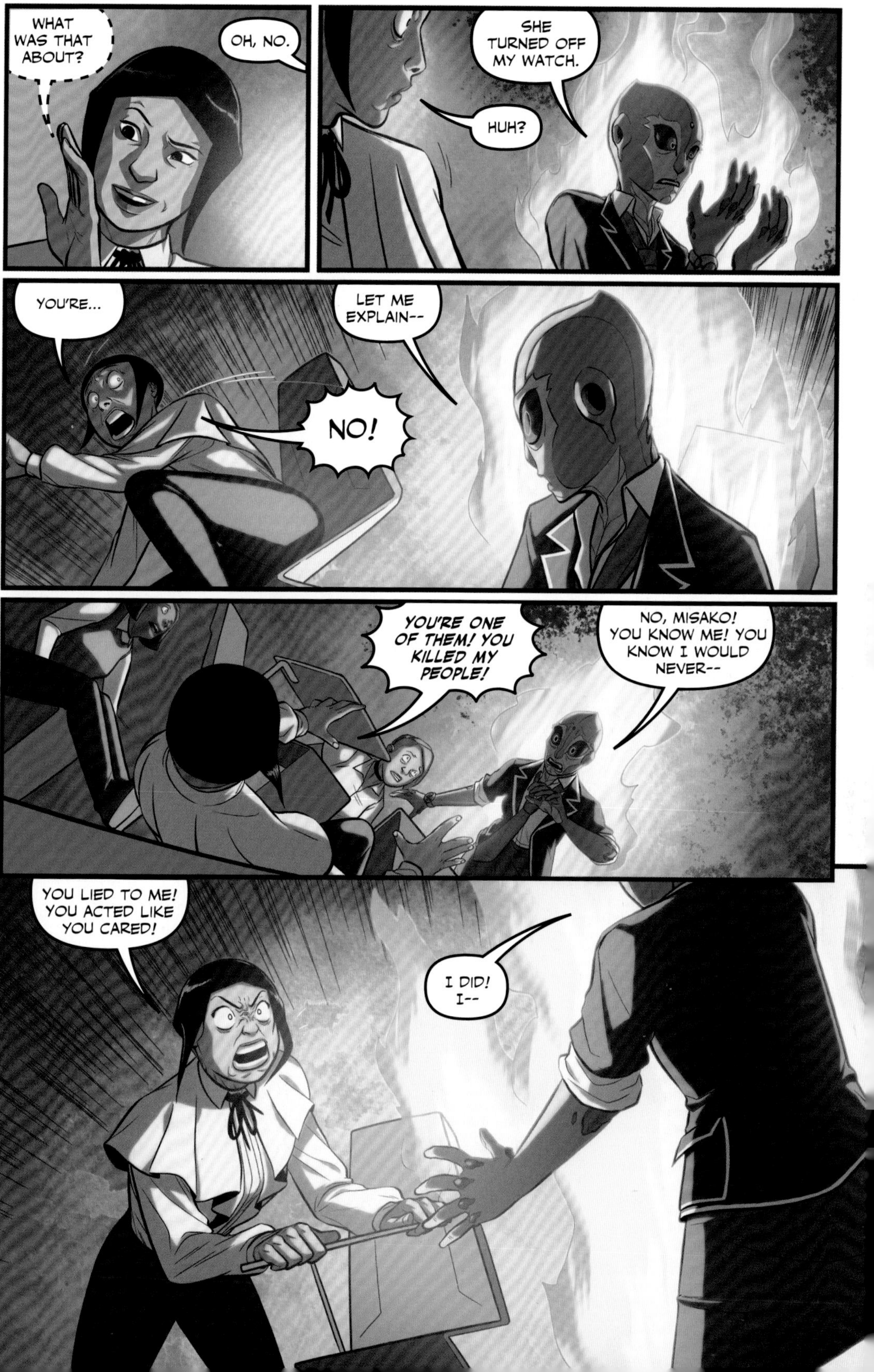
WHAT WAS THAT ABOUT?
OH, NO.
SHE TURNED OFF MY WATCH.
HUH?
YOU'RE...
LET ME EXPLAIN--
NO!
YOU'RE ONE OF THEM! YOU KILLED MY PEOPLE!
NO, MISAKO! YOU KNOW ME! YOU KNOW I WOULD NEVER--
YOU LIED TO ME! YOU ACTED LIKE YOU CARED!
I DID! I--

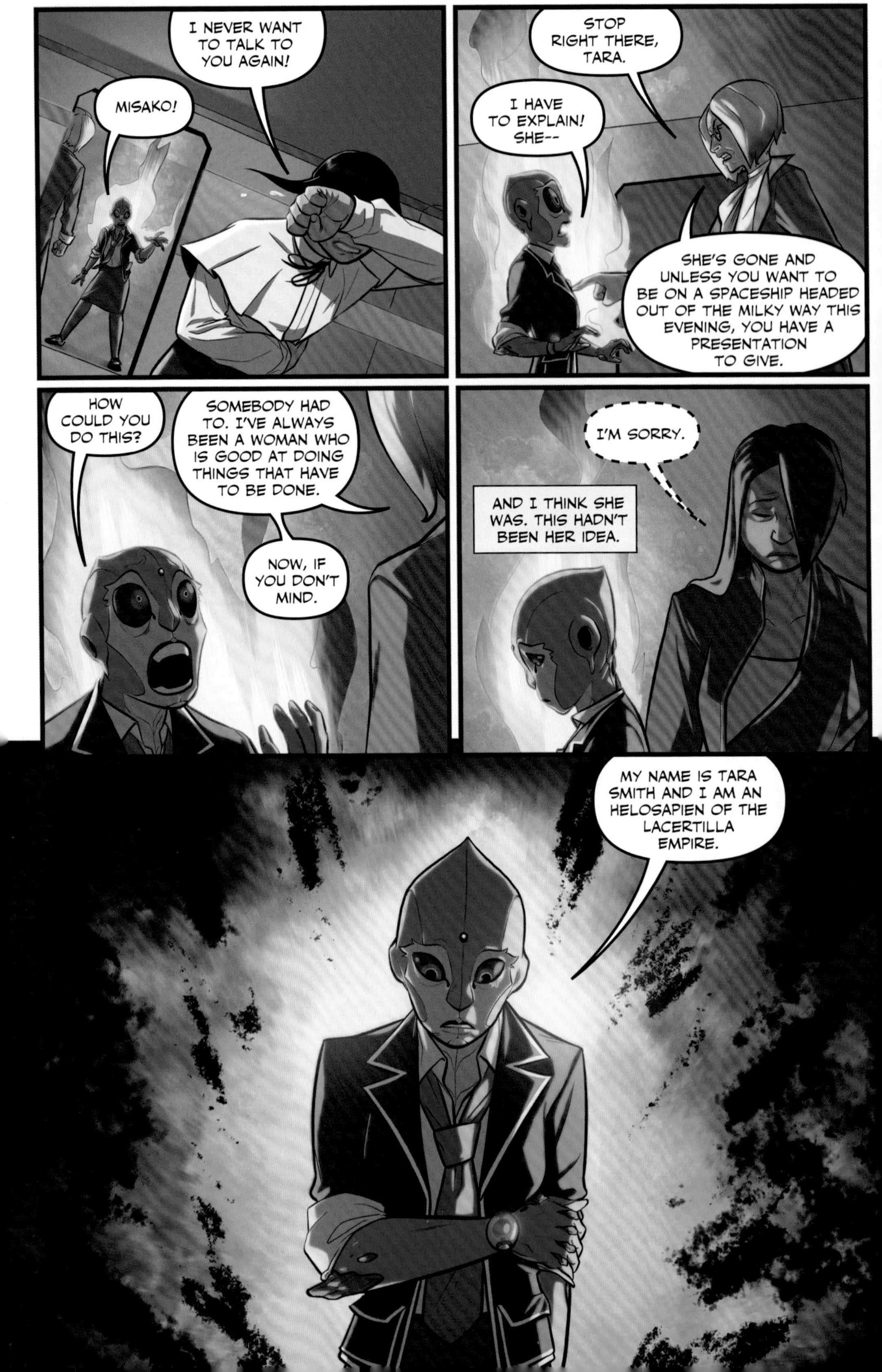
I NEVER WANT TO TALK TO YOU AGAIN!
MISAKO!
STOP RIGHT THERE, TARA.
I HAVE TO EXPLAIN! SHE--
SHE'S GONE AND UNLESS YOU WANT TO BE ON A SPACESHIP HEADED OUT OF THE MILKY WAY THIS EVENING, YOU HAVE A PRESENTATION TO GIVE.
HOW COULD YOU DO THIS?
SOMEBODY HAD TO. I'VE ALWAYS BEEN A WOMAN WHO IS GOOD AT DOING THINGS THAT HAVE TO BE DONE.
NOW, IF YOU DON'T MIND.
I'M SORRY.
AND I THINK SHE WAS. THIS HADN'T BEEN HER IDEA.
MY NAME IS TARA SMITH AND I AM AN HELOSAPIEN OF THE LACERTILLA EMPIRE.

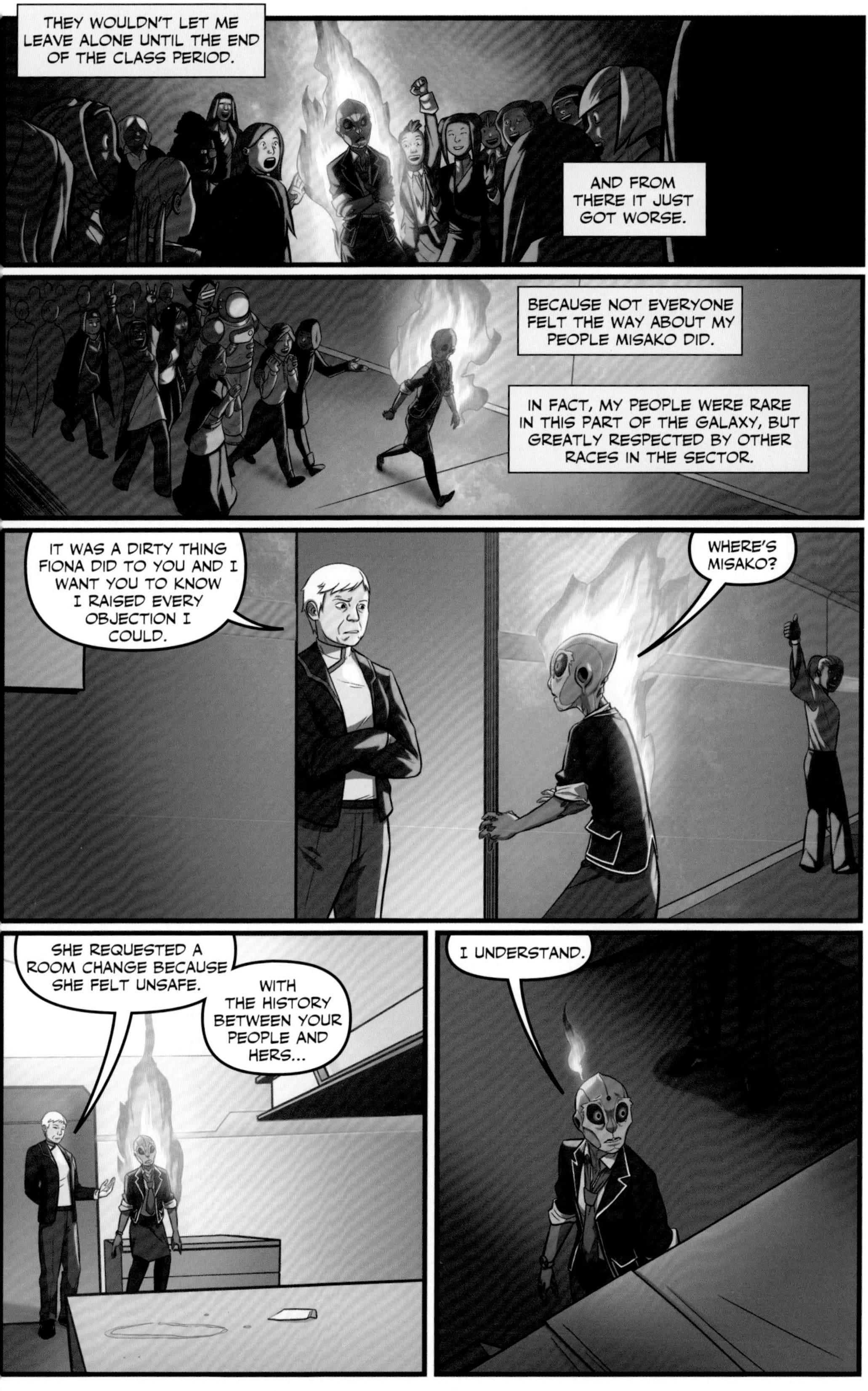
THEY WOULDN'T LET ME LEAVE ALONE UNTIL THE END OF THE CLASS PERIOD.
AND FROM THERE IT JUST GOT WORSE.
BECAUSE NOT EVERYONE FELT THE WAY ABOUT MY PEOPLE MISAKO DID.
IN FACT, MY PEOPLE WERE RARE IN THIS PART OF THE GALAXY, BUT GREATLY RESPECTED BY OTHER RACES IN THE SECTOR.
IT WAS A DIRTY THING FIONA DID TO YOU AND I WANT YOU TO KNOW I RAISED EVERY OBJECTION I COULD.
WHERE'S MISAKO?
SHE REQUESTED A ROOM CHANGE BECAUSE SHE FELT UNSAFE.
WITH THE HISTORY BETWEEN YOUR PEOPLE AND HERS...
I UNDERSTAND.

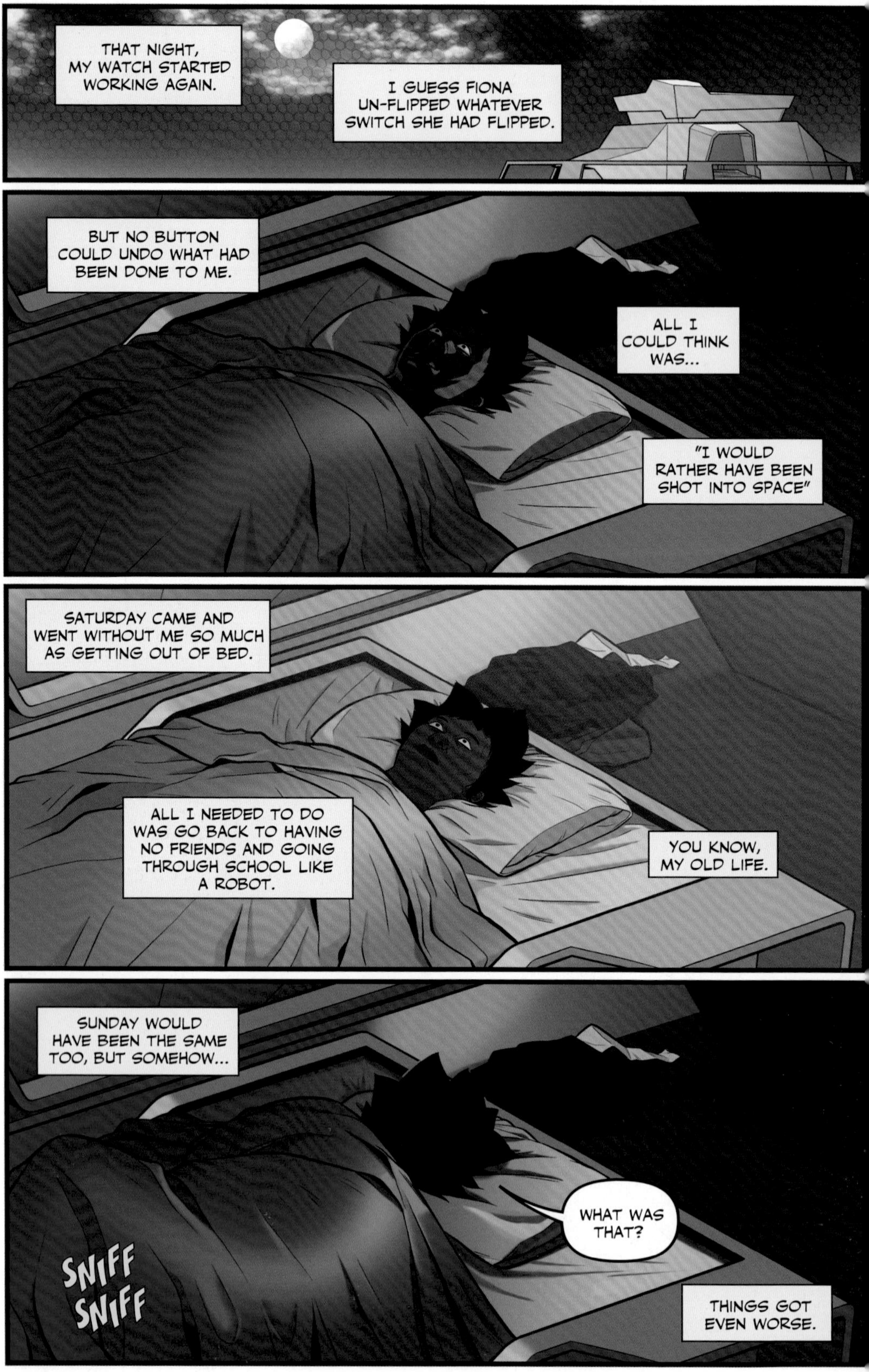
THAT NIGHT, MY WATCH STARTED WORKING AGAIN.
I GUESS FIONA UN-FLIPPED WHATEVER SWITCH SHE HAD FLIPPED.
BUT NO BUTTON COULD UNDO WHAT HAD BEEN DONE TO ME.
ALL I COULD THINK WAS...
"I WOULD RATHER HAVE BEEN SHOT INTO SPACE"
SATURDAY CAME AND WENT WITHOUT ME SO MUCH AS GETTING OUT OF BED.
ALL I NEEDED TO DO WAS GO BACK TO HAVING NO FRIENDS AND GOING THROUGH SCHOOL LIKE A ROBOT.
YOU KNOW, MY OLD LIFE.
SUNDAY WOULD HAVE BEEN THE SAME TOO, BUT SOMEHOW...
WHAT WAS THAT?
SNIFF SNIFF
THINGS GOT EVEN WORSE.

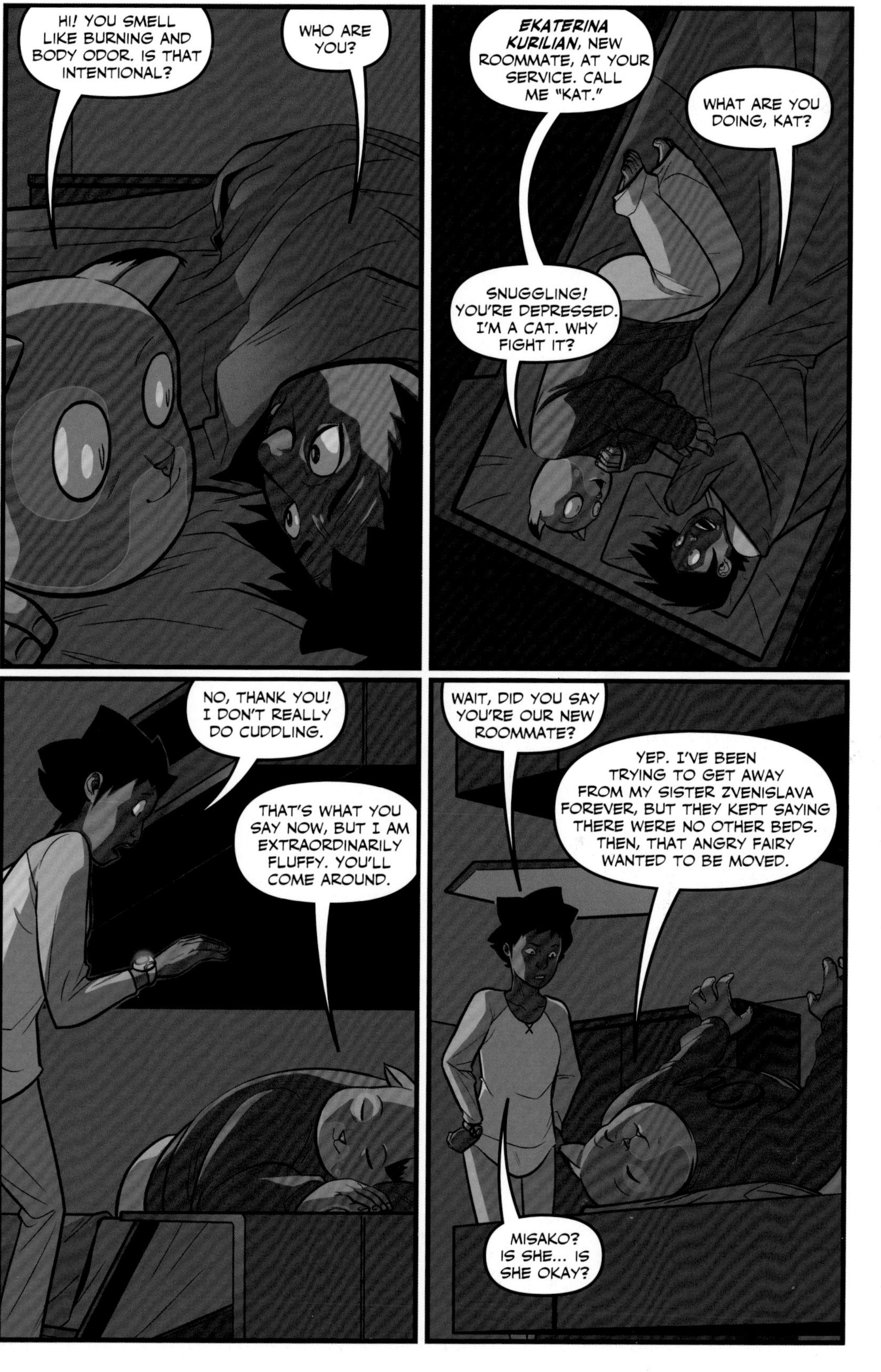
HI! YOU SMELL LIKE BURNING AND BODY ODOR. IS THAT INTENTIONAL?
WHO ARE YOU?
EKATERINA KURILIAN, NEW ROOMMATE, AT YOUR SERVICE. CALL ME "KAT."
WHAT ARE YOU DOING, KAT?
SNUGGLING! YOU'RE DEPRESSED. I'M A CAT. WHY FIGHT IT?
NO, THANK YOU! I DON'T REALLY DO CUDDLING.
THAT'S WHAT YOU SAY NOW, BUT I AM EXTRAORDINARILY FLUFFY. YOU'LL COME AROUND.
WAIT, DID YOU SAY YOU'RE OUR NEW ROOMMATE?
YEP. I'VE BEEN TRYING TO GET AWAY FROM MY SISTER ZVENISLAVA FOREVER, BUT THEY KEPT SAYING THERE WERE NO OTHER BEDS. THEN, THAT ANGRY FAIRY WANTED TO BE MOVED.
MISAKO? IS SHE... IS SHE OKAY?

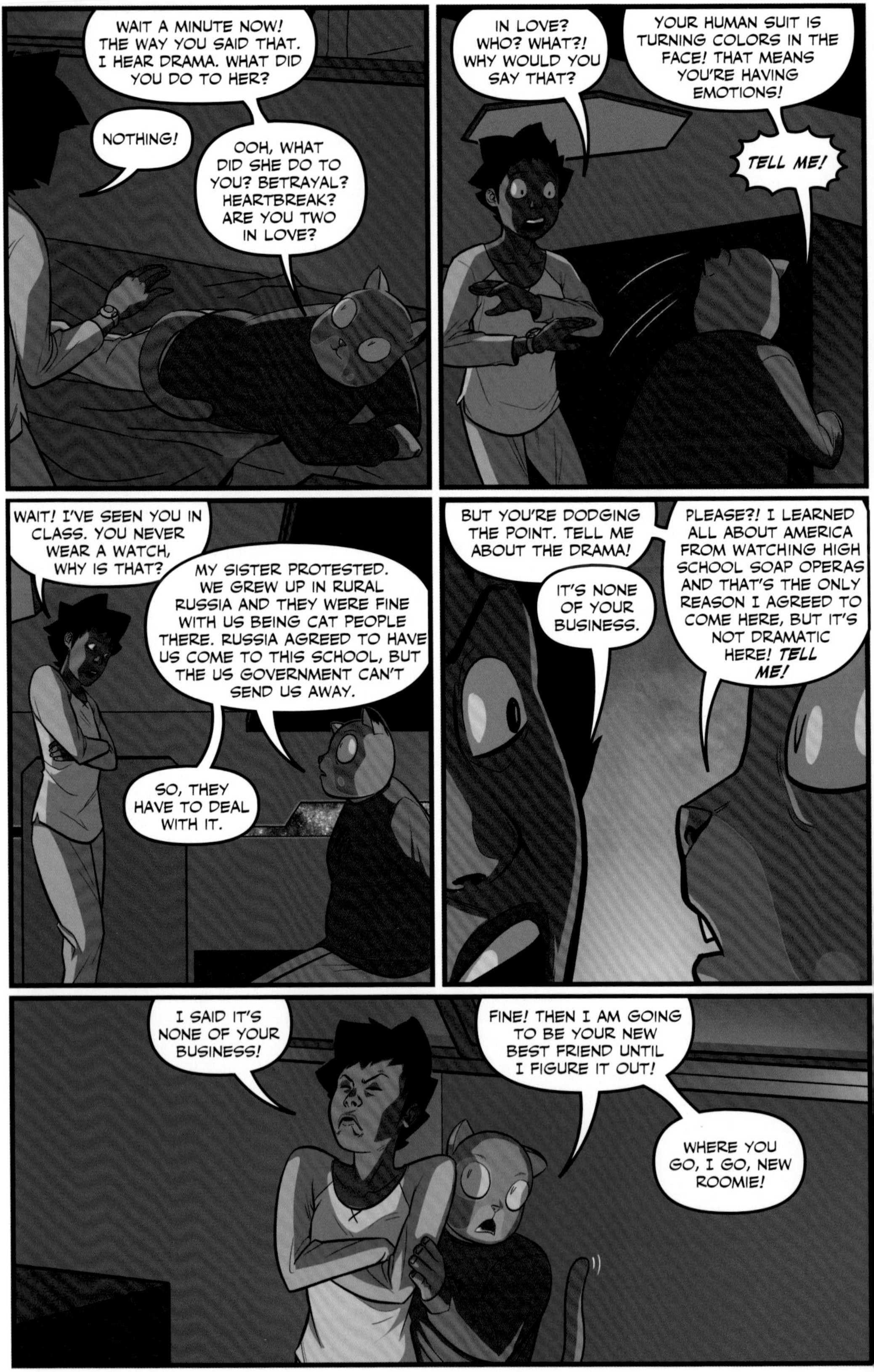
WAIT A MINUTE NOW! THE WAY YOU SAID THAT. I HEAR DRAMA. WHAT DID YOU DO TO HER?
NOTHING!
OOH, WHAT DID SHE DO TO YOU? BETRAYAL? HEARTBREAK? ARE YOU TWO IN LOVE?
IN LOVE? WHO? WHAT?! WHY WOULD YOU SAY THAT?
YOUR HUMAN SUIT IS TURNING COLORS IN THE FACE! THAT MEANS YOU'RE HAVING EMOTIONS!
TELL ME!
WAIT! I'VE SEEN YOU IN CLASS. YOU NEVER WEAR A WATCH, WHY IS THAT?
MY SISTER PROTESTED. WE GREW UP IN RURAL RUSSIA AND THEY WERE FINE WITH US BEING CAT PEOPLE THERE. RUSSIA AGREED TO HAVE US COME TO THIS SCHOOL, BUT THE US GOVERNMENT CAN'T SEND US AWAY.
SO, THEY HAVE TO DEAL WITH IT.
BUT YOU'RE DODGING THE POINT. TELL ME ABOUT THE DRAMA!
IT'S NONE OF YOUR BUSINESS.
PLEASE?! I LEARNED ALL ABOUT AMERICA FROM WATCHING HIGH SCHOOL SOAP OPERAS AND THAT'S THE ONLY REASON I AGREED TO COME HERE, BUT IT'S NOT DRAMATIC HERE! TELL ME!
I SAID IT'S NONE OF YOUR BUSINESS!
FINE! THEN I AM GOING TO BE YOUR NEW BEST FRIEND UNTIL I FIGURE IT OUT!
WHERE YOU GO, I GO, NEW ROOMIE!

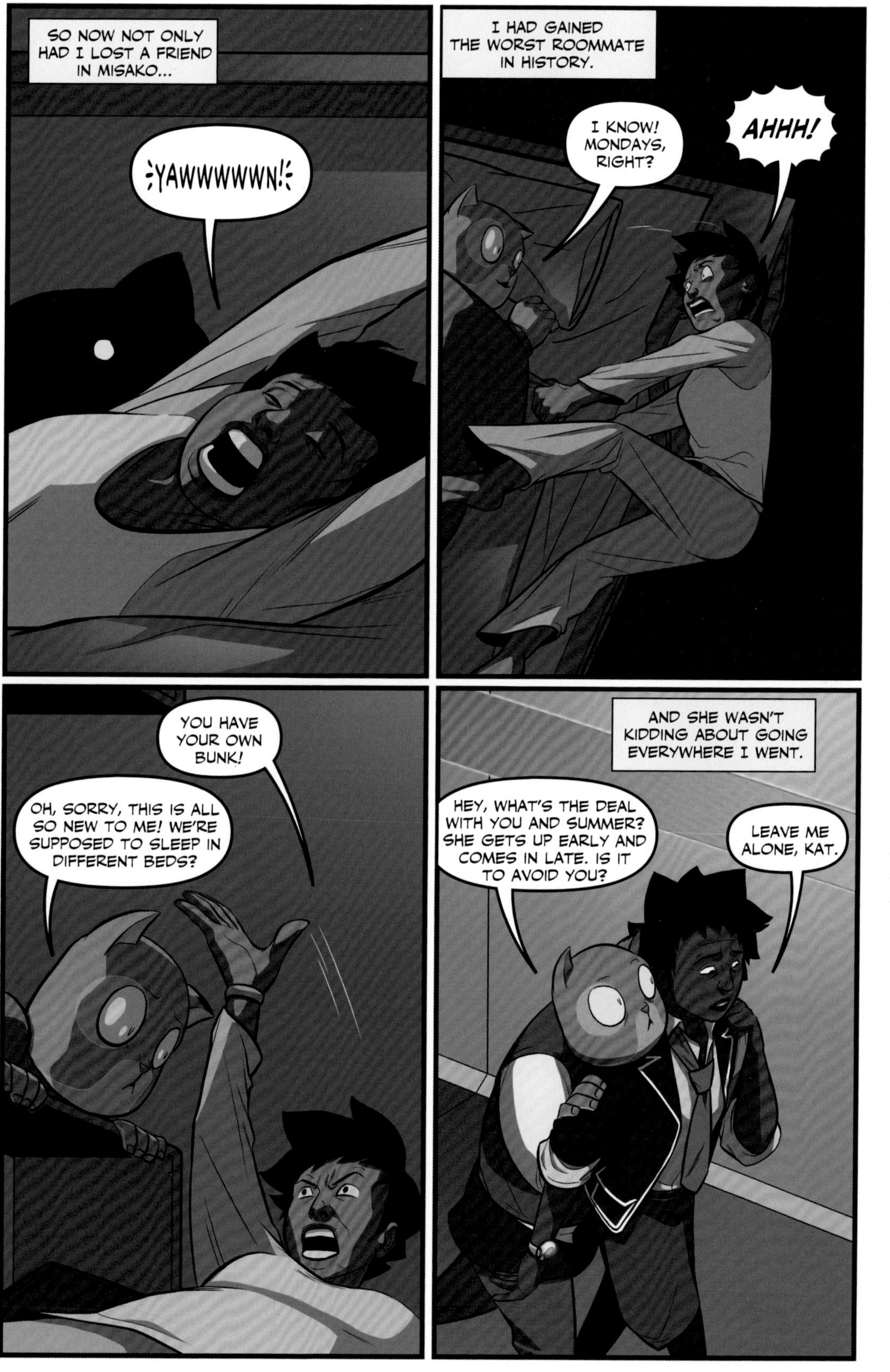
SO NOW NOT ONLY HAD I LOST A FRIEND IN MISAKO...
YAWWWWWN!
I HAD GAINED THE WORST ROOMMATE IN HISTORY.
I KNOW! MONDAYS, RIGHT?
AHHH!
YOU HAVE YOUR OWN BUNK!
OH, SORRY, THIS IS ALL SO NEW TO ME! WE'RE SUPPOSED TO SLEEP IN DIFFERENT BEDS?
AND SHE WASN'T KIDDING ABOUT GOING EVERYWHERE I WENT.
HEY, WHAT'S THE DEAL WITH YOU AND SUMMER? SHE GETS UP EARLY AND COMES IN LATE. IS IT TO AVOID YOU?
LEAVE ME ALONE, KAT.

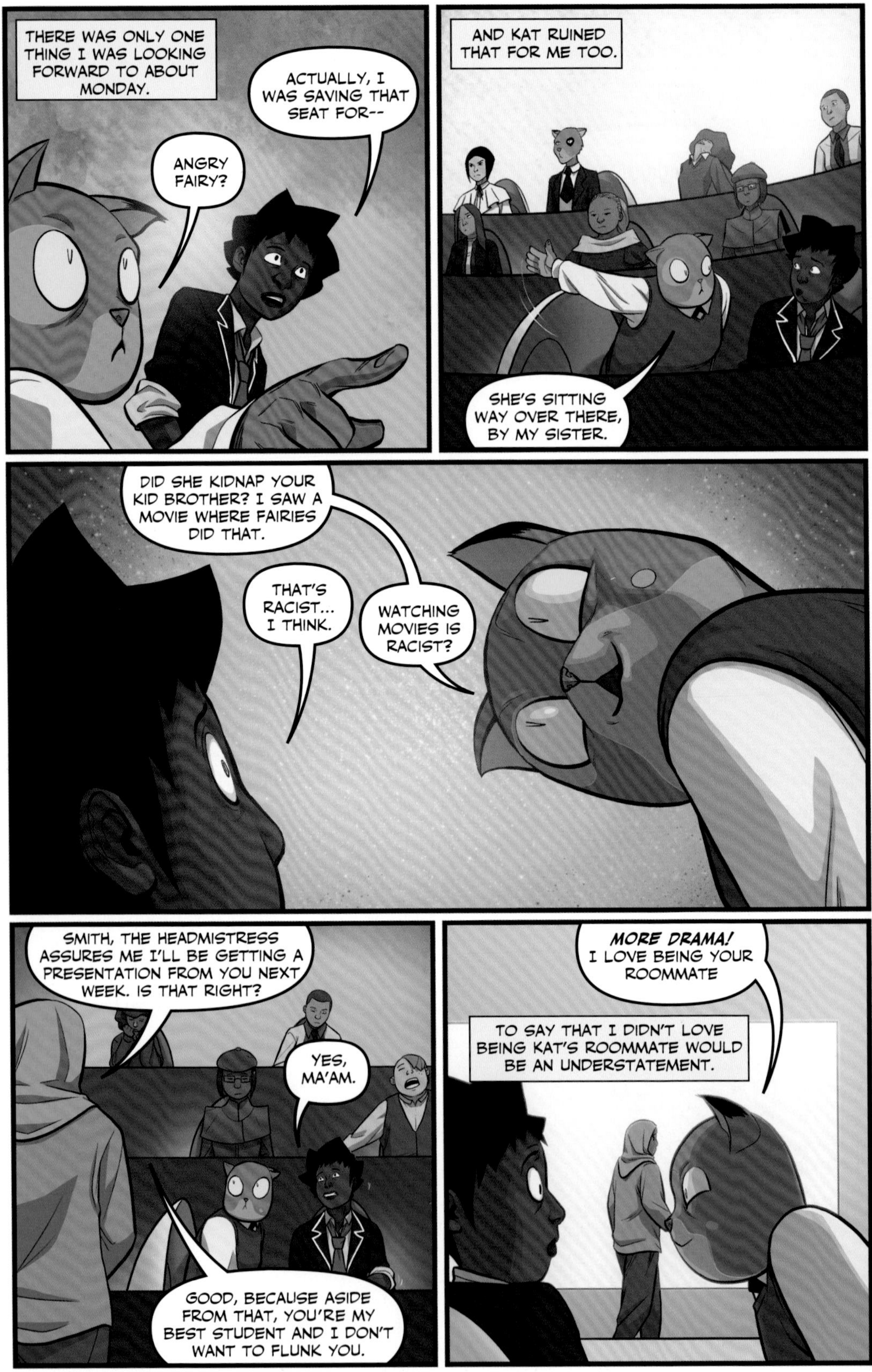

THERE WAS ONLY ONE THING I WAS LOOKING FORWARD TO ABOUT MONDAY.
ACTUALLY, I WAS SAVING THAT SEAT FOR--
ANGRY FAIRY?
AND KAT RUINED THAT FOR ME TOO.
SHE'S SITTING WAY OVER THERE, BY MY SISTER.
DID SHE KIDNAP YOUR KID BROTHER? I SAW A MOVIE WHERE FAIRIES DID THAT.
THAT'S RACIST... I THINK.
WATCHING MOVIES IS RACIST?
SMITH, THE HEADMISTRESS ASSURES ME I'LL BE GETTING A PRESENTATION FROM YOU NEXT WEEK. IS THAT RIGHT?
YES, MA'AM.
GOOD, BECAUSE ASIDE FROM THAT, YOU'RE MY BEST STUDENT AND I DON'T WANT TO FLUNK YOU.
MORE DRAMA! I LOVE BEING YOUR ROOMMATE
TO SAY THAT I DIDN'T LOVE BEING KAT'S ROOMMATE WOULD BE AN UNDERSTATEMENT.

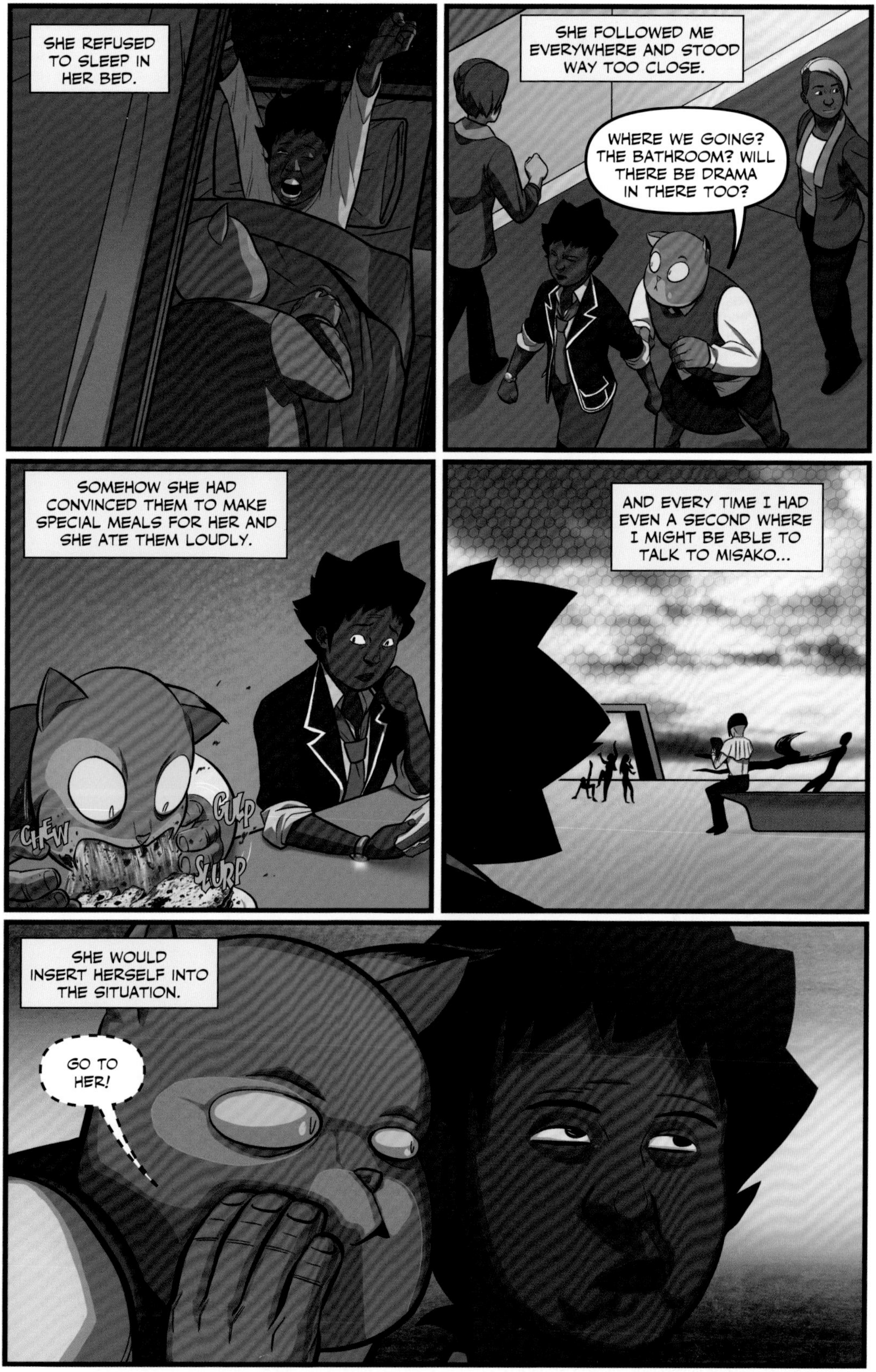
SHE REFUSED TO SLEEP IN HER BED.
SHE FOLLOWED ME EVERYWHERE AND STOOD WAY TOO CLOSE.
WHERE WE GOING? THE BATHROOM? WILL THERE BE DRAMA IN THERE TOO?
SOMEHOW SHE HAD CONVINCED THEM TO MAKE SPECIAL MEALS FOR HER AND SHE ATE THEM LOUDLY.
CHEW
GULP
SLURP
AND EVERY TIME I HAD EVEN A SECOND WHERE I MIGHT BE ABLE TO TALK TO MISAKO...
SHE WOULD INSERT HERSELF INTO THE SITUATION.
GO TO HER!

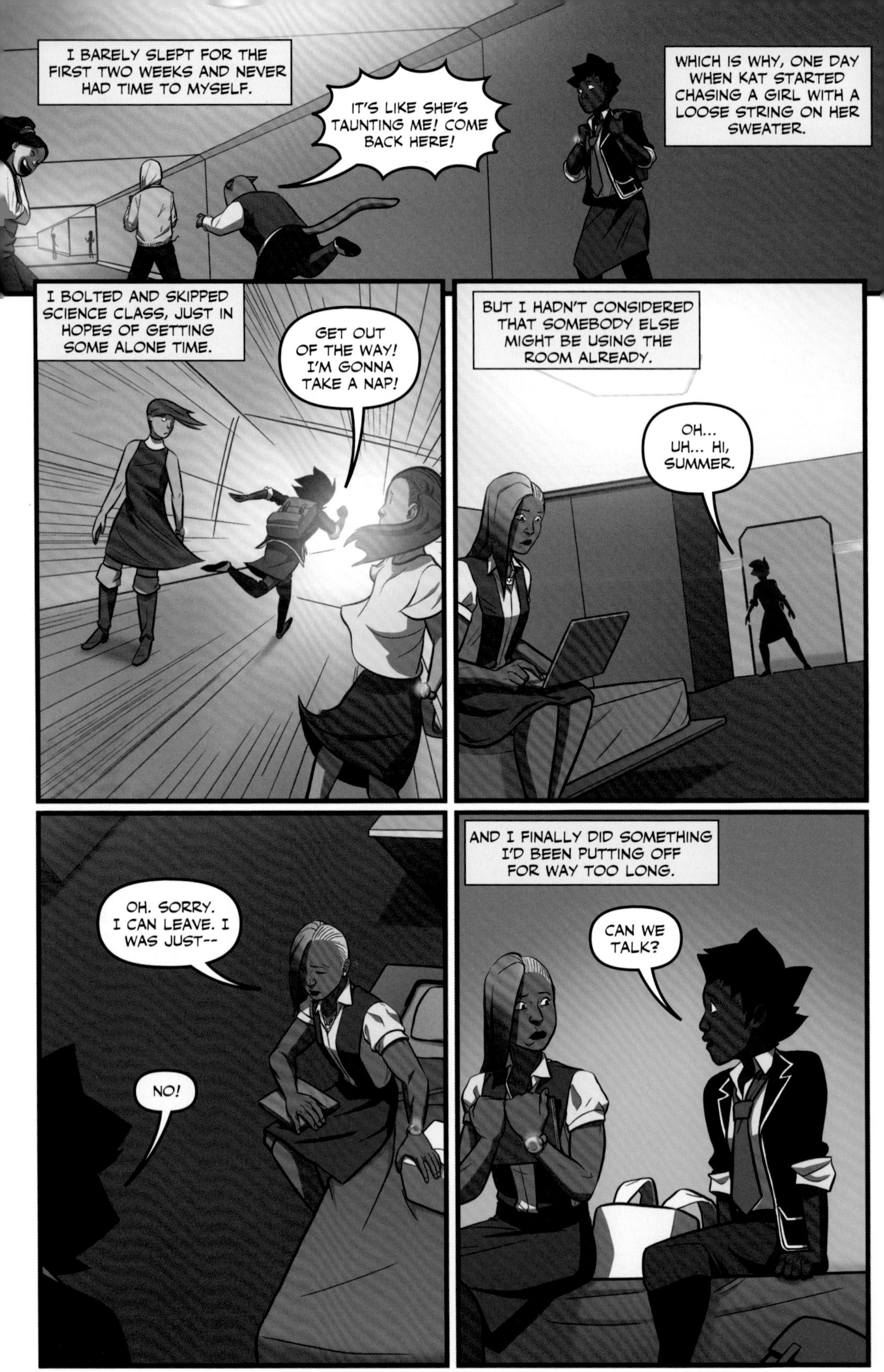
I BARELY SLEPT FOR THE FIRST TWO WEEKS AND NEVER HAD TIME TO MYSELF.
IT'S LIKE SHE'S TAUNTING ME! COME BACK HERE!
WHICH IS WHY, ONE DAY WHEN KAT STARTED CHASING A GIRL WITH A LOOSE STRING ON HER SWEATER.
I BOLTED AND SKIPPED SCIENCE CLASS, JUST IN HOPES OF GETTING SOME ALONE TIME.
GET OUT OF THE WAY! I'M GONNA TAKE A NAP!
BUT I HADN'T CONSIDERED THAT SOMEBODY ELSE MIGHT BE USING THE ROOM ALREADY.
OH... UH... HI, SUMMER.
OH. SORRY. I CAN LEAVE. I WAS JUST--
NO!
AND I FINALLY DID SOMETHING I'D BEEN PUTTING OFF FOR WAY TOO LONG.
CAN WE TALK?

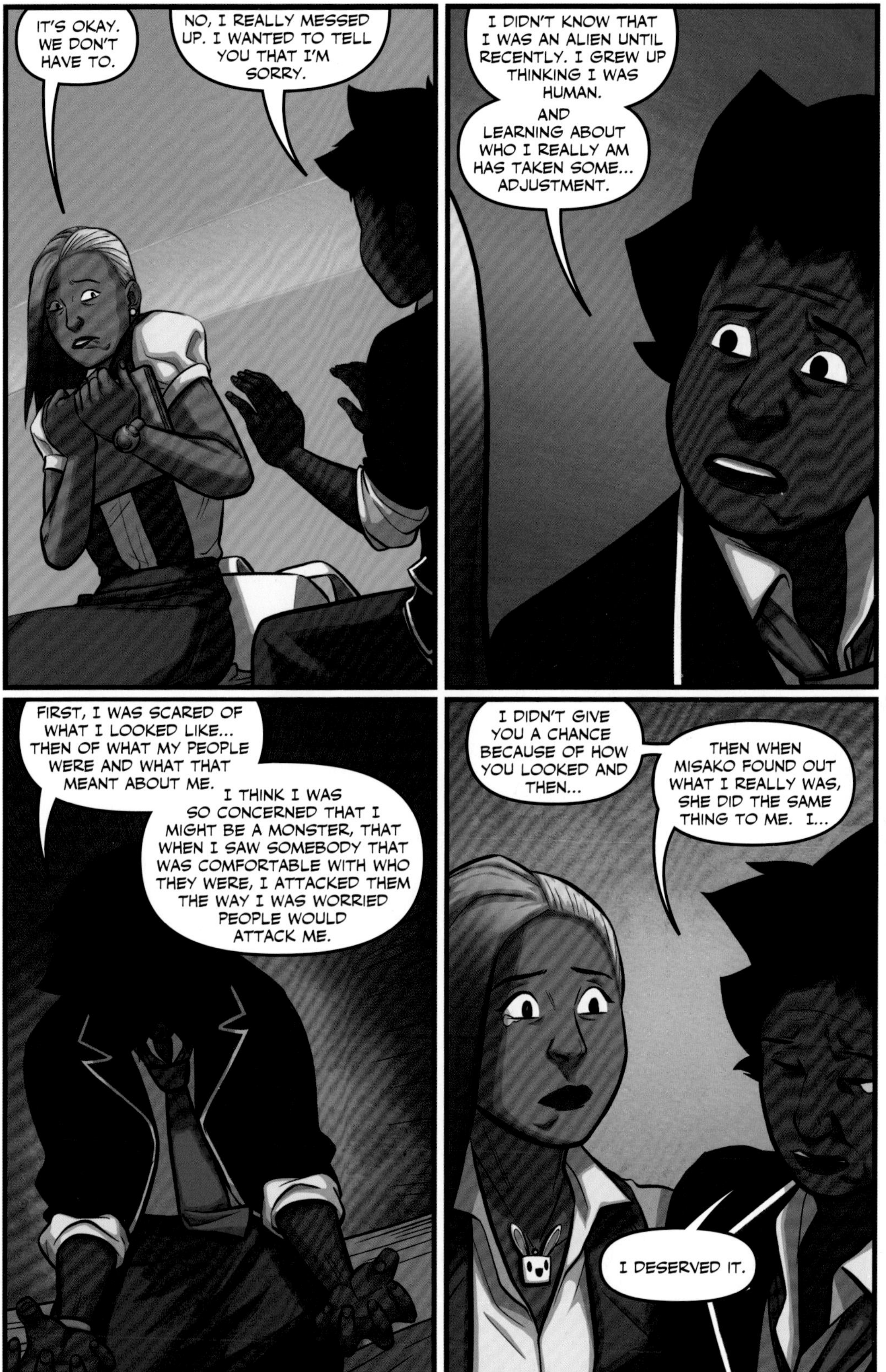
IT'S OKAY. WE DON'T HAVE TO.
NO, I REALLY MESSED UP. I WANTED TO TELL YOU THAT I'M SORRY.
I DIDN'T KNOW THAT I WAS AN ALIEN UNTIL RECENTLY. I GREW UP THINKING I WAS HUMAN.
AND LEARNING ABOUT WHO I REALLY AM HAS TAKEN SOME... ADJUSTMENT.
FIRST, I WAS SCARED OF WHAT I LOOKED LIKE... THEN OF WHAT MY PEOPLE WERE AND WHAT THAT MEANT ABOUT ME.
I THINK I WAS SO CONCERNED THAT I MIGHT BE A MONSTER, THAT WHEN I SAW SOMEBODY THAT WAS COMFORTABLE WITH WHO THEY WERE, I ATTACKED THEM THE WAY I WAS WORRIED PEOPLE WOULD ATTACK ME.
I DIDN'T GIVE YOU A CHANCE BECAUSE OF HOW YOU LOOKED AND THEN...
THEN WHEN MISAKO FOUND OUT WHAT I REALLY WAS, SHE DID THE SAME THING TO ME. I...
I DESERVED IT.

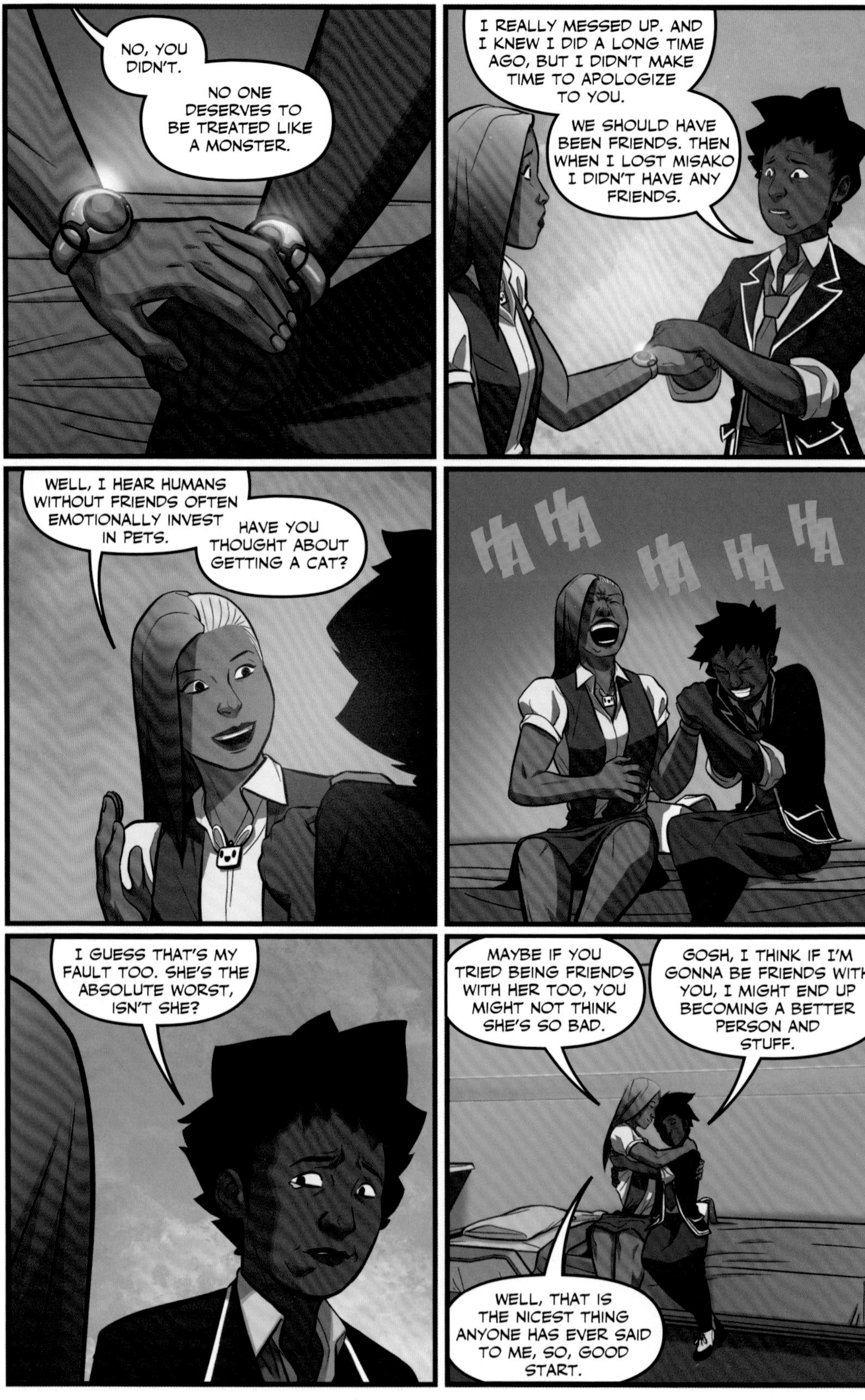
NO, YOU DIDN'T.
NO ONE DESERVES TO BE TREATED LIKE A MONSTER.
I REALLY MESSED UP. AND I KNEW I DID A LONG TIME AGO, BUT I DIDN'T MAKE TIME TO APOLOGIZE TO YOU.
WE SHOULD HAVE BEEN FRIENDS. THEN WHEN I LOST MISAKO I DIDN'T HAVE ANY FRIENDS.
WELL, I HEAR HUMANS WITHOUT FRIENDS OFTEN EMOTIONALLY INVEST IN PETS.
HAVE YOU THOUGHT ABOUT GETTING A CAT?
HA HA HA HA HA
I GUESS THAT'S MY FAULT TOO. SHE'S THE ABSOLUTE WORST, ISN'T SHE?
MAYBE IF YOU TRIED BEING FRIENDS WITH HER TOO, YOU MIGHT NOT THINK SHE'S SO BAD.
GOSH, I THINK IF I'M GONNA BE FRIENDS WITH YOU, I MIGHT END UP BECOMING A BETTER PERSON AND STUFF.
WELL, THAT IS THE NICEST THING ANYONE HAS EVER SAID TO ME, SO, GOOD START.

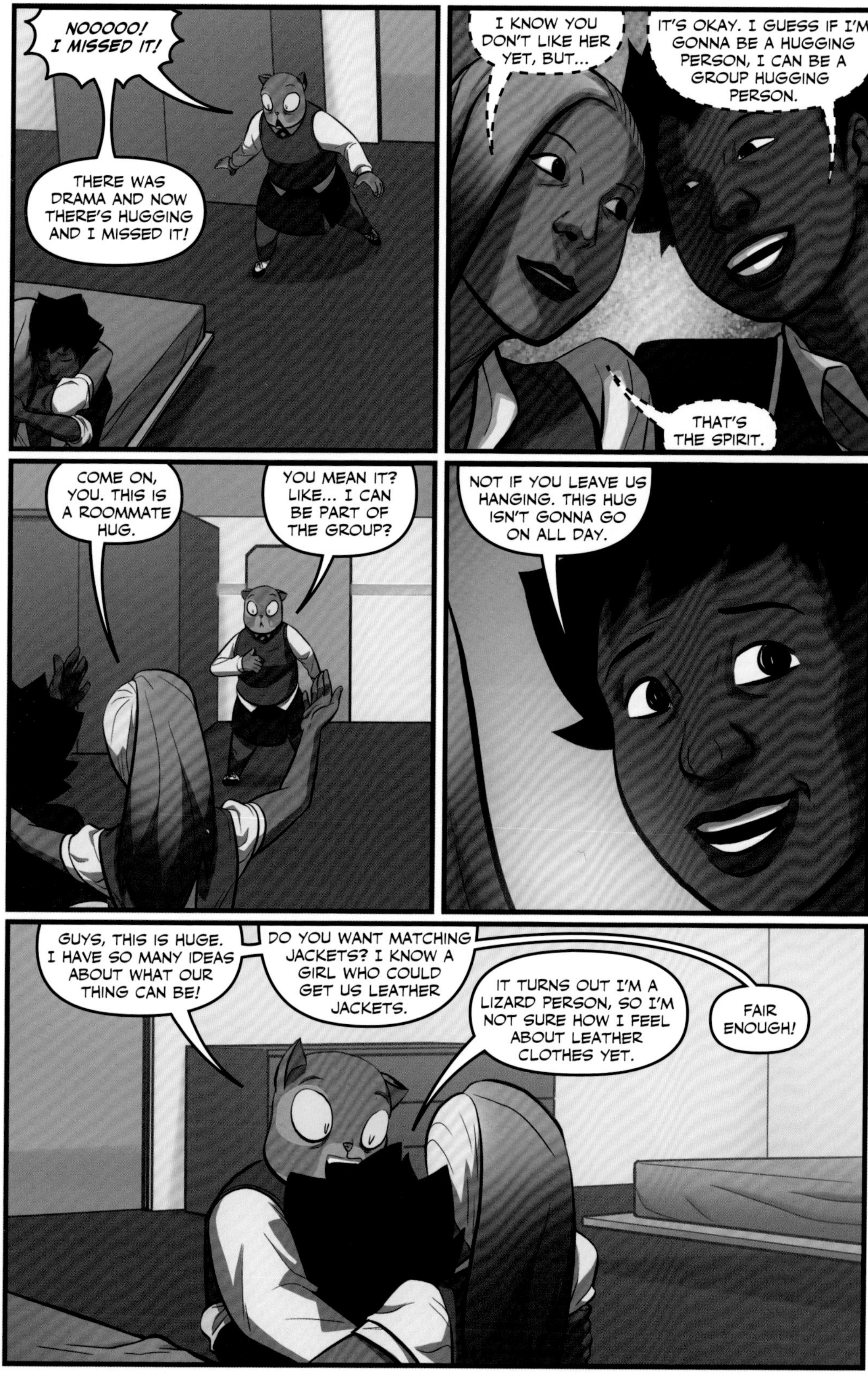
NOOOOO! I MISSED IT!
THERE WAS DRAMA AND NOW THERE'S HUGGING AND I MISSED IT!
I KNOW YOU DON'T LIKE HER YET, BUT...
IT'S OKAY. I GUESS IF I'M GONNA BE A HUGGING PERSON, I CAN BE A GROUP HUGGING PERSON.
THAT'S THE SPIRIT.
COME ON, YOU. THIS IS A ROOMMATE HUG.
YOU MEAN IT? LIKE... I CAN BE PART OF THE GROUP?
NOT IF YOU LEAVE US HANGING. THIS HUG ISN'T GONNA GO ON ALL DAY.
GUYS, THIS IS HUGE. I HAVE SO MANY IDEAS ABOUT WHAT OUR THING CAN BE!
DO YOU WANT MATCHING JACKETS? I KNOW A GIRL WHO COULD GET US LEATHER JACKETS.
IT TURNS OUT I'M A LIZARD PERSON, SO I'M NOT SURE HOW I FEEL ABOUT LEATHER CLOTHES YET.
FAIR ENOUGH!

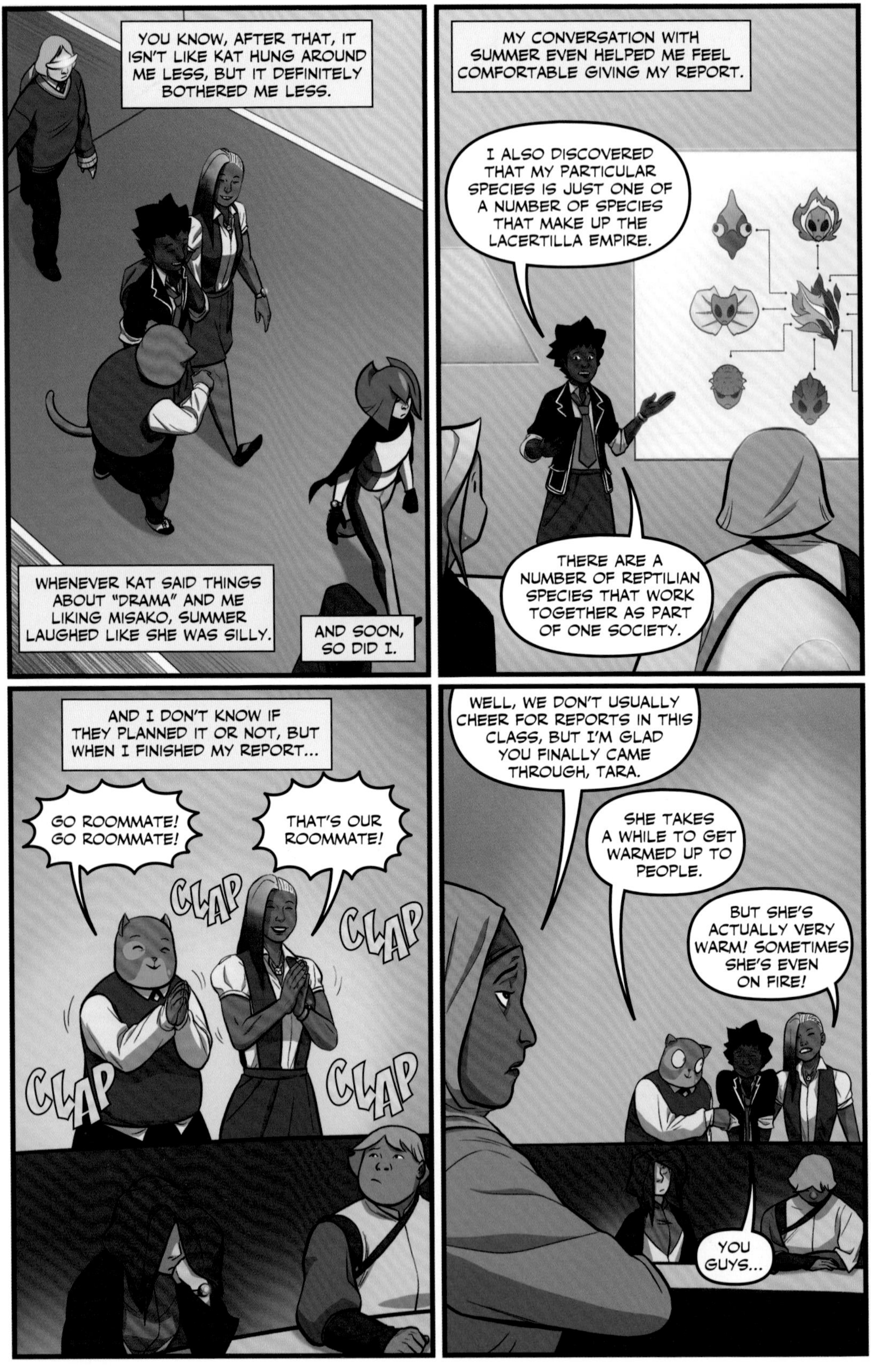
YOU KNOW, AFTER THAT, IT ISN'T LIKE KAT HUNG AROUND ME LESS, BUT IT DEFINITELY BOTHERED ME LESS.
WHENEVER KAT SAID THINGS ABOUT "DRAMA" AND ME LIKING MISAKO, SUMMER LAUGHED LIKE SHE WAS SILLY.
AND SOON, SO DID I.
MY CONVERSATION WITH SUMMER EVEN HELPED ME FEEL COMFORTABLE GIVING MY REPORT.
I ALSO DISCOVERED THAT MY PARTICULAR SPECIES IS JUST ONE OF A NUMBER OF SPECIES THAT MAKE UP THE LACERTILLA EMPIRE.
THERE ARE A NUMBER OF REPTILIAN SPECIES THAT WORK TOGETHER AS PART OF ONE SOCIETY.
AND I DON'T KNOW IF THEY PLANNED IT OR NOT, BUT WHEN I FINISHED MY REPORT...
GO ROOMMATE! GO ROOMMATE!
THAT'S OUR ROOMMATE!
CLAP
CLAP
CLAP
CLAP
WELL, WE DON'T USUALLY CHEER FOR REPORTS IN THIS CLASS, BUT I'M GLAD YOU FINALLY CAME THROUGH, TARA.
SHE TAKES A WHILE TO GET WARMED UP TO PEOPLE.
BUT SHE'S ACTUALLY VERY WARM! SOMETIMES SHE'S EVEN ON FIRE!
YOU GUYS...

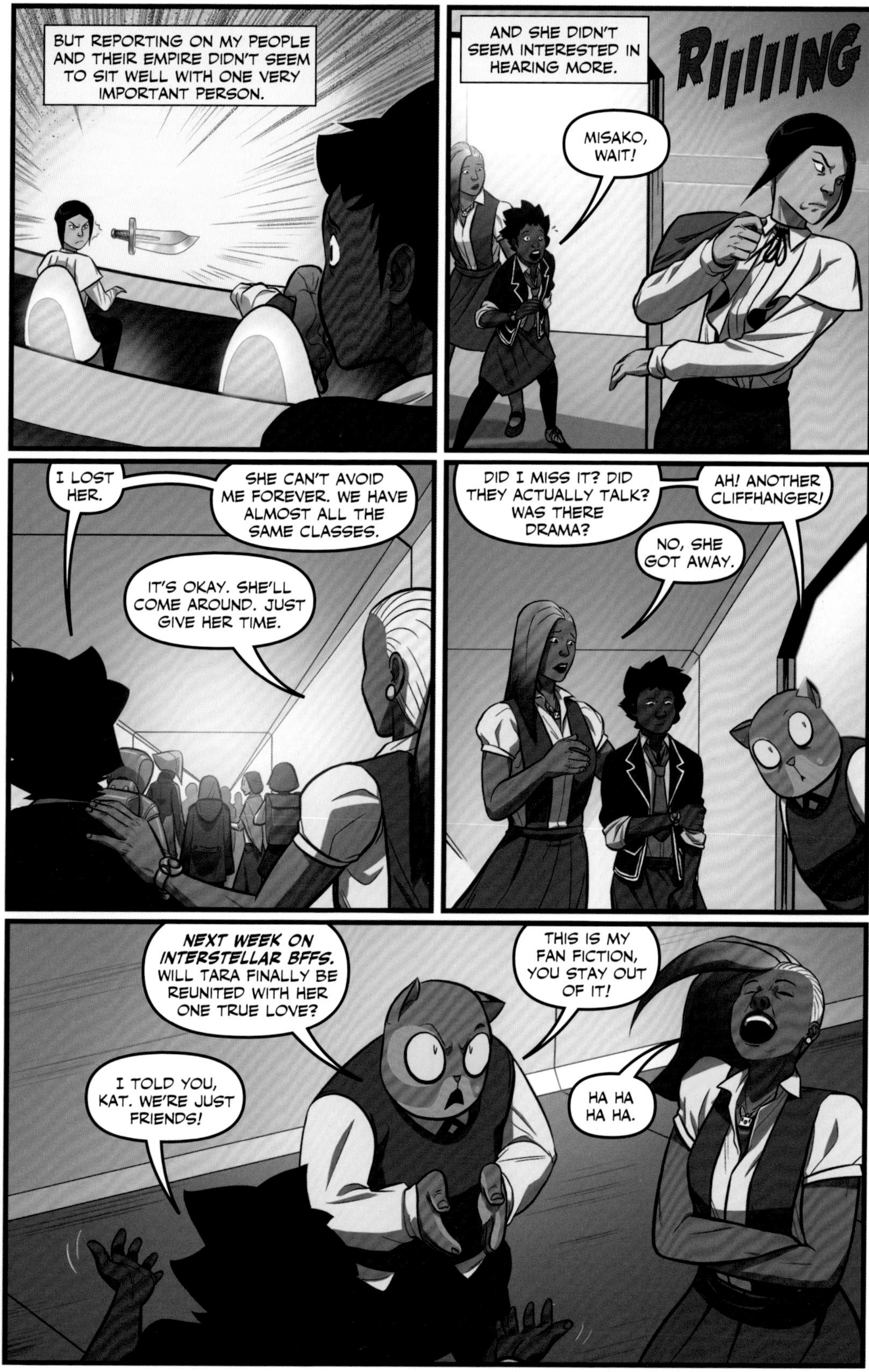
BUT REPORTING ON MY PEOPLE AND THEIR EMPIRE DIDN'T SEEM TO SIT WELL WITH ONE VERY IMPORTANT PERSON.
AND SHE DIDN'T SEEM INTERESTED IN HEARING MORE.
RIIIIING
MISAKO, WAIT!
I LOST HER.
SHE CAN'T AVOID ME FOREVER. WE HAVE ALMOST ALL THE SAME CLASSES.
IT'S OKAY. SHE'LL COME AROUND. JUST GIVE HER TIME.
DID I MISS IT? DID THEY ACTUALLY TALK? WAS THERE DRAMA?
AH! ANOTHER CLIFFHANGER!
NO, SHE GOT AWAY.
NEXT WEEK ON INTERSTELLAR BFFS. WILL TARA FINALLY BE REUNITED WITH HER ONE TRUE LOVE?
THIS IS MY FAN FICTION, YOU STAY OUT OF IT!
I TOLD YOU, KAT. WE'RE JUST FRIENDS!
HA HA HA HA.

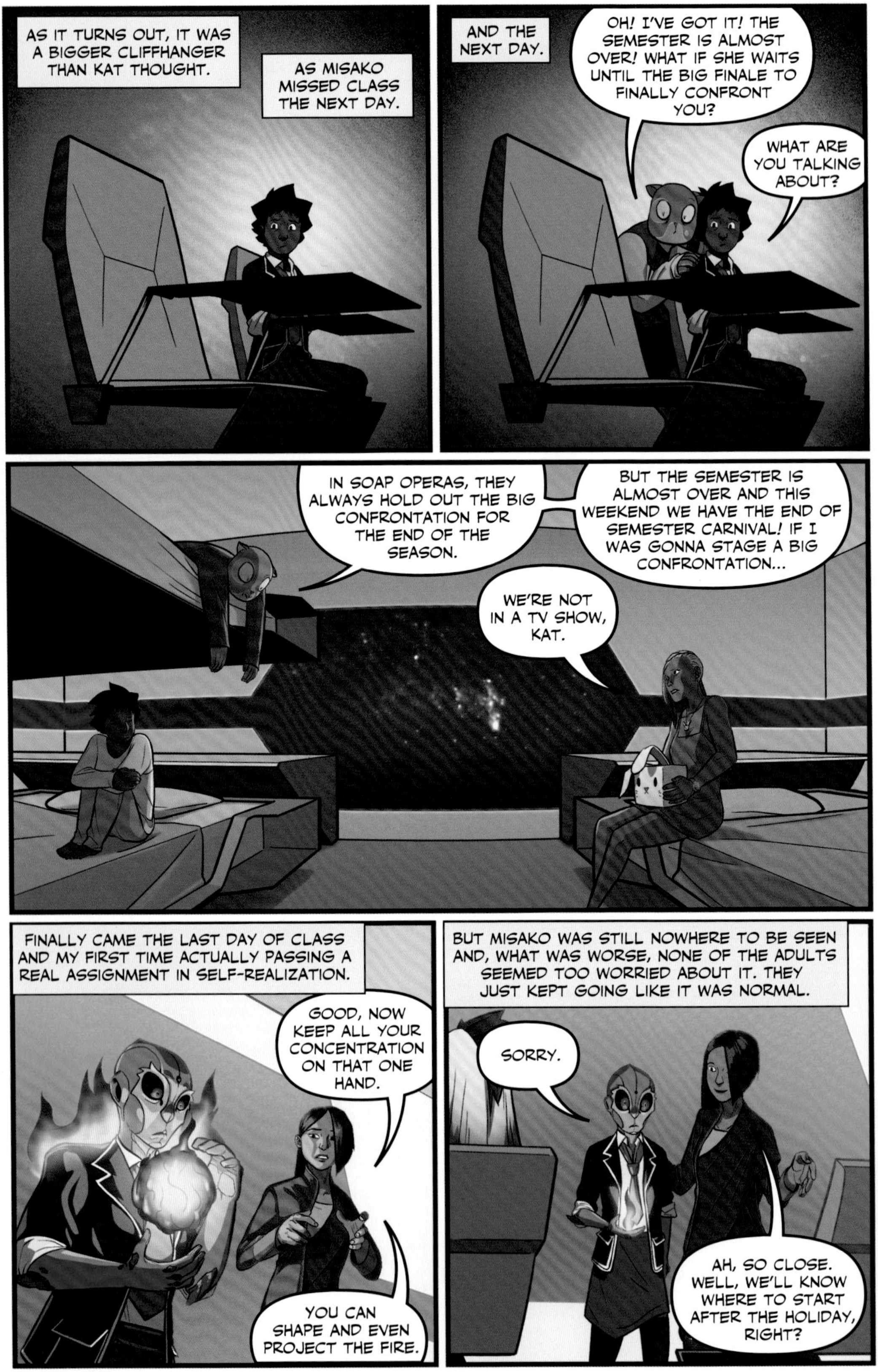
AS IT TURNS OUT, IT WAS A BIGGER CLIFFHANGER THAN KAT THOUGHT.
AS MISAKO MISSED CLASS THE NEXT DAY.
AND THE NEXT DAY.
OH! I'VE GOT IT! THE SEMESTER IS ALMOST OVER! WHAT IF SHE WAITS UNTIL THE BIG FINALE TO FINALLY CONFRONT YOU?
WHAT ARE YOU TALKING ABOUT?
IN SOAP OPERAS, THEY ALWAYS HOLD OUT THE BIG CONFRONTATION FOR THE END OF THE SEASON.
BUT THE SEMESTER IS ALMOST OVER AND THIS WEEKEND WE HAVE THE END OF SEMESTER CARNIVAL! IF I WAS GONNA STAGE A BIG CONFRONTATION...
WE'RE NOT IN A TV SHOW, KAT.
FINALLY CAME THE LAST DAY OF CLASS AND MY FIRST TIME ACTUALLY PASSING A REAL ASSIGNMENT IN SELF-REALIZATION.
GOOD, NOW KEEP ALL YOUR CONCENTRATION ON THAT ONE HAND.
YOU CAN SHAPE AND EVEN PROJECT THE FIRE.
BUT MISAKO WAS STILL NOWHERE TO BE SEEN AND, WHAT WAS WORSE, NONE OF THE ADULTS SEEMED TOO WORRIED ABOUT IT. THEY JUST KEPT GOING LIKE IT WAS NORMAL.
SORRY.
AH, SO CLOSE. WELL, WE'LL KNOW WHERE TO START AFTER THE HOLIDAY, RIGHT?

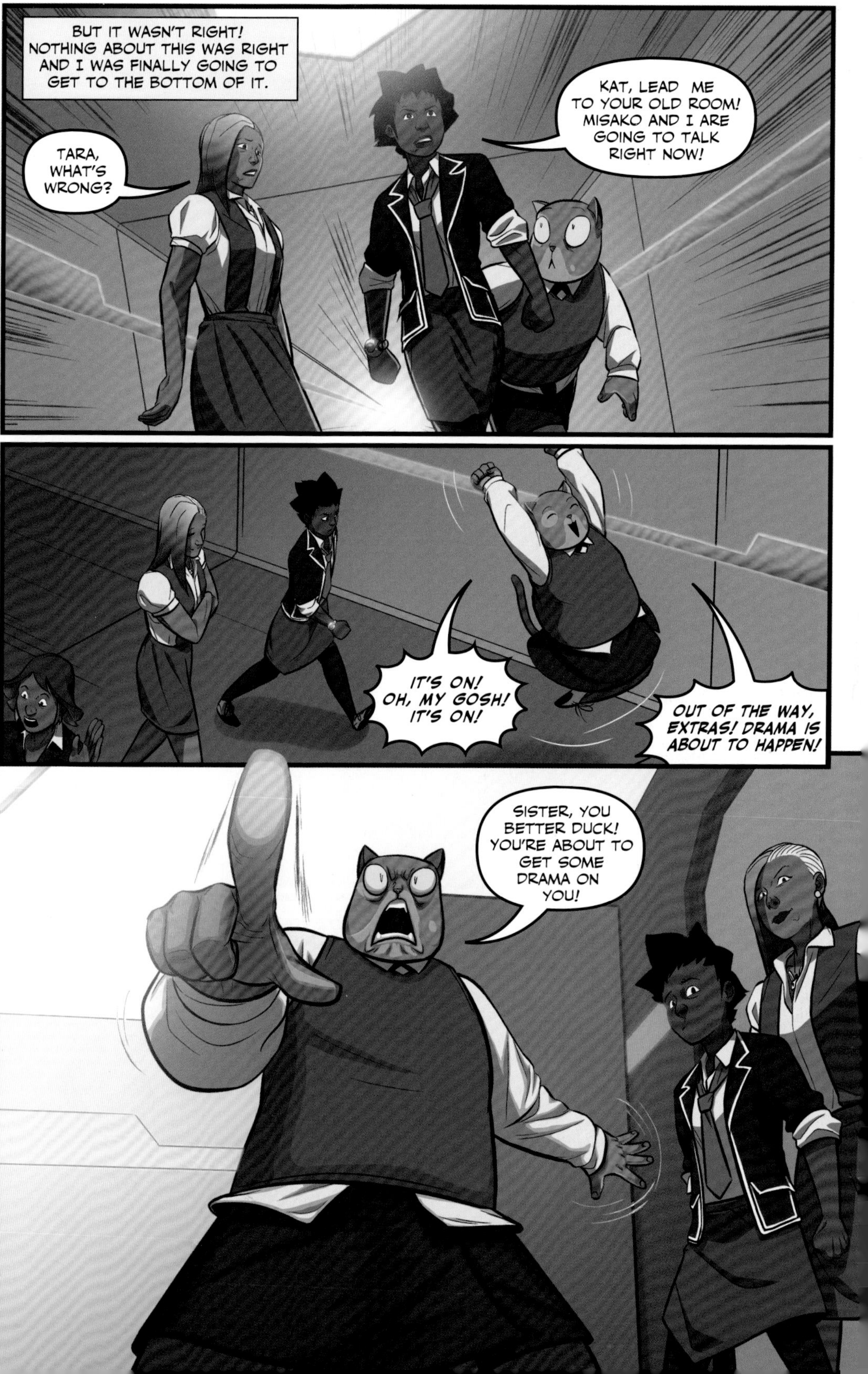
BUT IT WASN'T RIGHT! NOTHING ABOUT THIS WAS RIGHT AND I WAS FINALLY GOING TO GET TO THE BOTTOM OF IT.
TARA, WHAT'S WRONG?
KAT, LEAD ME TO YOUR OLD ROOM! MISAKO AND I ARE GOING TO TALK RIGHT NOW!
IT'S ON! OH, MY GOSH! IT'S ON!
OUT OF THE WAY, EXTRAS! DRAMA IS ABOUT TO HAPPEN!
SISTER, YOU BETTER DUCK! YOU'RE ABOUT TO GET SOME DRAMA ON YOU!

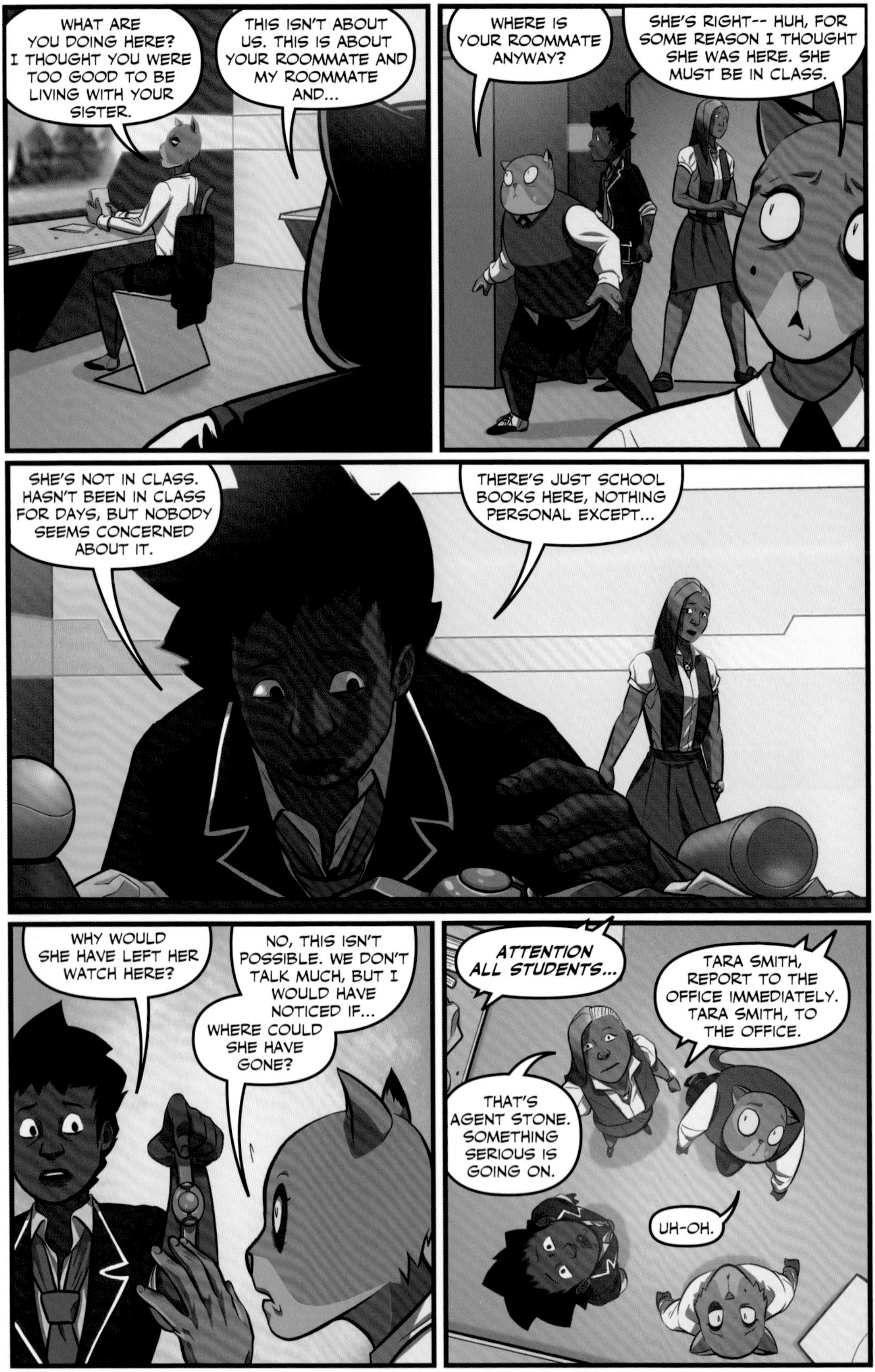
WHAT ARE YOU DOING HERE? I THOUGHT YOU WERE TOO GOOD TO BE LIVING WITH YOUR SISTER.
THIS ISN'T ABOUT US. THIS IS ABOUT YOUR ROOMMATE AND MY ROOMMATE AND...
WHERE IS YOUR ROOMMATE ANYWAY?
SHE'S RIGHT-- HUH, FOR SOME REASON I THOUGHT SHE WAS HERE. SHE MUST BE IN CLASS.
SHE'S NOT IN CLASS. HASN'T BEEN IN CLASS FOR DAYS, BUT NOBODY SEEMS CONCERNED ABOUT IT.
THERE'S JUST SCHOOL BOOKS HERE, NOTHING PERSONAL EXCEPT...
WHY WOULD SHE HAVE LEFT HER WATCH HERE?
NO, THIS ISN'T POSSIBLE. WE DON'T TALK MUCH, BUT I WOULD HAVE NOTICED IF...
WHERE COULD SHE HAVE GONE?
ATTENTION ALL STUDENTS...
TARA SMITH, REPORT TO THE OFFICE IMMEDIATELY. TARA SMITH, TO THE OFFICE.
THAT'S AGENT STONE. SOMETHING SERIOUS IS GOING ON.
UH-OH.

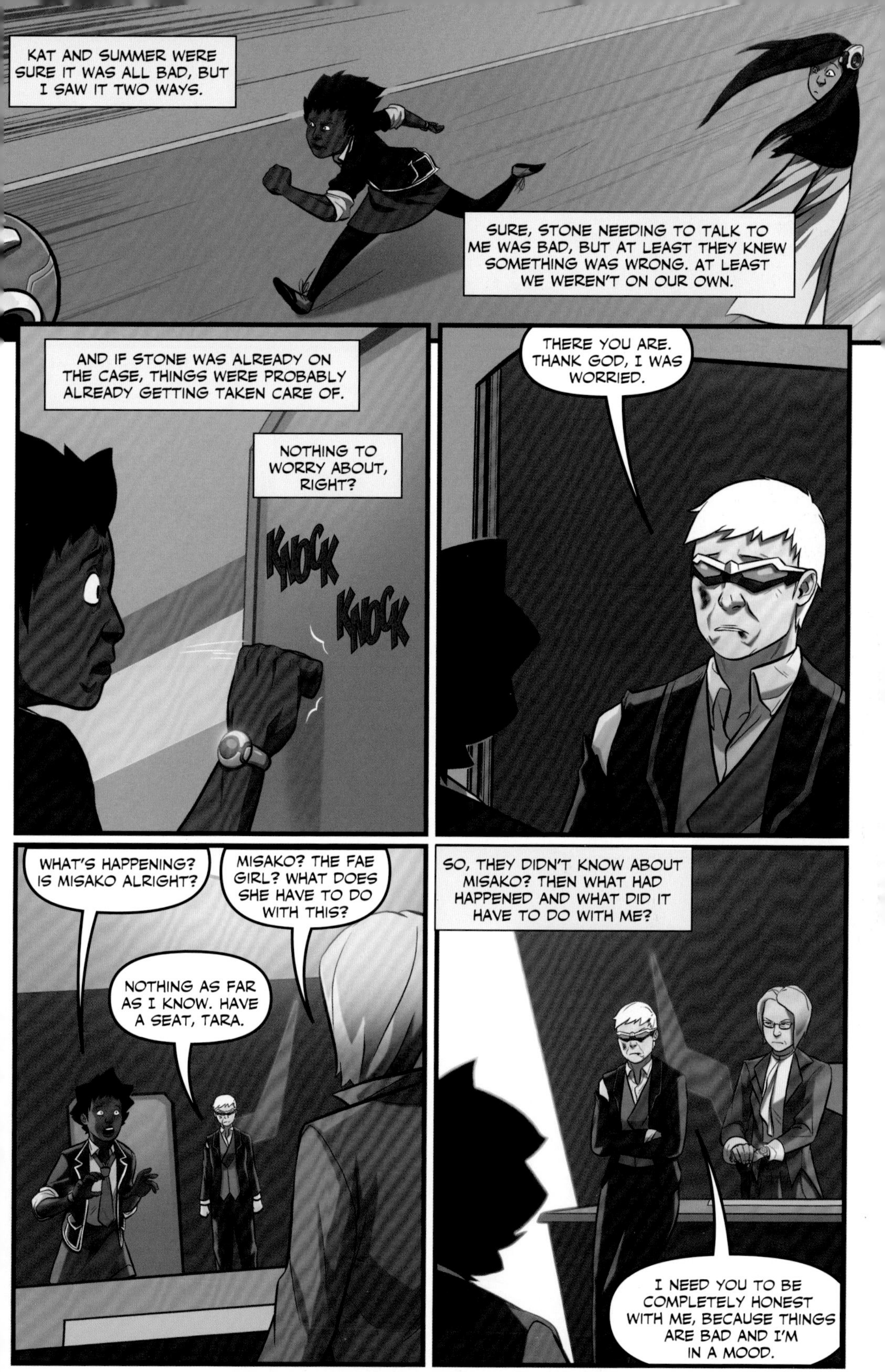
KAT AND SUMMER WERE SURE IT WAS ALL BAD, BUT I SAW IT TWO WAYS.
SURE, STONE NEEDING TO TALK TO ME WAS BAD, BUT AT LEAST THEY KNEW SOMETHING WAS WRONG. AT LEAST WE WEREN'T ON OUR OWN.
AND IF STONE WAS ALREADY ON THE CASE, THINGS WERE PROBABLY ALREADY GETTING TAKEN CARE OF.
NOTHING TO WORRY ABOUT, RIGHT?
KNOCK
KNOCK
THERE YOU ARE. THANK GOD, I WAS WORRIED.
WHAT'S HAPPENING? IS MISAKO ALRIGHT?
MISAKO? THE FAE GIRL? WHAT DOES SHE HAVE TO DO WITH THIS?
NOTHING AS FAR AS I KNOW. HAVE A SEAT, TARA.
SO, THEY DIDN'T KNOW ABOUT MISAKO? THEN WHAT HAD HAPPENED AND WHAT DID IT HAVE TO DO WITH ME?
I NEED YOU TO BE COMPLETELY HONEST WITH ME, BECAUSE THINGS ARE BAD AND I'M IN A MOOD.

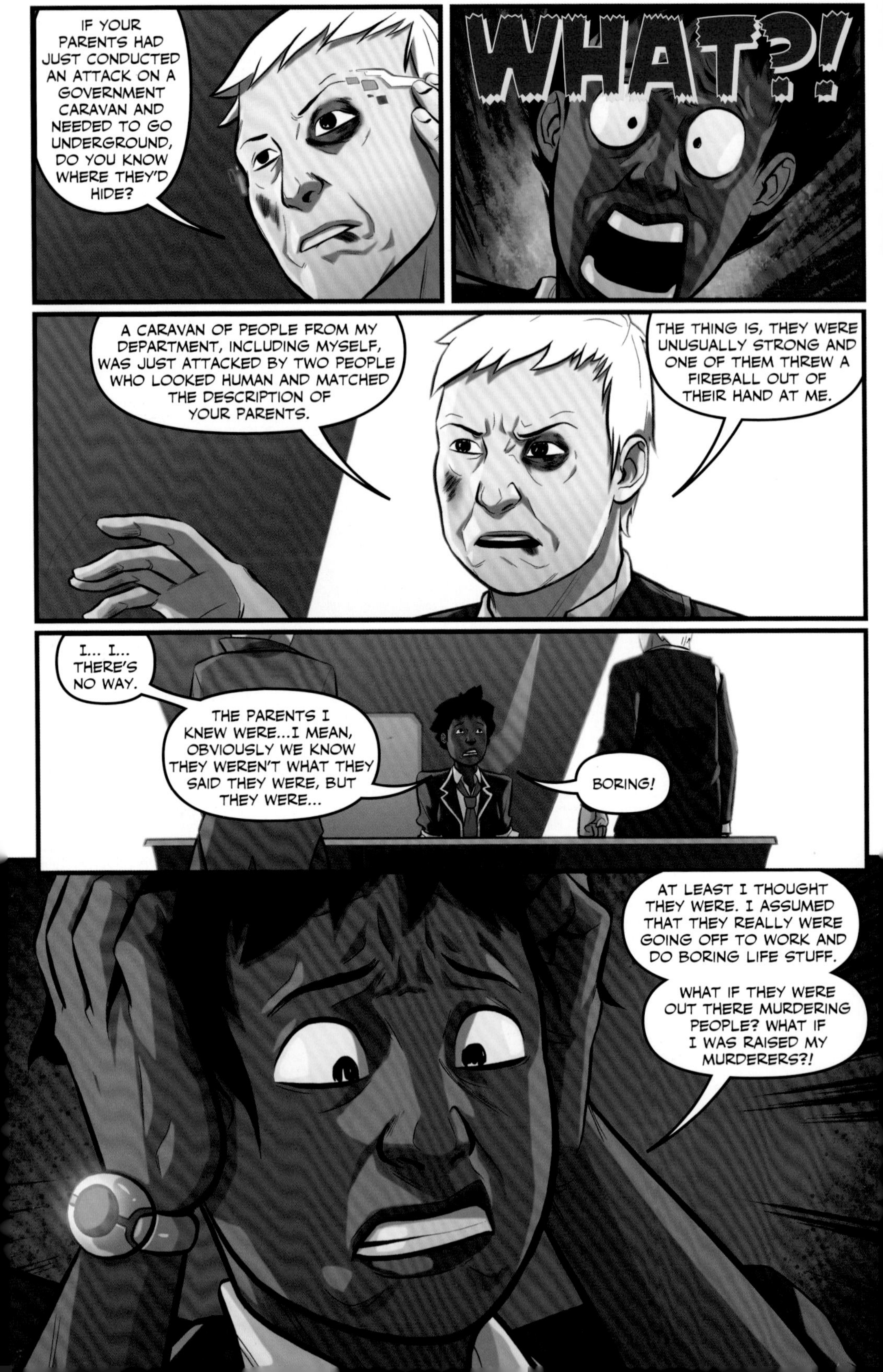
IF YOUR PARENTS HAD JUST CONDUCTED AN ATTACK ON A GOVERNMENT CARAVAN AND NEEDED TO GO UNDERGROUND, DO YOU KNOW WHERE THEY'D HIDE?
WHAT?!
A CARAVAN OF PEOPLE FROM MY DEPARTMENT, INCLUDING MYSELF, WAS JUST ATTACKED BY TWO PEOPLE WHO LOOKED HUMAN AND MATCHED THE DESCRIPTION OF YOUR PARENTS.
THE THING IS, THEY WERE UNUSUALLY STRONG AND ONE OF THEM THREW A FIREBALL OUT OF THEIR HAND AT ME.
I... I... THERE'S NO WAY.
THE PARENTS I KNEW WERE...I MEAN, OBVIOUSLY WE KNOW THEY WEREN'T WHAT THEY SAID THEY WERE, BUT THEY WERE...
BORING!
AT LEAST I THOUGHT THEY WERE. I ASSUMED THAT THEY REALLY WERE GOING OFF TO WORK AND DO BORING LIFE STUFF.
WHAT IF THEY WERE OUT THERE MURDERING PEOPLE? WHAT IF I WAS RAISED MY MURDERERS?!

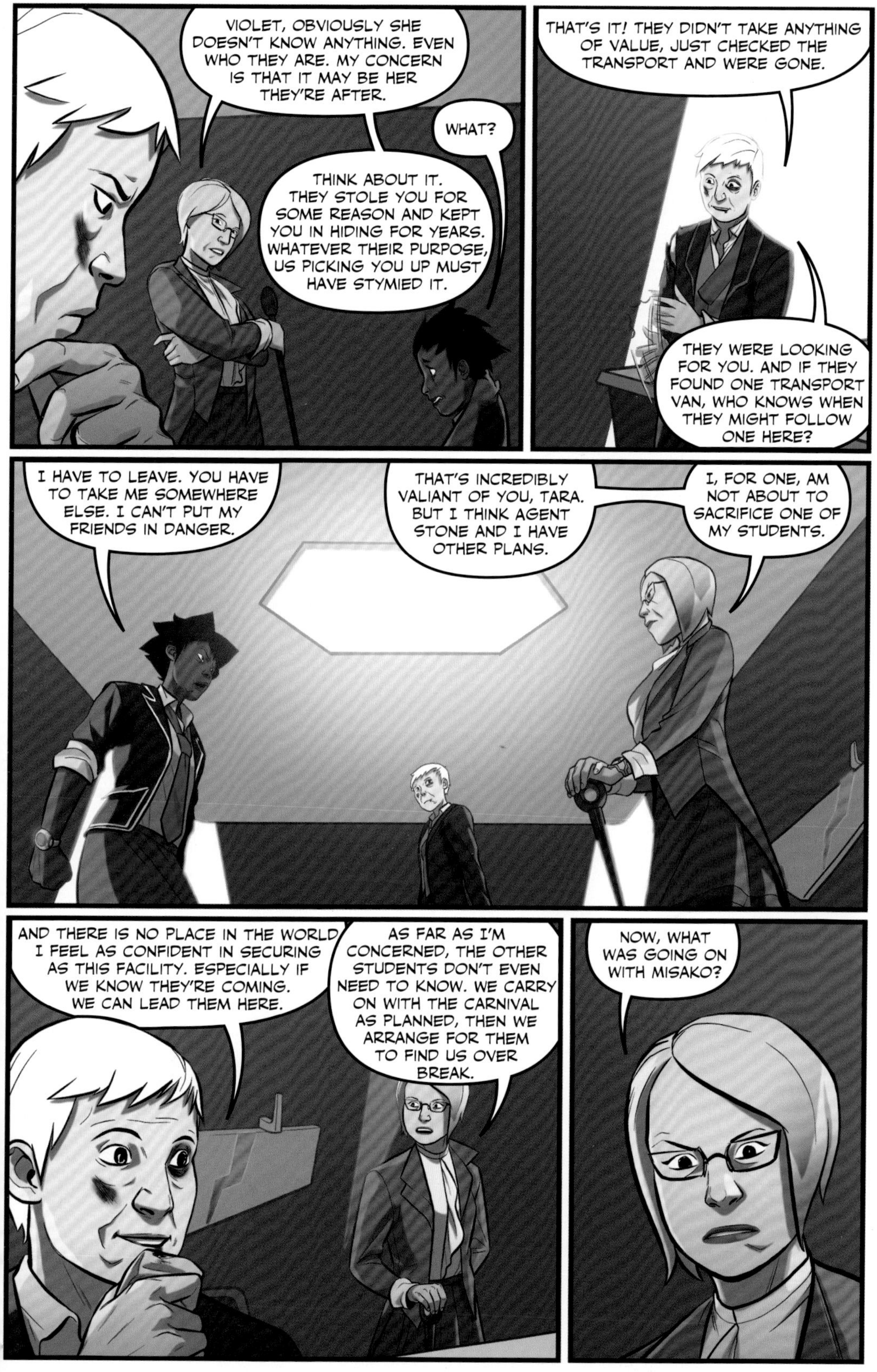
VIOLET, OBVIOUSLY SHE DOESN'T KNOW ANYTHING. EVEN WHO THEY ARE. MY CONCERN IS THAT IT MAY BE HER THEY'RE AFTER.
WHAT?
THINK ABOUT IT. THEY STOLE YOU FOR SOME REASON AND KEPT YOU IN HIDING FOR YEARS. WHATEVER THEIR PURPOSE, US PICKING YOU UP MUST HAVE STYMIED IT.
THAT'S IT! THEY DIDN'T TAKE ANYTHING OF VALUE, JUST CHECKED THE TRANSPORT AND WERE GONE.
THEY WERE LOOKING FOR YOU. AND IF THEY FOUND ONE TRANSPORT VAN, WHO KNOWS WHEN THEY MIGHT FOLLOW ONE HERE?
I HAVE TO LEAVE. YOU HAVE TO TAKE ME SOMEWHERE ELSE. I CAN'T PUT MY FRIENDS IN DANGER.
THAT'S INCREDIBLY VALIANT OF YOU, TARA. BUT I THINK AGENT STONE AND I HAVE OTHER PLANS.
I, FOR ONE, AM NOT ABOUT TO SACRIFICE ONE OF MY STUDENTS.
AND THERE IS NO PLACE IN THE WORLD I FEEL AS CONFIDENT IN SECURING AS THIS FACILITY. ESPECIALLY IF WE KNOW THEY'RE COMING. WE CAN LEAD THEM HERE.
AS FAR AS I'M CONCERNED, THE OTHER STUDENTS DON'T EVEN NEED TO KNOW. WE CARRY ON WITH THE CARNIVAL AS PLANNED, THEN WE ARRANGE FOR THEM TO FIND US OVER BREAK.
NOW, WHAT WAS GOING ON WITH MISAKO?

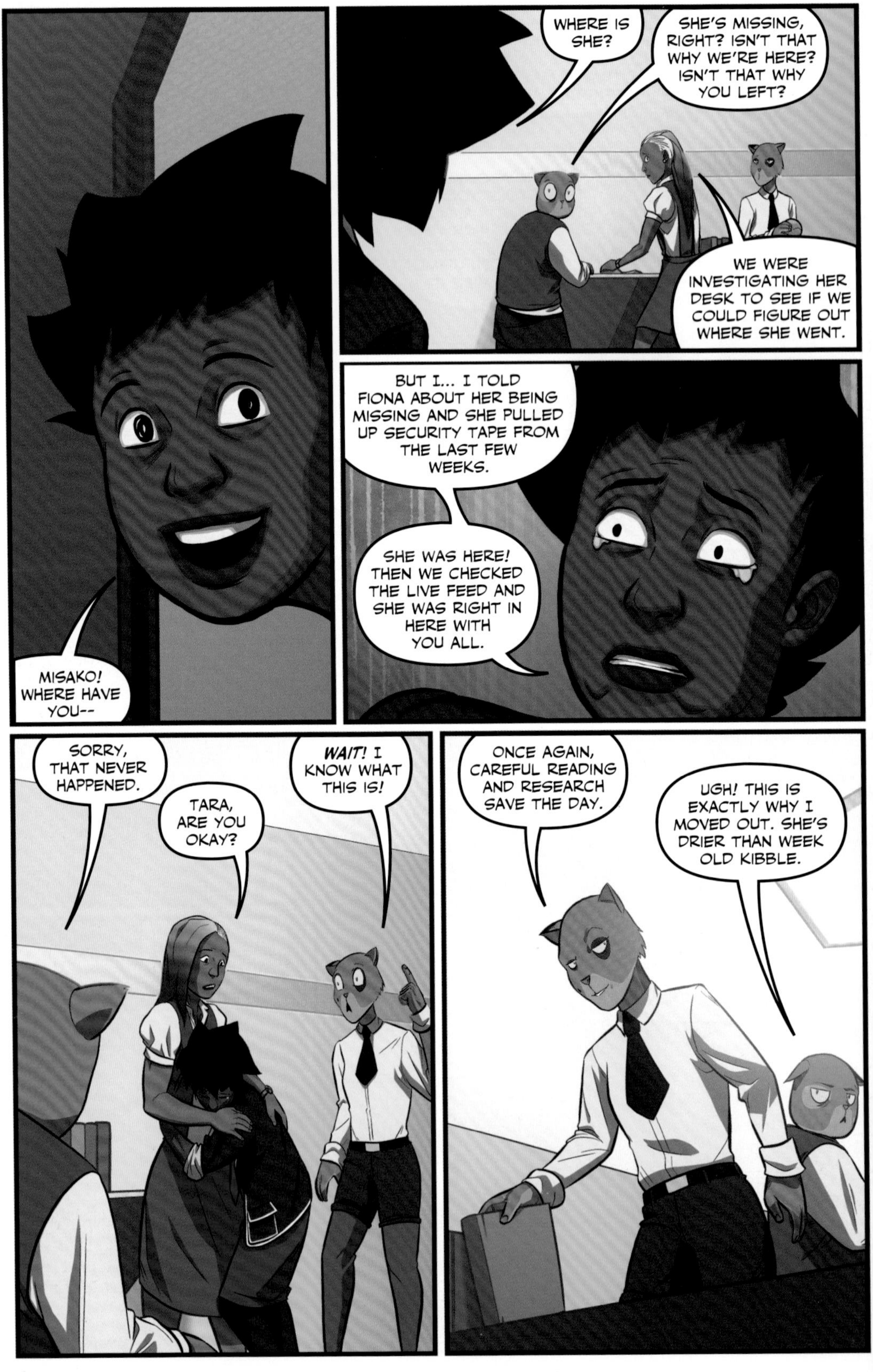
MISAKO! WHERE HAVE YOU--
WHERE IS SHE?
SHE'S MISSING, RIGHT? ISN'T THAT WHY WE'RE HERE? ISN'T THAT WHY YOU LEFT?
WE WERE INVESTIGATING HER DESK TO SEE IF WE COULD FIGURE OUT WHERE SHE WENT.
BUT I... I TOLD FIONA ABOUT HER BEING MISSING AND SHE PULLED UP SECURITY TAPE FROM THE LAST FEW WEEKS.
SHE WAS HERE! THEN WE CHECKED THE LIVE FEED AND SHE WAS RIGHT IN HERE WITH YOU ALL.
SORRY, THAT NEVER HAPPENED.
TARA, ARE YOU OKAY?
WAIT! I KNOW WHAT THIS IS!
ONCE AGAIN, CAREFUL READING AND RESEARCH SAVE THE DAY.
UGH! THIS IS EXACTLY WHY I MOVED OUT. SHE'S DRIER THAN WEEK OLD KIBBLE.

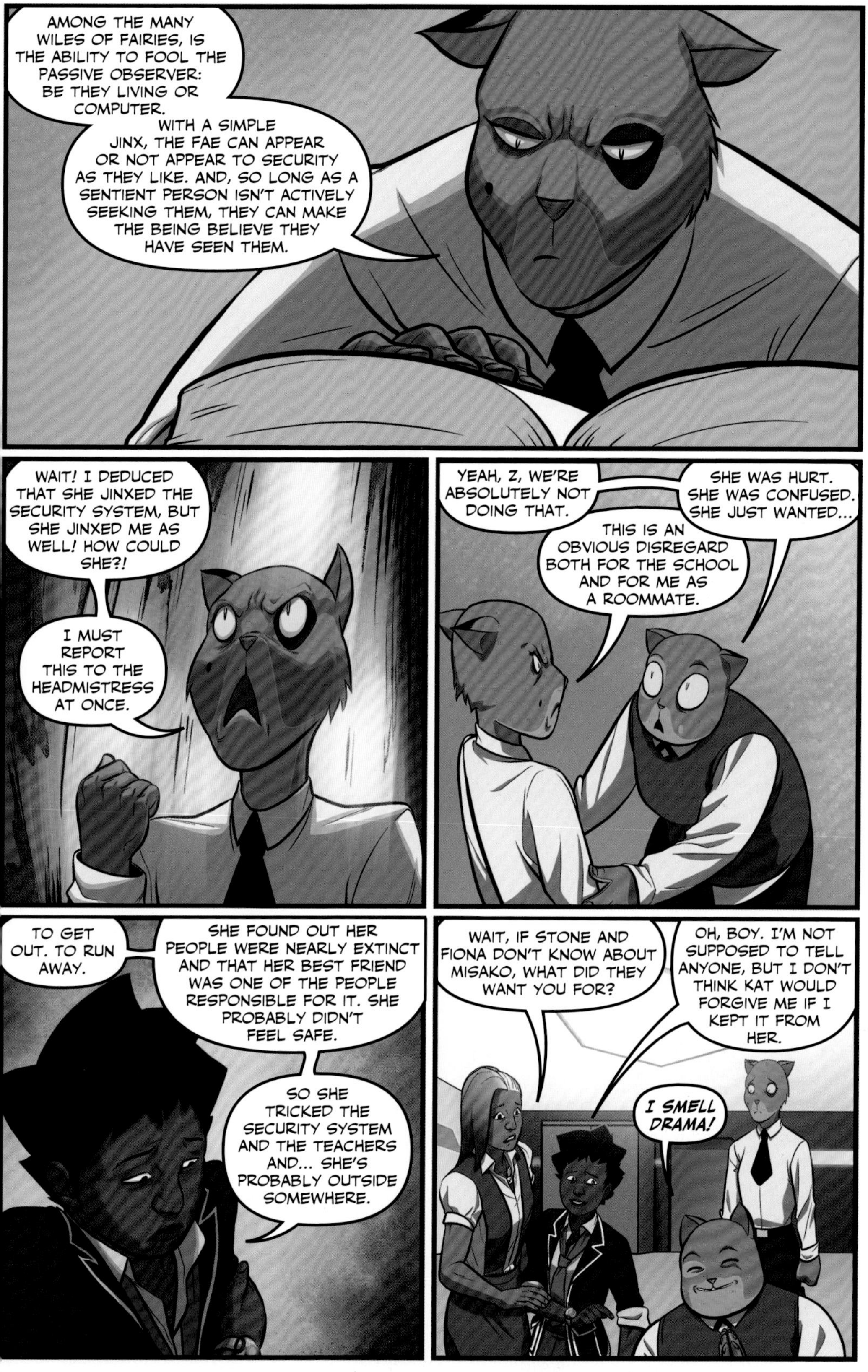
AMONG THE MANY WILES OF FAIRIES, IS THE ABILITY TO FOOL THE PASSIVE OBSERVER: BE THEY LIVING OR COMPUTER.
WITH A SIMPLE JINX, THE FAE CAN APPEAR OR NOT APPEAR TO SECURITY AS THEY LIKE. AND, SO LONG AS A SENTIENT PERSON ISN'T ACTIVELY SEEKING THEM, THEY CAN MAKE THE BEING BELIEVE THEY HAVE SEEN THEM.
WAIT! I DEDUCED THAT SHE JINXED THE SECURITY SYSTEM, BUT SHE JINXED ME AS WELL! HOW COULD SHE?!
I MUST REPORT THIS TO THE HEADMISTRESS AT ONCE.
YEAH, Z, WE'RE ABSOLUTELY NOT DOING THAT.
THIS IS AN OBVIOUS DISREGARD BOTH FOR THE SCHOOL AND FOR ME AS A ROOMMATE.
SHE WAS HURT. SHE WAS CONFUSED. SHE JUST WANTED...
TO GET OUT. TO RUN AWAY.
SHE FOUND OUT HER PEOPLE WERE NEARLY EXTINCT AND THAT HER BEST FRIEND WAS ONE OF THE PEOPLE RESPONSIBLE FOR IT. SHE PROBABLY DIDN'T FEEL SAFE.
SO SHE TRICKED THE SECURITY SYSTEM AND THE TEACHERS AND... SHE'S PROBABLY OUTSIDE SOMEWHERE.
WAIT, IF STONE AND FIONA DON'T KNOW ABOUT MISAKO, WHAT DID THEY WANT YOU FOR?
OH, BOY. I'M NOT SUPPOSED TO TELL ANYONE, BUT I DON'T THINK KAT WOULD FORGIVE ME IF I KEPT IT FROM HER.
I SMELL DRAMA!

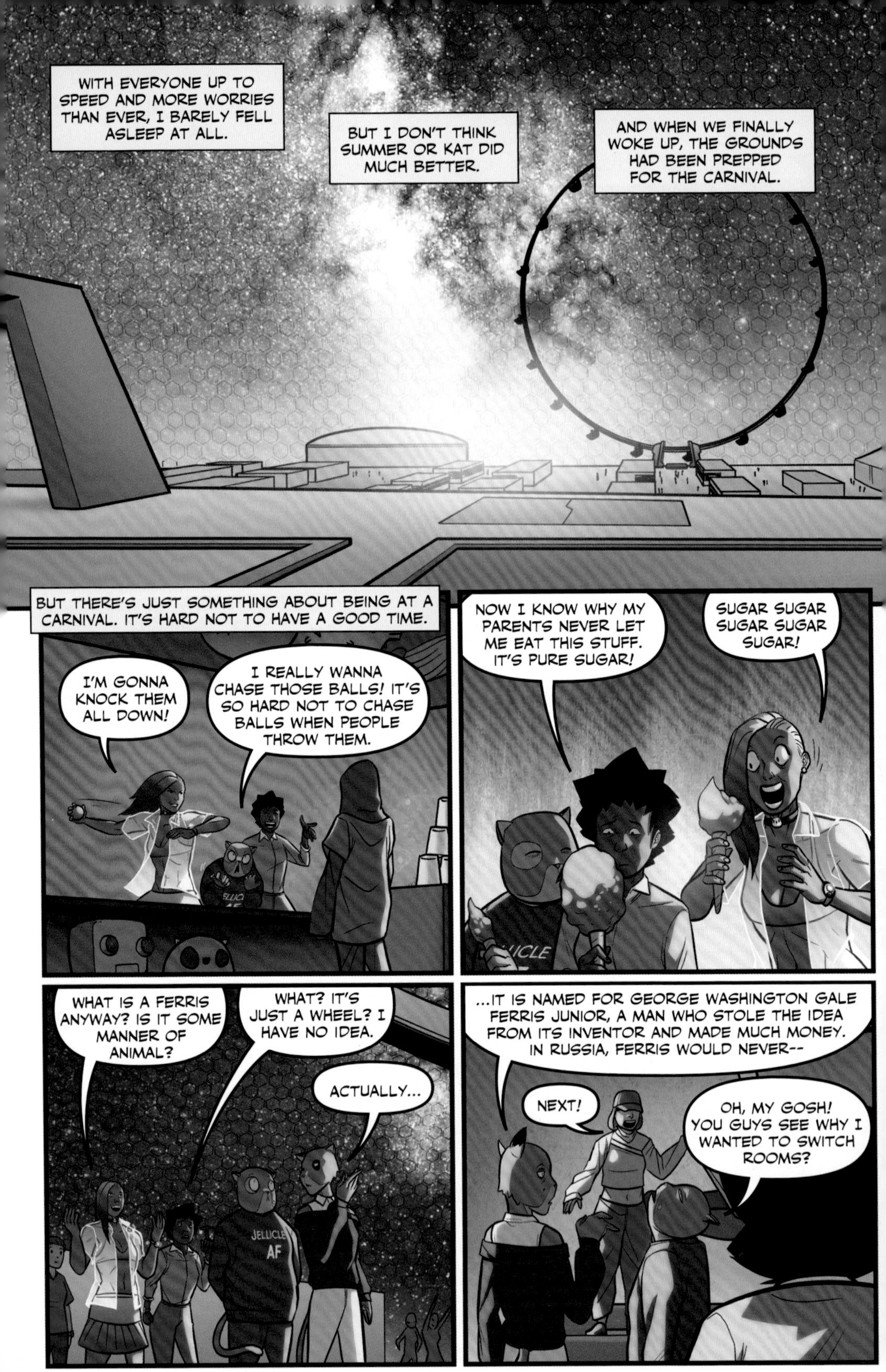
WITH EVERYONE UP TO SPEED AND MORE WORRIES THAN EVER, I BARELY FELL ASLEEP AT ALL.
BUT I DON'T THINK SUMMER OR KAT DID MUCH BETTER.
AND WHEN WE FINALLY WOKE UP, THE GROUNDS HAD BEEN PREPPED FOR THE CARNIVAL.
BUT THERE'S JUST SOMETHING ABOUT BEING AT A CARNIVAL. IT'S HARD NOT TO HAVE A GOOD TIME.
I'M GONNA KNOCK THEM ALL DOWN!
I REALLY WANNA CHASE THOSE BALLS! IT'S SO HARD NOT TO CHASE BALLS WHEN PEOPLE THROW THEM.
NOW I KNOW WHY MY PARENTS NEVER LET ME EAT THIS STUFF. IT'S PURE SUGAR!
SUGAR SUGAR SUGAR SUGAR SUGAR!
WHAT IS A FERRIS ANYWAY? IS IT SOME MANNER OF ANIMAL?
WHAT? IT'S JUST A WHEEL? I HAVE NO IDEA.
ACTUALLY...
JELLICLE AF
...IT IS NAMED FOR GEORGE WASHINGTON GALE FERRIS JUNIOR, A MAN WHO STOLE THE IDEA FROM ITS INVENTOR AND MADE MUCH MONEY. IN RUSSIA, FERRIS WOULD NEVER--
NEXT!
OH, MY GOSH! YOU GUYS SEE WHY I WANTED TO SWITCH ROOMS?

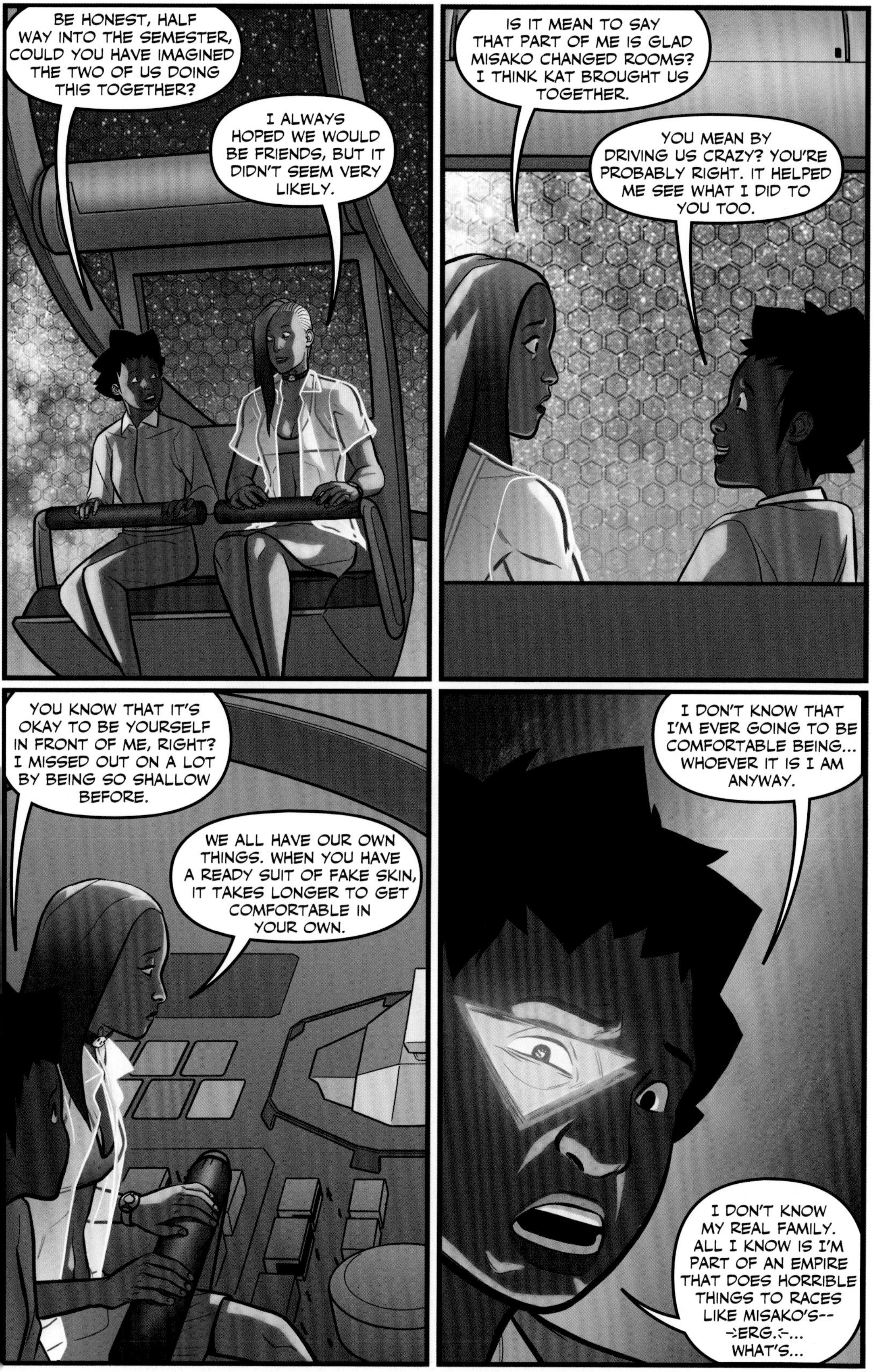
BE HONEST, HALF WAY INTO THE SEMESTER, COULD YOU HAVE IMAGINED THE TWO OF US DOING THIS TOGETHER?
I ALWAYS HOPED WE WOULD BE FRIENDS, BUT IT DIDN'T SEEM VERY LIKELY.
IS IT MEAN TO SAY THAT PART OF ME IS GLAD MISAKO CHANGED ROOMS? I THINK KAT BROUGHT US TOGETHER.
YOU MEAN BY DRIVING US CRAZY? YOU'RE PROBABLY RIGHT. IT HELPED ME SEE WHAT I DID TO YOU TOO.
YOU KNOW THAT IT'S OKAY TO BE YOURSELF IN FRONT OF ME, RIGHT? I MISSED OUT ON A LOT BY BEING SO SHALLOW BEFORE.
WE ALL HAVE OUR OWN THINGS. WHEN YOU HAVE A READY SUIT OF FAKE SKIN, IT TAKES LONGER TO GET COMFORTABLE IN YOUR OWN.
I DON'T KNOW THAT I'M EVER GOING TO BE COMFORTABLE BEING... WHOEVER IT IS I AM ANYWAY.
I DON'T KNOW MY REAL FAMILY. ALL I KNOW IS I'M PART OF AN EMPIRE THAT DOES HORRIBLE THINGS TO RACES LIKE MISAKO'S-- ›ERG.‹... WHAT'S...

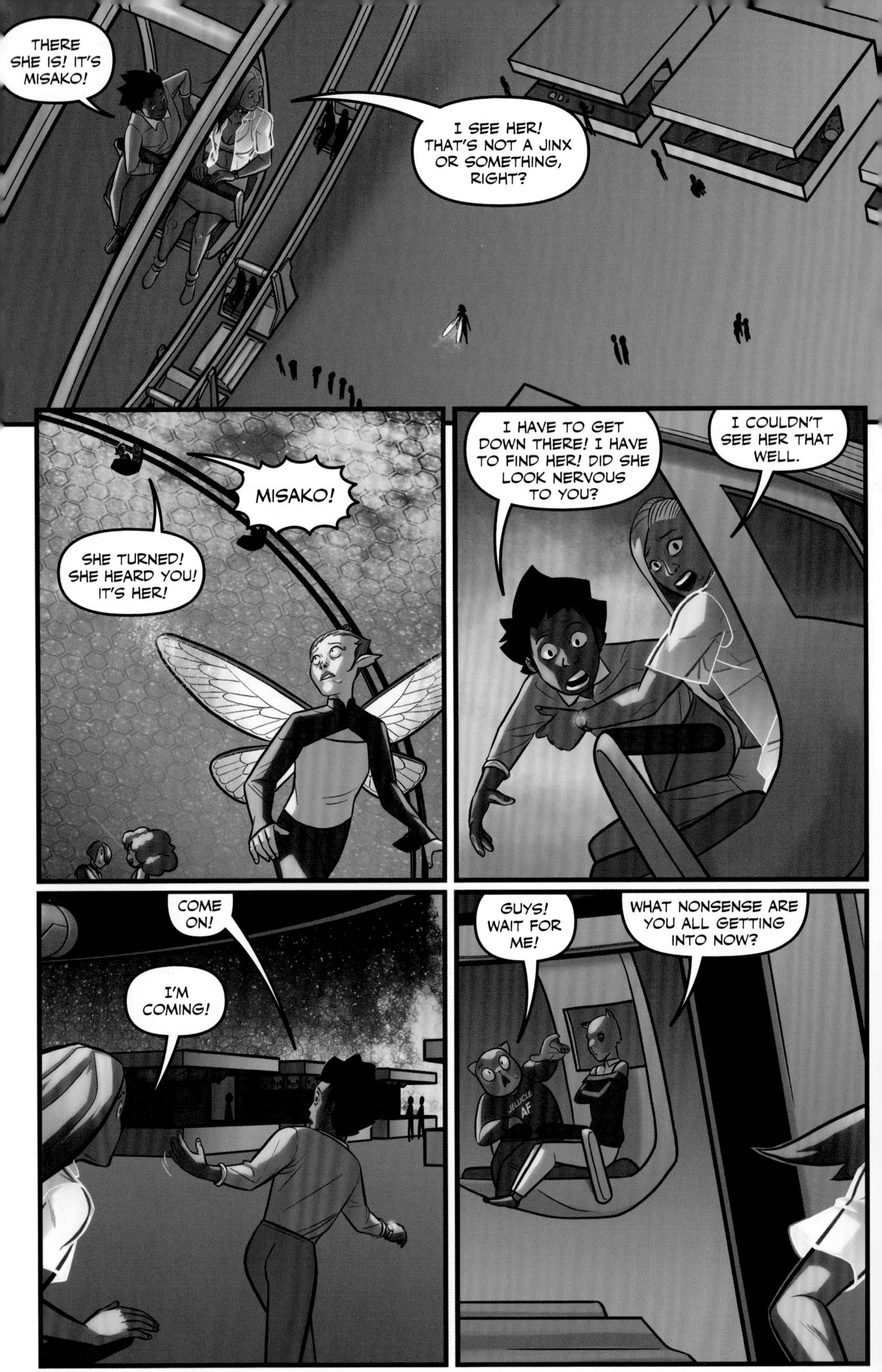
THERE SHE IS! IT'S MISAKO!
I SEE HER! THAT'S NOT A JINX OR SOMETHING, RIGHT?
MISAKO!
SHE TURNED! SHE HEARD YOU! IT'S HER!
I HAVE TO GET DOWN THERE! I HAVE TO FIND HER! DID SHE LOOK NERVOUS TO YOU?
I COULDN'T SEE HER THAT WELL.
COME ON!
I'M COMING!
GUYS! WAIT FOR ME!
WHAT NONSENSE ARE YOU ALL GETTING INTO NOW?
JELLICLE AF

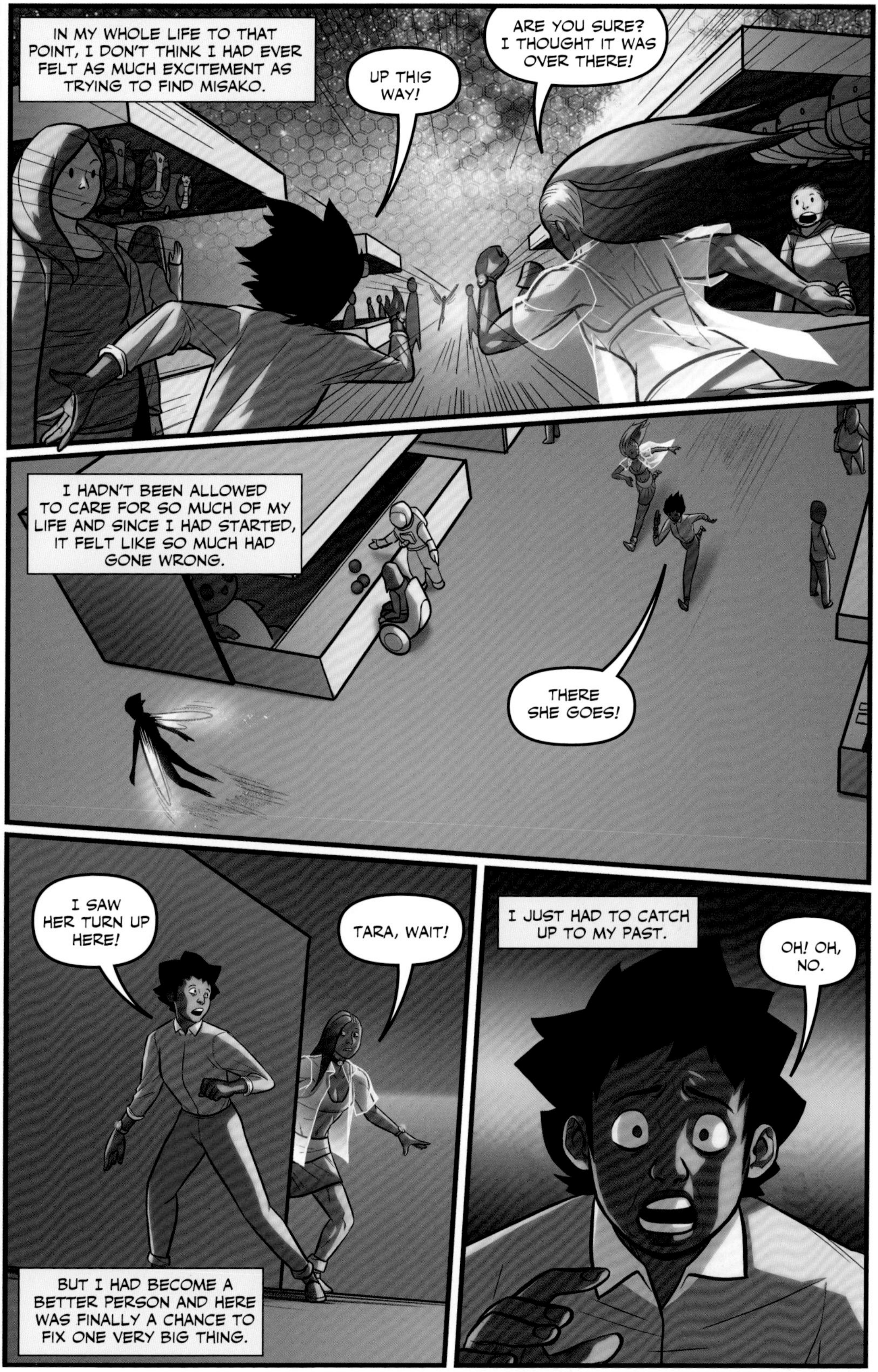
IN MY WHOLE LIFE TO THAT POINT, I DON'T THINK I HAD EVER FELT AS MUCH EXCITEMENT AS TRYING TO FIND MISAKO.
UP THIS WAY!
ARE YOU SURE? I THOUGHT IT WAS OVER THERE!
I HADN'T BEEN ALLOWED TO CARE FOR SO MUCH OF MY LIFE AND SINCE I HAD STARTED, IT FELT LIKE SO MUCH HAD GONE WRONG.
THERE SHE GOES!
I SAW HER TURN UP HERE!
TARA, WAIT!
BUT I HAD BECOME A BETTER PERSON AND HERE WAS FINALLY A CHANCE TO FIX ONE VERY BIG THING.
I JUST HAD TO CATCH UP TO MY PAST.
OH! OH, NO.

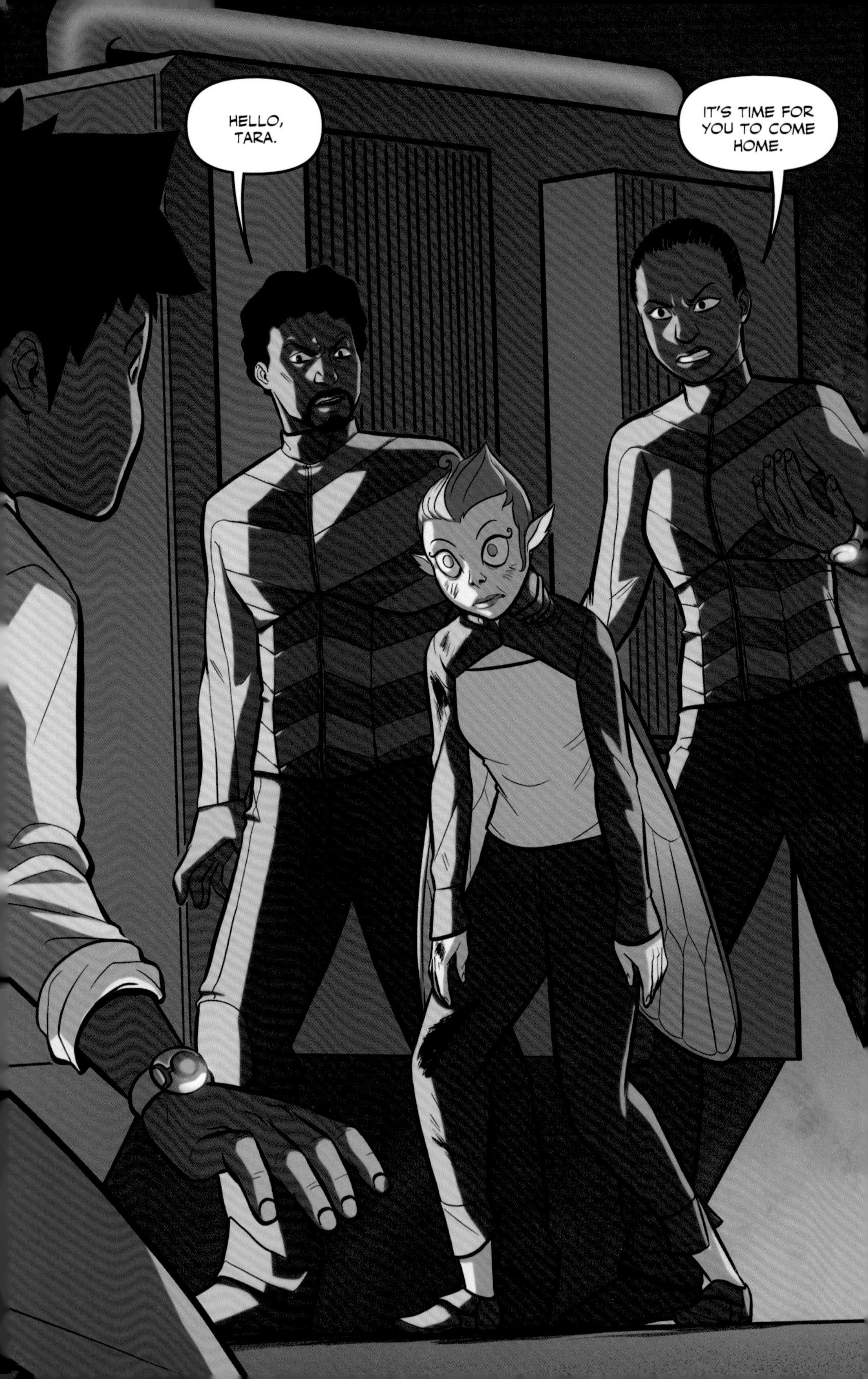
HELLO, TARA.
IT'S TIME FOR YOU TO COME HOME.

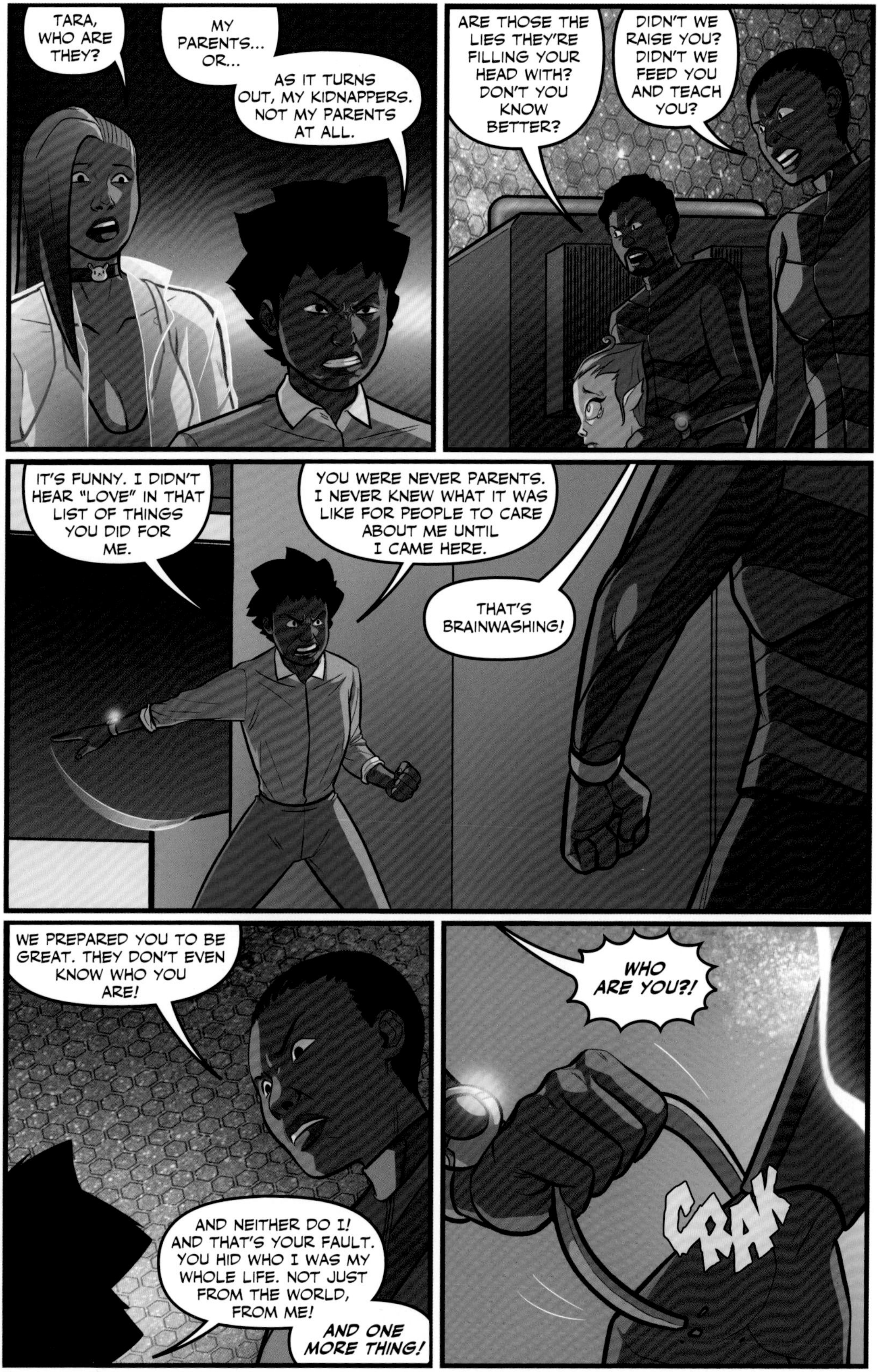
TARA, WHO ARE THEY?
MY PARENTS... OR...
AS IT TURNS OUT, MY KIDNAPPERS. NOT MY PARENTS AT ALL.
ARE THOSE THE LIES THEY'RE FILLING YOUR HEAD WITH? DON'T YOU KNOW BETTER?
DIDN'T WE RAISE YOU? DIDN'T WE FEED YOU AND TEACH YOU?
IT'S FUNNY. I DIDN'T HEAR "LOVE" IN THAT LIST OF THINGS YOU DID FOR ME.
YOU WERE NEVER PARENTS. I NEVER KNEW WHAT IT WAS LIKE FOR PEOPLE TO CARE ABOUT ME UNTIL I CAME HERE.
THAT'S BRAINWASHING!
WE PREPARED YOU TO BE GREAT. THEY DON'T EVEN KNOW WHO YOU ARE!
AND NEITHER DO I! AND THAT'S YOUR FAULT. YOU HID WHO I WAS MY WHOLE LIFE. NOT JUST FROM THE WORLD, FROM ME!
AND ONE MORE THING!
WHO ARE YOU?!
CRAK

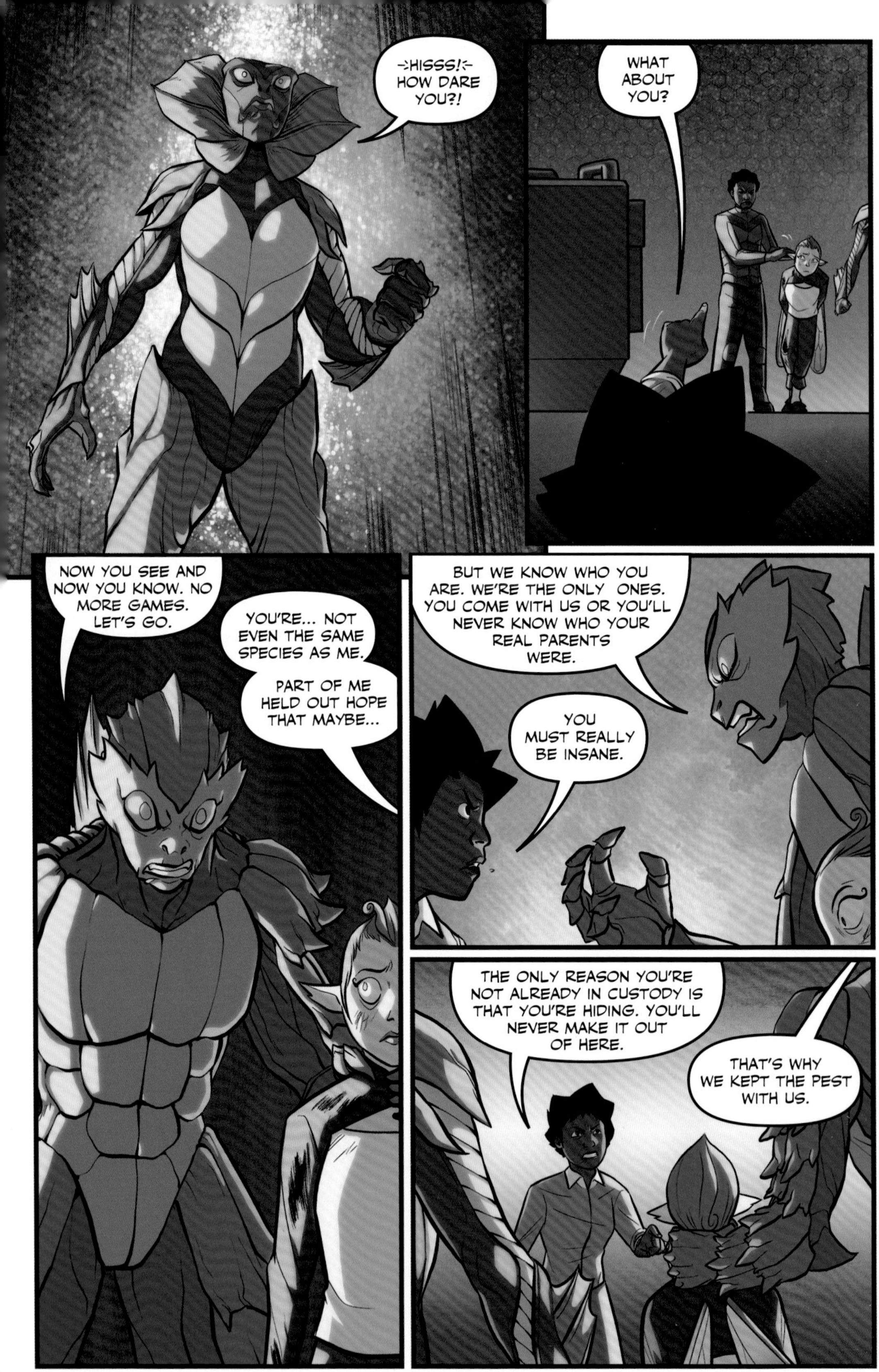

-HISSS!- HOW DARE YOU?!
WHAT ABOUT YOU?
NOW YOU SEE AND NOW YOU KNOW. NO MORE GAMES. LET'S GO.
YOU'RE... NOT EVEN THE SAME SPECIES AS ME.
PART OF ME HELD OUT HOPE THAT MAYBE...
BUT WE KNOW WHO YOU ARE. WE'RE THE ONLY ONES. YOU COME WITH US OR YOU'LL NEVER KNOW WHO YOUR REAL PARENTS WERE.
YOU MUST REALLY BE INSANE.
THE ONLY REASON YOU'RE NOT ALREADY IN CUSTODY IS THAT YOU'RE HIDING. YOU'LL NEVER MAKE IT OUT OF HERE.
THAT'S WHY WE KEPT THE PEST WITH US.

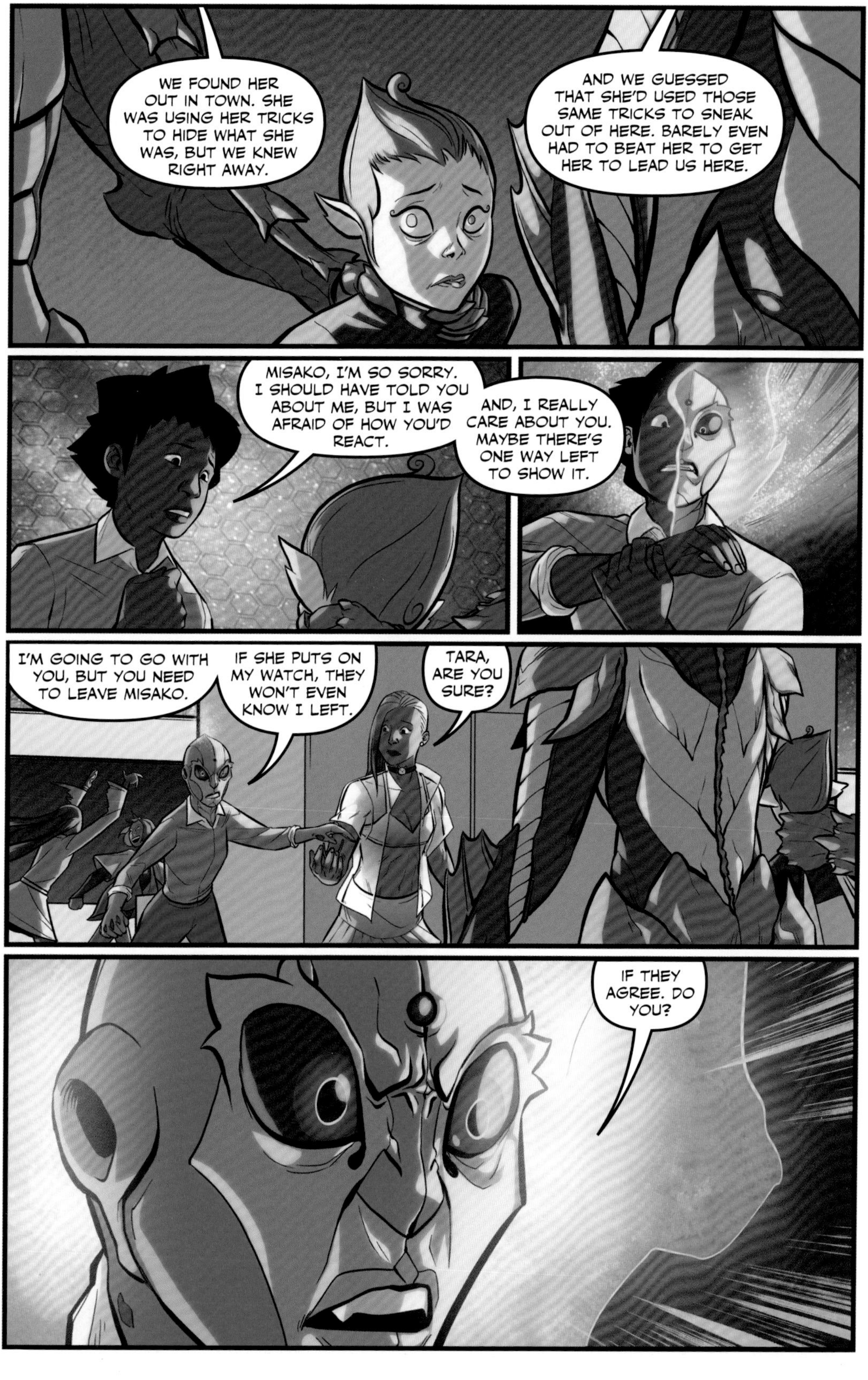
WE FOUND HER OUT IN TOWN. SHE WAS USING HER TRICKS TO HIDE WHAT SHE WAS, BUT WE KNEW RIGHT AWAY.
AND WE GUESSED THAT SHE'D USED THOSE SAME TRICKS TO SNEAK OUT OF HERE. BARELY EVEN HAD TO BEAT HER TO GET HER TO LEAD US HERE.
MISAKO, I'M SO SORRY. I SHOULD HAVE TOLD YOU ABOUT ME, BUT I WAS AFRAID OF HOW YOU'D REACT.
AND, I REALLY CARE ABOUT YOU. MAYBE THERE'S ONE WAY LEFT TO SHOW IT.
I'M GOING TO GO WITH YOU, BUT YOU NEED TO LEAVE MISAKO.
IF SHE PUTS ON MY WATCH, THEY WON'T EVEN KNOW I LEFT.
TARA, ARE YOU SURE?
IF THEY AGREE. DO YOU?

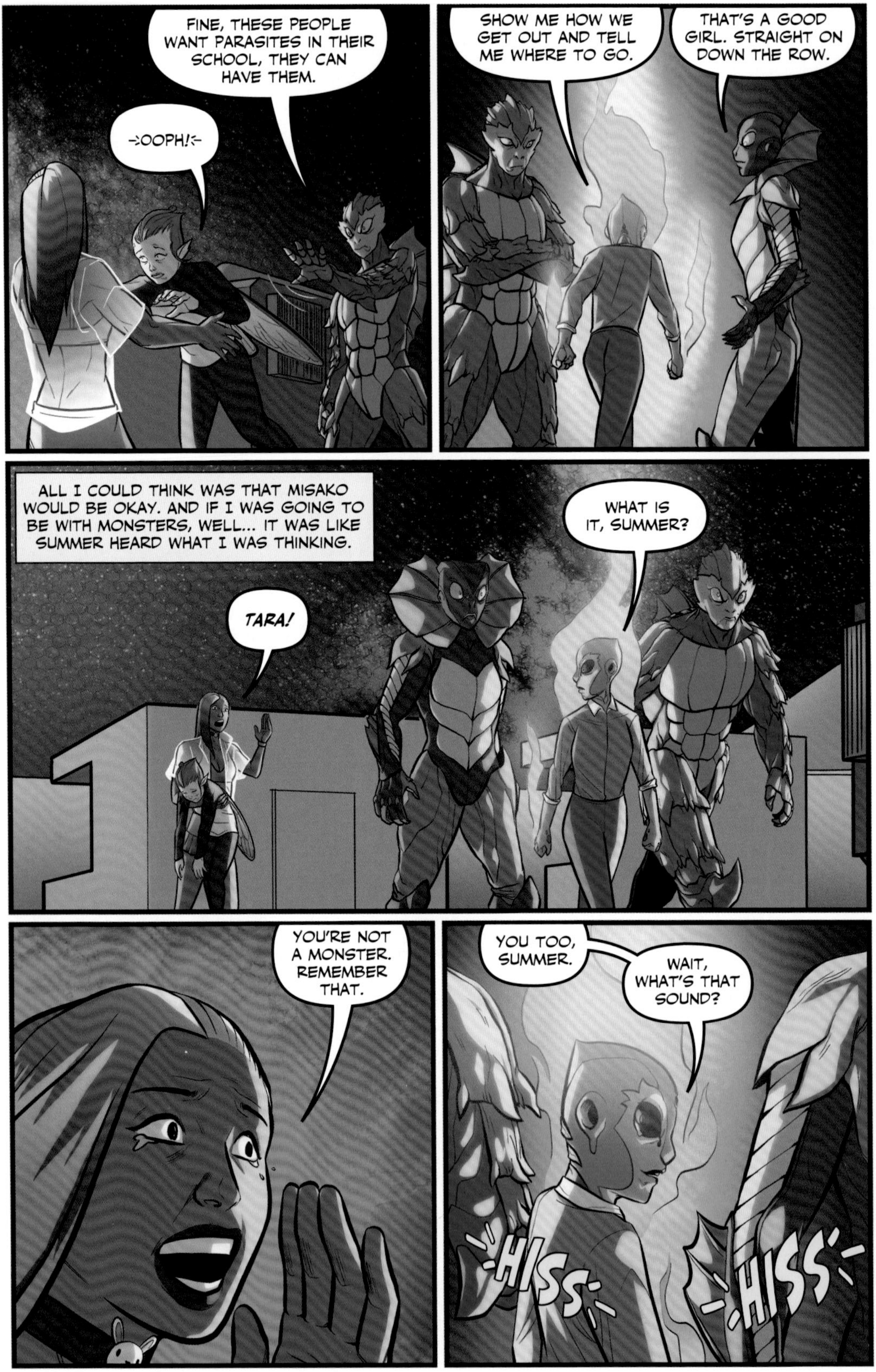
FINE, THESE PEOPLE WANT PARASITES IN THEIR SCHOOL, THEY CAN HAVE THEM.
-OOPH!-
SHOW ME HOW WE GET OUT AND TELL ME WHERE TO GO.
THAT'S A GOOD GIRL. STRAIGHT ON DOWN THE ROW.
ALL I COULD THINK WAS THAT MISAKO WOULD BE OKAY. AND IF I WAS GOING TO BE WITH MONSTERS, WELL... IT WAS LIKE SUMMER HEARD WHAT I WAS THINKING.
TARA!
WHAT IS IT, SUMMER?
YOU'RE NOT A MONSTER. REMEMBER THAT.
YOU TOO, SUMMER.
WAIT, WHAT'S THAT SOUND?
HISS
HISS

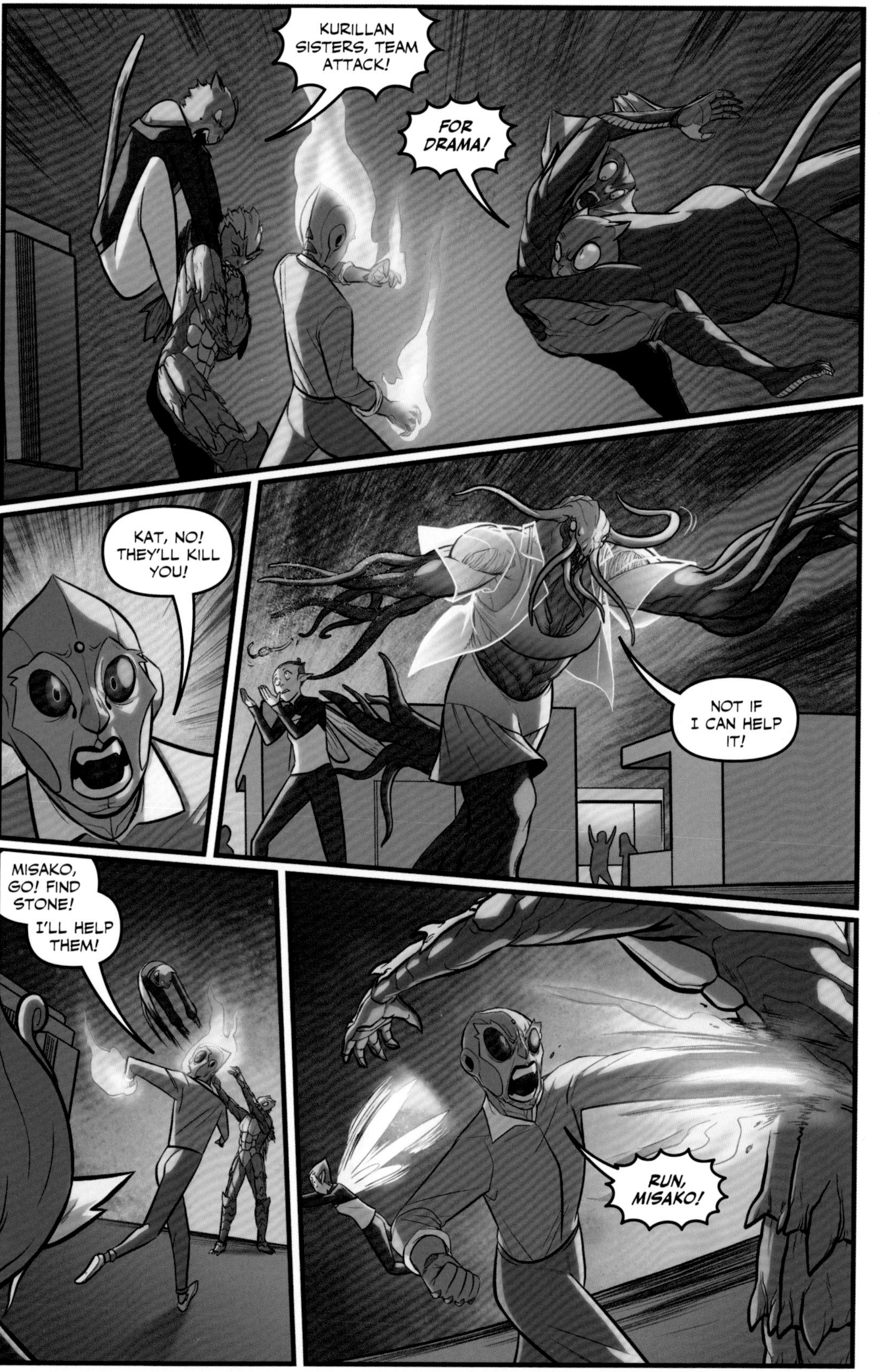
KURILLAN SISTERS, TEAM ATTACK!
FOR DRAMA!
KAT, NO! THEY'LL KILL YOU!
NOT IF I CAN HELP IT!
MISAKO, GO! FIND STONE!
I'LL HELP THEM!
RUN, MISAKO!

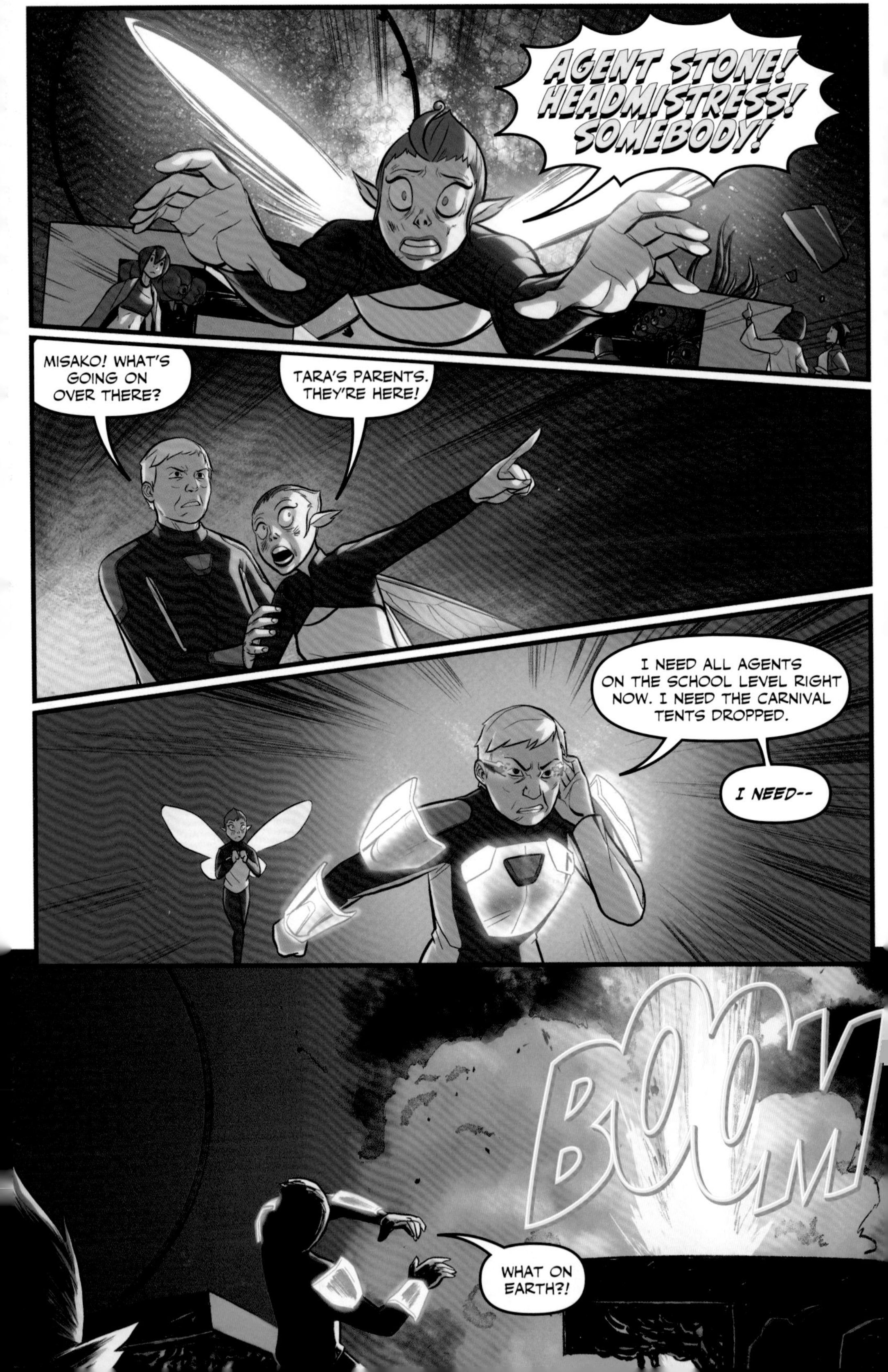
AGENT STONE! HEADMISTRESS! SOMEBODY!
MISAKO! WHAT'S GOING ON OVER THERE?
TARA'S PARENTS. THEY'RE HERE!
I NEED ALL AGENTS ON THE SCHOOL LEVEL RIGHT NOW. I NEED THE CARNIVAL TENTS DROPPED.
I NEED--
BOOM
WHAT ON EARTH?!

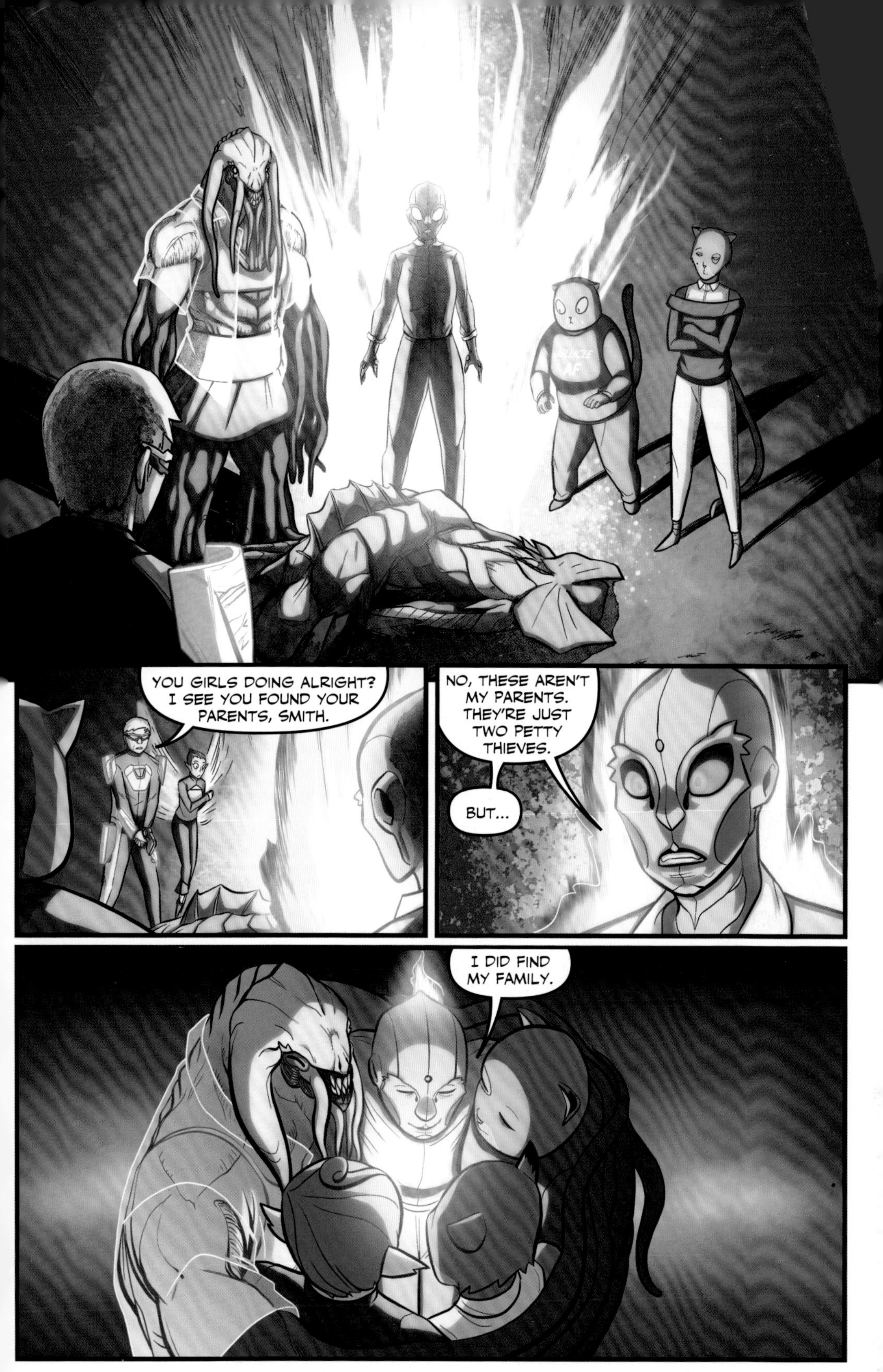
YOU GIRLS DOING ALRIGHT? I SEE YOU FOUND YOUR PARENTS, SMITH.
NO, THESE AREN'T MY PARENTS. THEY'RE JUST TWO PETTY THIEVES.
BUT...
I DID FIND MY FAMILY.

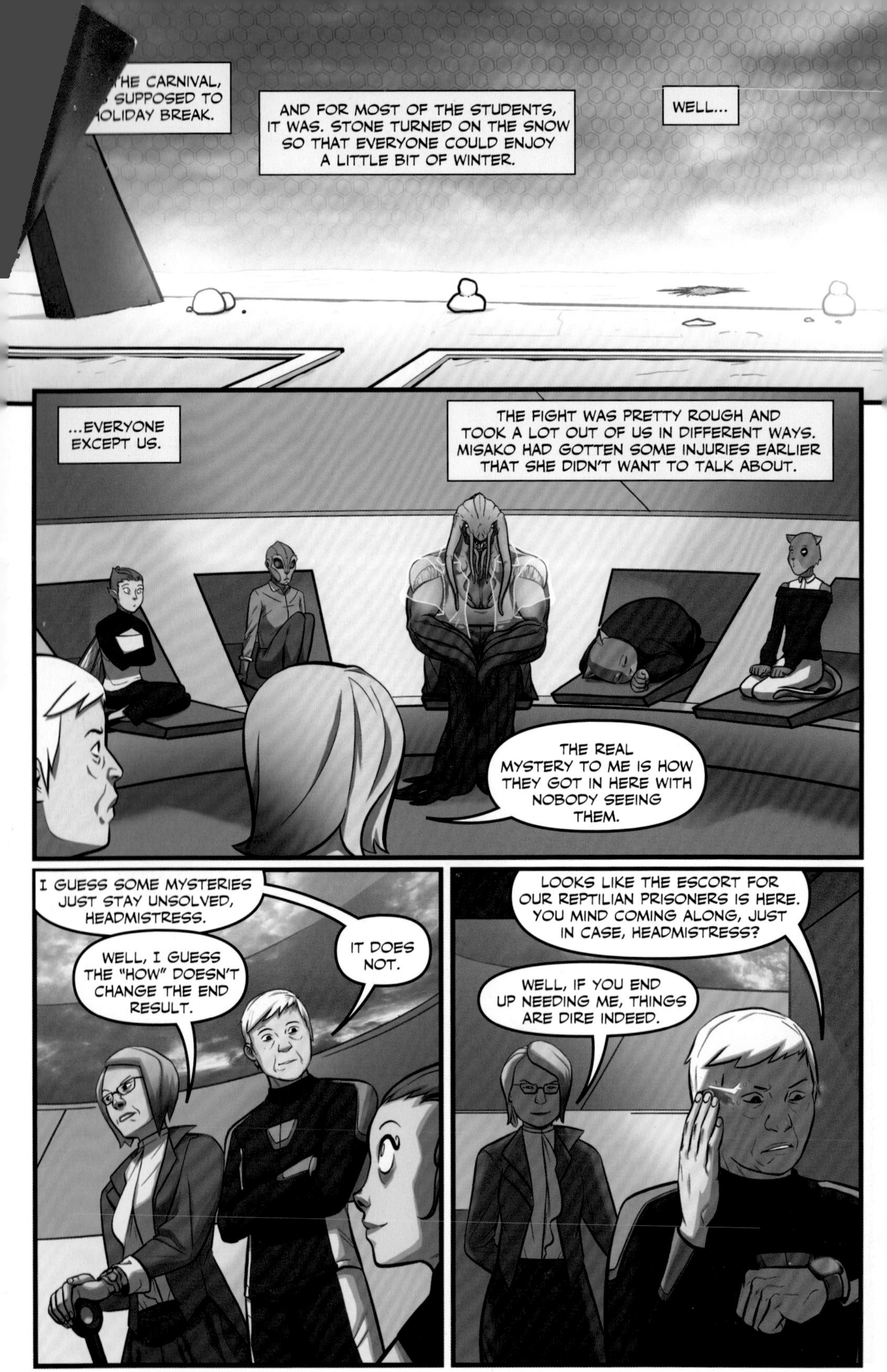

THE CARNIVAL,
SUPPOSED TO
HOLIDAY BREAK.
AND FOR MOST OF THE STUDENTS, IT WAS. STONE TURNED ON THE SNOW SO THAT EVERYONE COULD ENJOY A LITTLE BIT OF WINTER.
WELL...
...EVERYONE EXCEPT US.
THE FIGHT WAS PRETTY ROUGH AND TOOK A LOT OUT OF US IN DIFFERENT WAYS. MISAKO HAD GOTTEN SOME INJURIES EARLIER THAT SHE DIDN'T WANT TO TALK ABOUT.
THE REAL MYSTERY TO ME IS HOW THEY GOT IN HERE WITH NOBODY SEEING THEM.
I GUESS SOME MYSTERIES JUST STAY UNSOLVED, HEADMISTRESS.
IT DOES NOT.
WELL, I GUESS THE "HOW" DOESN'T CHANGE THE END RESULT.
LOOKS LIKE THE ESCORT FOR OUR REPTILIAN PRISONERS IS HERE. YOU MIND COMING ALONG, JUST IN CASE, HEADMISTRESS?
WELL, IF YOU END UP NEEDING ME, THINGS ARE DIRE INDEED.

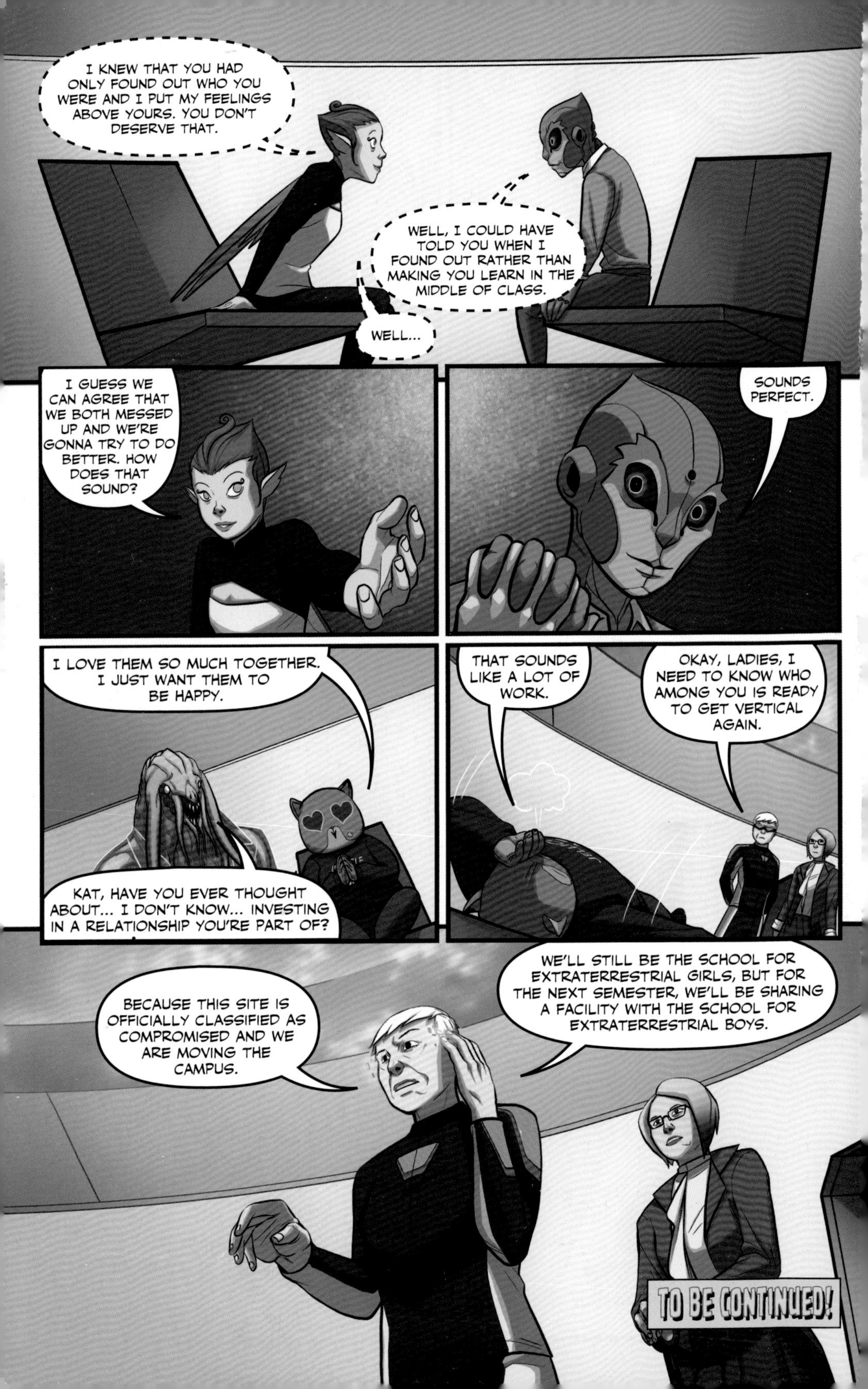
I KNEW THAT YOU HAD ONLY FOUND OUT WHO YOU WERE AND I PUT MY FEELINGS ABOVE YOURS. YOU DON'T DESERVE THAT.
WELL, I COULD HAVE TOLD YOU WHEN I FOUND OUT RATHER THAN MAKING YOU LEARN IN THE MIDDLE OF CLASS.
WELL...
I GUESS WE CAN AGREE THAT WE BOTH MESSED UP AND WE'RE GONNA TRY TO DO BETTER. HOW DOES THAT SOUND?
SOUNDS PERFECT.
I LOVE THEM SO MUCH TOGETHER. I JUST WANT THEM TO BE HAPPY.
KAT, HAVE YOU EVER THOUGHT ABOUT... I DON'T KNOW... INVESTING IN A RELATIONSHIP YOU'RE PART OF?
THAT SOUNDS LIKE A LOT OF WORK.
OKAY, LADIES, I NEED TO KNOW WHO AMONG YOU IS READY TO GET VERTICAL AGAIN.
BECAUSE THIS SITE IS OFFICIALLY CLASSIFIED AS COMPROMISED AND WE ARE MOVING THE CAMPUS.
WE'LL STILL BE THE SCHOOL FOR EXTRATERRESTRIAL GIRLS, BUT FOR THE NEXT SEMESTER, WE'LL BE SHARING A FACILITY WITH THE SCHOOL FOR EXTRATERRESTRIAL BOYS.
TO BE CONTINUED!

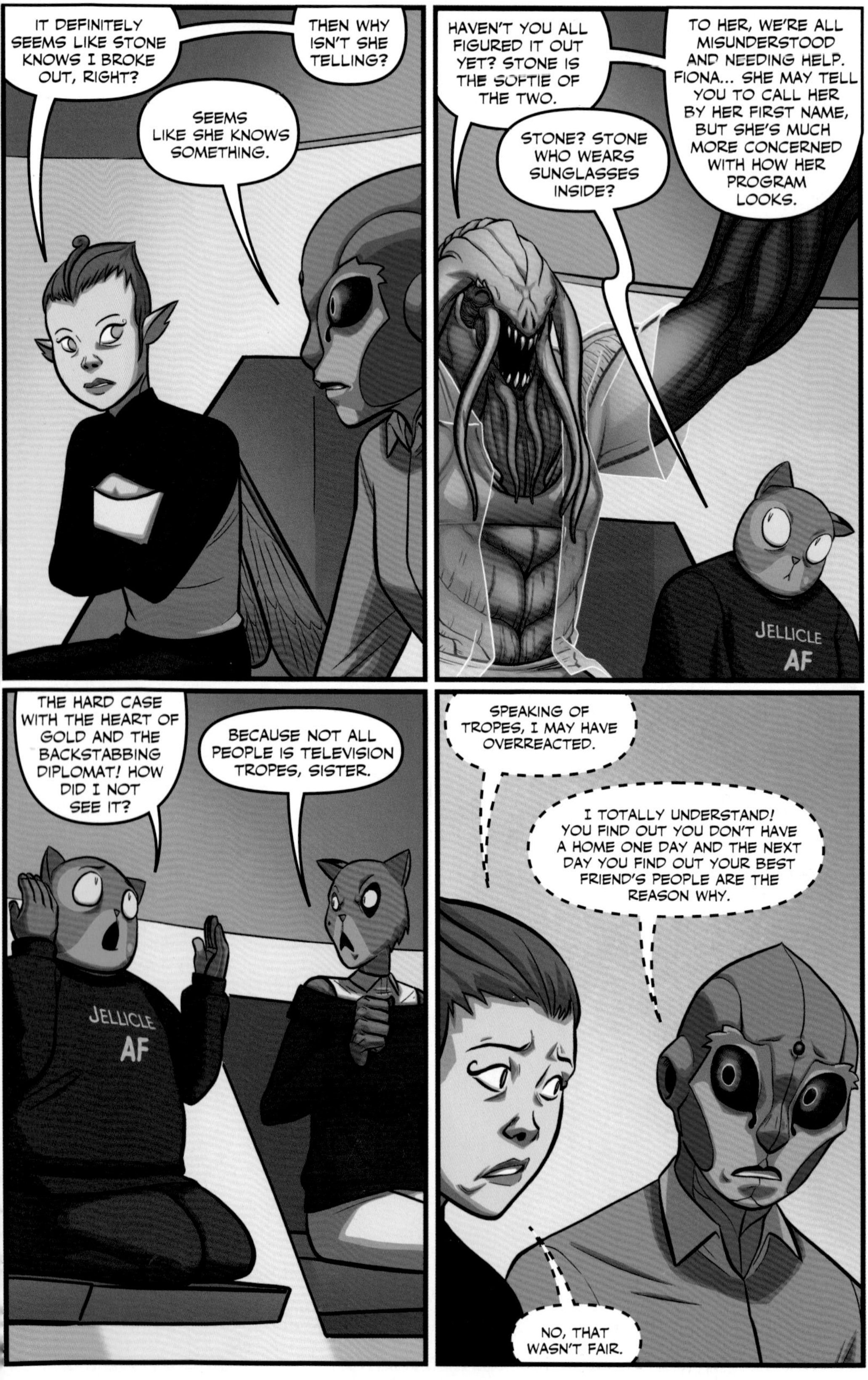
IT DEFINITELY SEEMS LIKE STONE KNOWS I BROKE OUT, RIGHT?
THEN WHY ISN'T SHE TELLING?
SEEMS LIKE SHE KNOWS SOMETHING.
HAVEN'T YOU ALL FIGURED IT OUT YET? STONE IS THE SOFTIE OF THE TWO.
TO HER, WE'RE ALL MISUNDERSTOOD AND NEEDING HELP. FIONA... SHE MAY TELL YOU TO CALL HER BY HER FIRST NAME, BUT SHE'S MUCH MORE CONCERNED WITH HOW HER PROGRAM LOOKS.
STONE? STONE WHO WEARS SUNGLASSES INSIDE?
JELLICLE AF
THE HARD CASE WITH THE HEART OF GOLD AND THE BACKSTABBING DIPLOMAT! HOW DID I NOT SEE IT?
BECAUSE NOT ALL PEOPLE IS TELEVISION TROPES, SISTER.
JELLICLE AF
SPEAKING OF TROPES, I MAY HAVE OVERREACTED.
I TOTALLY UNDERSTAND! YOU FIND OUT YOU DON'T HAVE A HOME ONE DAY AND THE NEXT DAY YOU FIND OUT YOUR BEST FRIEND'S PEOPLE ARE THE REASON WHY.
NO, THAT WASN'T FAIR.